Horace Ho is a Taiwanese writer and a professor in Comparative Literature at Chinese Culture University in Taipei. His writing has received numerous accolades, including the United Daily News Literature Prize.

The Tree Fort on Carnation Lane is his first book to be translated into English.

Darryl Sterk has translated numerous short stories by Taiwanese writers for *The Taipei Chinese Pen*, *Asymptote* and *Pathlight*. His novel translation includes Wu Ming-Yi's *The Man with the Compound Eyes*, and Chang Ying-Tai's *The Bear Whispers to Me*. He is a professor in Translation and Interpretation at National Taiwan Univerisy.

As a scholar he works on the representation of Taiwan's indigenous peoples in film and fiction.

HORACE HO

The Tree Fort on Carnation Lane

A Novel

Translated from the Chinese
by Darryl Sterk

Balestier Press
71-75 Shelton Street, London WC2H 9JQ
www.balestier.com

The Tree Fort on Carnation Lane
Original title: 花街樹屋
Copyright © Horace Ho, 2013
English translation copyright © Darryl Sterk, 2017

First published in English by Balestier Press in 2017

ISBN 978 0 9932154 8 3

The publisher gratefully acknowledges the support of
the National Museum of Taiwan Literature.

*The Tree Fort on
Carnation Lane*

1

A Crumpled Green Bill

I have no idea where that hundred dollar bill came from. The adults said I stole it, pilfered it out of the pocket of a pair of suit trousers my father left hanging over the bedroom door. I remember they had me surrounded and were shouting at me when I found myself kneeling before the family altar. It must have been evening, because, as I recall, it was dark out. The light in the family room was off, and the bulbs from the two electric candles on the altar cast a reddish glow on their faces. Of course, maybe their faces were red because they'd seen red. My parents launched volleys of Mandarin at me, with my dutifully widowed grandmother firing off Taiwanese remonstrations from the flank. I was crying, and my mother was crying too. They were stamping their feet and gesticulating. They all kept pointing at my right hand, which—lo and behold—was clutching a crumpled green bill worth about five United States dollars. It was like it had grown out of my palm, as if it were part of my own flesh.

My earliest memory. I'm not proud of it, but I thought of myself as a thief before I had any conception of my own identity or any notion of anything as basic as my gender.

If the scene weren't so shocking I wouldn't have remembered it, or I'd have forgotten it long ago. After all, it happened thirty-five years ago when I was all of three years old. A survey of some friends showed that most people's first memories form when they are five or six. One saw his Ma cooking in the kitchen one hazy afternoon, another was sitting smocked in the yellow school bus and yanking on the plait of the girl sitting beside him, stuff like that. Nobody's first memory starts with him or her kneeling at the age of three in front of the family altar.

I remember they were nearly apoplectic, my father, mother and grandmother. They were so enraged that they forgot I was only a child.

Though nobody hit me, someone did quite forcefully jab me in the back of the head a couple of times. Judging by the angle of my head and based on their positioning in relation to where I was kneeling, I presume that it was my father, who was standing behind me. I must have spent upwards of an hour kneeling in front of that altar. Of course, at that age I had no concept of time, so that upwards of an hour is a mere estimate I've made as an adult. During that whole hour, if that is how long it was, Grandma and Pa yelled at me constantly. I'm not sure if they were yelling at me together or whether they took turns. I just remember how oppressive their yells—and my mother's sobs—were, how they stood so close they raised an airtight wall around me. And no matter where I turned to climb that wall, someone would push me back. First I learned that what I had done was steal. Then I knew what it was like to feel helpless.

I don't blame them. I have to thank them really. If not for my fear of the helplessness I felt at being walled in by my elders, I might have gone on to burglary, or joined a gang like the boy next door. They had good reason to be so hard on me. After all, the neighbourhood we lived in was a less than ideal place to raise a kid. We'd settled down in Taipei City's sordid southwest, in a side street off a famous tourist nightmarket, located just south of the even more famous—infamous, actually—Carnation Lane. Night and day, johns, drunks, drifters and possible criminals flitted past our place. I remember that I wasn't the only one getting yelled at that evening. My mother took the opportunity to give my father a piece of her mind:

"I told you we should never have settled down in a place like this. See! Now our baby boy has gone bad. Are you satisfied?"

Of course, this is more than likely my imagination, because I grew up listening to my mother talking about moving away, as if it were her lifelong dream. Unfortunately, my father was never able to make her dream come true.

I can understand why my elders were so angry, but I still don't get how a three-year-old kid like me could have had any notion of money. Or what kind of worldly desires could have possessed me to filch a hundred dollars. Or how, at less than a metre tall, I had managed to reach my hand into the pocket of my father's trousers. It's unpleasant to think that I was already hung up on money so early in life. But no matter how hard I try to remember, I can't go any earlier: kneeling there is the first thing I recall. The harder I try, the more details occur to me, embellishing the memory. Of course, some of these details might also be my overactive imagination, because people are as good at imagining things as they are at forgetting them. The more time passes, the more the boundary between imagination and memory blurs. What's frustrating is that these details only clarify after I knelt in front of the altar: I still don't know how and why I got my hands on that crumpled hundred dollar bill.

2

Waaaaa-llet Mine

Ling-ling's first word was "Mama", her second "Papa". Then came "wallet".

The word wallet isn't easy for her to pronounce. She draws out the "wa", as if to practise moulding her mouth into the proper shape, before finally issuing a decisive "let". She's just started to talk, but before her linguistic faculty began forming she already evinced an interest in wallets. Whenever she riots in the high chair, refusing to eat like a good little girl, I give her my wallet. It buys me at least twenty minutes of quiet time, enough to feed her half a bowl of congee.

"I wonder if this has anything to do with Taurus being her rising sign," says Amanda, looking at Ling-ling worriedly. "A Cancerian shouldn't be so fond of money."

Amanda believes in astrology the way I believe in genetics. But now I know that Ling-ling's predilection for wallets has nothing to do with either astrology or genetics. That's the Internet for you. You just do a search and learn that a kid playing with a parent's wallet is no big deal. There's no reason to punish a kid who hasn't grown a memory yet by forcing him to kneel in front of the family altar. Sure, you could see early childhood Mammonism in it, if you wanted. It's a consumerist age, after all. Kids these days! They follow their parents into Toys"R"Us and Costco, where they get told they can't eat or play with the products in the cart, because they're "other people's things". But once you go down a narrow lane, arrive before the gatekeeper, and the adult you're with takes out his or her wallet and pays, the things in the cart can, as if by magic, suddenly be eaten, or played with, because now they're "Daddy's" or even "mine". The ownership of things changes just like that with the flash of a wallet. What young child wouldn't be curious? How could he not find a way to get his hands on the wallet Daddy left in his trouser pocket?

I'm not at all worried about Ling-ling having some kind of precocious fondness for filthy lucre, because most of the time the bill compartment of my wallet is empty. Ling-ling enjoys divesting the wallet of its contents, but usually that only amounts to a few cards—business cards, my health insurance, ID, EasyCard for the MRT, driver's and scooter licences, even my Costco card and library card, the sort of thing a pickpocket would bin in the first public washroom he passed (though he might keep the EasyCard, which still has a few hundred dollars in stored value). I am sure that as long as I don't yell at her when she stands on her tiptoes, grasps the edge of the table, and reaches for my wallet without permission—as long as I don't punish her by making her kneel in front of the family altar —Ling-ling will forget her early fondness by the time she's all grown up. Without suffering some unusual trauma, who can remember anything that happens before the age of two?

Amanda bends down, snatches the wallet from Ling-ling's hand and collects the cards scattered on the floor. Ling-ling starts wailing.

"Waaaaa-llet." Her tears are flowing, her nose running. "Mine."

Amanda hasn't given me back my wallet or put it back on the table.

I draw a baby wipe and wipe the mess of mucus and tears from Ling-ling's face, taking out my mobile phone for her to play with. She releases a few more sobs before succumbing to the phone's charms, the colourful screen and the key tones. Then she sits and plays, utterly absorbed. A disastrous loss of control has been averted, thanks not just to the phone but also to Ling-ling's outstanding forgetfulness. The brevity of her memory staunches her tears.

I reach out and stroke her face. It's warm and soft and smooth to the touch, without the slightest wrinkle or blemish, like her memory at this age. She will probably not, like me, remember things that happen to her over the next year. She might never know that I crawled on the floor like a horse for her to ride on, or how many times I bathed her and changed her nappy. If Ling-ling were to be abducted I would be easily erased from her memory; I would have no part in her wistful reminiscences. It would be as if I had never existed.

Scary. The possibility is frightening.

"Would Ling-ling remember us?' I ask Amanda, my gaze lingering on Ling-ling. "If she were separated from us now, I mean, if she never saw us again. Do you think she'd remember us?"

"What are you talking about?"

"Considering that in the twenty-two months since Ling-ling was born I've been with her twenty-four/seven. I've bathed her six hundred times, fed her eighteen hundred meals. If anything happened to her like in the Society section of the newspaper, say she was abducted by human traffickers or went missing or something, what do you think? Would she remember me?"

"Remember you? Didn't you just ask if she would remember us?"

"Well, you know, if Ling-ling didn't remember me, there's no way she'd remember you. How much time do you spend with her each day? You've got your career and I'm a stay at home dad! If she didn't even remember me, these two years I've given up work so I could take care of the baby would go to waste, right?"

"You didn't give up work; work gave up on you," Amanda corrects me. "If your old department hadn't gone bankrupt, you would never have let your college teaching gig go. You wouldn't be the most overqualified nanny in Taiwan."

"It didn't go bankrupt, it just wasn't able to enrol any students. It's just a temporary closure."

"What's the difference? In any case you're out of a job."

"I could still teach somewhere else… Hey, I thought we made this decision together. Since the department was closing, I would just stay at home for a few years and take care of Ling-ling. We would have to get by on a single salary, but by economizing we could make ends meet. You didn't want Ling-ling to be sent somewhere unfamiliar, to a daycare or that nanny's place, remember?"

"I don't blame you for staying home to take care of the baby. It's just that there were three thousand dollar bills in your wallet the other day. Where did they go?"

Amanda raises my wallet and opens it with her thumbs, like pulling apart a tangerine, to show me that there's nothing inside except for the monogrammed lining. "Waaaaa-llet." Cue Ling-ling. Her little face looks up, then her tiny hands reach up: "Mine."

Amanda lets Ling-ling grab the wallet out of her hands. My daughter now has both phone and wallet.

I try to extricate my phone, but Ling-ling uses my wallet to bat my hand away. She is still none too clear about the concept of ownership, though she understands possession. Anything she labels "mine" is as good as gone unless we immediately correct her, repeating that it is "Daddy's" or "Mummy's".

I give it another try. This time she screams, as if to assert sovereignty. I give up.

"Don't you have enough money? Some major purchase you needed to make?" Amanda won't let the matter drop.

"I took it out."

"You took it out?"

"Sunday is Ilya's funeral, remember? I put the money in an envelope, and left it in the drawer. I'll take it with me on Sunday."

"Oh…" Amanda's tone has softened. "We can list the money for the white envelope as a joint expense."

"Don't be like this. He was my friend. I want to use my own money."

"Ilya Chiang was my friend too."

"No, he wasn't."

"I knew him for years. How can you say we weren't friends?"

"Of course you were. But you're not any more."

I do want Amanda to understand how I feel, but there isn't any point explaining. She must be thinking: here he goes again, the resident Assistant Professor of Cryptology up to his old tricks. Idle at home, he's got nothing better to do than encrypt the simple concept of "friend" and turn a readily intelligible message into apparent nonsense.

Of course, that's not what I intended to say or what I meant. After all, my research area is recovery: my specialism is decryption, not encryption. Ilya was no longer Amanda's friend because we didn't meet Ilya together. She only met Ilya after we started dating and it was only because he was my friend that she considered him hers. She was friends with him for less than eight years, while I met him before we were ten. Ilya appeared in my life long before Amanda. He was on the scene, at least in many of the scenes, before she came along. Deciding to step inside the panorama of my world meant she had to accept Ilya as a friend, a part of our connubial life, as a person we would be seeing a lot of and that she had to be nice to. Now that Ilya has disappeared from the face of the earth, logically the friendship he and Amanda formed should come to an end, because he will never again come over to see us.

But I have to admit that I wanted to use my own money for the white envelope not to be fair, but for selfish, personal reasons. While Ilya was still alive, I always wanted Amanda to consider him her friend, which indeed she did. But since Ilya died I've been feeling selfish; I want exclusivity. I don't want to treat this sum of money as a joint expense. I don't want Amanda's money to be added in, diluting the purity of my friendship with Ilya.

Like I said, there's no point explaining.

3

There's Always Someone Better Up There

This soupcon of selfishness seems rather silly when I see the flood of mourners at the memorial service. Though Ilya was a well-known pianist I never expected him to have so many friends. When I reach the mortuary there are no more empty seats inside the mourning hall and the walkway by the door, the steps up to the door and even the car park at the base of the steps are packed. All the funeral guests are about the same age as me. They must all have been Ilya's friends.

I squeeze through the crowd and pass the white envelope to the person collecting the condolence money at a table by the entrance. There is no guest book on the table, only a big poster of black and white piano keys. This seems strange. I am no expert in these matters; my personal experience is limited to my grandmother's and my father's funerals. But I'm sure I've never heard of getting people to sign a poster instead of a guest book on such an occasion. I pick up a black marker and look for an empty key among the densely penned signatures. Just as I am about to sign I have a sense of déjà vu. Perhaps I'm reminded of Ilya's wedding three years before, perhaps of the petition booth at the protest against ractopamine in imported American beef.

Daniel Fang, I write. To indicate my attendance. And as a protest, though I don't yet know what I am protesting against.

A picture of Ilya hangs over the altar inside the mourning hall, beside it a big projection screen, which has got to be two metres wide. They are playing a recording of a stage recital. It's not the National Concert Hall. Based on the rounded wall at the back of the stage and the foreign audience, I guess it's from a recital Ilya did two years ago at the Konzerthaus in Vienna. I stand by the door awhile, wanting to watch a performance I couldn't attend in person, but the heavy floral fragrance pervading the mourning hall forces me out. I find the smell of perfume lilies so morbid. Maybe they aren't perfume lilies. Maybe I don't know what I'm smelling. Even if they are, maybe I'm wrong to lay all the blame on one flower. Surely people don't use just one kind in funeral flower arrangements. All I know about this is what I observed at two family funerals: in both cases I was standing up front, my eyes stinging and my nose smarting from the pong of all the potted perfume lilies on the flower stands behind me.

My grandmother contracted cancer of the oesophagus, my father of the stomach, ten years apart.

Three years ago, Ilya's guests had signed another poster, printed with a picture of Ilya and his bride. I forget her name: her marriage to Ilya lasted all of a year, too brief a time for her name to register in my mental database. I just remember that she was a nurse, because she reminded me to go for a regular colonoscopy even though I was only in my early thirties. Cancer of the digestive tract runs in the family.

This was reasonable advice, based on our current understanding of genetics. If cancer really does run in the Fang family digestive tract, you might be able to tell what generation I belong to according to which of my organs is afflicted. Even so, I still haven't followed Ilya's ex-wife's advice and gone for an examination, because in the end cancer was not the reason why I had to attend my grandmother's and father's funerals.

My grandmother died of a stroke, my father of a heart attack, also ten years apart.

And Ilya? He killed himself. Found hanging from a tree by the riverside. Slipped a rope minim around his neck and took his leave of our dear planet earth.

"But why?"

"He was doing just fine. How could this happen?"

At Grandma's and Pa's funerals, I kept hearing comments and questions like this in the conversations of friends and relatives. Yeah, she was doing just fine. The doctor cut the tumour out, she finished the chemo. The doctor announced his five year survival rate, he was optimistic. We were like spectators at a baseball game that went nine extra innings. We dragged our tired bodies and happy moods home from the hospital, only to receive the sad news that the patient had dropped dead. Nobody knew why it had turned out that way.

Now, in the car park of the same funeral home, I'm hearing the same exclamations in the pleasantries exchanged by the mourners. Yeah, things were going really well for him. I walk past this one group on purpose and pretend to look at the titles and names on the gift wreaths. In each group there seems to be a speaker holding forth on his recent meeting with Ilya, detailing the place and time like a criminal witness giving a statement to the police. Yeah, yeah, last month we had hot pot together. Who knew it would be for the last time? Yeah, he always drove to my place, but that day he took the bus. Come to think of it, he was acting kind of strange. I can't help but take note of the timing of these meetings. I really didn't want to hear that in the month before Ilya left this world, or in the two weeks before his death, or even in the last few days of his life, he had time to meet so many friends. When was the last time I saw him? Half a year ago? He made time for all these people before doing himself in, but didn't give me any notice, didn't so much as drop me a line. I don't even have the right to say he was doing just fine.

The ceremony is mostly over. The MC announces the names of the groups in attendance, so each group can line up and pay their respects. I'm in no hurry to go in, because I'm not part of any of the groups. I can only wait until the end and say farewell to Ilya as an individual. I see quite a few politicians come out of the funeral home, all VIPs, the kind that's often in the news. With some of them, I know their names; with others, I can't think of who they are. There are green Democratic Progressive Party politicians and blue Kuomintang politicians. But regardless they all walk out like they have somewhere to be in a hurry. I also see some people I can't quite place but who nevertheless look a bit familiar, probably people in the music industry. They wouldn't appear on television as much, but might very well appear on the covers of the classical music compact discs I collect. Just like the politicians, these people don't stick around.

Like the pavement in front of a cinema after a movie ends, there are more and more people in the car park in front of the funeral home. They are shaking hands, exchanging cards, handing each other cigarettes, joining the existing groups or forming new ones. Everyone is talking about the Ilya he or she knew. Some are in a hurry to interrupt whoever is talking, to assert the right to speak by telling a story about Ilya. Others just keep on repeating the same questions: Why? How could this happen? He was doing just fine…

I walk among the groups. Nobody recognizes me. Nobody knows about my friendship with Ilya. I feel a bit angry, actually.

Why? How could this happen?

Not even Mrs Chiang recognizes me.

I didn't expect she'd come, on account of the custom according to which the white-haired shouldn't send off the black-haired: she shouldn't be here. She is anyway, though she didn't stand with Ilya's cousins when the guests were paying their respects. Mrs Chiang is sitting way at the back of the mourning hall, watching the memorial like a spectator.

When most people have already left, I finally re-enter the hall and approach the coffin to light incense to Ilya. I look over at Mrs Chiang. She is still looking over from her corner. She is looking at me, but still doesn't seem to recognize me. But she looks all right. Emotionally she can't be all right: she is a widow, and Ilya was her only child. Nobody in such circumstances could be all right. What I mean is that her hair isn't a mess, and she hasn't broken down. Her make-up is immaculate, no tear streaks at all. She sits there clad all in black, looking perfectly composed, expressionless. I think she looked the same at Ilya's wedding. The only difference was that at the wedding she wore red.

After offering incense, I hesitate, then walk over. I'm positive now she doesn't know who I am. Here she is in the corner, looking across the hall, checking out everyone who comes in to offer incense, but hasn't given me a second glance. I didn't say anything to her on the day of Ilya's wedding. Today it seems necessary to pay my respects.

"Hello, Mrs Chiang."

I regret saying anything as soon as I open my mouth. I've misjudged the situation. Mrs Chiang probably decided to sit in the corner because she broke custom to come and doesn't want anyone to see her. By walking over to greet her, I have exposed her presence, perhaps embarrassing her.

"It's Daniel. Do you remember me?" Mrs Chiang's expression is blank. I feel like I am introducing myself to a complete stranger. "Ilya's elementary school classmate. The one who lived by the nightmarket."

"Daniel?" she says, eyes widening. "It's you! I almost didn't recognize you. How you've changed! You're a lot thinner than you were as a boy."

"Maybe I just look thinner because I'm taller now."

"No, you're really a lot thinner. I remember you were a pudgy kid, with a face like a balloon. I often told Ilya: 'Don't be such a picky eater. You've got to eat more or you won't have energy to play the piano. Look at your classmate Daniel! So adorable! When people see you two standing side by side they'll think I'm not feeding you.'"

"Ilya was really particular about food," I say. "If he hadn't become a pianist, he would have been a master chef or gourmand or something."

"What could he do besides play the piano? I often told Ilya: 'If you're tired, don't play. You can be successful at anything you put your mind to.' Would he listen? No, he just kept practising."

"Did Ilya like practising?"

"Of course he did. Doesn't it go without saying? But for some things you need talent. You can't force it. You know how stubborn he was. He had to be the best. I used to tell him: 'Don't compare yourself with the kids in the neighbourhood, because there's always someone better up there. What does it prove if you beat the local kids? They have to go and help their folks set up stands in the market at night. What time do they have to practise?'"

To my surprise, Mrs Chiang talks about Ilya as if nothing could be more natural. As if Ilya isn't lying beneath a sheet in a coffin. As if he is getting ready to perform somewhere. Somehow the vibe I'm getting from Mrs Chiang isn't right. I don't mean messing up the idiom "there's always someone better out there". Maybe "up there" wasn't just a slip of the tongue. Maybe Mrs Chiang said it that way on purpose, meaning that even if you were the best pianist in the world, there might be some virtuoso extraterrestrials floating around up in outer space. No, it's something else, but I can't put my finger on what it is. Just like I couldn't figure out what I was protesting against at the entrance to the funeral hall.

"I don't remember who was learning piano besides Ilya. But you're right, a lot of our classmates had to go help out at the nightmarket."

"Yes, they did. They weren't as fortunate as you, with a father running a variety show and all. How is your father? I don't know how long it's been. He must be retired by now? Or is he still performing? Is he still as hot on the drums as he used to be?"

"He passed away about ten years ago."

"He passed away?" Mrs Chiang said. "How could this happen?"

"It happens to everyone."

"That's not what I meant."

"He got stomach cancer. But he died of a heart attack."

Now I know what the problem is. My father was never in the spotlight in his life, or in any light. He used to sit by day in the grubby ticket booth of a cinema, selling tickets for B movies or strip shows, and at night he'd ride on his scooter to all of the little inns in the area, delivering the lists of occupants to the police. The one who went up on stage was Brand's dad. Brand's dad was a regular potentate of percussion back in the day, a successful manager of a song-and-dance variety troupe. And now he was a congressman, so influential that even water would hang on his words. Mrs Chiang has mistaken me for my elementary classmate Brand Lin.

"Your father was a good man."

"That's what the pastor at the funeral said."

"Pastor? He was a Christian? I thought your family was Buddhist. Didn't you used to go to temple to offer incense first thing in the morning on New Year's Day?"

"It was my mother who was a Christian. She got baptized as soon as he died."

"Didn't your parents get a divorce?"

"I'm not sure whether they got a divorce or not, but they were living together until my father's death. It's true my mother always wanted to leave the nightmarket."

"How strange," she says. "I imagine a lot of people came to attend your father's funeral."

"Not as many people as have come to attend Ilya's funeral."

"Over half at least?"

"No, not even a tenth. We only set up five rows, but not even three were full."

"Oh? I thought your father had a wide acquaintance. How can

people be so cold?"

I'm not going to tell her the truth, that my father wasn't the leader of the troupe, that she's mistaken me for that little fatso classmate of mine, Brand. My specialism is cryptology, so I know that everything I've said since Mrs Chiang's initial misrecognition has helped encrypt the truth, making it harder and harder for her to decode as her misunderstanding grows more and more baroque. I have no choice, of course, because as a man I've lost whatever qualities I had as a boy. Mrs Chiang can hardly identify me now, if I ever made an impression on her. If I told her I wasn't Mr Lin's fat little boy, Mrs Chiang might not know who I was, and our whole conversation would become even more embarrassing than it already is, or even impossible to carry on. Then again, I never anticipated she'd have so much to say. I was just planning to say "I'm sorry for your loss" or "Take good care" and hear her say "Thank you, I will" in reply. Then I could leave the mourning hall and escape the smell of perfume lily.

"Mrs Chiang, I should go." I feel like I should just say what I came over to say and end the conversation: "You take good care now."

Mrs Chiang doesn't answer "Thanks" or "I will". She opens her eyes wide, like she's realized the milk is past the use-by date after drinking half the carton. She looks at me suspiciously.

"Did you just tell me to take care?"

"Yes."

"You're telling me to take care?"

I hesitate. "I meant that we must all take good care."

"No, you said: 'You take good care now.'"

"I guess I did."

"Did you tell me to take care out of pity?"

"No no no, I..."

"Why should I have to take care? You must think me pathetic, like I don't have anything to live for now that Ilya's gone. That's why you told me to take care."

"No, that's not what I meant."

"No need to tell me to take good care. I'm not one of those weak women who can't take a blow. I lost my husband, but I carried on, and now I'm doing fine. Now Ilya's gone, but I've survived loss before and there's no reason to think that loss will make me despair now. I don't need your pity. I don't need Ilya. I've got my own life to lead. Ilya was just one of the people in it. Not all of it, not at all. You should pity Ilya. He was the weak one. No, he doesn't deserve pity either. He was brave enough to kill himself, so don't tell me he was weak. And since he's decided he didn't want us, we have no reason to be sad for him or for ourselves. Wouldn't that be foolish?"

My jaw drops and I stare at Mrs Chiang, mute. I can't tell if her words express what she is really thinking, or whether they were ciphers in a code she's invented to conceal her emotions. She remains expressionless. I can't identify what she's feeling, much less describe it.

Leaving the hall, I meet the me Mrs Chiang thought I was: Brand Lin, the only one at the funeral who knows me. He drives a shiny new sapphire BMW roadster right into the mortuary car park with some bodacious babe sitting beside him. The hardtop is down, just like the low-cut skintight top the girl is wearing, allowing folks an ample view of the luxury interior. The bereaved family members and the funeral guests forget their sorrow at his arrival, as he brings something of the fuel-injected vigour of a car show into the ashen gloom of the funeral home.

"I'm late! Is it over yet?" Brand asks.

"The part that's over is over," I say. "But Ilya is still inside, so you still have a chance to see him."

Brand raises an eyebrow, squinting at me slightly. I know what this expression of his means. As kids, we three used to crouch under the pailou – the gateway to the market, made of two columns with a lintel crosspiece that displays the name of the market – on the south side of the pailou road, sipping our slurpees from the convenience store, the first generation of kids to do so. Brand would always finish first and look at me like that and say: "Ilya sucks slowly cause he's got sensitive teeth. What's your excuse?"

"I should hurry up then." Then he says: "You wait here, I'll be right back."

"Don't leave me, Brand-meister. You know your girl gets scared if you leave her all by herself." The car show babe pouts her lips, cocks her head and tosses her hair to reveal flawless skin on the nape of her neck that seldom sees the sun. I imagine that a girl like that would find herself very busy riding in a car like this. Hair to rearrange and all.

"Just stay in the car," Brand says. He leans over the car door and presses a button on the driver's side.

Like some giant beetle opening its elytra, the roadster begins raising the steel panel located on its rear end, startling onlookers standing too near into retreat. Propping up something like a glossy hard shell travel case, two steel arms emerge from the black hole beneath the panel and arch forward towards the windshield. Unblinking, the woman stares up as the travel case separates into two steel arcs and closes upon her head. But what a change came over her just now! The moment before Brand pressed the button she was still the consummate socialite, flaunting her physical charms, hoping to use a coquettish tone and a flirtatious demeanour to make her man change his mind. But when she looked up and saw that posh plaything undergo a manly metamorphosis, unadorned excitement flashed through her heavy foundation. Half-hidden behind the jet-black arcs of her false lashes, her eyes pulsed with light, and her lips, soaked with rouge, formed a nimble O.

I don't know the woman in the car, but I do know that look. Every time I unwrap a new toy, or a packet of her favourite cookies, Ling-ling, too, will look up with the same fascination, her eyes tracking the thing in which she is so very interested. The process by which an open top turns into a hardtop is certainly new to me, but ninety per cent of the time my gaze remains glued to the woman's face: I didn't want to miss for one moment an expression that has become so familiar but whose true value I understand only now.

But by this time the two steel arcs have fused into the roof, and the rear windshield and the panel at the back have lowered into place. The automatic tinted windows are up. I can't see a thing.

4

Those Times Are Gone

Ling-ling has just learned to speak, and it's like she has all these things she can't wait to say. She can name a number of physical things on picture cards or around her, and she understands a few pronouns, demonstratives and genitives. But she mostly gets things off her chest with onomatopoeia: "Dis… uuuuh… oooooh," she might say, with the utmost solemnity, before nodding emphatically and grinning. Then she rides around on her toy truck.

Of course, I never know what she thinks she's just told me. But I can understand her urgent need to express herself. Almost two, she must need an outlet as much as anyone.

As do I. First I lost my teaching job, then Ling-ling was born: suddenly my life quieted down. I no longer had to save my voice. When I was teaching, I always used to take a packet of Eight Immortals throat soothers, and prepare a microphone and a bottle of mineral water, reminding myself to modulate my voice. Amanda and I went out a few times every week, occasionally with my friends, mostly with her friends. She works in one of the twenty top multinationals in Taiwan, and got the job right after graduation. Eight years ago when we met, I'd just started my PhD, and she was a lowly sales manager at the company headquarters. She kept getting promoted, and was already a manager when I finally finished my dissertation. She was way ahead of me in terms of income and connections, even after I got a job as an assistant professor of Cryptology. But I didn't really mind. Before Ling-ling was born, we had some good times. We had time and money, and were both outgoing. We were people people. We'd go for hot pot, sing karaoke, or find a little bar and hole ourselves up for an entire evening. We didn't have that many friends in common, but it seemed our regular engagements had the regular periodicity of the planets in their orbits: our paths would cross, diverge and come together again.

We would revisit old memories for the umpteenth time. We would tell lame jokes under the influence of alcohol or the atmosphere, slapping the table or our knees. We would lower our voices, put our foreheads together and gossip about some absent friend. We always felt there was more to say, that a single evening wasn't enough. After we'd get home Amanda and I would sometimes take our seats at the kitchen island we'd got the designer to put between the kitchen and the family room, have a half glass of red wine, and continue the conversation deep into the night.

Those times are gone.

With Ling-ling's birth, those bland, repetitive, somehow irresistible gatherings we never wanted to miss fizzled out. The kitchen island was taken over by milk bottles and sippy cups of various sizes and a bottle sterilization machine. The loveseat in the family room got moved to the wall to make space for a foam mat—Ling-ling's play area. Every time we came home we'd have to navigate an obstacle course—a potty trainer, a baby walker, a Rockin' Tunes Giraffe and a box of nappies —on the way from door to bedroom. The dining room is piled with baby clothes that are all either too big or too small. The whole home environment changed, becoming unconducive to conversation, until Ling-ling began to speak.

5

Brand

I don't think I'll mention meeting Brand.

Of course Amanda knows Brand, but she only met him when she became my girlfriend. I'm not sure if she considers Brand a friend the way she considered Ilya a friend.

I'm not even sure if I can count Brand as my friend.

Like Mrs Chiang, the last time I saw Brand was at Ilya's wedding, and of course the car show babe he's brought to the memorial wasn't the lady companion he brought to the wedding, a famous model whose photo I'd often seen in the paper. She wore a low-cut full-length sparkling dress with a slit up to the thigh, like she was going to the Oscars. Amanda said: "Lucky Brand didn't bring this kind of girl when we got married, or none of the male guests would have been looking at the bride." She disappeared from the Entertainment section about two years ago, but I still remember her name. Unlike Ilya's ex-wife's name. All I remember about Ilya's ex-wife is that she told me to go get a colonoscopy.

I don't remember my own wedding very clearly. Six years have gone by, and all that's left of that busy, happy day in my mind are some disconnected scenes and images, like a random playlist of video clips and stills. I imagine the discontinuity is due to the fact that the photographer and all the wedding guests kept blinding me with the flashes on their cameras. These devices have become so sophisticated, tempting us to relinquish the task of remembering. The technology of memory has accelerated memory loss. I can remember the details of stealing a hundred dollars out of my father's wallet thirty-five years ago, but not of the most important day of my life.

I don't remember which lady friend Brand brought when Amanda and I got married. Of course, she must appear in the DVD. It's just that in the intervening six years I've never had the courage to replay the only film in which I've ever had a leading role. But I do remember that at that time Brand was still Brand, not yet Brand-meister, but also not Little B or Lin or even kid, names people called him a dozen years ago when he first started working at the production company. Mrs Chiang just knew that Brand's dad was one of the more successful people in our neighbourhood, but not that the son had used his old man's political and commercial connections to break into the entertainment biz, or that he had outdone his old man and was now the president of a well-known media talent agency. Ilya must never have mentioned Brand's success to his mother. I never had to. My mother never fails to tell me when she sees Brand or even hears his name mentioned: "Your elementary classmate Brand was on the news again!" I am surprised that my mother finds it so easy to recognize Brand when she can't even recognize her own son: "I can barely recognize you all skinny like this," she often says.

Brand works behind the scenes, so he doesn't appear that often on television, but every time he does he gets a bit fatter. Brand has probably only grown about ten centimetres since elementary school, but his girth has doubled. He looks even fatter on my mother's new widescreen television. But she is always able to recognize him and remember how we used to hang out (or how we used to hang out with him). She might not have recognized Ilya, because mostly he would just go home and practise piano instead of coming out to play. She probably doesn't know that as an adult I saw a lot more of Ilya than I have of Brand, that even though as kids Brand and I were like Liu and Wang from the famous Taiwanese film, like Laurel and Hardy, now I only ever see Brand at weddings, funerals and other formal occasions.

It's been three years since we last met, but Brand doesn't give me the slightest feeling of distance. It's like we just went out last night, ended up drinking until dawn and have only now managed to make it to the mortuary. As expected, Brand is a man of his word: he emerges from the mourning hall, now all but deserted, in no time, out of breath. I find his haste gratifying, because it wouldn't have given him time to talk to Mrs Chiang or even to see who else was still in the mourning hall; there's no chance Mrs Chiang has found out I am not the man she thought I was. The embarrassment of my conversation with Mrs

Chiang can stay in the mourning hall.

"How'd you get here?" Brand asks.

"By bus."

"Get in. I'll give you a ride." Brand opens the passenger door and calls inside: "Get out. You're taking a cab."

The roadster shudders, I guess because the chick is stomping her feet in displeasure. She gets out of the car and, despite being fully a head taller than Brand, steps meekly to the side and offers a courteous smile to the guy who has just stolen her seat.

Without further ado I hop in and close the well-constructed door, hoping to shut the embarrassment out. The leather seat still carries the body heat of the woman's naked thighs and the air conditioner vents are blasting an icy stream of her perfume. The warmth and the scent that I will inadvertently carry home with me will take some explaining. But before facing Amanda I will have to rack my brains to figure out what to say to dispel another kind of embarrassment, which I have shut into the car, the kind of embarrassment two grown men feel when they are seat-belted into the same vehicle but can't think of anything to say.

Brand drives onto the elevated highway. When he steps on the accelerator, I am immediately pressed back into the seat like in a plane on the runway. This kind of speed, the kind the 125 CC Kymko Jacky I used to ride when I was eighteen or nineteen couldn't reach even when I maxed it out, dampens the embarrassment. I no longer feel any need to try to think of something to say to break the silence. Although we haven't seen each other in three years, I don't feel the least sense of estrangement, though he is Brand-meister now and not Brand like he used to be. We know each other too well, and even if we don't see each other for thirty years we will probably dispense with the polite formalities. The awkwardness I felt initially was because of the silence, but there's no necessary connection between silence and estrangement. Especially now that Brand's main task is gripping the wheel, shuttling us through traffic, slamming on the brakes for a speed camera, unsticking us from our seats. Talking to me should not be his top priority.

But when I glance at the dashboard and see that the needle has gone higher than my height in centimetres, Brand suddenly speaks.

"I saw it coming," he says, matter-of-factly, gazing ahead. "I knew this would happen, sooner or later."

I give no response, because I am not sure if he is saying this to me. I feel like Ilya is with us somehow. Though there are only two seats, it's like Ilya is in the car, perhaps hiding in the black hole beneath the boot, just like the three of us used to tuck ourselves into that tiny tree fort. I don't bother telling Brand he's missed my exit. As the sapphire roadster rumbles on and on, the cars ahead of us keep retreating towards us, seemingly fixed in place as we overtake them. I have the sense that time has stopped, or even started flowing in reverse.

6

The Tree Fort

The tree fort was Ilya's idea. If I'm not remembering wrong, we built the fort the summer after sixth grade, when we were twelve.

In those days I always liked to go and hang out at Brand's. His family operated a travelling extravaganza. He lived right on the main street of the nightmarket district, and the roll-up iron door on the first floor of the Huang household was higher than the corrugated plastic eaves on mine. It was so high that when we played badminton under the covered walkway out front, we would rarely have to replay a point because the shuttlecock had hit the ceiling. Just this was enough to impress Ilya, and me, who had both grown up on narrow, winding alleys; but there was more to Brand's house than that. It had three storeys, with what we called an "ironskin" addition on the roof, a shack with metal siding. My mother said the Huangs lived in a townhouse, which meant it was all yours, floor to roof. In our neighbourhood, there weren't many people with the means to own a townhouse. Brand must have been extremely lucky to live in a house like that, we thought. One time I said: "Well, our house's got two storeys, and it's all ours, bottom to top, just like Brand's, so I guess our house is a townhouse too." My mother said: "Silly boy, go take a good look at what kind of a place you're living in." She raised her voice, as if to make sure my father, who was sitting at the kitchen table shelling peanuts and drinking rice wine, would overhear. "We live in what people call a code violation, a house jerry-built out of scrap wood, metal, canvas and plastic. Understand? A townhouse is a Western-style domicile made of bricks. Don't you be going round saying you live in a townhouse, or I'll be the laughing stock of the whole neighbourhood."

The manual roll-up iron door to Brand's house always seemed to be up, and there were always people coming and going or sitting around that tree stump of a tea table and drinking tea. It was clearly a prime storefront location, but Brand's dad had only put in that big tea table and some stools made of cypress wood, along with a metal desk with a matching cabinet, as well as two potted money trees covered in little red bows and fake ingots. The remaining space went unused, a complete waste. Brand said the furniture arrangement was on account of Fengshui geomancy and the Five Phases: fire, metal, wood, earth and water. According to Brand, his full name—林鑫煌—provided wood 木, metal 金, and fire 火. His father's given name—淼坤—supplied the water 水 and the earth 土. Imagine that the son was called Brand Golden Grove, the father Muddy Waters Grove, and you get the idea. "A deficiency in any of the phases is detrimental," Mr Lin would say. "Bad for health and bad for business. If you ensure the phases are balanced, you won't get all paranoid when something doesn't go your way, blaming it on a lack of this or a lack of that."

Brand's and his dad's lives were still unbalanced somehow, because Brand lacked a mother, his father a wife.

Brand's father would light two sticks of incense every day at dawn and dusk, sticking one in the censer on the altar and the other in the slot by the entryway. Several New Year's Days in a row he would get up before dawn and secure a spot in the line at the temple gate, and one time he really did get to poke the first stick of incense of the year in the giant censer, in the hope of ensuring good luck for the coming year. Too bad the balance of the Five Phases and his pious beliefs couldn't fill the void that Brand's mother's departure had left.

According to Brand, there was certainly no lack of women in his father's life. His dad had so many lady visitors that Brand learned not to call any particular "Auntie" by name, to avoid a mix-up and a rolling of the eyes. Living in a place like this, finding a woman is the least of a man's worries, as his father had said. What his father could not find so easily was a woman who would cook and clean for him. Even if such a woman appeared, Brand was not about to call her "Ma". Brand said that if his father ever forced him to call an "Auntie" "Ma", he would up and run away.

Ilya felt the same way. He, too, was missing someone. Before we started elementary school, in the days when we were still riding our tricycles up and down the alleyways, Ilya's father went out one morning and never came back again. Someone found his motorcycle upstream on the levee, and his body turned up downstream in a mangrove swamp close to the mouth of the Tamsui River, crawling with bluebottle flies and a fiddler crab brandishing its gigantic propodus. Bodies washed up on the riverbank in our neighbourhood from time to time. A drowned person was nothing, but Ilya's dad's drowning caused a sensation, because he was a civil servant, a waterways inspector for the Environment Protection Agency. On one side of the levee on which he'd left his motorcycle was a chemical factory inside an ironskin warehouse that used to release effluent illegally into the river, while on the other side, a backhoe was scooping sand into the back of a truck. As for Mr Chiang's corpse, which turned up miles downstream, no water had accumulated in his lungs, but there was a gaping hole in the back of his head, big enough for the crab to crawl in and out of. The grown-ups who drank tea and played go under the banyan tree in the temple courtyard played armchair detectives, coming up with various unlikely explanations of the clues. There was only one thing on which everyone agreed, which was that Ilya's father was killed in the line of duty, which meant that Mrs Chiang was entitled to a large bereavement payout.

"Let's build a tree fort," Ilya blurted to me and Brand the summer of the sixth year after his father's death.

His proposal met with our instant approval. The summer holidays were so long, and our parents placed so many restrictions on where we could play. Mrs Chiang wouldn't let Ilya go through the watergate —the nearest gate in the levee—afraid the river that had taken her husband from her would also inflict some unforeseen fate upon her child. Brand's house was three storeys high, and his dad let him scamper up and down, but he also kept the iron door at the top of the stairs bolted shut, refusing Brand access to the rooftop addition. And though my mother basically let me run wild, she often warned me, grim-faced and in a stern tone of voice, that I was never to cross the pailou road. She gave no reason, but everyone knew the winding lane off the nightmarket street was hiding something that us kids were not supposed to see, which was her main reason for wanting to move away from the neighbourhood. The levee to the west and the pailou road to the north slashed away at our stomping ground. All that was left to us was a skewed grid of noisy city streets parked with adult means of production and transportation: food stands and scooters, mostly. The narrow covered walkways afforded space for hole-in-the-wall fried rice noodles and squid stew eateries to set out tables and stools, for hardware supply shops to stack water buckets and folding ladders, for clothes shops to display discount items, and for motorcycle sales and repair shops to do oil changes or repair tyres. They also served as open-air inns where bums could stay the night or outdoor addiction clinics where drunks could go to dry out. So although the food stalls in the nightmarket appeared only at dusk and parked in their assigned spaces along the covered walkways, it felt like we were living in a vast market all day long. Our space to roam was so limited, the summer holidays so long as to seem endless. Ilya's idea came at the right time. Building a tree fort would give us something to do.

"How do you build a tree fort?" me and Brand asked.

"All you need to build a tree fort is a tree and some wood, and we've got no lack of either," Ilya said. In the yard behind Brand's place, there was an uninhabited Japanese-style house and a mango tree. The tiled roof of the house had caved in, and the frame had collapsed, a long time since, while the luxuriant mango tree in the yard loomed over Brand's three storey mansion. We had been too scared of ghosts to dare to climb the wall and explore, but one of the local building supply shops had begun storing lumber there sometime before the summer holidays began. After several truckloads of assorted boards and planks were unloaded and stacked up in the yard, we had ourselves a new playground. We didn't have to scramble over the wall to get there, or to squeeze through the hole in the half-rotten red wooden gate. The woodpile in the yard was almost as high as the wall. We could waltz into Brand's place, walk right past the adults steeping tea at the cypress wood table, go up to Brand's room on the second floor at the back, open the window and jump, and we would land safely on our lumber playground.

Problem was, we were city kids, and none of us had ever seen a tree fort or knew what one was supposed to look like.

"That's easy," Ilya said. On the way back from a piano lesson, he came over to show us a children's encyclopaedia he'd brought. "There are two kinds of tree forts, your lookout-type and your residence-type." Ilya opened to a page with coloured illustrations and read the explanation. "A lookout-type tree fort is for defensive or security purposes, of simple construction, but built on relatively tall trees. A residence-type tree fort is for habitation, with walls and a roof to keep out wind and rain." Intrigued by the little black people in the illustration, who were clad in grass skirts, armed with spears and climbing up and down the tree fort, me and Brand stopped following what Ilya was saying.

"So which type are we going to build?" Brand asked.

"We're going to build a lookout, the higher the better," Ilya said.

"But what are we supposed to be on the lookout for?" I asked.

"What are we supposed to be on the lookout for?" Ilya repeated, seemingly uncomprehendingly.

"Yeah, what are we supposed to be on the lookout for?"

"For your future. Moron."

7

Phonics Envy

"Little pig, little pig, let me come in," I say, in the voice of the big bad wolf.

Ling-ling has heard the story a million times, but she is still listening happily on my knee, and when the big bad wolf visits the second little pig she preempts me: "Liiiiiiittle… piiiiig!" And she huffs and she puffs up her little cheeks and blows spittle all over the picture book.

"One more time!" When the big bad wolf has fallen into the pot full of water and been boiled up and eaten for supper, Ling-ling begs me to tell the story of the three little pigs again.

"You've heard it three times already! Daddy'll tell you the story of the frog prince, all right?"

Ling-ling looks up and raises three fingers on her right hand: "One more time."

"That's not how you say one more time," I say, counting on Ling-ling's fingers. "Holding out three fingers means three more times. One, two, three. One more time is like this." I extend my index finger.

"One more time, one more time, one more time!" Ling-ling brushes my hand away, kicks her legs and starts crying.

And so the big bad wolf makes another visit to the house of the three little pigs. This time I change the wording. The first little pig builds a code violation that the big bad wolf blows down with a huff and a puff. The second little pig builds a tree fort that gets blown down along with the tree. The third builds a townhouse, which the wolf cannot blow down no matter how hard he tries. The townhouse doesn't have a chimney, so there's nowhere for him to climb in, and anyway he couldn't have climbed that high. So the big bad wolf has to forget about the third little pig and go try his luck with the little sheep instead.

Ling-ling blinks, like she hasn't noticed that the buildings are different. She's at the age of cognitive confusion. She can't tell A and 4 apart, and often mixes up you and me and back and front.

I'm in no hurry to correct her; sooner or later she'll get it. But Amanda is very concerned.

"What'll we do? Ling-ling's almost two, but she can't say three or four yet," says Amanda. Just out of the shower, head wrapped in a towel like a Sikh lady, she is busy spreading cream on her cheeks with two fingers in front of the vanity. "And she still can't figure out the difference between 6 and 9: which circle goes up and which goes down."

"6 and 9 look a lot alike, don't you think? Put them together into 69 and let them roll around on the floor and it doesn't matter who's on the bottom and who's on the top," I say with a grin. While her hands are busy, I sneak behind her back and put my hands inside her bathrobe. "Blame the Arabs for designing easily confused numerals."

"Don't you think Ling-ling's a slow learner? The accountant at work's kid is only a year and a half and can already read the phonics," she says, twisting her body and hip-checking me. "Not in front of the baby."

"So what if she sees. She doesn't know what we're doing."

"You don't think she understands anything. Don't underestimate her."

"Didn't you just say she's a slow learner? Now you're afraid she understands everything."

"You're confusing two totally different kinds of understanding."

"Well, I guess it's the cryptographer in me. In cipher design, confusion is the core of data security. First we confuse, then we diffuse. Confusion means that each character of the ciphertext should depend…"

"There you go again."

Amanda rolls her eyes, unties the towel from her hair and turns on the dryer to indicate she doesn't want to hear any more. She looks down, stands in front of the mirror, one hand on her hairdryer, the other hand tousling her hair like she is trying to get some irritating thought out of her head.

At the sound of the dryer, Ling-ling goes to hide in the family room and play with blocks on the foam floor. I turn on the stereo and let her listen to one of the Happy Kid Song cycles on YouTube. Then I return to the bedroom to continue the conversation.

"Don't you think it's cute that Ling-ling can't say three or four, like she's at sixes and sevens?"

"I should say you're the one at sixes and sevens. Or should I say sixes and nines? Sorry, lame joke."

"Why do we have to be in such a hurry for our daughter to understand? Any kid learning to speak will go through a period of linguistic confusion. Ling-ling can't count from one to ten, or read the phonics, yet. But what's the harm? She'll be fine. This is how kids at her age are supposed to be: confusion is normal, not to mention cute."

"Yeah, really cute."

"I bet you hadn't discovered how similar 8 and B are. I'd never noticed, or I'd forgotten. But Ling-ling has helped me rediscover the similarity. To little children, the two symbols look the same, just two circles one on top of the other. We adults have to tell circles from half-circles, and if you can't tell them apart as an adult you'll get laughed at, or worse. Ling-ling can't tell red from yellow, or the difference between a duck and a chicken. But she's not even two! She has the right to be confused."

Amanda doesn't pay me any attention. She tosses the dryer aside. Tousling her damp hair, she walks to the computer, pulls out the chair and sits down. I follow her there and see a new crop growing in the farm she just harvested after coming home from work. I can't understand why the whole world is crazy about this boring game. I just know that to Amanda, debating early childhood development seems a lot less fun than virtual watering and weeding. I have less than two years of teaching experience, but in class I often noticed that instead of taking notes students would draw circles or write the same character over and over again. People seem to use repetition as a form of resistance. Students resist dull lectures; my wife, her husband's loquaciousness. I know I am barking up the wrong tree, but whether at school or at home I somehow have to keep talking.

"Haven't you noticed the charmingly silly expression that often appears on toddlers' faces? I think it's the outward shape of confusion. In their eyes, the world is full of easily confusable pairs like A and 8. She must not understand why she's supposed to call you Mummy and me Daddy. Remember when she kept getting us mixed up? I dare say, this is the time in her life when she feels the safest. She doesn't even know what danger is. Why do we need to be in a rush for her to leave this most fortunate stage in her life?"

"The company accountant's kid can read the phonics."

"So you said."

"And the twenty-six letters. And he can count from one to fifty."

"Great!"

"When I completed my postpartum month and my two months of maternity leave, she was only eight months pregnant. She was always bugging me with questions about what it was like. And now? She wouldn't ask me anything, because her kid is four months younger than Ling-ling but can do so many things Ling-ling can't."

"Good for him."

"When she found out that Ling-ling couldn't sort blocks by shape, you know what she said? She said: 'What? Your kid can't tell triangles from squares? I can't believe it! Our Bei-bei got tired of sorting games before he turned one.' She said it so loud the whole office heard. You should have heard her tone of voice."

"So what?"

Amanda takes a deep breath and lets go of the mouse.

"What's with your attitude? I'm trying to have a serious discussion."

"What attitude?"

"It's like you couldn't care less."

"Wait a second, who's the one who couldn't care less first? Who went and dried her hair just now when I was speaking? And who started planting virtual vegetables?"

"I was listening to everything you said. Can't I multitask? Not like you. Yes, you've been standing there not doing anything and you still haven't heard anything I've said. It's like nothing I say is important to you, like I'm making a mountain out of a molehill. Who's the hypocrite?"

With a kick of the leg and a twist of the waist, she slides the swivel chair away from the desk half a step and half-turns to face me. I am shocked at how effortlessly she can complete such a complicated sliding and twisting manoeuvre. Must be the result of long practice in the swivel chair in her office cubicle.

"How do you know I wasn't listening? You're not making a mountain out of a molehill, you're making a big deal out of nothing."

"You mean there's nothing wrong with Ling-ling?"

"I mean you don't have to compare our daughter with what's her name's kid at your company."

"This isn't about what's her name, it's about Ling-ling. I'm worried about her. She's a slow learner, at least linguistically. My colleague sent her daughter to a daycare where they stimulate right brain development, and in just six months she can eat by herself and use the toilet. And Ling-ling? She spends all day at home with you and what has she learned?"

"You mean to say our Ling-ling's dumb?"

"My daughter isn't dumb, it's just that nobody's teaching her."

"What are you supposed to teach a toddler? I teach her to sing songs and I read stories to her. Isn't that enough?"

"Other people's kids can already read the letters of the alphabet."

"Who cares about other people's kids? We're not English speakers. There'll be time to study English later on."

"Later on it'll be too late."

"Did you learn the letters of the alphabet by the time you were two? No? But now you're working at a multinational."

"The world's a different place now. You've been a stay at home dad too long. You don't know what's going on out there."

"Now you're blaming me for not going out to work?"

"No I'm not."

"Didn't we agree that I'd take care of Ling-ling until she went to kindergarten?"

"Did I say I blame you for staying at home?"

"Not exactly, but that's your attitude."

"Since when are you so sensitive?"

"Me sensitive?"

"You are sensitive. And you've changed. The slightest criticism and you lose it."

"Aren't you the one that lost it first?"

"No I didn't."

"Yes you did."

Now we're both standing up and yelling at each other.

When Amanda was pregnant we promised each other we'd never fight over parenting. But over the past year we've had a number of nasty fights. I feel like Amanda is insinuating that I should go out and find a job, but we made an agreement that she doesn't want to break. All she can do is pressure me on phonics.

"If you want me to go out and find a job, then say so. You don't have to beat around the bush."

"Daniel Fang!" Amanda's face darkens. "Now I'm angry."

Screeeeeeeeeech! An explosion of sound ends our fight. However emotionally confused and diffused we feel, we both act on the same parental instinct, charging towards the source of the screech, the family room where Ling-ling is playing. I embrace Ling-ling as she rushes towards me, frantic arms extended, while Amanda leaps to the television cabinet to twist off the knob on the amplifier.

The deafening noise disappears, and it is quiet for two seconds. The next explosion comes when Ling-ling bursts out crying.

"Who told you to twist the knob? Don't do it again!"

Ling-ling buries her face in my shoulder, covering my black cardigan in snot and tears.

"It's all right, honey." Amanda comes over and pats Ling-ling's back. "Don't cry, honey, don't cry."

But Ling-ling won't stop crying. She cries until both our hearts soften.

"Don't be scared, that was just music. It's all right."

Amanda and I comfort her together.

8

Two Sets of Russian Dolls

"Music scares me," said Ilya.

His words were almost drowned out by waves of music.

That was the last time I saw him. We met in a bar we used to frequent. Now, half a year later I've finally fished up the memory and tossed it on land, just like I'd fished Ilya's confession out of the noise of the bar in the first place.

"What? The c…rap music they play in this bar scares you?"

"Lame joke. No, I'm scared of music, any music," he said. This time he spoke loud enough to drown out the sound of the rapper.

"Are you kidding? You're a great pianist."

Ilya'd just come back from a tour in Europe. After Christmas he was heading to Japan for a charity concert celebrating the two hundredth anniversary of Chopin's birth. He didn't have time to go to my house in the suburbs, which was at any rate no longer a place to have a conversation, so we met in a bar downtown and had a two hour chat. He hadn't forgotten Amanda or Ling-ling, and asked how they were doing. He'd even brought back a present for Ling-ling. "It's a set of Russian dolls. I bought two in a market by a church, one for Ling-ling, one for myself."

I tried to remember what else we talked about that night half a year before, his complexion, expression, tone and body language. Maybe it was extremely meaningful, that meeting, the last of our lives. Maybe he slipped the key into our conversation that evening, the key to the code he'd left behind for me to decipher and tell everyone what they wanted to know. (Why? How could this happen? He was doing so well!) Maybe, though, it was just an ordinary meeting in a bar, just part of our routine as friends, and I am blowing it out of all proportion because it was the last time I saw him. Or maybe I was oblivious to what he was trying to tell me the whole time, because I'd had too much to drink or was busy eyeing the hot babe's bust at the next table's. At any rate, the fact that it was the "last time" has gilded the memory, making me remember it with a certain solemnity.

"I don't know what you're afraid of," I remember saying. "You know, sometimes I think you do the same work as me. As I see it, the notes in a score are like the symbols in a code, and a pianist has the same task as a code-breaker. The difference is that there's only a single key to a code, whereas there are many possible interpretations of a score."

"You're right," Ilya said, I think. "The same piece of music can be interpreted in different ways by different people or by the same person on different occasions. It could never be the same. You can't hear the differences. I'm not saying I don't respect your ear, but that you only hear one version, the one I play in in the auditorium or the one the recording technician decides is the best. You can't hear all the practising I do before I perform. Endless practice sessions, infinite interpretations. Ironically, the most perfect interpretation, if it exists, is always the one you play in practice. My best performances are in the practice room without anyone else to hear. I've never played perfectly on stage. It would be impossible. The lights, the tails, the white shirt, and all the onlookers in the darkness – who could play his best in such a pressure cooker? I would rather wear shorts and a singlet on stage, to approach the level of relaxation I can enjoy when I'm practising at home."

First and final memories are the hardest to forget, people say. Thirty years later, I can still remember my very first memory, kneeling in front of the family altar with a hundred dollar bill in my fist. You'd think I'd be able to remember my final meeting with Ilya half a year ago even more vividly, but I actually can't. I can't remember when exactly Ilya elaborated upon his fear of music. Maybe when we tapped glasses on the first toast, maybe when happy hour was about to end, maybe after we had downed a half dozen beers. Maybe he didn't even say all these things on that particular occasion. Maybe I've suffered a retrieval error, combining memories of different times and places into a conversation I believe we had on our final evening together. I can't remember how

Ilya sounded, whether he was gripping the glistening beer bottle or whether he was taking apart the Russian dolls one by one and putting them together again. All I can do is assume I've given an adequate account of our conversation.

Thus far, however surprising Ilya's words were, I mostly knew what he meant. But the things he went on to say, whenever or wherever he said them, were beyond me at the time, and still are.

It might have gone something like this: "Call it interpretive difference. A trendy academic way of putting it, I guess. And we could very well ignore the academics and just keep on practising. The problem is even if you ignore it, difference still exists, and a lot of it is emotional. Yes, emotional. I'm not a robot after all. I can't practise to the point where each performance is the same. So I don't think you can say that our jobs are the same. No. As you said, you're looking for a single answer, while I'll give you a different answer every time. You can call it interpretive difference, but 'interpretation' is just a convenient subterfuge, a way of rationalizing difference without resolving it, especially the differences that arise in the same human being. The inconsistencies over time. Because that's what happens to me. If I interpret a piece of music differently every time, then how should the music interpret me? If you treat someone differently every time, then how is he supposed to treat you? He'd never be able to understand you. It's ironic, isn't it? You think you know a piece of music, but it doesn't know you, not at all. When you come to this realization, then you think: what right do I have to go and interpret it? How can I face music and not feel afraid?"

Of course, that wasn't the only topic of conversation that night. That's just the part I've managed to remember. Memory is unavoidably selective, and with selectiveness come gaps. Maybe Ilya spoke clearly enough that evening, and it is the gaps in my memory that have created difficulties of understanding after the fact. Just like when a code has been compromised so much it's become incoherent, even with the key.

The gaps in memory create spaces in which the imagination runs wild, making assumptions and jumping to conclusions, splicing connections and twisting the truth. I decide to quit trying to find meaning in my doubtful memories of six months ago, but when I do my memory replays the conversation I had with Mrs Chiang.

"You should pity Ilya. He was the weak one."

Of course, her statement has also surfaced selectively, whatever the principle of selection is. The conversation she had with me, or with the person she thought I was, is still fresh in my mind. Ilya's funeral is still recent, so my memory of it has had less time to decay, and should be relatively free of gaps and distortions. But enough time has passed for a flip in my understanding of what Mrs Chiang said. When Mrs Chiang said Ilya was weak, I thought she meant he lacked the courage to face life. But after trying to remember that conversation at the bar six months ago, I feel like Ilya's problem wasn't life in general, that what Ilya lost the courage to face wasn't life but music.

Could one interpret his fear of music as fear of failure? Maybe, but that wouldn't be the only interpretation, certainly not now. The first thing someone who leaves the feast early loses is the right to interpret, let alone control interpretation. He can't stop people from turning his departure into a topic of conversation, from speculating freely about his motivation. Just as any musician would have a different interpretation of a certain piece of music, so everyone might have a different interpretation of a certain person's death.

My guess, that he was afraid of failure, probably sounds implausible, given how successful Ilya was. Whose distance from failure could have been greater? The standing he enjoyed in the music world never surprised me, because to me it was always yesterday's news.

We always knew Ilya would make it, even when we were kids.

9

Spider and Egret

The tree fort was finished but me and Brand hadn't seen our futures yet.

But it's not like we hadn't seen anything. We climbed into the fort from the woodpile and looked all around and discovered we weren't living in a grand nightmarket, as we'd assumed, but under a patchwork of ramshackle roofs. Some of tile, some of sheet metal, some of corrugated plastic, and some of water-repellent fabric: yes, some roofs were tarpaulins, battened down and sealed with a coat of pitch. There were a lot of strange things on the roofs: discarded tyres, mossy bricks, hollow concrete blocks, clay gardening pots, earthen jars and rotten railway ties. The roofs were all connected, fitted together like the pieces of a gigantic jigsaw puzzle, a puzzle so uneven that it looked like it had been dropped or stepped on.

Our tree fort wasn't too sturdy either. Calling it a fort was being charitable. Actually, it was just a few boards fastened to the branches to form a platform, with some shorter boards angling up to improvise a roof: it was a simple lean-to. When the wind blew we would clutch hold of the sturdy trunk, afraid the boards would escape the bondage of nail and rope and return whence they had come: the woodpile down below.

Standing up there on the makeshift platform of our fort and gazing out at the crude roofs of the dwellings in our community was dispiriting. But thanks to the height of the mango tree we made an unexpected discovery. Our fort was higher than the pailou gateways, higher than the levee, so reminiscent of a prison wall. From our lookout, we saw how constrained our stomping ground really was, as well as the no-go areas, the parts of our neighbourhood our parents had cordoned off and declared off limits. Ilya saw the river on the other side of the levee. For the first time in his life, Brand didn't have to look up to see the rooftop addition. And I saw another puzzle, to the north of the pailou road. The only difference was that the pieces on our side didn't fit so tightly together as the ones on the north side did: folks there had used green, blue or blue-and-white striped canvas sheets to cover the gaps between the roofs, like they were worried about getting sunburned or rained on or something. Along one lane they'd even stretched canvas sheets from the eaves on the covered walkways all the way to the ground so nobody could see what was going on inside, no matter where they were.

"Do you see?" Ilya shouted in the wind, his arms wrapped around the trunk. "I never thought we were so close to the river."

"I can't see anything," I said.

"Me neither," Brand said. "I always thought Dad had installed windows in the addition."

Ilya hadn't noticed how disappointed we sounded. He was like a hyperactive monkey, climbing all around. "See, I told you guys we should build a lookout, the higher the better," he said proudly. Straddling a branch, he broke off a twig, stripped off the leaves, and started conducting the river, the sandbars, the white egrets and the smoke-spewing sand dredgers, closing his eyes every so often, a look of intense enjoyment on his face. Then, as if he'd remembered something important he had to do, he tossed his baton aside, climbed down the tree and left.

That's the way Ilya was. Me and Brand were used to it. He'd always leave us halfway through a game, and the older we got the less he was allowed to play with us. That year, Mrs Chiang had enrolled him in a bunch of cram school classes. On top of that, he had to practise piano six hours every day. He hadn't even had time to come help me and Brand build the fort.

"Why's Ilya so pleased with himself? The tree fort wasn't his doing," said Brand.

"Yeah, we built the tree fort, but he's prouder of it than we are."

"What's up with that?" asked Brand, raising an eyebrow and narrowing his eyes.

"Maybe he saw the future," I suggested.

I wasn't sure whether Ilya had seen his future from the fort, but I had already glimpsed it, not from the fort but from the "piano room" in his house. Me and Brand went this one time to Ilya's place to listen to him play the piano. His house was in a winding alley, even further from the main street than mine. It was a miracle that the movers managed to get a grand piano down that alley and squeeze it into a shack with the tyres on the roof, into a space that couldn't have been more than ten pings, about thirty square metres. My dad said the piano was more expensive than a car, and that Mrs Chiang must have bought it with Ilya's daddy's bereavement benefit. My mom said there was something wrong with the woman, spending money on a piano rather than on a trip out of this hellhole. Not to mention that sticking an instrument so big it belonged in a school auditorium in her house left no space for a television or a dinner table. Brand said he couldn't understand how Ilya could practise piano without the neighbours complaining. There were jazz drums, an electric piano and a saxophone on the third floor of Brand's house, in a practice room for the troupe. But his dad had damped the room by edging the walls with polystyrene and the door with sponge. Brand called it the studio. As far as we could see, Mrs Chiang hadn't taken any precautions to prevent the sound of Ilya's practising from disturbing the neighbours.

Mrs Chiang must not consider the sound of the piano noise, I told Brand. As for why the neighbours didn't complain, well, they weren't exactly quiet. They didn't need a grand piano to make noise: they brawled, gave booze-inspired monologues, beat the kids, belted out karaoke hits, recited Buddhist scripture over a microphone to a wooden clapper accompaniment, or tried to imitate the hysterical canned laughter of the television variety shows. None of them had the right to protest about Ilya's six hours of piano practice. Nobody even thought to protest. They might even have felt that the sound of Ilya's grand piano added a certain sophistication to the lane. Ilya's piano allowed folks to forget they were living in wretched poverty under rotting roofs in the middle of a slum.

But my mother was right: the grand piano really filled the place up. When Mrs Chiang opened the door and let me and Brand in, we had to squeeze along the wall and stand at the end of the instrument, because there wasn't space for any other furniture. Ilya was sitting on the only chair, facing the row of shiny black and white keys, smiling awkwardly at us. He said his mother was worried about how he would perform on stage in the upcoming competition, when all eyes would be on him. She'd asked him to invite me and Brand to come watch him play, to accustom him to an audience.

Actually, Ilya didn't have to explain. We knew what his mother had in mind. Me and Brand had never gone to a piano competition before, but we knew there wouldn't be anyone standing by the piano like we were doing. Not to say we didn't get anything out of it; it was really interesting watching someone practise from so close up. When Ilya started to play I was captivated by his hand motions, which reminded me of the movements of two animals. His left hand was like a startled spider flitting up and down so fast you couldn't see its steps, while his right was like a high-stepping white egret strolling slowly in a rice paddy. Soon the egret turned into a second spider, a frenzied treble spider that raced up and down with the bass spider on the left. Then both spiders turned into long-legged egrets stepping elegantly on the keys. At that the performance ended, leaving only a humming echo in our ears.

Two animals had appeared before my eyes, as had Ilya's future. I'd seen him wearing tails like a magician and standing on the stage performing in front of a full house in a magnificent concert hall, winning fame, fortune, influence and everything else with his spider-egret hands. But this vision of Ilya's future soon dissolved into another. After Ilya had finished playing that dance duet for spider and egret he hadn't looked up at me or Brand, just stared expressionless at the keyboard as if waiting for something. I couldn't help remembering his mother in the next room. Though I couldn't hear her I had a powerful sense of her presence. We'd heard her rinsing the greens and the rice, but as soon as Ilya started playing, the sound of splashing in the next room vanished, only to resume after his little performance was done. Only then did Ilya's face relax into a smile.

"That was Chopin's Third Prelude. I still can't get it right. My mother says the balance between my left and right hands is off."

We never went to hear him play again. Brand said he greatly admired Ilya for his musical talent, and for being willing to go along with his mother and spend all his time at the keyboard. Brand's dad had tried to teach him how to play drums, but he failed, because although him and his father's names balanced out the Five Phases, Brand had no sense of rhythm. In his hands, drum sticks were like unwieldy bamboo poles. At the drums, he was like an old man shuffling along on his cane. No matter how hard he tried he couldn't play a seamless running rhythm, a sizzling beat, like his old man. And every time Brand played a drum beat wrong, his dad's drum stick would fall in perfect time and rap him on the back of the hand. Brand said he practised for three months before he'd had enough. Whenever his dad told him to practise he wanted to scream and yell and cry for help, knowing that it wouldn't do any good: with all the polystyrene nobody would hear him scream, not even if he burst his vocal cords. So he thought of a way to end his torment once and for all. With the spirit of the samurai warrior who cuts off his snake-bitten hand to stop the flow of poison, he took a penknife to his dad's expensive jazz drum set. Then he sat on the ground, closed his eyes and waited for a beating that never came. When his father saw his beloved drum set eviscerated, he was momentarily speechless, but when finally he spoke his voice was tender, a tone Brand had never heard before. "I was wrong, son," his dad said. "I shouldn't have been so heavy-handed, locking you up and forcing you to practise. Now you're free. Go out and play."

I forget where Brand told me this. Maybe in the tree fort, maybe under the pailou gateway. All I remember is that Brand never told Ilya about his life-changing experience. Brand said that Ilya was certain to succeed, but that success would come at great cost: he would never be able to rebel against parental authority the way Brand had. Brand looked uncomfortable, though. I guessed his father's tender tone had taken him by surprise, made him wonder whether his impulsive choice would cause him hardship later on in life.

But he didn't really have anything to worry about. Though his future wasn't visible from the fort, we could see his townhouse right next door. Even if he couldn't enjoy a musical career like Ilya, he at least had the townhouse and the variety show band to inherit. Unlike me. I had both my parents, but neither of them seemed likely to leave me anything. And neither had any feel for music. There wasn't a single musical instrument at my house. The only thing you could blow a sound on was one of my dad's empty liquor bottles.

"What do you need an instrument for? You just keep studying, because there's a house of gold in those textbooks of yours. That house of gold sure as hell isn't located in our neighbourhood," my mother said. "You just put your heart into your studies, and someday you'll buy a house and take Ma far away from here."

Blame Ilya for proposing a lookout, for forcing us to think about the future before we were ready and to notice everything lacking in the present. I wasn't a talented student. My grades at school put me a long way away from a house of gold, further than the distance from Ilya's house to the main road. I didn't have any musical talent either. I never studied an instrument, and I wasn't Pavarotti: when the music teacher was getting us ready for a choral competition, she told me to just open and close my mouth for show. I was never meant to be an athlete: I was always the first to get knocked out in dodgeball, and had never had a place on the relay team. It seemed like I lacked talent for a lot of things. Which sometimes made me resent my parents for being in such a rush to combine their X and Y chromosomes. That, I was sure, was the reason for my sense of lack.

I know that was unfair of me, because congenital or environmental disadvantages aside, my parents didn't deprive me, and even gave me something other kids only dreamed about. There was always paper around the house. Pa often brought back posters and leaflets from the cinema, as well as "storyline" fliers with blurbs and previews for new films. Ma used the posters as tablecloths, and I folded the fliers into paper aeroplanes and boats. Then she noticed the fliers were only printed on one side, and thought it was a waste to turn them into boats or planes. Better to paint or write something on the blank side. She gave me a brush and an inkpot, and I found that the cards were just the right size to practise writing characters on, one per card. I wrote big standard script characters, like capital letters in English. Eventually, I discovered an interest in calligraphy. I covered countless cards in characters in all the scripts, and from third grade on all the awards I won were for calligraphy competitions. There were all sorts of competitions, for Filial Piety Month, Sino-Japanese Exchange, the

Anniversary of Generalissimo Chiang Kai-shek's Blessed Birth, Eye Health, and Crime Prevention. My award certificates from school or extracurricular competitions covered one whole wall of the family room.

"If you want to do well you've got to write well," my dad said. "Look at me. I never did well at school because I never learned proper penmanship."

He liked to watch me write, sitting across from me at the table, drinking spirits and shelling peanuts while I inked characters on cards. My grandmother, who had never been to school, didn't recognize the characters I wrote, or what all the awards I'd brought home were for, but would often make supposedly offhand remarks to the neighbours to show off my achievements. She'd say: "Don't be deceived, that dopey-looking grandson of mine does so well at school they're always giving him awards." If I remember rightly, that was the second time they'd ever agreed on anything. The first time was when they'd caught me with the hundred dollar bill and decided that if they didn't kneel me before the ancestral altar I'd turn into a thief. Now my mother and father and long-widowed grandmother would praise me unreservedly in Mandarin and Taiwanese, unanimous in their conviction that there was a direct relationship between writing well and doing well at school. Of course, they couldn't know that by the time I'd grown up, nobody would use a pen, let alone a brush, to write characters any more. Computers would soon be ubiquitous.

10
Daddy's Perpetual Motion Machine

Ling-ling climbs onto the red slide, smiles and waves at me, then slides down.

I've been sitting here on the concrete bench by the playground for almost half an hour. As soon as I brought Ling-ling to the park, she ran to the jungle gym. Not big enough to climb about and bash around on the platform of rollers, tubes and ladders with the older kids, she just walked carefully up the six or seven steps of the slide with her hands on the railing, sat at the edge, then slid down with a smile, enjoying one of the first thrills of her life.

The sun is cooking the nappy bag I put on the concrete bench. Ling-ling's hair is all damp, but she shows no sign of slowing down. I time her with my watch. It takes her ten seconds to climb up the slide, five seconds to sit down and wave, less than two seconds to slide down, and three seconds to stand up and run back to the steps. If not for other kids dawdling before the stairs or the slide, getting in her way, Ling-ling could theoretically complete three cycles a minute.

When Ling-ling waves at me for the sixty-seventh time it finally occurs to me I can use the time to read something. I open the bag and get out the Costco leaflet from among the nappies, wipes, tissues, cup, bib, plastic bowl and spoon. I brought it as a diversion for Ling-ling, who likes things with colourful designs, especially when she won't sit still and let me feed her. But I've discovered I quite like to read the ad copy in the explosion bubbles as a way of passing time.

"Daddy, look!"

"Daddy's looking at you."

Import lace bras push breasts up, get your cleavage in a cup, $599 before the 15th. The mixed race model's left breast has a red mole on it, doesn't it? Or is it a rash? Or a misprint?

"Daddy, look!"

Ling-ling is yelling. Her hands are clutching the railing as she waits at the top of the slide with two or three kids about the same size behind her, unsure what to do now that the line has stopped moving.

As soon as I gaze over she slides down. Maybe what keeps Ling-ling moving isn't the slide but my gaze. But my gaze doesn't belong exclusively to Ling-ling, and though it can't determine the cause of the underwear model's discolouration it can certainly fan out through the entire playground or even part of the park beyond. The kids in the playground are mostly under five. It doesn't take a cryptologist to figure out why. It isn't a holiday, so all the school age children are in school. That leaves only the kids kindergartens refuse to take, the ones who need one-on-two or even one-on-one supervision. As a result, there are an equal number of tykes and adults in and around the playground. Some of the adults are sitting on a concrete bench like me. Some are waiting under a tree. Some are standing by the slide, the rocking horse, or the sandbox. Each adult's gaze has turned into a kite string. Each lets a little perpetual motion machine swoop and climb, without ever letting it out of sight.

Sitting in an amusement area under the sun, listening to birdsong and children's laughter, I should be happy, but the longer I sit there the more disconcerted I feel. There are boys and girls running and jumping on the jungle gym and the sponge matting on the ground, but almost all of the adults are women. There are only a few men, all elderly, their faces wrinkly, their hair white. In the whole community park, there is only one able-bodied guy. There he is, the one in his late thirties. Sitting on a concrete bench by the playground, he's checking out an underwear advertisement in a Costco catalogue. No wonder he looks ill at ease.

"Go way!"

It's Ling-ling's voice, belligerent and shrill. There's an ongoing incident on the slide. I return my gaze to Ling-ling just in time to see her shove the little boy behind her. He is about the same age and height as her. He doesn't fall over, just stumbles back a step and bumps into another kid, a little girl with sparse hair.

I bolt towards the slide, noting two other adults headed in the same direction, one from the gazebo, the other from under a tree. We reach the slide at about the same time. The little girl is sitting on the ground, bawling. Ling-ling is blocking the entrance to the slide, refusing to let the little boy climb up.

"Ling-ling, what did I tell you about pushing people?" I say.

"Go way!" repeats Ling-ling, pursing her lips.

"What did Daddy tell you? You have to play with the other children."

"I don't want to!"

"I'm so sorry." I grab Ling-ling's hand and apologize to the little boy's mother.

"They're just kids, it's nothing," the lady from the gazebo says. She is holding a mobile phone with the cover open and has a pair of sunglasses hanging at the throat of her white blouse. Her tone of voice compels me to take another look. "Go over there and play, you, and don't get in the way."

"Is she okay?" This is no time to let my mind wander! I hurry to apologize to the other mother, whose little girl, I notice, has a purple mark at the corner of her eye. At first I think she's injured, but looking closely I see that it is a birthmark. The woman is tiny and dark-skinned. She doesn't reply, just pulls the little girl away, anxiously patting her trousers and arranging her shirt. "Don't crying! Don't crying!" she keeps repeating, in English. Worry and fear are written all over her dark face.

I return to my spot on the concrete bench. I don't want to look at the model in the lace bra any more. I only have eyes for the young mother in the play area, curious as to her identity. Anyone able-bodied would probably be at work on a weekday. The rest are "mainland brides" who haven't got their work permits yet, Indonesian or Filipina maids, retired grandparents, and of course house-husbands in early middle age standing around looking ill at ease, holding a Costco catalogue.

Ling-ling is playing on the slide, the sun is getting higher and higher. Almost all of the kids and adults have left the play area, but Ling-ling shows no sign of slowing down. She keeps going and going, climbing up, waving, sliding down and climbing up again.

11

The Treasure Trove

Ilya said we should each put some personal treasure in the tree fort, to make it feel like a secret base.

Brand immediately nodded to voice enthusiastic affirmation, but I was a bit peeved. Me and Brand had done all the work building the tree fort, but Ilya could enjoy it and declare how we were going to use it, when his only contribution was moving his lips.

"You're not as smart as Ilya, so stop complaining. Just do as he says," Brand said.

After making the proposal Ilya went home to practise, leaving me and Brand sitting on the woodpile trying to figure out where to store the stuff. The fort wouldn't provide shelter from the wind and rain and no matter what it wasn't a good hiding place. We sat there, feeling glum. Brand watched the windowless addition on the roof of his house, while I looked north of the pailou road, at the raggedy sea of coloured canvas awnings luffing like sails in the wind. Suddenly, both of us had ideas. Brand said he could bring a plastic rubbish bin from home with a lid to keep the treasures dry. I suggested we could remove some more wood from the pile to make a little hole: put the bin in there and we'd have a kind of storage chamber, or a treasure trove.

Making the hole wouldn't be hard at all. To set up the fort, we had needed to get nails and ropes. We wouldn't need anything to make a hole, just take out some boards and rearrange the rest like building blocks. We'd have a space for our things in no time. The only worry was centipedes. Every time we moved a board a centipede would scurry out or fall on our legs. Fortunately, they were about the size of caterpillars, not long enough to scare anyone. We'd stomp them or kick them all the way onto the rotten tiles of the roof next door.

Ilya had opinions about Brand's idea. He thought putting treasures in a rubbish bin was an insult. But when he saw the hole, or cave, we'd made, and especially when we demonstrated how to pull a few boards across to conceal the entrance, he was so excited he felt like tossing Mrs Chiang onto the roof next door. He didn't want to go home and practise.

I could understand the way he felt, because of all the space: the treasure trove had room enough for the three of us to crouch down inside, while his family room was so full of that grand piano that me and Brand had felt a bit claustrophobic. Actually, I felt the same way at home, because the situation at my house wasn't much different: most of the space in the family room was taken up by my grandmother's mahogany altar, my mother's Singer sewing machine, and Pa's glass whisky case, always empty. All that furniture left too little space for the four of us to spend time together. If three of us were there and the fourth came in, one of us would have to leave. Sometimes Grandma would push open the door and talk with a neighbour in the lane, sometimes Ma would retreat into the kitchen to cut meat and rinse greens for lunch or dinner. When none of the adults wanted to leave they'd tell me to go out and play or go do calligraphy at the table.

Soon Ilya came with an armful of the treasures he wanted to store in the treasure trove: a Boy Scout rope, a pair of black plastic glasses, a watch that didn't tick, and a camping stove with a broken burner and an immaculate pot. Me and Brand stood at the edge of the trove and watched Ilya put his things into the rubbish bin with a solemn look on his face, thinking a bin was the right place for them. Ilya said they belonged to his dad. When his mother had cleared out the house to make room for the piano two years before, his dad's personal effects had all been stuffed in plastic bags and cardboard boxes and tossed in the bin. Everything was gone, except these few things Ilya had managed to salvage without his mother finding out.

Brand just brought two things: a penknife and a metal build super alloy mobile suit, a kind of transformer toy based on a Japanese cartoon. Both were made of metal, but were worth very different amounts of money. Every kid in the class had a penknife, but only Brand could afford a mobile suit, which could move every joint and fold into a car.

The presence of a mobile suit lent lustre to our humble tree fort, firing up our resolve to protect and camouflage the place lest other kids in the neighbourhood discover it. As for the penknife, Brand didn't say anything, just put it in the rubbish bin. Ilya didn't even notice, but I knew this was the knife that had given Brand his freedom. In his mind the value of the knife was many times greater than the expensive Japanese toy.

I didn't bring anything. Which left Ilya feeling a bit peeved, because he thought I wasn't participating. If this had been Brand's idea he would have thrown his ample weight around, grabbing my collar and saying in a grown up's tone of voice: "You don't respect me?" But Ilya wasn't Brand. His family didn't have a mishmash of people coming to the house to drink tea. The only person he had at home was a mother who'd only ever wanted to become a music teacher. He just gave me a cold stare and climbed up the tree to catch a glimpse of his future.

I didn't do it on purpose, not participating in Ilya's game. I really didn't know what to bring, what things deserved to be treasured. I didn't have a mobile suit. I didn't have a Lego set. Both of my parents were still around, but even if they'd died all they'd have left me would have been empty liquor bottles and complaints that rang through our code violation of a shack.

There was a little iron box under my bed with all the different brands of ballpoint pens I'd ever used in my six years of elementary school, but I was afraid that if I brought it Brand and Ilya'd laugh at me. It also contained a brush as big as a paintbrush from when I won the Counterespionage Calligraphy Competition. About five centimetres in diameter, it could have sucked up all the ink in the pot. To me it was trash. There were a few buttons and a couple of flattened liquor bottle caps. I forget why I'd kept them; perhaps because I was too lazy to throw them out.

The only thing I used to take out of the metal box to play with was a set of acrylic Chinese chess pieces with a few pieces missing. I didn't have a board, and the missing pieces would have made the game unplayable. All I could do was arrange them, red and black, in battle arrays, pretending they were two warring armies. I surveyed war games in my imagination. Among the pieces was a chipped black footsoldier. (The paint on the right leg of the character for person 人 inside the character for pawn had fallen off: it had turned into 卒). Only this one piece was incomplete, and that's why I liked him best. I liked to tell a tragic story about him. Like the steadfast one-legged tin soldier in the Hans Christian Andersen fairytale, the one-legged footsoldier had some kind of congenital deformity and was ostracized and bullied by his peers. In the wars I waged in my imagination, he was always the last one standing. Of course, at first nobody had any regard for him. But facing the oncoming force of the red side, black advisers and elephants were surrounded and slain by mere footsoldiers; and when the feeble old black general was finally encircled, and the other pieces on the nearly decimated black side were all quaking with terror, unable to come up with a plan to rescue their liege, it was that one-legged (or sometimes one-armed or one-eyed) footsoldier who slipped behind enemy lines, took the general on his back and ran the gauntlet, spiriting him out of harm's way. Of course, sometimes he would be mortally wounded while completing his sacred mission, but by the time of his demise he would have already won the respect and admiration of all who had looked down on him before. They formed a circle around the unknown soldier and held a solemn memorial for the greatest champion who had ever lived. Sometimes several tears would fall from my eyes onto the floor in the vicinity of that heroic plastic personage.

I didn't dare bring my chess set, because if they knew I was playing war games with chess pieces they would have doubted my sanity, and because unlike those crappy things Ilya brought or Brand's penknife, the chess pieces weren't symbolic of a specific change in my life, even if the one-legged footsoldier was a kind of talisman of personal transformation.

Brand said: "Everyone has at least one significant thing. Think hard."

Brand was right and wrong. Everyone has something that is personally meaningful, but it's not necessarily something you can show other people. I didn't have to think hard to know what that special something was for me: a certain dog-eared hundred dollar bill. The problem was that the green bill I had clutched was no longer in circulation. Even if the currency had not changed from green to red, my father would have spent that bill, as he spent any money that came into his hands. Even if he hadn't spent the bill, and had kept it in his wallet a decade, I would not have had the guts to steal it a second time. When I realized I was a thief at the age of three I lost the courage to steal anything ever again.

Ilya suddenly started climbing down the tree, and jumped onto the woodpile from halfway up. We thought he was going home to practise piano, until he motioned for me and Brand to join him in the treasure trove.

"What are you doing?" Brand asked.

"Shhhh! There's someone on your roof," Ilya said. "Pull the cover."

I didn't know why we had to hide, but to go along with Ilya's game we squatted in the treasure trove and looked towards the roof of Brand's house through the cracks in the woodpile. Ilya was right: there was someone on the roof. Brand pressed himself flat on the ground, forgetting that nobody could possibly see him from the roof. His fat cowering form knocked me onto my backside, but I'd still got a glimpse of the person on the roof, who had only briefly poked his head out.

"What's your dad doing on the roof? Doesn't he have guests down below?" I said massaging my bum.

"Be quiet," said Ilya. "They might hear us."

More people appeared on the roof, surveying the vicinity like Brand's father had just done. They seemed as afraid of being discovered as us. We could only see half a head or a third of a body above the low wall around the roof. Those people kept coming up and going back down. Judging from their movements, they seemed to be busy moving things into the addition on the roof.

"Who are those guys?" I said.

"I don't know," said Brand.

"What are they moving?"

"Dunno."

"Why don't you know? It's your house."

"So many people come and go every day. If you were me, would you be able to recognize everyone?"

"You must recognize at least one?"

"Sure, I recognize my dad."

"Tell me something I don't know. Even I recognize your dad."

Crouching in the treasure trove, I started to resent that orange plastic bin for the amount of space it was taking up. Brand's girth was pressing me against the wall. I was having trouble breathing. Ilya's situation wasn't much better. He was holding the plastic bin with one hand and propping himself on the floor with his other, afraid he might crush the bin if he leaned his full weight against it. Brand hadn't noticed our plight. He was looking up unblinking through the cracks between the boards at every move those people made on the roof of his house, completely oblivious to the centipede that had fallen onto his leg and was preparing to march into that forbidden zone between his thighs.

12

The First Performance of Their Lives

Ilya saw Ling-ling once, but Ling-ling will never see Ilya, her classical pianist uncle. She was just two days old that day, and her eyes were closed most of the time. She wasn't ready to gaze back at the light and shadow of the world.

I fast-forward in my memory of Ilya and reach the day he went to the hospital to see Amanda and Ling-ling. She wasn't Ling-ling then; her name hadn't been born yet. She was sleeping in a clear plastic cradle in a little pushcart, with a pink name tag with Daughter of Amanda Liang and her birthdate (she was a Taurus, with Cancer in the ascendant). Ilya got to the hospital, went into the post-natal ward, and said hi to Amanda. He was hoping to see the newborn, but we hadn't opted to have her in the same room as her mother. Visiting hours hadn't started yet. Ilya was a bit disappointed.

We walked down the stairs to the ground floor. Ilya said he'd brought something special, but that we had to go outside to enjoy it. I knew what he meant by something special. He'd mentioned at some point that he'd celebrate the birth of my first child with Cuban cigars. In my understanding, a cigar is customary for a boy, a box of chocolates for a girl, but Ilya didn't bother with the custom. And of course I couldn't refuse, especially because those two Cuban cigars were packaged in an intricately decorated wooden box. If you didn't open it, you'd never know it wasn't a box of chocolates.

Even the clearest memory has patches of haze. You'd think it'd be the peripheral parts of any unforgettable memory that go blurry, but sometimes they're the parts that stay in focus. The place where Ilya and I smoked cigars, outside the main door of the hospital, resembled a memory to begin with: a group of patients congregated in the shadow of a towering building in a haze of smoke. Some sat in wheelchairs, some trailed IVs, some had casts or bandages on arms or legs. All wore hospital gowns striped pink or blue, and every one of them was smoking. One guy kept looking up and blowing smoke rings. Our presence among these people was strange, not just because of the two Cuban obelisks Ilya had brought, but also because they were trapped in hospital by illness, and we weren't. They could only slip downstairs during meal or medication breaks, and we could leave anytime we wanted. They were indulging an addiction, we a one-off extravagance. They were sick, and we were celebrating one of the few events in a lifetime that really deserves celebration.

We smoked the cigars on a curved concrete bench, a raised flower bed behind us, a stainless steel tube of an ashtray in front. At first we talked about the delivery, how Amanda's waters broke in the middle of the night, how the taxi driver drove as fast as he could without jarring the mother too much, how the foetus got stuck in the birth canal so long that the doctor had to use suction. Later I discovered that delivery for women is just like mandatory military service for men, that when mothers get together they can talk about childbirth forever. Ilya was like a woman forced to listen to army stories. Unable to participate, he just stayed politely quiet, not really listening.

A middle-aged man came over to borrow a light, relieving Ilya and me of the awkwardness of the topic of conversation. He was wearing a corduroy suit, with an unlit cigarette hanging from his mouth. Coming out of the front door, he'd gone through the motions of checking his pockets. He'd approached the smoking area and eyed the seven or eight people in it. In the end he chose us.

"You know why he chose us?" Ilya asked after the man left.

"Cause he forgot his lighter."

"That's not what I meant. I meant of all the people in the smoking area, why'd he ask us, two guys smoking cigars?"

"Maybe he likes the smell?"

"Course not," Ilya said. "Didn't you notice that we're the only people sitting here not wearing gowns. Think about it: smoking is such an unhealthy activity. The guy didn't want to ask for a light from someone sick, like he was scared bad luck would have rubbed off on the lighter. That's why he chose us, two healthy-looking guys. Problem is, how does he know we're healthy just because we're not wearing robes? Maybe we're sick psychologically or even physically. Maybe we're worse off than the people wearing the robes."

"He just asked for a light so he could have a fix. He's addicted. There's no need to overinterpret."

"No, it was a gesture of resistance," Ilya said. He was twirling the cigar like a pen between his index, middle and ring fingers. I remember being a bit dazed, maybe because the smoke was too strong, maybe because he was twirling the cigar, or maybe because I still hadn't recovered from the shock of fatherhood. Ilya didn't notice, just kept fiddling with the cigar. He became talkative where he'd been reticent before, and once he'd started he showed no sign of stopping.

"Take a good look at these people," said Ilya. "You think they're here because they can't stand it? That they go through all this trouble with their wheelchairs and IVs, come all the way down to have a smoke because they need one in the worst way? No way! It's a form of resistance. Why is it that you want to smoke the most when you're not allowed to? Because our minds rebel, consciously or not, against anything that limits our freedom. Take a look at their striped clothing. Doesn't it remind you of a prison uniform? All they smell is sanitizer and medication, and all they hear is someone moaning in the next bed. They're being held like convicts in an unhealthy and unfree place. Course they'd want to slip out and enjoy a moment to themselves. It's not addiction, it's an unconscious resistance. Against their unhealthy bodies and confined surroundings, where their freedom is restricted at every turn. They're trying to show that they're just the way they were. They indulge a vice to prove they have the ability to get better, to assert that they can return to normal."

"You make them sound so pathetic. Aren't they just having a smoke?" I asked.

Ilya had always had his own unique point of view. At the time he'd just married and released his second or third album. I remember reading in the music review in the paper: "I've never heard such a talented young pianist, with so many of his own ideas." I couldn't see how a pianist could add his own ideas to a piece of music someone else had written. But I was impressed that the critic could summarize what was important in a single sentence. That he could listen to the piece as Ilya played it and identify what was particular about the performance.

It's just that it's a bit stressful to talk with someone who is full of ideas. They can go on flights of fantasy, leaving their interlocutors stuck on earth. They say what they want, and make things hard for those of us who aren't quite as sharp, who don't have the gift of the gab, and who seem responsible for any awkward silences that appear in the conversation.

Ilya and I went upstairs. The curtains were still closed on the newborn viewing room, though there were quite a few relatives and friends standing around outside. There were signs every metre or so saying "Don't Tap the Glass or Talk Loudly". Which reminds me that right by the buttons in the lift was a sign saying "Don't Press with Medical Gloves." But why is it that when I remember the day Ilya came to see my daughter I recall all sorts of irrelevant details, peripheral parts of the experience that should have blurred, like in a portrait by a professional photographer? Things like "Don't Throw Needles or Syringes in a Regular Rubbish Bin." "Promotions for Formulas, Suckers, Bottles and Pacifiers are Strictly Prohibited." "No Use of Mobile Phones or Other Electronic Devices Allowed." I am helplessly unable to prevent those prohibitions from embellishing my penultimate memory of Ilya. This was the maternity ward, a place where new life comes into the world, a place with ungainsayable signs and unquestionable rules. "Prohibited." "Don't." "No." There were so many symbols circled in red. I can't remember any signs saying "permitted", "welcome" or "may".

Then the curtain was pulled open.

Though I'd just pushed Ling-ling from Amanda's room in the maternity ward to the nursery an hour before, I still had to check the number attached to the swaddling clothes before I could tell Ilya which plastic cradle she was in. In front of us was a little baby boy with curly hair, while Ling-ling (aka No. 36, Daughter of Amanda Liang) was five steps away. The family groups standing in front of the window played a game of horizontal musical chairs, just without the music or the chairs. It was like a whirlwind had blown through. It was like waiting on the platform when a train comes in and discovering it's not going to stop in front of you.

Ilya looked down and stared at Ling-ling, whose eyes were tightly closed. He stared at her quite a while before looking side to side. As if he'd seen something novel, he leaned closer for a better look, interrupting a clamour of commentary when he hit his forehead on the glass, startling everyone but the infants. I rushed to pull him out of the human wall in front of the window.

"It's really a magnificent sight, so many tiny babies," said Ilya, rubbing his forehead. "Look at their little heads, not yet as big as my fist."

"You've never been to a hospital nursery? I can't be the first friend of yours to have a baby."

"Lots of friends have had babies. But this is the first time I've been to a nursery to see a friend's newborn. It was really a magnificent performance. The kids behind the window are on a stage almost, and then the curtain opens and they all appear in a row. This is the first performance of their lives. No need to rehearse or practise. Everything is natural, and they're at their best when they come on stage. It was so amazing, so perfect that I almost gave them a standing ovation."

"It's a good thing you didn't," I said, pointing at a "Don't Tap the Glass or Talk Loudly" sign.

"When the curtain parted, you know what I heard?" said Ilya, oblivious. He went ahead and answered his own question. "I heard Mozart's B-flat minor violin concerto, Köchel 378. I never used to choose Mozart to perform. His pieces are too simple to show off technique. But just now when I saw the puckered faces of the infants, the piece played itself, like an X-ray through my skull."

I was curious about the music, because I hadn't heard any music in the delivery room. When I saw the doctor pull my daughter from between my wife's two naked legs, all I heard was a buzzing sound that reminded me of target practice: fire, recoil, then the world goes suddenly silent and all you hear is a buzzing echo of air. I don't understand music, but I do know Mozart. Later I found the piece on YouTube and it sounded very pleasant. It's light and flowing from the start, and the piano and violin are wonderfully matched, like a dialogue between mother and newborn (although I don't know which one is the newborn, which one the mother). I googled the piece, but didn't find anyone who had registered the same reaction, just a saying attributed to Albert Einstein: "Only the young and old can play Mozart well."

Ilya and I walked into the lift. There was a cleaning lady inside, behind a cart. She raised a rubber glove, extended her index finger and pressed one of the buttons, right next to the "Don't Press With Medical Gloves" sign. I looked over at Ilya, thinking he'd say it was a kind of unconscious protest, but he hadn't noticed.

"What a nice feeling when the curtain opened!" I think is what Ilya was saying. "You know? How I wish I could hide behind the curtain and see it slowly open. The curtain doesn't part at a concert. Before I walk on stage, the lights are on and the audience has taken their seats, and conductor and orchestra are all in place. I don't have the chance to catch my breath or prepare. When I go on stage, I have to start performing as soon as I sit down."

The door to the lift opened and Ilya's sense of excitement disappeared, but he kept talking. "There's no curtain on my stage, and when I finish performing the curtain is still hanging open. It's still hanging open when the last audience member leaves. The curtain never closes," Ilya said, disconsolately. "I don't have a second of privacy on stage. Everything is on display for the audience. I'd be bored, if I were in the audience. Wouldn't it be more interesting if the curtain opened and closed? Like just now when the visiting hour was over and the curtain closed, how did you know what the kids were doing in their cradles? Maybe they crawled out, joined hands and started singing children's songs. Maybe those pushcarts are go-karts, for racing. Don't you think that places we can't see are full of possibility?"

"They're just newborns. They can't crawl out and sing or race cars," I said seriously.

"I know," said Ilya. "But who knows? You're not a maternity nurse."

"Your wife's a nurse. Won't you find out when you have a baby?" I encouraged him. "Have one soon. Then our kids'll only be a year apart. They can play together."

"No way, not in the short term, anyway," Ilya said, looking over. "We got a divorce."

"You're kidding?"

"No, we did."

"When?"

"Last month."

"What did your mother say?"

I remember I didn't seem surprised. I didn't try to conceal it. These days getting a divorce is nothing special. You can buy a generic divorce agreement at Costco, and bring it home with your toilet paper, detergent, frozen dumplings and bathroom mop, and put it on the dinner table and wait for your spouse to sign. But I couldn't have been completely unsurprised. Your closest friend doesn't get a divorce just every day. But relatively speaking, I'd been a lot more surprised when Ilya married that nurse whose name I've forgotten than when he divorced her. It was very sudden, a flash wedding. The first time I saw her, half a head taller than Ilya, was on the day of the wedding. In fact, when they were walking down the aisle, Ilya had probably not been alone with her more than a couple of times. She'd been picked out, or up, by Mrs Chiang at the park one morning. Mrs Chiang practised Chi Kung, Chinese breath meditation, in the same park where the nurse's mother did Tai Chi. Two retired women somehow struck up a conversation, and discovered they both had marriageable children whose spinsterhood and bachelorhood had become a worry. They were obviously very pleased with the products of their labours and loins. After making their respective sales pitches, the two arranged to bring photos the next time. While Ilya was at home practising for public recitals or recording sessions and the nurse was at the hospital taking blood samples, giving injections or changing dressings, their mothers were going on dates in the park for them. I remember I didn't ask why he'd got a divorce. It didn't seem like a very sensible question. It was a decision between two adults. Understanding the reason couldn't change the fact that they'd signed. And if I'd asked I'd have only heard his side of the story, a superficial account designed to justify his decision, no doubt. The truth of the matter was like Ilya said, hiding behind some curtain somewhere, full of tragedy and absurdity. I didn't really care. But I was still curious: what did Mrs Chiang think?

"She said: 'Lucky for me, I was smart enough to decide to let you two move out as soon as you got married,'" Ilya said.

"Why did she say that?"

"You're the same as Brand."

"How am I the same as Brand?"

"You don't ask why I divorced, just how my mother reacted."

"You told Brand?" Then I asked: "What did your mother mean?"

Ilya sighed.

"She said: 'I'm a widow, you're my only son. Had we all lived under the same roof, the neighbours would have said the wife left because of her wicked mother-in-law.'"

"Makes sense."

"Brand said the same thing."

By then we'd walked out of the hospital and across a car park belonging to a neighbouring building. Ilya said: "You're just like Brand." For the second time. But I didn't notice the expression on his face. Maybe at the time I did notice, but since then the memory has receded into the shadows. What I do remember of my final moments with Ilya that evening is a damn background detail on the building behind him, a huge red acrylic sign with white lettering: "Private Property. Unauthorised Vehicles Prohibited."

13
Life Cryptology

Strictly speaking, I'm not unemployed. Though I don't have an actual income, I do work of the utmost sacredness and purity. But in the eyes of others, it seems shameful for a fellow in early middle age to work as a nanny. In losing my job and my title I am in danger of losing my dignity as a man.

At some point I'll decide to switch "jobs". But before I do I want to pay a visit to my dissertation adviser, Professor Safe, former chair of both the department and the graduate institute. He was always urging us to confront the disciplinary and employment crisis of the field of comparative informatics. "Don't assume you've got a future with diss-in-hand. There's no necessary mathematical, logical, semiotic or codificational connection between a degree and a future. Don't get your hopes up."

"Then what are we doing here taking a PhD?" we would ask.

"To find a better job," Professor Safe would reply, unhesitatingly.

Professor Safe didn't dare guarantee the future of a PhD student, but he did try to arrange a way out for me. My specialism was cryptology. After I passed the oral defence, he exercised his influence to get me employed as a regular faculty member, with an elective course for me to teach. So many students signed up for the course I got a call from Academic Affairs asking if I wanted to switch to a bigger classroom to allow more students to take "such a meaningful course". I refused, because therein lay a small misunderstanding. The course name I'd sent was Cryptology in Daily Life, but I guess that was too many letters for the system; and when Academic Affairs had put it on the course selection website, it had turned into Life Cryptology. A simple change! Which made a course about the relationship between mathematical principles and logic into something esoteric-sounding. I knew that I was not going to be the one to champion rationality against mysticism, and wasn't surprised by the reaction to the first and only revelation in the course. When I stood behind the podium and announced that the purpose of the course was not to crack the code of existence, that it would have nothing in common with bestsellers or blockbusters, that it was more about logic than life, that it was mainly an examination of the principles and practices of encryption and decryption in daily life, so many students dropped the course that I was almost unable to offer it. At the next department meeting, the new chair said, pitilessly: "See what you've done!"

Professor Safe has just recovered from a serious illness. He had surgery; the doctor left a shunt in his heart. I didn't go see him in the hospital because I didn't even know he was sick. His wife didn't tell anyone, not even his daughter in New Jersey. They put on their backpacks and went out to hail a taxi. On the way to the road they nodded to their neighbours and said hello, as if they were off to buy groceries, not to check Professor in at the hospital for surgery.

"How's your baby?" asks Professor Safe, smiling.

"She's fine," I say. "Two years old last week."

"Oh, two already. A little girl, not a baby any more."

Professor Safe is sitting in an armchair in the family room. Beside him, on a small round table, is his vacuum flask with the flaking paint and his pipe with a straw for a mouthpiece. I am intimately familiar with both objects. He used to take the vacuum flask everywhere he went, to class and to meetings. As for the straw, which has quite a few bite marks, it was always poking its head out of one of the pockets of his flannel blazer. We used to laugh at him for being so stingy, so attached to his crap flask and pipe, but seeing those two things now is powerfully reassuring. It is as if everything is the same as it was before.

Unfortunately, things aren't the same. Professor Safe's decision to keep me on as assistant professor was his last act as chair of the Department of Comparative Informatics. He brought two folders to the department meeting that year: one was my application for a faculty position, the other his application for delayed retirement. Our department had a history of less than a decade and Professor Safe had been chair for eight years. He'd already delayed retirement once, four years ago, but he'd just turned sixty-five, so a second application shouldn't be a problem. Unexpectedly, the committee resolved to pass my application and reject Safe's. "Resolved" is one way of describing what the committee did. Later I found out that "someone" insisted that we only pass one of the two applications, either Professor Safe's delayed retirement or my promotion.

Professor Safe's wife brings out a plate of cut fruit from the kitchen and puts it on the tea table. "Help yourself," she says to me, offering a wedge on a toothpick to her husband. "You have some, too, dear."

Professor Safe doesn't react; a piece of light yellow fruit comes to a stop in front of his mouth. "No, thanks," he says. Just like he used to lecture us in class: "Everyone says, an apple a day, but apple's got less vitamin A than watermelon, less vitamin C than papaya, less energy than banana, less potassium than strawberry. But it's the most expensive. Where's the logic in that?" Without waiting for me to reply, he adds: "It just goes to show what can happen when you neglect to compare information from different sources, when you accept things on faith."

"You have a point, but it's not a piece of apple," his wife says.

"Well, what is it? Pear? I don't want pear either. Pear's even less nutritious than apple."

"It's not a piece of pear."

"If it's not apple or pear then what the heck is it?"

"Would I feed anything strange to your guest? This is a stone pit peach."

"Stonepit as in the famous pottery town south of Taipei?"

"No, stone pit is a local variety of peach."

"Have I tried it before?"

"You have. Eat."

Professor Safe takes the toothpick and looks at the wedge of peach suspiciously. He examines it for a while before sending it into his mouth and giving it a taste. "Mmmm… sweet. And tasty." He tells me: "You try one too."

I've never tried this kind of peach before, and don't want to try now, so I just sip tea from the mug his wife has left on the table. Professor

Safe keeps popping wedges of peach. "What kind of peach did you say it was?"

"Stone pit."

"Pretty tasty. Have I tried it before?"

"It's your favourite," she says. "Don't you remember? Your cousin Shawn had a hillside orchard in Nantou. The peaches were ripe in July or August, during your summer holidays. Any chance you got, you used to drive to central Taiwan to steep tea with him and stay a few days, and you'd always bring back a few crates."

"Now I remember! I haven't seen Shawn in the longest time. We should go visit him."

"Shawn's passed on. Two years ago on New Year's Eve. He died of a stroke."

"Passed on?" Professor Safe puts down the toothpick like he's suddenly lost interest in peaches. He picks up the pipe on the side table and puts it in his mouth. "How old is the baby?"

"Two years old."

"Two years already? She's a little girl now, not a baby."

I glance at his wife, who nods at me, confirming my suspicions. I want to get up and leave but don't want to be impolite. I've not been there very long. I came to talk about the work I hope to do, to ask him for a reference letter. He used to be quite well connected, was generally decent, and, within academia, was renowned and respected. He just needed to say the word and anyone would oblige him. His second application to delay retirement was an exception. He never expected he would be treated that way on his own turf by former students, old friends he'd built the department with, colleagues who understood him better than anyone. How could they refuse to let him stay on for another two years? They didn't dislike him. In fact, at his honorary retirement banquet many people who had voted against him at the meeting shed sincere tears at the departure of a mentor. They liked him, but liked even more the position and title he'd occupied for eight years. They'd had a hard time with administration over the first delayed retirement, and my faculty application gave them a reason to get him to give up his position, a rationalization for their betrayal that would spare them excessive guilt.

It was just a simple power struggle. The surprising thing was that as chair of the Department of Comparative Informatics, Professor Safe never saw it coming. He'd created the department to help deal with the frightening explosion of information in modern society, concerned that people only knew how to absorb information not analyse it or assess its value or truth. "More information isn't any use unless it helps you form a new gestalt of a situation or adopt a new perspective on the truth," Safe would say in his speeches to prospective students or write in department leaflets, to stress that without comparison and analysis information was dangerous. He inspired new students with confidence that they were going to acquire a professional skill that would see us through anything, that we just had to take the tiller and navigate our way through the flood. What we didn't realize was that we were selectively absorbing the information Safe was sending us. We neglected to compare Safe with other sources. Which was why we did a collective face-plant in the crisis-ridden discipline of comparative informatics, why we were ultimately sucked into the vortex of unemployment.

Nonetheless, mastery in the field of comparative informatics didn't necessarily impart wisdom. The linguists, mathematicians, electronics experts, statisticians and computer scientists in our department who were so adept at analysing information failed to foresee the inherent risk in a power struggle. They failed to keep in mind that our university had once been a private vocational college and didn't have the same equipment or resources as a typical university, and that the only reason our programme passed muster with the Ministry of Education was because of Safe's connections and people skills. Every single Ministry reviewer knew Professor Safe personally. When his colleagues forced him to hand over the baton, they'd totally forgotten about the four-year departmental review the following year. Safe's surprise retirement soon became academic gossip, and the Ministry officials somehow got wind that his application to stay on had been rejected by his own people. They were none too friendly when they arrived to conduct the review. Although it wasn't a punitive expedition, it certainly wasn't like it used to be, when they'd just chat and check out a few things and that was the end of it. This time, they pored over the department documentation, and even interviewed students. They were a model of diligence.

That's the simplicity and danger of a play for power. The new chair got his position by playing the game, but less than a year later had to stop admitting students after the department failed the review. I lost my teaching position, becoming the most overeducated full-time nanny in the nation.

"Kids today face a difficult future," says Professor Safe. I notice that when he moves the pipe away, the corner of his mouth trembles slightly, like he is chewing what he has to say before uttering the words. "Information in modern society has proliferated to such an extent that people can't handle it any more. I can't imagine what it'll be like in another two decades. In the past it was just television, radio, print. Now it's computers and mobile phones. An unimaginably vast amount of information is sent out by arrays of devices twenty-four/seven. And here we are, woefully limited, each of us a broken net. All we can do is let the information, useful or not, flow through the holes in the net. The information we can capture is out of all proportion to the total."

"I feel the same way."

"Modernity involves two types of informational partiality. First, the information we receive about any individual situation is partial, in the sense of limited. Second, information is partial, in the sense that it lacks objectivity: instead of possessing a truth value, it reflects the intentions of its producer. In general, modern people have a worrying tendency to make decisions based on limited information of dubious value. The blind faith in information I see all too often tells me we have entered a new era of superstition."

"It's sad, but true."

"So you see how important comparative informatics is. All information production, transmission and reception involves ideology. In layman's terms, it is inextricably linked to power. If you don't have the ability to assess information, to get information from different sources and perspectives, then you will, completely obliviously, be manipulated by the information you do receive." Professor Safe puts down the pipe and raises his hands, extending thumb and little finger and shaking them in front of his chest. "A lack of information-intelligence might result in a loss of subjectivity. Without information-intelligence, you're a puppet. You walk around with all these strings attached to you without realizing it."

"Professor Safe, you've always emphasized the importance of information literacy," I say.

The wall behind Professor Safe's armchair is covered in photos, awards, diplomas and banners. My gaze passes over him and stops on a colour photograph in a gold frame. It's Safe and the former president of the university, both in suits, standing in front of the brand new academic building. They are smiling widely, while behind them a red banner hangs from the third floor to the first: "Congratulations on the Founding of the Department of Comparative Informatics," or some such wording. In fact, all was not smooth-going when Safe founded the department. Where did comparative informatics, a discipline nobody'd ever heard of, belong, in the School of Management? Or Commerce? Or was it a branch of the Social Sciences? Just this issue was cause for many interminable university meetings, and as everyone knows the greatest source of resistance to the founding of the department was the middle-aged suited fellow with his arm round Professor Safe's shoulder in the picture.

I have no interest in the picture, because the message it sends is completely partial, static and artificial. My gaze comes to rest on that photograph only because I want to avoid looking at Professor Safe's lips. Under his salt and pepper beard his lips are trembling, no longer under conscious control. The sight sends me into a paroxysm of guilt. It seems that a shunt in the heart is not Professor Safe's only problem, that his mind has gone sharply downhill in just a few short years. No matter what, I can't eliminate retirement as a factor. And since he retired on account of my employment, I feel partly responsible for his subsequent decline. In fact, one of the reasons why I've come to visit him today is to apologize.

"Professor Safe, I'm so sorry: I might have to go find another job."

"It's a great pity!" Professor Safe sighs. "It pains me that people aren't in the habit of 'reading' information. They just know how to receive information, but not how to 'read' it. They think they just need to increase the amount of information they're receiving to increase their factual understanding. But they're making a big mistake."

"Daniel wants to talk to you about work, dear. Why are you still lecturing?" asks his wife.

"Work? What do you want to talk about?"

"I don't think I'll be able to find a teaching position for the time being. I'm thinking about giving the private sector a try. Maybe at first the salary wouldn't be any better than I was making as an academic, but I imagine that with experience I might make quite a bit more than a professor in five to ten years."

"Didn't you graduate a couple of years ago? Where've you been working all this time?" he asks.

I can't help glancing at his wife again. She nods again, this time offering me a faint smile. The informational content of her smile is unclear, but I find it illuminating nonetheless. I suddenly feel a bit restless sitting here.

"Thanks, Professor Safe, for recommending that I stay in the department as a teacher. I didn't live up to your expectations. We didn't live up to your expectations. The department didn't pass the review the year after you left. The school forced us to cease admissions."

"What does that mean, to cease admissions?" Professor Safe turns to ask his wife.

"The department you created doesn't exist any more. The tree fell and the monkeys scattered," she said.

"Scattered..." Professor Safe says, with a regretful expression on his face. "When?"

"It's been two years."

"So what have you been doing the past two years?"

"Taking care of my daughter."

"Oh, I forgot you have a baby," he says, tapping his forehead, then reaches out for the vacuum flask and takes a sip. "How old is she?"

"Two years old now!"

"Two years old... you can't say she's a baby any more."

Now I'm sure there's something wrong with Professor Safe's mind. He's repeating questions, forgetful of my repeated answers and unable to recognize simple, everyday objects. All of which points to the possibility of dementia, age-related amnesia. I feel sorry for his wife. If memory is an information-rich original, then amnesia is the most extreme steganography, a secret writing that conceals parts of a message, fragmenting it and turning it into the hardest code to crack. There are many kinds of steganography in cryptology, but there always has to be a way to restore the original message, in a rule-based, systematic manner. Poor Mrs Safe! Amnesia's concealment is more like erasure: it is lawless and irreversible. Professor Safe hasn't forgotten who she is, but is forgetting who she was. And all she can do is watch.

"I've always emphasized the crisis of the discipline of comparative informatics," says Professor Safe. "Every discipline has its own anxieties, but none are as great as ours. We doubt the essential definition of the discipline and worry about its future for fear that one day the field might die."

I have no idea where my teacher's memory has taken him. Or should I say I don't know what parts of his memory have been concealed, or erased. It seems like his disciplinary knowledge remains untouched, so far.

"This discipline of ours often comes under criticism. People say we're just a bunch of sceptics. That we doubt other people and ourselves, without proposing a unique perspective. But as the information tsunami looms over us, doubt is no longer a dirty word. It's become a virtue, which not everyone is able to cultivate."

"It's not easy to understand what you're saying," I say, emboldened. "Sometimes I feel like academic language is a kind of code, whereby a simple message is rendered unnecessarily complex."

"I've said it before: don't assume that a PhD assures you a job. There's no direct mathematical, logical, semiotic or codificational connection between a degree and a future. But I like your field of study, cryptology, because it's turned you into a classic sceptic." Professor Safe looks at me intently, his eyes radiating heat, almost sending my gaze into hiding a second time. But this time his lips hold my gaze: they've stopped quivering. "You must feel that doubt is nothing special, certainly nothing to be proud of. But I sense you've been having a hard time lately. Am I right? In the prime of life. You must feel that what you lack the least right now is doubt. But believe me: doubt isn't a bad thing. No matter whether you have doubts about values, beliefs or life itself, it's all right. Of course you should doubt, because all things deserving doubt were created by people with a lack of it. In the past you felt yourself in the right in your belief, and you believed in it wholeheartedly, whatever it was, but now you've got a good reason to doubt. This is natural, don't worry…"

I see a brightness in his eyes, and wonder whether his amnesia is intermittent. If he's now back to normal, I can raise the issue I went there to discuss. Maybe his mental clarity has just now shone through the fog to penetrate like an X-ray to the essence of things. Like what he said just now. Even though I didn't say anything in reply, I found it quite thoughtful and poignant. I'm reminded of my own father. Fathers always know their sons, people say. They might not ask, they might not say anything, but they know what their sons are thinking. Except that my father never said anything so thoughtful to me, not once in his life. I started my PhD the second year after he died, and often felt Professor Safe was like the father I'd never had. Of course he was nothing like my father. My father had never been on stage in his life, unlike Professor Safe, who got up on stage every day. Professor Safe never cut a dashing figure, but he had a strong presence, accompanied by vacuum flask and pipe. Professor Safe directed my PhD thesis, but now I need further guidance. Work isn't all I want to talk to him about. I want to tell him about Ilya's death and about raising my daughter. I guess I want him to offer a one-on-one special studies course: Topics in Life Cryptology. I have too many questions to ask him, questions about the present, questions for the future. Time allowing, I even want to ask about the past. Like how and why a hundred dollar bill ended up in my three-year-old hand.

"Don't worry," he says. "I'll write a recommendation letter to the current chair of the Department of Comparative Informatics. He'll arrange a faculty position for you at the university. He was my student. He'll listen to what I say."

"No need to go to the trouble," I say, disappointed.

"No trouble. I'll write it now. You wait." Professor Safe tells his wife: "Please get me a pen and paper. Let's not make Daniel wait."

His wife and I exchange glances. She is still smiling at me. I know he's forgotten all about the ugly power struggle that ousted him. Just this should make me happy. But I can't help feeling sad. We're both living in an era of information, but there's precious little information he and I are capable of exchanging, nor can I tell him what I really want to say.

"Have some more fruit," says his wife, offering him a wedge of peach.

"I don't like apple."

"It's a piece of stone pit peach."

"Have I had it before?"

"Yes, you have. It's your favourite," she says. "Eat."

14

North of the North of the Nightmarket

According to Brand, the adults had their own secret base.

Lately his father had kept the roll-up iron door down, leaving the wicket door as the only way in or out. There were still a lot of people coming and going, but instead of steeping tea on the first floor, most of them went right upstairs, not to practise in the soundproofed studio on the third floor but to visit the rooftop addition, just like we'd seen that afternoon.

"What are they doing in the rooftop addition?" I asked.

I'd known something was up at Brand's house ever since the day a centipede almost got into his underpants. Every time I went in through the wicket door, the tea drinkers stopped talking and stared at me like I'd disturbed their conversation. This happened a few times before they simply told me to go play somewhere else. From that day on I had to squeeze under that half-rotten red wooden gate to be able to get to our fort in the mango tree and treasure trove in the woodpile. But Brand insisted on continuing to jump over the fence through the window in his room, because his bum was so big that he had trouble squeezing through the hole in the gate.

"I think my dad's getting ready to do something big," Brand said mysteriously, rubbing his bum, which his father had almost beaten to a pulp with a drum stick. That was the price he'd had to pay for the discovery of the secret: Brand had gone against his father's prohibition and sneaked up to check out the addition while the gate to the roof was unlocked, thinking that he'd get forgiven, just like the time he took a knife to his father's drum set. Well, his dad caught him coming down from the roof, and drummed a cadenza on his backside in the studio. Nobody heard his cries of pain. Nobody heard him beg for mercy. His father had really done a good job on the soundproofing.

Brand was going to wait until the three of us were together in the tree fort before telling us his momentous discovery, but we hadn't seen Ilya in several days. Last time Ilya'd looked distraught, complaining that his mother had extended his daily practice time from six to eight hours. Me and Brand hadn't seen him since. I guessed that Mrs Chiang had found out about the tree fort and forbidden Ilya from coming to the woodpile lest he get a splinter. Brand said Mrs Chiang must be worried about the upcoming piano competition. Whatever the reason, the effect was the same. Now when you went past Ilya's house on that winding alleyway you'd hear crazy scales alternating with an elegant andante. Brand must have felt that the announcement of a momentous secret deserved an audience or that the momentousness of the secret was directly proportional to the number of people who heard it, because he held it in for a couple of days, during which time he kept dragging me past Ilya's house to see if he could come out and talk. But he didn't get the chance to tell Ilya. We didn't dare interrupt, and when he finished practising we would hear his mother critique his performance. One time we even heard Mrs Chiang critique me and Brand.

"Your mind is elsewhere," she shouted. "You've stayed home for all of two days, and all you want to do is go out with your beastly friends. Get your priorities straight."

Sitting in the tree fort, I continued to enjoy looking out at the rotten roofs and the coloured canvas sheets of the shacks north of the pailou road. But Brand seemed to have lost interest in the addition on the roof of his house. Instead, he would stare at the ground, just like the tea drinkers on the ground floor of his house, who only looked up when someone walked by outside. Mrs Chiang's criticism had caused Brand to lose hope. He decided not to wait for Ilya. He came right out and told me about the amazing discovery he had made. He took out a piece of paper that had been folded several times and handed it to me with a great air of mystery.

"Get a load of what my father and his friends have been printing in the addition," Brand said.

It was about half the size of a *Mandarin Daily News*, a tabloid-sized paper for children. It was densely printed in black characters with comics and pictures, like the children's newspaper. The difference was that the headlines were written with a brush or marker. One headline said: "FREEDOM OF SPEECH A CONSTITUTIONAL RIGHT". Another said: "PARTY-STATE HARMS DEMOCRACY". Honestly, the calligraphy would have been a lot better if they'd let me do it.

"Is your dad printing his own newspaper?"

"It is not a newspaper, it's a pamphlet."

"What's the difference?"

"My dad says that a newspaper is a channel for government propaganda, that everything in the newspaper is a lie and that the pamphlets they're printing are the true voice of the people."

Brand said they were storing a lot of neat stuff in the addition. He'd seen a weird machine about half the size of a car that was covered in cylinders and levers and rollers and pipes. If you touched it something gummy would come off on your hand, not like engine oil, more like paint. It was an ink that was hard to wash off. There were quite a few giant shelves, each taller than a grown man, on which giant wooden boxes were stacked. Inside these boxes were innumerable little metal "stamps", which reminded Brand of name chops, except that instead of a name, each was engraved with a single character. There were also huge rolls of fabric and reams of white paper many times bigger than a B3 sheet of drawing paper. In the corner there was a bunch of wooden poles each about the length of a mop handle and a big table covered in mats, paste, ink, utility knives, iron rulers, ruling pens, transparent tape and coated graph paper. The floor was littered with cigarette butts, drink cans, shredded paper, broken knives, used Styrofoam bowls and bamboo chopsticks. "And there was a strange smell," Brand said. "Like smoke, urine, instant noodles, paint and perfume, all mixed together." Brand was so excited it was like he had just returned from a jungle adventure. He made his discoveries sound so mysterious that I suspected he had been to a distant land and not to the rooftop addition, located directly above the room in which he slept, fooled around and did his homework, just a few flights of stairs away.

"You think I'm making it up?" asked Brand, raising an eyebrow and narrowing his eyes.

"That much stuff'd take some time to move up there."

"You don't believe me, do you?"

"I don't disbelieve you. But it's been a long time since your dad forbade you from going up to the roof. Why haven't you gone up before?"

"As if you're any different! It's been a long time since your mum forbade you from crossing the pailou road, and you've never crossed it, have you?"

Brand wasn't wrong, but he wasn't exactly right either. It's true I wouldn't dare to venture beyond the limits my mother had set for me, not because I wasn't curious but because if I crossed the line and got caught I might get forced to kneel in front of the altar again. I could just imagine it. My mother would start crying and reciting the litany of my father's transgressions. She'd say: "Here he is, still in elementary school, following the bums into Carnation Lane, monkey see monkey do. All because you don't have the means to move us to a better neighbourhood." The part Brand was wrong about was that I actually had crossed the line.

Many years before, when I was maybe five or six years old, my mother took me into the forbidden zone north of the pailou road, which I had been told ever since I was little never to enter. I remember walking a long, long way, and that I had to keep myself in line, because she was carrying bags of clothes and didn't have a hand free. I gathered she didn't really want to take me along, because every time she had to wait for me to catch up or chase after me when I ran ahead, her voice was even more severe than usual. "If you wanted to play you should've stayed home with Grandma like I told you to," Ma said, more than once. Of course I knew we hadn't come to play, and that we weren't leaving home or anything like that. She had an objective, to deliver bags of clean clothes to customers and take their dirty clothes back home. It was difficult work. She did it not so much to supplement the family income as to display her stubborn determination to move. Problem was that Dad was usually too drunk to notice the hint, and the menial labour she was doing was hardly lucrative. Ma did not seem to have very many customers, nor did her customers appear to have very much money. As a result they led a fairly strange life. They were all young women living at the destination of my mother's long journey, a tiled, reinforced concrete building hidden in an alley off the main street of a district to the north of the north of the nightmarket. All the buildings there were tall and new, and there were so many they blocked the view. If some kid here built a tree fort twice as high as the one we had built by the nightmarket, he wouldn't have been able to see anything. I didn't really like the place. Forbidding walls towered all around. I felt stifled. But to my mother it was the other way around. When we walked down our winding alley in the slum, she always lowered her head and walked as fast as she could, like she was angry at someone. But when she reached the district to the north of the north of the nightmarket, she walked slower, looked around, and even hummed a tune, as if those new buildings and straight boulevards had lifted her spirits.

Brand claimed me and him were just the same: his father didn't let him go up to the addition, while my mother didn't let me cross the pailou road. And if Ilya had been there Brand might have said all three of us were the same, because each one of us had a line he could not cross. But there was no way I would accept Brand's claim. He had no idea what they were storing in the addition until a few days before, but I knew about the Bird Houses and the Tofu Tenements north of the pailou road and how they concealed everything us kids were not supposed to see. Brand didn't know that before Ilya's father's corpse had washed up downriver, turning the levee into a line that Ilya could not cross, I'd already gone north of the pailou road, north of the north of the nightmarket, with my mother.

Unlike the memory of me kneeling in front of the altar at the age of three, I very seldom recall that time I went on a clothes delivery with my mother. All the trip left in my memory was a few fragmentary but indelible impressions of that tower in the lane. I remember going up flight after flight of stairs without feeling like we'd really got inside the building. There were no wide, heavy, metal security doors that you saw in a typical walk-up apartment. There were just dim, narrow hallways so long you couldn't see the end of them. Outside the sun was shining brilliantly, and there'd been a glare off the tiles on the top floors, but the light did not crawl very far up the stairs or along the hallways, where there were no windows, only doors, door after wooden door, each one exactly the same. The only source of light was a single bulb on the ceiling, which kept hissing on and off, like a scene out of a nightmare.

I followed close behind my mother, trying to walk a line down the centre of the hallway, like I was crossing a log bridge. I was worried I might trip and fall over jumbles of footwear and debris that had been tossed outside the doors. Ma would occasionally knock on one of the doors and softly call the name of the woman living inside. Knock knock. Lily? Those wooden doors did not have numbers, and Ma called only names, or rather nicknames. I don't know how my mother got the names right. Knock knock knock. Nana? Nana?? Even harder to understand was the U-turn my mother's tone had made. At home, she was always belligerent and loud, whether she was reproaching my father for his many faults or yelling like a loudspeaker for me to come home for dinner. But in that hallway, she was all soft-spoken and polite, almost obsequiously so. Knock knock. Nina? Knock knock knock. Nina?? I might never forget the nightmarish scene: door after wooden door, each the exact same colour and design, each creaking open agonizingly slowly. When Ma knocked, we had to wait the longest time for the inhabitant to answer. The inhabitant, whether she was Lily, Nana or Nina, was always a woman who came to the door most unwillingly. One was wearing a nightgown, her face as white as a sheet, like one of those lady ghosts I'd seen on television. Every time a door opened, a cloud of smoke poured out when the door opened, probably just cigarette smoke, but the first time it happened it scared me so badly I wrapped my arms around my mother's thigh. For some reason, my mother didn't take the opportunity to teach me good manners, like she would have done anywhere else. She didn't force me to say hello, call the girls Auntie or Big Sister. She just exchanged bags of clean clothes for bags of dirty clothes, at which point the door that had opened with such reluctance would immediately slam shut. One woman was only wearing a camisole. She might have been wearing knickers, but I didn't particularly notice at the time as I wasn't yet six years old: the unfamiliar world behind the wooden door aroused my curiosity more than the scantily clad woman. In the room I spied a man without a shirt on sleeping prone on a bed. Beside the bed was a vanity unit covered in cosmetics containers, and in front of that was a side table bedecked with empty beer bottles lying on their sides. After the door closed my mother had another bag of dirty laundry to wash.

We kept walking down that sunless corridor knocking on door after door and exchanging bags of laundry with women in nightgowns or loose-fitting clothes. Though it was the middle of the day everyone in the building seemed to be sleeping. All the women who opened the doors looked haggard, like we had just woken them up. Their voices were hoarse and phlegmatic. They mostly opened the door to torso width, some just a crack, just wide enough for a hand to reach out to exchange a bag of clean clothes for a bag of dirty laundry. In which case I didn't get the chance to peek in and confirm whether there was a vanity unit and a half-nude man sleeping on a big bed.

I could've refuted Brand by telling him about my ascent into hell, but I didn't, without knowing exactly why at the time. I had to wait until many years after the fact, by which time the memory had fragmented, before the reason for my reticence became suddenly clear to me. I didn't tell him because it was nothing to brag about. And if I had told him, I might not have been able to convince him to keep it a secret.

"At least I had the guts to go up to the addition. Not like you. I don't think you'd dare to cross the pailou road," Brand said.

"Who says?"

"Admit it, you don't dare. You even drink a slurpee slow, like a girl."

"And what if I dare?"

"If you dare to cross the road, I'll give you my mobile suit. Then we could count that as your treasure. You'd have a treasure to stick in our secret base."

"What about you?" I asked. "If you give me the mobile suit, all you'll have left would be a penknife. Maybe that wouldn't be enough to satisfy Ilya."

"I've got something even better to put in the treasure trove," Brand said. "Don't you worry."

He took out the densely printed pamphlet, leaned back and relaxed against the tree trunk with his legs crossed, and lifted it high, grinning. He proudly flipped it over, admiring it, as if a teacher had just handed him a certificate of merit.

15
The Virtues of Scepticism

Professor Safe said that my research in cryptology has turned me into a classic sceptic. I actually don't know exactly what he meant. I lived in a continuous state of doubt when I was writing my dissertation. At the time I'd already passed the oral exam for my proposal, but I still worried I'd chosen the wrong topic, research design and methodology. I even doubted my motivation for taking a PhD and the meaning of getting the degree. Other than that I just can't figure out what if any connection there is between cryptology and scepticism.

Philosophy isn't my specialization. All I know about scepticism is that it's an attitude of judgemental neutrality. Facing surface appearances, sceptics don't voice affirmation or opposition lightly. Sceptics are often described as naysayers, because they're likely to doubt popular beliefs. But historically there's a difference: naysayers denied God's existence, sceptics just doubted it. In the past they sometimes forgot to doubt what might happen to them if they voiced their doubt about, say, whether the sun goes around the earth. Living in societies that did not guarantee freedom of speech, they were excommunicated, flogged, put in prison, caged and drowned, sent to the gallows, or burned to death. It sounds strange to say, but many sceptics ended up martyrs. Even stranger, secular power always seems to be in the hands of people who have never doubted anything in their lives.

It goes without saying that I could never be that kind of sceptic. Obviously, I don't have the strength of personality to assert my own perspective. Faced with the unwavering faith of people in power, I've only ever voiced doubt once. That was enough. I've never done it since. My mother was convinced that as long as I did well at school I could buy a big house for her to live in. All I said was that I didn't know what the point of memorizing the multiplication tables was now that we had calculators, and that if she wanted me to make money, it would be quicker to set up a stand in the nightmarket and let me sell ready-made clothes. That's when I learned where doubting the beliefs of the power-holders leads. To a tragic conclusion. Ignoring my grandmother's attempt to restrain her, my mother picked up the Y-shaped bamboo laundry pole used to hang wet clothes out to dry. She chased me out the door, down the narrow winding alley, onto the nightmarket street, all the way to the pailou gateway. She only stopped chasing me when she realized I was going to run across the pailou road.

"You should be more like your friend Ilya and listen to what your mother says!"

When I was a kid, Ilya's name was the proverbial salt rubbed into a wound, the stone tossed into the well into which you've fallen. Parents would always cite his good example as a goad to their children when they'd done wrong or failed to make the grade. But what the adults didn't realize is that overstimulation can lead to desensitization. I'd got used to the comparison. And admitted to myself that there are some people you can never catch. It's not that you're stuck in place, not trying to get ahead, just that some people are advancing lines you can never catch up with, let alone cross, no matter how much you sacrifice, no matter how hard you try.

I'm talking about none other than Ilya.

But even if you accept your limitations, it's still not pleasant to see someone succeed gloriously, especially not at times when you're having a hard time or suffering from self-doubt. Especially not when it's someone you grew up with. You always knew that he would succeed someday, but you never knew how successful he would be.

I'm still talking about Ilya.

I'm not sure how he was discovered. Success accumulates, of course; it doesn't happen overnight, though it sure seems that way when you see strangers succeed. Or friends you haven't heard from in a long time. Either way, fame always appears suddenly, and is impossible to overlook.

That's the way it was with Ilya. Suddenly, he was the pianist everyone was talking about. I saw his name in the paper. I saw his name on posters stuck on telephone poles. I saw his name on the homepages of major orchestras. His face appeared on television, in the display windows of the record shops, in subway ads. Suddenly everyone seemed to know him. I should have been happy for him. I had always imagined him successful, but he only actually became successful when we turned thirty. Which was surprisingly late, but better late than never. I should have been proud of him, too, and proud that twenty years earlier I had already recognized his potential. His eventual triumph was proof that I had an eye for talent.

Professor Safe's affirmation of scepticism recalls my state of mind in the depths of dissertation hell, as well as Ilya's concurrent success.

I search through my memories of five or six years before, and don't find much to be proud of or happy about. All I can find is a sense of shame I still feel now. Ilya had risen to fame, become a household name, and I would have said I was proud to know him. But the sad thing was I was only one of many people who could say the same thing. Our friendship had been diluted by all the people who suddenly knew him, or knew about him. Now that everyone knew about Ilya, I didn't dare tell people I was his friend, afraid that I would sound like a name-dropper. Ilya issued his first solo album to popular acclaim, and I felt a sense of loss. I felt like I had lost a friend.

It was wrong of me to feel that way. Ilya didn't become distant or anything. At the time Amanda and I had just celebrated our first wedding anniversary. Ilya would come over to our riverside flat almost every Friday night with beer, peanuts and takeaway. He would come late, mostly after nine o'clock. And whenever he came he seemed more at ease than I was. The twenty-five ping flat belongs to me and Amanda, but the amount of me in it is meagre. Literally. Amanda's pharmacist father paid for it. In cash. I paid part of the cost of the renovation and the furniture, a small part as I was still in graduate school. My father-in-law came to see the place once after we moved in. He hasn't bothered us since. Amanda and I showed him around, or followed him around as he checked the finishing on the wooden cabinet, squatted beside the toilet bowl and used his finger to see whether the sealant along the sink and the wall was even. He'd even brought a little night-light to test the outlets. He was talking and laughing with Amanda, praising the interior design and the furniture she had so carefully chosen. But when

I took him out to the balcony to show him the glorious river view from twenty-three storeys up, he caught me off guard: He stopped smiling, gave me a meaningful glance and said: "I know! I paid for it." I thought he was going to go on to remind me to take good care of his daughter, to treat her right, not make her angry. But he didn't. He just kept on inspecting the installation of the gas and air conditioner lines. If he'd had enough time, I believe he would've taken out a little hammer to tap the tiles on the railing to make sure they were solid. Waiting by his side, I gazed over the sunlit river and the levee and the roofs of the shacks and hovels in the ghetto on the other side. I saw, among the patchwork puzzle of roofs, two familiar red gates. Only then did I realize that we'd bought a flat in a brand new residential tower right across from the old neighbourhood. All that separated me from the nightmarket was a murky stream.

Ilya seemed to be in a good mood every time he came. It was like he wasn't visiting so much as coming home. As if he'd put up some of the money for the little flat, as if he had a stake in it. His attitude actually pleased me. At least one of us could feel at ease in the place that my pharmacist father-in-law had bought. And with him there I actually started to feel at ease too. I really enjoyed chatting with Ilya on Friday nights. Even though he decided the topic of conversation every time and even though we always talked about the music world. Like which composer was fond of self-promotion, which conductor was always trying to curry favour, which musical director was moonlighting with several orchestras in a bid for power. And the more scandalous the story, the more dramatically Ilya told it, and the more incensed he sounded. He talked to me like I was another big name musician, as if I knew the bastards he was talking about personally. When in fact I'd only read their names in the media. Ilya didn't just bring beer, peanuts and takeaway of a Friday night. He also brought a lot of eye-popping gossip, as if he wanted to tell me what people are really like. And just when he was reaching the climax of some story, giddy and red-eared with beer, he would suddenly stand up and shout: "It's that time again! Time for us to take in the riverscape." Then he would stroll onto the balcony on which I always felt queasy, stand by the waist-high wall and look down at the city lights.

It can be windy up here. When Amanda saw Ilya leaning over the wall she panicked, afraid a gust of wind might blow him over. That didn't worry me. Ilya had never been afraid of heights. He'd told us to build the tree fort as tall as possible. I was just wondering what he could see from the twenty-third floor now that he was famous and successful. You couldn't see the dilapidated roofs of the slum dwellings on the other side of the river at night, but the nightmarket was bright. The line of lights of the food stands along the nightmarket street was a shining wand, the entire area a burning torch, and Ilya's gaze was as a moth to the flame. Which made me think that maybe what Ilya was gazing at was not the nightmarket but his past.

Of the three of us, Ilya was the first to move away. The year we graduated from university he went to Brussels to study music. His mother sold everything. She sold that tiny shack with the used tyres on the roof. She even sold the grand piano. And she went with Ilya to Belgium. I don't know if they could put a new grand piano in the house they rented in Belgium. I just know that three years later he had moved to Paris. Mrs Chiang had sold everything in Brussels and taken her son to France. I said Mrs Chiang was like a piece of luggage Ilya was carrying around: no matter where he went he took her with him. Brand said it was the other way round, that Ilya was a piece of luggage that Mrs Chiang was carrying around and which her gaze would never leave for an instant.

No matter what, Ilya was a success. On his promotional posters I saw the kind of face that you'd see on a successful person: resolute, satisfied and confident. I remember looking at it across the window of the display in the record shop, like we were looking at each other through the glass. Seated along a keyboard in tails, he was smiling warmly into the camera. Then I heard the sound of water from the tap, as if Mrs Chiang was rinsing the greens and rice offstage somewhere, out of frame. I didn't hear him say "I still can't get it right," because he had achieved perfection: there wasn't the faintest hint of doubt in his eyes. Though thin, he looked steely and single-minded, determined and decisive, like he knew all the preparation he had done – for more than ten or even twenty years – was for today. Which also made people assume that this was the expression he always had on his face, all this time.

Of course I knew the photograph was a lie. I'm not a musician, but I do know how such photographs are taken from when Amanda and I got married. In a few of our studio wedding photos I'm wearing tails and lensless glasses, facing the camera with a smile. I also had safety pins in my clothes, foundation on my face and gel in my hair. In the studio, out of frame, were umbrella lamps, reflectors, high spec camera equipment and powerful touch up software. All of which rendered several images that transcended my potential for personal perfection. I knew that wasn't me, that the smile had appeared on my face not because I was anticipating the pleasures of matrimony, but because I was imitating the professional smile of which the photographer had given an impromptu demonstration. That's how I knew that Ilya in the photograph wasn't Ilya. That decisive expression belonged on his mother's face, because that's the only expression she had worn for twenty years.

But it was Ilya who'd succeeded. And at the time his success gave me the chance to compare the relative merits of scepticism and decisiveness.

Ilya's success reminds me again of the year I spent writing my dissertation.

If you define doubt as the sum of all your uncertainties about what you're doing, then doubt was the main reason for my lack of progress in my dissertation. Maybe my self-doubt had nothing much to do with philosophical scepticism, but I certainly suffered like some of the sceptics did. I felt trapped in a prison made of books, or strapped to a woodpile that had been set alight.

From my dissertation year I returned to Professor Safe's scepticism.

Too much hesitation over too many choices will turn you like a top, spinning you in place. Sometimes the only effective way of achieving success is single-mindedness. A single-mindedness based on faith. It seems like you have to believe in something to succeed. Whether it's your own faith or whether it belongs to those who have power over you.

16

Crossing the Line

It wasn't for Brand's mobile suit that I decided to cross the line, though I admit it was an incentive. Brand had discovered a different side of his father and of the other adults who drank afternoon tea on the first floor. And for the first time he'd gone up to the rooftop addition, and given me an extravagant, perhaps somewhat embellished description of what he had discovered there. I finally realized how ignorant we were about the environment we'd grown up in.

This realization made me a bit angry. I wasn't angry at the adults for laying down the law and limiting the range of our activities. I was angry at myself for realizing the possibility of crossing the line too late. It was a strange feeling. All these years the lines were there. We all knew where we stood, and had become accustomed to the restrictions on our lives. We totally accepted them and had never thought of rebelling. And now one of us had taken a leap. Brand had gone first, leaving me feeling a bit ashamed. If I didn't follow suit, I'd seem oblivious to how unreasonable my mother's limitation was. On the other hand, if I followed Brand's lead and crashed against the walls the adults had cooped us up in, I would seem like a copycat. After all, crossing the line was a game someone else had thought of. Playing someone else's game might not be the wisest thing to do.

But no matter what, the line had to be crossed. I was twelve years old already. I had the right to know what I wanted to know. What was more, Brand had already crossed the pailou road and was waiting for me under the gateway on the other side.

"Come over," Brand yelled. "Didn't you say you weren't afraid to cross the road?"

"I'm coming."

"Hurry up. There aren't any traffic lights."

"I said I'm coming."

"If you're coming then come. What else is there to say?"

"What are you yelling about? They're my legs, not yours to order around."

"No, I can't control your legs. So you just stand there like a good little boy."

"Why do I have to listen to you?"

"Who cares who you have to listen to? In any case, here you are. You've crossed the road," Brand said. "Smile! That mobile suit is already yours."

Only when Brand spoke did I realize that I was already standing under the pailou gateway on the north side of the road. I looked around and suddenly felt a little bit deflated. Of course I knew the two gateways were exactly the same. But standing on the south side, I always felt that the gateway on the other side was a tiny bit taller, the base a little bit thicker. Now that I had taken the risk of kneeling in front of the altar by crossing the street, I saw it wasn't so: there was no difference. Even more disappointing was that the road that I had never dared to cross until now didn't seem as wide as I had expected. Although I had crossed the line it didn't seem like I had crossed anything. I couldn't help feeling let down.

"Hurry up," Brand said. "There are no adults out doing business during the day, so nobody will see you're here. But if we stay here too long, I can't guarantee you won't get noticed."

Brand had dragged me into the north of the nightmarket. If he hadn't mentioned it I would have been all right, but now that he had I started to feel a bit nervous. Of course, I knew that at this time of day most of the shopfronts in the nightmarket were closed, their iron doors rolled down. But unlike Brand I didn't find that reassuring. There were only a few people on the tiled walkway beneath the plastic arch-shaped awning over the nightmarket street, but for the same reason a couple of elementary students all of a hundred and fifty centimetres tall would stand out. I couldn't set my heart at rest. Thank God Brand knew the way. After we walked by a couple of Chinese medicinal aphrodisiac shops, he pulled me down a winding lane, away from the nightmarket street where we were so conspicuous. I knew where Brand was taking me. I had crossed the pailou road, gone past the other gateway, but hadn't gone all the way, just like Brand when he'd made it up the stairs without going inside the addition. To really break the taboo, we had to go inside and see what the adults did not want us to see. Obviously, Brand had gone north of the pailou road before. Brand was forbidden from visiting the addition on the roof, not from crossing the pailou road. I guessed Brand didn't think that coming here was a big deal. For him, it wasn't exciting or new, or even worth mentioning. The reason why he was pleased to be my guide was because that was a role he liked to play. It was just like when we jumped the "super string". We'd tie a bunch of elastic bands together into a super string, which we kept raising from our ankles to our knees to our hips to our chests to our necks, by which point it was too high for most of us to cross. Brand had invented a combination overhead kick-scissor kick: he would leap into thin air like a soccer superstar about to boot the ball backwards, then somehow reverse his momentum in mid-air and like a professional wrestler slam the super string down to the ground in the shape of a V. Then the rest of us could just line up and hop across. Brand was pleased to play this role. Defying the pull of gravity, he displayed the particular flexibility of the plump. I hated the high jump, that feeling of facing an insuperable limitation, of having no way to get over. And I didn't like having to rely on someone to lower the standard, like I was a little chick under the protection of the mother hen.

"Let's go back," I said.

"What's the rush? We haven't seen what we came here to see."

"It's not worth it. They're selling the same things here as they sell where we live."

"Calm down. Just follow me, and I guarantee you will see something that you have never seen before," he said with a mysterious smile.

My heart was pounding, my entire body burning up. I saw up ahead what we had seen from the tree fort, the green, blue and striped blue-and-white canvas sheets of various sizes tied at all different angles and in various ways between the low eaves of the roofs of the shacks. From the tree fort, of course, we could not see what was underneath the sheets, and I'd assumed they were to block the sun and rain. Only now did I realize that they put up the sheets to prevent people outside the lane from seeing in. And that wasn't my only discovery. Walking up the deserted nightmarket street just now, I thought everyone was taking an afternoon nap, but if they were it must have been a short nap: for here were all these people. The lane we had turned on to was packed. It was like a traditional produce market, except that nobody was carrying a shopping basket or bag and everyone in the lane was a man. But the men were all moving slowly along and looking sideways, like shoppers do. They were all very impolitely staring at the windows and doors on both sides of the lane.

Brand kept walking intently forward, head down. The lane was winding but he very skilfully kept himself right in the middle like he was traversing a mountain ridge. I stuck close behind, afraid that he might suddenly disappear and leave me trapped in a canvas covered realm, unable to find my way out. The feeling was a lot like when I was six and I went north of the north of the nightmarket with my mother. Both times, my guide was in a hurry, while I was afraid I'd get left behind, but also curious. The lane was certainly unnerving, like the tower of strange women, but it wasn't deserted, or dark. Sunlight oozed through the canopy of blue plastic sheeting, turning turquoise, slipped through the gaps in the eaves, sprinkling down like a waterfall, or shone through holes in the canvas awnings like laser beams. The lane was a motley lake of light and shade, like a tropical rainforest, like a savage glade. From time to time faint trails of smoke floated by the faces of the men walking in the lane, perhaps from cigarettes, from sausage grills, or from the censers in which people burned spirit money. But I've always imagined the wisps of smoke wafting out of the open doors and windows, on account of the tower I visited with my mother at the age of six, in which clouds of smoke floated out when the doors opened so unwillingly. Somewhere deep in the memory area of my brain, I imagined that the women themselves were fuming when they opened the doors. The women in the towers were behind the doors, while the women in the lane were standing in front of the doors, lined up in a row, like they were waiting on a platform for a train. Nobody's dress was dishevelled, but all were skimpy. Unlike when I was six years old, their clothing was enough to make me feel embarrassed. Like when I was six, my curiosity fell into the world behind the doors. But I could barely see anything, because the women in front of the doorways formed a human wall. The wall looked turreted, because each woman was a different height and weight. All I could make out of the world behind these brazen bodies was that it was not very bright. It was like the fruit stands in the nightmarket that radiated a gorgeous artificial red. I wondered whether this gaudy red was candlelight from the altars in the family rooms in these homes. But it was hard for me to satisfy my curiosity, because my inward gaze could not pass the wall of women without meeting an outward gaze. I don't know why I avoided their gazes, when none of the men in the lane did. Now I knew that the men weren't staring impolitely at the windows or doors of homes on either side of the lane; they were staring impolitely at those women ringed in red light. They kept inching forward like a process of peristalsis, exchanging insinuating glances with the women. I soon noticed that mostly these men just lobbed glances at the women and did not try to squeeze through the glowing wall. I gathered it took great courage to do so, not just because of the tightly woven, riotously patterned fabric of lascivious looks, but also because ever since I was a boy I had heard legends of how fierce these women were: how they would charge out, grab your arm, rip off your glasses and your watch, and drag you in through those low red doorways. I didn't see anyone get dragged in, but like Brand, I kept to the centre of the lane, for fear I would be surrounded by bright red faces and revealing outfits, like when I was three years old and forced to kneel in front of the altar.

We shouldn't have come here. Now I knew why my mother had forbidden me from ever crossing the pailou road and why she was always talking about moving. I never thought the place we lived was so close to Carnation Lane, the same feeling I had the first time I climbed into the tree fort with Ilya. But I couldn't whoop with excitement like Ilya had when he'd glimpsed the egrets, the sandbars, the windswept river, the first wide-open view of his life. In the motley light that spilled through the canvas awnings and mixed in a claustrophobic maze with the gorgeous rich red light from inside the rooms, I saw countless pairs of intent eyes meet across a narrow gap, each gaze radiating malicious intentions.

I felt a bit sorry that I had crossed my mother. There was a stench in the lane that made you want to run away, which I'd noticed soon after entering. No wonder my mother avoided this place like the plague; no wonder she was so desperate to move away. Now I understood how she felt, unable to leave, because that was how I felt that day. Especially when Brand, my guide along that winding lane, suddenly disappeared. I was following close behind, and he was just ahead, and he was in my field of vision, and everyone else must have been able to see him, too, and then he vanished into thin air. I thought he was playing a practical joke on me, just like he sometimes did when we jumped the super string. Usually, when he stomped the string down onto the ground in the shape of a V, he would let us line up and jump over one by one; but sometimes he would release the string on purpose right when some unfortunate kid was jumping across. Maybe he was hiding off to the side, delighting in the frantic expression on my face. I swore at him under my breath, but couldn't shake the feeling I had only myself to blame. I had a guilty conscience, because just now my curiosity had got the better of me. I had not kept Brand in my line of sight; my eyes had wandered from the centre of the lane to the walls of women on either side. Maybe at some point after I got the wandering eye, Brand got dragged inside.

I didn't know whether to keep going or to turn back. I knew that though Brand liked to play practical jokes, he wasn't a jerk; he was a loyal friend who wouldn't leave me here all by myself at a time and place like this. Though the mysterious smile that often appeared on his face was enough to inspire doubt, I decided to believe in him. I couldn't leave by myself without saying anything.

I stopped moving, just stood there in the centre of the lane, so that when Brand was released he would be able to find me. But I immediately discovered that standing there would create two problems. First, there were two lanes of traffic moving in opposite directions, very slowly. Standing stationary in the centre of the lane would make me stand out more than my age and height. Second, nobody here in the lane was looking ahead. I'd stood there for less than a minute and been rear-ended by quite a few fellows, and told to fuck off a few times. I'd even been shoved by this particularly uncouth guy.

I had to keep going for my own safety. And now, I didn't have to avoid the glances of those girls. To find Brand, I had a legitimate reason to look to the two sides of the lane, into the windows and doorways to the left and to the right, just like the other men. Soon I'd won me a lot of praise. "Will you get a load of that: a smooth-faced lad with a hard on!" somebody said, patting me on the shoulder. "Are you here to deflower, or are you here to be deflowered?" somebody else asked, tousling my hair. Maybe they were making fun of me. Surely they misunderstood why I was there. But I didn't care, because at least they saw me as the same as them. I had become one of the guys wriggling along in the lane, just a bit younger and shorter. They didn't jostle me or push me any more, nor did they swear at me. I felt that I had won their approbation, that they looked upon me with friendly eyes.

The further I walked the narrower the lane became. There was no point walking down the centre of the lane any more, because the women on either side were already so close I could have reached out and touched them, so close that they could have reached out and dragged me in before I even had the chance to call for help. I smelled their body odour, a stench of perfume. My mother had never bought perfume. She said perfume had alcohol in it, and if she brought any home my father would use it to wash down his peanuts. I'd never smelled this particular perfume on her, but I had smelled it somewhere before. The only possibility I could think of was those bags of dirty laundry. It's just that the smell on the laundry wasn't so strong, while the smell on these women was so strong it was like a cloud of fog. The fog enveloped them like a shield, giving them protection against harassment or violation. Maybe the shield was why I didn't see any expressions that made me uncomfortable. I was now so close to them that if they had sneezed and forgotten to cover their mouths, I might have been hit by liquid projectile bullets. In that moving crowd I walked at close range past face after static face. Luckily, those women put one at ease. No matter how red their faces, how slack their smiles, whether they were standing in a doorway or behind a grated window, I saw no scary expressions like those on the faces of the pale and emaciated women who had opened the doors so unwillingly in the tower of strange women.

With one exception.

That exception belonged to a girl in a nightgown.

If I had not been looking for Brand—if I had not been gazing left and right into those doorways—I would not have seen the face of that girl, who was hiding behind the human wall. You could tell she was so much younger than the others, maybe about the same age as me, or at most one or two years older. She had a lot less colour on her face, just a gaudy sheen of red. Her face was static just like the others. I should've kept moving forward, but her nightgown stopped me short. It was a white ankle-length nightgown, with a thick lace edge like the icing on a birthday cake. I had seen this kind of nightgown before, in a picture book of European fairytales Ilya had lent me. There were a lot of girls in nightgowns in the book. Little European girls, it seemed, all wore nightgowns to bed. Their fathers and mothers all read bedtime stories to them until their eyes closed. After their parents had left, those girls would sneak out of bed and walk around barefoot. One carried a candle downstairs and stole into the kitchen to find things to eat or feed to the kitten she was keeping in her wardrobe. Another carried a teddy bear to the window and rode the moon, which had turned into a little boat, up to the stars to play.

I am not positive that the girl was wearing a nightgown. Maybe she was just wearing a regular blouse, a blouse so big it covered her knees and reminded me of the pictures in Ilya's book, giving that savage dappled lane the ambience of a fairytale. But the girl didn't seem to be able to go anywhere. She was trapped in a doorway behind the human wall, and all she could do was cast her gaze at the crowd that was moving slowly by outside. People went to and fro in the lane, and her gaze encountered mine. I don't understand why she kept looking at me, a boy about the same age as her, but she did. She stared at me like a magnet with a gaze so hot it was scalding. I would rather have looked at an insinuating glance or a lazy smile, because in her eyes I saw, simply and unmistakably, an expression of revulsion that verged on fury. She seemed so furious I thought she might start breathing fire. She seemed to see through me. She seemed to know that I had broken the rules coming here, that I was somewhere I shouldn't be. I had never seen such a fierce look before. She seemed to use her gaze to accuse me of crossing the line and to blame me for becoming just like the other men in the lane.

I was terrified. But this time crossing the line was something I had done by myself. This time, I couldn't hide behind my mother like I'd done at the age of six. I was scared stiff. I forgot to keep moving forward to ensure my own safety. I stood there stuck in place, roasted by the burning gaze of that girl. Until finally somebody slapped me hard on the shoulder.

"Here you are! I've been looking all over for you."

The Master of the High Jump appeared from out of nowhere and saved me yet again.

"I didn't bring you here to show you this. Let's get out of here. The thing I'm taking you to see is just up ahead."

17
Lazy Habits

Verbs are a lazy habit.

When Ling-ling began to speak, almost every word she uttered was a noun. And since she's not yet two, all the words in her vocabulary are tangible and visible, concrete and haptic, if pronounced somewhat indistinctly and applied somewhat indiscriminately. She'll point at the computer monitor and say "televijun". She'll point at a dove and say "bud". She'll point at the sign to an English cram school and say "gilaffe" (because of the long-necked mascot of a ubiquitous local cram school chain). Each of these nouns is a vast semantic field applicable in many different situations. Each can contain subtleties I've never noticed, or which are known to her alone. But she cannot yet understand abstract, intangible things like air or time or life, things you can't touch with your hands or point at, things that take a lot of explaining.

Lately she's been adding a few simple verbs, each representing a single action, to her lexical repertoire. Very quickly, Ling-ling has discovered the utility of another part of speech. Before verbs appeared, Ling-ling used to totter over to the dinner table, stand on tiptoes, and strain her plump little hands towards the things on the table. She might grab the plastic container of seasoned seaweed, hold it close to get a good look, turn it over, bite the handle and the top, and tap the side. Or she might just throw it onto the floor. When verbs appeared in her vocabulary, such complicated and strenuous gestures disappeared. Ling-ling now knows she just has to use verbs like get and open and she can clearly express her intent. The more verbs she learns, the less body language she needs. I'm disappointed: I liked to observe her gestures and guess at their meaning, like breaking a code. I enjoyed interacting with her without words. She used to climb onto my leg, clutch at my hand and try to crawl onto my lap and into my arms. No longer does she raise her arms and look up at me with an imploring expression. Now she dispenses with her gestures, just says '"hug" to tell me to pick her up and sit her on the crook of my arm. That tells me she's tired and needs to be taken to bed and put to sleep.

After Ling-ling goes to sleep, I go into the study. Amanda is sitting at the desk staring at her laptop, but she isn't cultivating her farm. Her hands are flying over the keyboard, typing a message.

I stand behind her for a while before she speaks.

"Look at this," she says, swivelling her chair to the side. "I've already forwarded it to you. I want you to read it."

I bend down and look at the screen. The title of the essay on the screen is shocking: "Please Help: Child Abduction."

Please forward this message, and immeasurable karma will accrue to you
My daughter Hsuan-hsuan is 2 years old, and 90 cm tall
She has a green birthmark the size of a dollar coin at the corner of her right eye
While playing in the park today, she was snatched away by some middle-aged woman
At the time only my mother, who can't get around very easily, was present
Unable to catch that nasty woman, she now feels extremely guilty
She and my wife have been washing their faces with tears all day long
I beg you, kind sir or lady, to forward this letter to classmates, co-workers and friends
Please help us get our daughter back
It won't take too much of your time
Your help will give our whole family a thread of hope

"Isn't it scary?" Amanda says. "I never thought such a thing could happen in real life."

I sit in front of my own computer, and open my gmail. In just a single day, I have twelve unread messages and sixty-five spam messages. I open the inbox, and realize that though the new messages are from friends or acquaintances, the subject lines all say forward. There is no e-mail to me personally.

"I hear these people are members of a child trafficking ring, and they're very organized. They only steal children as young as Ling-ling. As soon as they nab them they put them on a fishing boat or on a container ship and send them abroad and sell them to foreigners, so that their parents have no chance of getting them back."

"In a container? Since when did Taiwan start exporting toddlers?"

"Don't ask me. That's what people say on the Internet. Do you know what happens to some of those children who are sent abroad?"

"Aren't they sold to rich, childless foreigners?"

"That's if they're lucky. The unlucky ones will fall into the clutches of a criminal gang. Little boys will be blinded, deafened or crippled, then dumped on the streets and forced to beg. Little girls aren't treated that way. They're taken care of for a few years, but well before they're adults they get pushed into the pit of fire. They become child prostitutes."

Scary. Was it even possible?

If Ling-ling were separated from us now, and if she never saw us again, would she remember us?

I open the shocking e-mail Amanda just forwarded, which was originally posted in an Internet chat room. The original post wasn't very long, but there are a lot of comments from all the people who have forwarded it. Reading the comments breaks my heart. "Please help forward this message to as many people as possible so we can bring these criminals to justice soon." "Oh my God, I won't dare take my kids to the park to play ever again." There's a long, dense stack of comments and handles. It's a bit like a traditional Chinese landscape painting on which generations of collectors have stamped their names. I reread the original post carefully. The poor father has neglected to indicate when and where his daughter was abducted. He's just left his name and mobile phone number. You can tell how upset the man must be.

"Don't you often take Ling-ling out during the day?"

"It's Ling-ling who wants me to take her out."

"This is no joke. When you take Ling-ling to the park to play do you keep your eye on the other adults there?"

"It's all people with kids."

I notice there's a photograph attached to the message, so I move my mouse to click it. I'd find it hard to open up to Amanda about my colleagues in the play area. Although she can't reproach me for my decision to be a stay at home dad, because it was our decision, she might not be too happy if she knew that my colleagues in the park are retired grandpas and grandmas, mainland Chinese brides and Indonesian maids.

"Are you sure that all the adults in the park are there with their kids? There are so many people in the park. Does your gaze ever leave Ling-ling?"

"I keep my eye on her at all times."

"Then are you keeping your eye out for suspicious individuals?"

"If my eyes never left Ling-ling, how could I notice whether there was anyone suspicious in the park?"

The girl in the photograph has stringy hair. She looks about the same age as Ling-ling. It's an ordinary face. And the background is an ordinary park on an ordinary afternoon. The picture is so ordinary it's chilling. It's a slice of life that makes me think of death, as if the person in the photograph is no longer living. Of course this girl must still be alive and well somewhere. It's only because I know that something happened to her that I feel sad. Presumably, after she was kidnapped, her parents went through all their pictures of their daughter to select one to go with the message, hoping someone would recognize her. They must have felt they were looking at pictures of a deceased family member, suddenly torn apart by ordinary images that now conveyed extraordinary pain. I try to imagine the feelings of her family, peering into a black hole that nobody could bear or escape.

Frightening. They might never see their child again.

"You'd better not take Ling-ling to the park so much."

"Then where should I take her? We can't stay at home all day, can we?"

"I think we should enrol Ling-ling in daycare as soon as possible."

I know what Amanda is trying to tell me, even if she wouldn't admit it. The problem isn't the park. The problem is that I don't have a job, and she thinks I should find one. Because it's only because I don't have a job that I take Ling-ling to the park, and there's no guarantee that she won't get abducted some day. Her logic is simple, but I'd best keep quiet. If I call her on it she'll get angry and accuse me of being too sensitive. I don't really understand her state of mind: she wants me to get a steady job, but can't admit it on account of the agreement we made.

"The park isn't that dangerous," I say. "It's no more dangerous than daycare. I've seen field trips of toddlers in the park."

Amanda doesn't reply, denying me the opportunity to recite the response I have mentally prepared. I was going to say that teachers at the daycare often have to take care of fifteen little kids. No matter what, a teacher can't look after Ling-ling as well as me.

To defend myself, I'd censored any information that might not be to my advantage, such as the fact that I let Ling-ling play by herself while I sit on a concrete bench appreciating the underwear models in a Costco advertisement. Of course, there are many hidden dangers in the park. For instance, all those schoolchildren wobbling around on bicycles, those unleashed dogs basking in the sun, or those kids about the same age as Ling-ling waiting in line to go down the slide.

"Hey!"

"What?" Amanda asks.

"The little girl who was kidnapped has a birthmark. Could it be the girl from last time?"

"What girl? When?"

"The girl from the playground. The girl Ling-ling shoved."

"Do they look similar?"

"I don't remember what she looked like, but I'm sure that she had a big birthmark like a bruise at the corner of her eye. At the time I assumed she'd hit her head when Ling-ling pushed her over."

"Then that's who it is!" Amanda jumps up. "How many children could have a birthmark in that exact place?"

"Calm down. Maybe I'm misremembering."

"Was there anybody with that little girl? Who went with her to the park?"

"She looked like a foreign maid. She was speaking English. I don't know what country she was from."

"She must be a member of a multinational child trafficking ring!"

"Unlikely. Would a member of a child trafficking ring take a child she had kidnapped to the park?"

"Maybe she would. Children that young would lose any memory of life before they were abducted. A child trafficker wouldn't worry about taking them to the park." Amanda walks over to the coat rack, opens her purse and gets out her phone.

"What are you going to do?"

"I'm going to call them."

"Aren't you overreacting? You've never seen that girl. Just relying on my description, how can you know that the girl that was kidnapped is the girl I saw in the park?"

"You said she had a birthmark at the corner of her eye. What are the odds?"

"You just saw that missing person notice today. I saw that girl in the park last month. The timing isn't right."

"Haven't you noticed? The missing person notice does not say when the child was kidnapped, and look how many times it's been forwarded. Obviously, it didn't happen recently."

"Do you know what time it is? Call them tomorrow."

"If it were your child, would you care about what time people who had information about her whereabouts called you?" Amanda says as she enters the number. "I think your biggest problem is that you lack execution. I don't want to be like you."

She takes her phone into the family room. I examine the birthmark in the picture, feeling like some corner of my mind is stained with a shadow of the same colour. Not having time to let the shadow spread, I try to recollect that brilliantly sunny afternoon, to recover any details concerning the girl who fell on the steps of the slide. I'm afraid Amanda might have trouble communicating with the person who answered the phone, that she might hand the phone over to me. Amanda has already taken action. And it seems like I should follow her and do something. But she has never been so impulsive before, calling someone's number from a missing person's notice on the basis of a piece of uncertain information I've just reported to her. If it isn't maternal instinct it's a woman's irrational petulance. Or maybe both, I can't help thinking.

I sneak a glance at Amanda pacing in the family room. I don't know whether her call has been answered, just that I've hung up on the unanswered call I just placed to my memory. How can I excavate the memory under such stressful conditions? Even if I could extract some impressions from the haze, I couldn't guarantee nothing had been added. Any embellishments would be no help in locating a missing person.

Luckily, when Amanda turns towards me, I see that her flip-style phone is already closed.

"What did they say?" I ask.

"They found the child already." Amanda tosses her phone on the table. "You know what? That notice is from three years ago. Their little girl is now five years old."

I sigh with relief. "How could this be?"

"He said it was all a misunderstanding. The child came back the very next day. He erased the original missing person's notice, but by that time it'd been forwarded many times. He didn't know what to do." Amanda sits down and stares at her laptop again. She doesn't say anything for a long time. Finally she sighs and says: "What should I do? I've forwarded it to ten people. Should I write them one by one to tell them the child has been found and not to forward the message?"

I don't offer her any suggestion, just trash the forwarded message. Forwarding messages is another lazy habit. This missing person's notice has circulated through blogs, chat rooms, Facebook and e-mail for three years, and will keep on flowing or drifting through the boundless virtual space of the Internet. The kidnapped girl in the photo has been frozen in time at the age of two. She will never grow up, and will never go home.

18

Harriet the Orangutan

Brand wouldn't tell me what we were going to see, just guaranteed I'd never seen it before. But he was wrong again. Quite a few years before, maybe when I was in fifth or sixth grade, my mother and father had sandwiched me on a scooter trip north to the zoo, where I saw all the animals in the cages.

It was an unforgettable day, partly because Dad wasn't drinking. I could never figure out what started first, my dad's drinking or my mother's complaining. She was always talking about moving, nagging my father about his drinking, actually about everything. She didn't just say we lived in a code violation. She also said that there were too many wolves, foxes and snakes in the neighbourhood, as if we were the ones living in a zoo. I don't remember whether we saw any wolves, foxes or snakes that day. But I do remember the elephants, the giraffes, the zebras and the camels. And also the kind of animal that Brand had dragged me through the rainforest of Carnation Lane to see.

"So what? I've seen apes before," I said.

"It's a great ape, not just an ape. And even if you saw one before at the zoo, it was in a cage. You couldn't reach out and touch it now, could you?"

"I didn't touch it. It was too far away."

"I bet you wouldn't dare touch one," Brand said, raising an eyebrow and narrowing his eyes. "You wouldn't even dare to get close."

We were sitting in the tree fort on a rare occasion when all three of us were free. The summer holidays were half over. Me and Brand went out roaming every day. We had suntanned faces and necks, while Ilya was white as a roll of toilet paper. Put our faces together and we would have looked like the black and white keys on Ilya's grand piano. Me and Brand didn't ask Ilya why he couldn't come out to play, afraid that if we did he'd rush home to practise. So we tried to outdo each other recounting our most recent exploits. Brand bragged about how he'd sneaked into the rooftop addition and told Ilya what he'd discovered there, and he opened the treasure trove and got out the pamphlet with the titles in bad calligraphy to show it off. I announced that I had audaciously crossed the line and gone deep into the rainforest off the nightmarket street to the north of the pailou road, and boasted about how I'd looked left and right at all the scantily clad women, wriggling along with the other men. For all our embellishments and exaggerations, Brand didn't mention that he had been beaten by his father, nor did I bring up the girl in the doorway with fire in her eyes. But it wouldn't have made any difference: Ilya didn't seem the least bit interested. He listened quietly, but kept looking across the levee at the river, the sandbars and the egrets, where his gaze had drifted as soon as he climbed up. Only when Brand mentioned the great ape did Ilya interrupt.

"What colour is its fur? Is it orange? Is it an orangutan?"

"Yeah, how'd you know? It must be an 'orange' utan," said Brand, correcting himself.

"But an orangutan is an endangered species. How could one appear in our neighbourhood?"

Brand took whatever Ilya said as the gospel truth, and would patiently relate whatever Ilya wanted to know. That day he explained that the beast had come with a troupe of circus performers and cure-all hawkers. They'd started towing their wagon of a stage to the open area by the gateway to the north of the pailou road the previous week, and were going to perform there for a month. The frontman of the troupe seemed to know, or at least know of, Brand's father, and had come to the house to steep tea and pay his respects, though he'd felt no qualms about borrowing a spotlight, a loudspeaker, a curtain and some other props to use in the show. Which is how Brand knew the troupe was staying in a seedy inn down Carnation Lane. All day long the orangutan was caged in the narrow fire access behind the inn; only at night did they lead it out and use it in the first part of the act, to attract as many people as possible to come and watch.

"You mean this orangutan performs in their show?" Ilya asked, eyes bright.

"Yeah, it can smoke and eat betel nut and put on a shirt. It also eats bananas."

"It can do all those things?"

"For now. I heard my father's friend say he was teaching that ape… I mean, that orangutan arithmetic. That's the next trick he wants to add to the orangutan's repertoire."

Ilya seemed really interested in that orangutan. He kept asking questions about it, which I thought was pointless, because the troupe only started performing at nine o'clock at night, which was way past Ilya's curfew. It was even too late for me to go out and see what kind of medicine these itinerant performers were selling. Why would Ilya care what kinds of performance the orangutan was giving? I had no idea. He was behaving really strangely that day. The longest he'd ever spent in the fort before hurrying home was half an hour. That day, he stayed out all afternoon, and demanded that me and Brand take him to see the orangutan.

Brand quickly agreed. I wasn't so sure.

"What's the problem?" Ilya asked. "You've already crossed that line. So what if you cross it again?"

Crossing the line wasn't the problem. Even though it was still there, it didn't matter to me any more. Strange how breaking a taboo once can deprive it of all force, freeing you to break it ninety-nine times or however many times you want. The problem was no longer the line. The problem was the orangutan. I imagined the orangutan would be taller than me when it stood up. And covered in orange fur from head to toe. With two horns on its head, it would look like an orange devil in a storybook. But the reason why I hesitated wasn't the invisible line or the scary ape. What I was most afraid of was another encounter with that girl. I didn't want to see that awful look again.

I didn't know how to tell Brand and Ilya how I felt. All I could do was follow them like a good little boy across the pailou road and onto Carnation Lane, repeating the creepy odyssey. This time I didn't dare to look left or right. We walked single file down the centre of the lane, with Brand in the lead. Soon he led us down the fire access behind that seedy inn.

As before, the ape was sitting on a big iron cage. Last time I'd only dared to look at it from afar from the entrance to the fire access. Brand had called me over quite a few times but I didn't dare approach. Ilya didn't even wait for Brand to open his mouth. He started right down the lane towards the orangutan. Brand had to put his hand on his friend's shoulder to stop him.

"Easy does it. Don't get too close. You'll scare it," Brand said.

"Or it'll scare us," I said.

"I don't think it's afraid of people," Ilya said. "But you're right, we'd better approach it slowly."

We walked down that fire access, the walls of which trickled with condensation from the air conditioners. We eased step by step towards the orangutan. To me our caution also seemed pointless: I thought we'd never scare it, and that it was already angry: I'd seen the orangutan look our way and bare its teeth and stare at us at the entrance to the lane. There were no canvas awnings here, so the late afternoon sun spilled down through the gaps between the eaves. It didn't light up the fire access much, but it did set the orangutan's fro of wiry fur aflame. How could anyone not think it was angry?

But Ilya wasn't scared at all. I stopped five metres away from the cage. Brand went closer than me, but still stayed two metres away. If that orangutan had been locked in the cage, two metres would have been fine. But it was sitting on wooden planks on the roof of the cage. I didn't know why it was sitting so obediently up there, why it didn't just run away. I worried it might suddenly stand up and rush us, which didn't seem to worry Ilya. He was like a boy possessed, inching towards that staring beast. He got really close, close enough to reach out and touch it, just like Brand had dared me to do. No, even closer, so close that his knees almost knocked the iron bars of the cage, close enough to feel the breath of the orangutan on his face. Suddenly the orangutan moved. Me and Brand called out, thinking that the orangutan was about to bite Ilya. But it didn't. It had just lifted its backside, retreated two steps, and turned, like it was peeved, or like it wanted to keep its distance.

"I guessed wrong. You seem a bit afraid of people," Ilya said.

He walked around the cage, wanting to get face-to-face with it, but the orangutan changed positions again and kept looking away. "Come here, you guys. It's just a bit shy," Ilya said. I looked at Brand. Neither of us dared take a single step closer. I guessed Brand must've felt a little bit taken aback, as if the orangutan wasn't his discovery any more, as if it was a pet that Ilya had been keeping for a long time. This was really surprising. Although we had seen Ilya turn his hands into a spider and an egret at the piano, we'd never imagined he would have a thing for real live animals. We were still hesitating two and five metres away, and he had faced down that orangutan, and reached out and held its hairy hand. He'd raised his palm and placed it against the ape's.

"What long fingers! I think playing the piano would suit you more than me," Ilya said.

Seeing Ilya holding the orangutan's hand, me and Brand got up the courage to go closer. But we'd only got two steps closer when a draught poured a formidable stench into our nostrils. It wasn't the smell of piss or shit. It wasn't the smell of rotten food or vomit. It was the orangutan's body odour, and it was way stinkier than any of the smells in our daily lives, even stinkier than a pack of stray dogs. I held my nose to block the stench. Continuing my advance, I noticed the stinky orangutan was chained at the neck, like a dog. The chain was really long, and fastened to the cage with a combination lock about half the size of a pack of cigarettes. No wonder it sat there so obediently. No wonder it didn't try to run away. The steel arc of the lock was thicker than my index finger, and the chain was so rusty it was practically the same colour as the orangutan, as if it had been dyed orange by the orangutan's fur, or as if it were an appendage to the orangutan's body.

Seeing the orangutan chained by the neck, we knew that even if it wanted to attack us it couldn't get very far. The chain gave me courage, but Ilya didn't seem too happy with it. He yanked at the chain and at where the chain was attached to the cage. He even tried dialling combinations on the lock. I stared at him unblinking, planning to run away if he happened upon the right combination or somehow managed to break the chain. Luckily, the chain was pretty solid; it covered Ilya's hands in rust, but didn't snap. "It's been chained up for a long time," Ilya said, gesturing at the ape's neck and shoulders to point out places where its skin was scraped or bald. "This must be from all the chafing," he said, obviously feeling sorry for the animal. "Look, all the fur on its neck and shoulders has been worn away."

Hearing Ilya put it that way made me feel for the poor creature too. Its neck and shoulders were hairless, and tufts of fur had fallen out at its elbows and knees. The rest of its body was covered in long fur, but not very thick. Its fur was so thin and fluffy that it didn't cover its light brown skin. It was a bit like when my grandmother undid her bun and let her hair hang loose. It looked almost elderly sitting on the cover of the cage like that. It just sat there slouching, letting its arms hang limply by its crossed legs and hanging its head, not moving a muscle. And its big protruding jaw was so slack it rested on its nearly hairless chest. No matter how many flies landed on its body or buzzed around it, no matter how close me and Brand tiptoed towards it, it didn't react at all. It was so indolent it was like: "Go ahead, flies, I couldn't get rid of you if I tried. Do with me what you like."

"Is it old?" I asked Ilya. "Look at how wrinkly its face is."

"Please. Orangutans have wrinkly faces when they're born," Brand rushed to say.

"Have you seen a baby orangutan?"

"Not in the flesh. But I saw one on television."

"Then do you know how old this orangutan is?"

"I guess it's five years old," Brand said. He turned and looked at Ilya. "What you think? Around five years old, right?"

"Up to your old tricks, again, eh?" I said, pointing at Brand's nose. "Orangutans only live to the age of ten. You just guessed a middle figure. So no matter how old Ilya guessed, you could say 'same difference.'"

"You're confusing orangutans with dogs. An orangutan can live to the age of forty," Ilya said.

Brand burst out laughing, and the indolent orangutan looked up at him, scaring off quite a few flies. I didn't mind Brand's mockery. I just thought it was a little bit unfair. Dogs were animals too. How come they only lived ten years while orangutans could live to forty? Why was it that we were all in the same class and Ilya knew how long orangutans can live, Brand that orangutans are wrinkly when they are born? Why didn't I know any of these things? Then I got angry, because that sickly-looking orangutan exposed two rows of yellow teeth and smiled a few seconds after Brand did, right before standing up, pursing its lips and hooting like it was the funniest thing it had ever heard in its life.

I initially thought the orangutan was imitating Brand, but it kept calling after Brand had stopped laughing. It kept calling and calling, when into the lane walked a man wearing a beret and carrying a water bucket and a plastic bag full of fruit in one hand and a metal frame and a flat black leather suitcase in the other. He tottered towards us. I guessed he was the keeper. "Scram! Go play somewhere else!" the man yelled. He put down the water bucket, and set the frame and the suitcase against the wall, freeing up his hands. He waved at us to git like he was shooing flies. "It just started hooting, we didn't touch it," I hurried to explain, but something in Brand's eyes told me to shut up. Brand went up and intervened: "You know Variety Lin," he said, using his father's nickname. "I'm his son. Remember me? You came to my house to drink tea." The man narrowed his eyes, then nodded suspiciously. Tongue emboldened, Brand said: "These are my classmates. They heard that your ape was a natural performer, and wanted to come over and meet the ape so they could go back and advertise the show for you. They'll tell their fathers and mothers and aunts and uncles and grandmas and grandpas and everyone else in the family to go to the pailou gateway to see you perform."

Brand's words had their desired effect. The man in the beret grinned at us, and said the orangutan was hungry. First he got out two bananas, then told us to step back lest it think we were going to fight it for food and slap us all the way to America. Ilya asked: "Do apes only eat two bananas a meal?" The man kicked away the bag of fruit and said: "Two bananas is just an appetizer. I have to teach the ape some tricks. If I feed it too much too soon, it won't be willing to learn."

I thought the orangutan was starving: when it saw the bananas, it jumped to the edge of the cage, still chained, reached out and grabbed the bananas from the man's hand. It didn't peel them, just shoved them in its mouth. It was so quick, so different from its lazy demeanour just now. I suddenly thought to ask the orangutan's age. The man said that he'd had it for less than two years, but when he got it from his friend the beast was already ten.

"It must be about twelve years old, about the same as us," Ilya said.

"Not exactly the same as you," the man said. "This ape don't have a dink. It's a girl."

The orangutan finished eating the bananas and extended a long arm towards the man, who smirked at it. He took a cigarette out of his pocket and put it in the orangutan's hand. The orangutan immediately put the cigarette in its mouth. But it didn't swallow it like a banana, just held the filter lightly between its lips. Then it reached out its hand again. "Wanna light?" the man asked. He got a Brilliant brand lighter out of his pocket and turned to ask us: "Any one of you got the guts to give this here ape a light?" When none of us replied, he started laughing. Just then, the orangutan took advantage of the man's distraction to steal the lighter and give itself a light. Then it started smoking its cigarette, looking just as practised as my father. Every so often it exhaled white shafts of smoke through its nostrils.

"Is this the first trick of the show?" Ilya asked.

"That's not a trick, she's addicted. If I didn't let her have a smoke for dessert, it'd put her in a bad mood," he said.

He took the lighter back from the orangutan and lit his own cigarette. Then he opened the X-frame metal rack and put the suitcase on top. Me and Brand pushed forward, wanting to see what was in the suitcase. But the man only opened the suitcase a crack, shoved his hand in, yanked out a club and a pair of pants, and closed it. Then came the ballyhoo. "Come on," he hollered. He tapped the leather suitcase with the club, like a conductor taps the music stand. "Thank you, ladies and gentlemen, for coming from far and wide to see your humble servant perform. Of course, I am not unaware that it's not me you have come to see but the star of our show. The star of our show is a regular Betelgeuse, a red hot orange beast of a star so big and bright it's practically the biggest and brightest star in the night sky. Of course, the star of our show, known far and wide, isn't really a star, but it is an orange beast and it is red hot. Without further ado, I present to you, all the way from the jungles of darkest Borneo, a 'red beast', also known as an orangutan! This particular orangutan goes by the name of Geuse, which is G-E-U-S-E as in the star, not J-U-I-C-E as in the beverage. Come on now, Geuse! Get up and bow to the audience!"

The orangutan glanced at the man but did not bow. It just blew another two shafts of smoke through its nostrils. Very quickly the cigarette in its hand burned down to the filter, but it would not throw the butt away.

"Oh sorry. I forgot: she doesn't pay any attention when she's smoking," the man explained. "Are you ready yet? You smokestack! How long does it take you to smoke a cigarette?"

Finally the orangutan threw away the butt, and the man hit the suitcase with the club again. "Now bow!"

The orangutan stood up, but didn't bow. It just extended a hairy arm towards the man. I don't know if it wanted bananas or cigarettes. But now the man was angry. He raised the club high, and cruelly clattered it against the metal cage. "I tell you to bow and here you keep begging. You've forgotten the very first lesson I taught you. Are you getting ready to embarrass me this evening?" the man howled. The orangutan immediately pulled back its hands and covered its head with its hands. Its comical appearance made me and Brand laugh. But Ilya did not seem to find it funny. He didn't seem interested in this kind of performance. He retreated to the wall and stood there. Just like the orangutan he put his hands on the small of his neck. "Stand straight!" The man shook the club and gave the leather suitcase a couple of thumps. This time, the orangutan stood up, thrust out its round chest and put its arms in the air. It looked like it was surrendering. "Bow!" the man barked. This time the orangutan obeyed. Without moving its arms or legs it bent at the waist like it had been broken in two, leaned forward and knocked its forehead against one of the planks of the cover of the cage. There it stayed, motionless. "Very good," the man said. "Get up!" It immediately sprang back to its original stance. The man took a little round treat the size of a piece of popcorn out of the plastic bag and tossed it to the orangutan. I looked over at the bag and saw inside a big bag of Dodo Pops, which generations of docile little boys and girls begged their parents to buy, even though as adults they would realize the pops tasted like you know what. I don't know what flavour it was. The ape swallowed it in one bite. Then the man tapped again on the suitcase. "All right, one more time: bow!"

We saw the ape bow three times and eat three more pops. Brand was dying to see it perform some other tricks. The man said: "One minute on stage, ten years of training." He also said that if we wanted to see the ape perform other tricks we'd have to wait. He had to practise the opening move a few more times to make sure there would be no mistake.

"It's so easy. How many more times do you need to practise it?" Brand asked.

"Hold your horses, kid. Wait and see: the beast will put on a pair of pants," the man said, one hand holding the bag, the other tapping the suitcase with the club.

"I don't want to watch any more," Ilya said. "Let's go home."

19
Good Times

Ilya's house was torn down eight years ago.

By that time it wasn't Ilya's house any more. After Mrs Chiang packed Ilya off to Belgium, the shack was home to some solitary old mainlander, one of the thousands of soldiers who came to Taiwan with Chiang Kai-shek in 1949. We never saw much of that old fellow, because he kept his doors and windows tightly shut all year long, and seldom came out. Less than two years later, the old guy disappeared. The new tenants were two indigenous brothers, though I don't know what tribe they belonged to. They were the opposite of the old fellow. Unless there was a typhoon or a cold snap, they kept the door open with a brick, and even took down the two board windows for ventilation, so that passers-by could see them sitting in their underwear in the little family room watching television and drinking. Soon we discovered more and more people living in the shack, men, women and children. Incredibly, seven or eight people managed to squeeze into that little shack: in a space of nine or ten pings, there was barely space for them to sleep. Then the aboriginals just up and left like the old fellow had. The door was boarded up, the windows sealed with plywood. Two years later Ilya's house and some of the houses in the area were torn down. First they tore off the roof and the door and windows, leaving a ruin of brick walls, like a set in an airsoft field. Soon an excavator came and cleared everything away.

The year the house was torn down was the year that Ilya finished his studies in Europe and came home. But he didn't make it home in time to see his house. Eight years ago he came home and stood in the space where he had practised the piano for more than ten years. He was standing in the middle of a freshly paved road fully six metres wide.

"My house is gone," said Ilya.

I remember he kept muttering this to himself, over and over.

I guess Ilya would have regretted seeing what had happened to his house. Seeing the house that he had grown up in gone probably wasn't a very pleasant experience. Ilya said the apartments he'd lived in in Belgium and France for six years were both quite nice. He opened his window to see a seagull soaring over a canal or a church out of the Middle Ages. But he often dreamed of his ramshackle house in the slum. Ilya said sometimes he would wake up and think he was sleeping in the tiny attic in that old shack. He would open his eyes before realizing he was in Europe, and that the ceiling was high overhead.

I rewind my memory to eight years ago, to Ilya soon after he returned to Taiwan. It was an important year for both of us, as I intuited at the time. He had just finished his degree abroad, and I had just been discharged from the military. Both twenty-seven, we were both fresh from somewhere else, and were preparing to make a fresh start. I don't remember exactly when he came back. He didn't come to see me right after he got off the plane. First he found a flat for him and his mother in the well-to-do east side. Then he found a job. He settled in before he got the idea into his head one afternoon to take the MRT halfway across the city to see the old neighbourhood. The exit to the station was right by the gateway at the entrance to the nightmarket.

Where we just happened to run into each other. He had been abroad for six years, during which time we had never called or written. Seeing Ilya's house razed to the ground, I thought I'd never see my childhood playmate again. I never thought that a fortuitous encounter at the MRT station would whisk us back to a jokey familiarity. It was as if Ilya had never left the country or even moved. It was as if just yesterday we had shared slurpees under the pailou gateway.

But six years had changed many things. I forget where I was going that day. I just remember seeing Ilya standing by himself on the stairs to the station. He looked like a tourist trying to figure out where he was on the map.

"Are you lost?" I asked.

"As if! I'm just shocked by where they built the entrance to the metro," Ilya said.

"It's actually called the MRT, not the metro. Are you from Paris or something? What's wrong with building the entrance here?"

"Nothing wrong with it. But I was just thinking, there was only this one open space in the nightmarket. Now that they've built the station here, where's the next travelling performance troupe going to set up, do their stunts and their song-and-dance numbers and hawk their cure-alls?"

"Those performance troupes don't exist any more."

"They don't? How do you know?"

"They disappeared a long time ago. Who wants to see that kind of show nowadays?" I asked.

Ilya didn't say he wanted to go anywhere in particular. So I took him to see his old home and down the old alleys and lanes of the neighbourhood. Ilya had lived there for twenty years. He didn't need me to lead the way. But I remember he followed me like he was sleepwalking. Or like an amnesiac coming home, someone for whom the mundane details of daily life would take on new meaning. The moss-covered corrugated plastic eaves. The two-wheel food carts waiting under canvas covers for the nightmarket to open and the evening crowds to stream in. The discarded car mats tossed on the grilles of the manholes to block the stench. I couldn't see these things. Ilya pointed them out one by one, as if I was the tourist, as if I was the amnesiac, not him.

Thinking about Ilya just back from France makes me recollect all the things that were happening that time. Osama Bin Laden flew the planes into the Twin Towers. My father succumbed to heart disease. Y2K came and went. I finished my military service. There was a once-in-a-century earthquake in central Taiwan. And the last whorehouse in Carnation Lane closed for business. I met Amanda and started to pursue her. There was a peaceful transfer of power from the blue Kuomintang to the green Democratic Progressive Party. And I entered a PhD programme in comparative informatics with a research focus on cryptology. I think of all sorts of personal, national and global events before discovering that I cannot rely on memory to put the events in chronological order. Did 9/11 happen in the same year as the 921 earthquake? Did I leave the army first or did Ilya come home first? Did the DPP take power first or did the last brothel close first? In less than a decade these events have obscured themselves, each in its own way. I remember Professor Safe saying that time is the simplest encryption device. It can disturb, erase or change the information in memory, leaving you unable to restore it, no matter how hard you try.

I give up trying to order the incidents, just continue roaming through my memories of eight years before. Ilya and I walked those dim, damp lanes and alleys, swung past the banyan tree in the temple square under which nobody was steeping tea any more, and returned to the pailou road. It was still daylight, and the blockade that would turn the nightmarket into a pedestrian zone had not been moved out yet. Various kinds of vehicles were entering and exiting the nightmarket street. Most of them were get-rich-quick Kei trucks, vans and light duty refrigerated trucks. They were delivering all kinds of food supplies to the nightmarket before the blockade began, because if they arrived too late they could only park on the pailou road and push the goods in on foot. There was one kind of vehicle to which the restriction did not apply. It was another kind of human-powered vehicle: the food carts of various sizes that did business in the market. Each of them had its own stall, assigned by the Nightmarket Management Committee and by a kind of authority nobody wanted to talk openly about: the mafia. But the carts wouldn't arrive that late, because only Moses could have parted the sea of people in the nightmarket.

Ilya climbed up on the stone base of the gateway. Vendors pushed their carts slowly from all directions towards the nightmarket, filing through the gateway towards the stalls they had rented along the covered walkways. Under the walkways, some vendors were setting out metal frames and plunking down boards on which they dumped piles of clothes and displayed their wares, while others were hanging cheap women's clothing on the gridwalls tied to the columns.

"Good times. My favourite time of day in the nightmarket used to be right about now," Ilya said. "Look! The crowds haven't appeared yet, but there are so many people busy already. Doesn't it look like a stage in a theatre before the audience enters or the curtain lifts?"

"The reason you liked this time of day is because you were almost never allowed to come out to the nightmarket at night," I reminded

Ilya. After school, me, Brand and Ilya often came to sit under the gateway on the south side of the pailou road. We drank slurpees and watched people set up their stands. If Brand were in a good mood and his fat arse didn't take up too much space, we could all sit together on the stone base. I did not want to deprive Ilya of a moment of nostalgia. But just back from France, he was wearing a black wool coat that he'd bought in Paris or Brussels. Standing up on that base which had not grown up with us, he looked pathetically small, and really stood out. I wished he would hurry up and come down.

"Before, I never knew why I liked this time of day, but now I know," said Ilya. "Look at these people. All of them are helping to set up the stage, all acting at the same time with the same goal in mind. This scene is so powerful, so full of vitality. What a poignant sight!"

"You just think they are full of vitality because you don't have to put your back into pushing one of those two-wheelers over the bumpy tiles and bricks."

"Do you mean to say that that these workers cannot feel the vitality they are releasing? Not necessarily. If the musician on the stage cannot feel the life in the music, how can he move the audience?"

"But these people are not musicians. You don't have to wheel the grand piano onto the stage. You are not the same as them."

"Hey, you're not the only one who grew up here. But it's strange that you have to grow up first before you see how great these people are. Look around. The nightmarket is so cramped and congested, but everyone finds his place. They all know what they should be doing, and even though everyone's space is so limited they never get in one another's way. Out of chaos order, a beautiful harmony. Tell me, if that isn't music, then what is it?"

Thinking back now, I feel like Ilya was saying things that were not easy to refute but at the same time hard to agree with. Brand said Ilya was different from us, and I always acknowledged that Ilya had his own way of seeing things. But at the time I just couldn't see any beauty or hear any music in the nightmarket. Ilya and his mother didn't rely on the nightmarket to make a living. We did not have to help set up a stand after school either; we were forbidden from messing around in the nightmarket. But no matter what, we were living in the greater market, the area around the nightmarket, twenty-four hours a day. Our neighbours along the narrow, winding alley were all street vendors. I never knew what their names were, just that they sold stinky tofu, roast squid, shaved ice with tapioca topping, or guavas.

The family that sold guavas had twin daughters. They must've been older than me by about five or six years. Their father was a bona fide alcoholic. Always dead drunk, even if he didn't drink himself to death. My father was practically a Puritan or a teetotaller by comparison. A couple of times every week, rain or shine, I'd see that drunk collapsed against the wall somewhere along the alley, his hair unkempt, his clothes covered in filth. He would be clutching an empty rice wine bottle and crying: "Mama, Mama." His two daughters were used to it; they had given up on him. Every time he sat there crying for his mother, no matter how close he was to the house, I never saw his daughters pay him any attention. They wouldn't come out and help him home, or take the bottle from his grasp, wipe the filth off his face and help him change into a pair of clean clothes. Their father's disgusting appearance didn't bother them. They were more concerned about how the guavas looked. I always saw them sitting on little stools in the doorway in front of a big aluminium basin of water, de-stemming and rinsing the guavas and then placing them on the green plastic steps of a wooden frame on the back of a two-wheel cart. At dusk, the twins would turn on the red cellophane light and push the load of guavas towards the market. Piled with fruit, the cart was very heavy, and the alley was not very smooth. There were short grades in a few places, and the twins were really thin. One on either side, they would push the guava cart along, calling one-two-THREE every time they neared a slope and breaking into a run to get enough momentum to make it partway up. Then they would arch their bodies, bury their heads between their arms, and lean into it, pushing the cart with all their might step by step to the top.

Ever since I can remember, perhaps before I knelt in front of the altar, the twins had pushed the guava cart every day past the door of our house. Their lives ebbed away on that rolling cart. I imagine Ilya never noticed them, because they pushed just one of over a hundred carts that set up in the nightmarket. Like all the other cart-owners, their goal was to become a small part of Ilya's set or mise-en-scène.

Ilya never knew the twins were later headline news and a topic of conversation for everybody in the neighbourhood. Maybe because of a congenital disease or malnutrition, they remained small and dark into their twenties. They never married. Their attitude towards marriage was the same as their attitude towards their father: indifference. They had already given up. All they cared about was how well the guavas would sell. The day before they made headlines, while Ilya was watching a seagull soaring over the canal in the early morning in Brussels, the twins set out as always in the late afternoon towards the nightmarket. One-two-THREE, they cried, pushing the cart up the rise at the railway crossing. Everything went as usual, until the left wheel chose the moment when the barrier came down and the bell started ringing to protest the fact that their father had been siphoning funds from the lubricant budget to buy booze for over a decade. The left wheel betrayed its companion on the other side and leaped onto a track on which it was never meant to run. One of the twins, who had long suspected the loyalty of the left wheel, immediately crouched down and used her knees to try to prop up the cart, filling in for the wheel by taking its place. But she could only slow the speed at which the cart tilted to the left. The other twin had to rush around to help keep it from falling over. They should have considered the danger they were in, and abandoned the cart. Why on earth did the perennially late north-bound train choose that day of all days to make a change? It arrived early for once, taking everyone completely by surprise. What happened next made it into the news the next morning. The cart, the carefully arranged rows of glistening de-stemmed guavas, the twin sisters and their pathetic father would never ever again appear in the nightmarket. The management committee quickly leased out the vacant stall to a new vendor, and several days later someone new wedged his cart in.

Ilya never heard about it, because he was in Belgium. Six years later he came back, stood on the stone base of the pailou gateway, rode the wind and cast his gaze around. And in a fairly typical tourist nightmarket, as hustling and bustling as always, he heard a symphony of life and perceived a harmonious beauty. As a boy, Ilya used to climb high up the tree, pluck a twig to use as a baton, and conduct the river, the sandbars and the egrets outside the levee. Seeing him up there on the stone base of the gate, I worried his next move might be even more embarrassing.

"You only see beauty because you've been away too long. Beauty depends on distance. Now get down or people will think you're a crazy bum standing up there with a goofy grin."

That finally got through to Ilya, who jumped down from the stone base, looking gloomy.

"You're right. What's the difference now between me and a street person? My old house has been torn down. There's no place for me anywhere else in the world."

"Don't say that. You just got back. You're only a temporary 'street walker'. Wait until you walk the streets some more. You'll get used to everything and feel at home again."

I motioned for him to follow. The forced closure of the public brothels north of the pailou road had increased the number of women standing like cardboard cutouts under the arcades or in the maze of lanes off the nightmarket street. They were the street walkers. We used to have to walk along a ridge down the centre of Carnation Lane to make it through the rainforest, to run the gauntlet of women. Now we had to avoid the covered walkway and walk down the slow lane of the street to stay safe.

"Maybe," Ilya said. "But right now my situation is a lot like theirs."

Ilya and I kept going. During the day you could tell the block was run-down: fat rats waddling across the eight metre road, unafraid of people or cats. People here were busy all night long, and during the day all they did was rest. They were too lazy or tired to bother to drive away the rats while the cats, which ate nightmarket delicacies all night long, couldn't be bothered trying to catch something mobile and uncooked. By night, however, the street would morph into a nightmarket tourists would find worth visiting. Colourful neon signs would flaunt whatever needed flaunting, and anything shameful would sink into the shadows. Witnessing the splendour and the decay, Ilya and I walked through the old neighbourhood, a pair of vagabond foreigners somnambulating side by side on the frontier of day and night.

20

SEX CULTURE INDUSTRY MEMORIAL PARK

As soon as I stand up, everyone looks up at me, all the people sitting on the bench in front of the general service desk holding numbered tickets. It's just like waiting to see the doctor at the hospital or a teller at the bank. Every time the next number is displayed and announced, people instinctively look first at the display, then at the fellow whose number has been called, and finally at the number on their ticket, to calculate the distance between the two.

But this isn't a hospital or a bank. It's the Employment Services Division at the Bureau of Labour Affairs. All the people waiting have the same distinctive expression. Their faces aren't twisted with illness. They don't look anxious about money. Rather, they look vaguely ashamed or cringing, like someone has refused or hurt them. They look at you very sympathetically, knowing that you have come for the same reason. "Good luck finding a job!" trumpet the volunteer ladies in orange vests as they walk through the crowd with exaggerated cheer. Maybe being overly cheerful is part of the job description. After all, this isn't a funeral home. Why the long face? Cheer up! Maybe your next job is just around the corner.

The display and the intercom tell me to go to desk three. The lady serving me looks like she's in her fifties, about the same age as the volunteer ladies. The difference is she's not wearing a vest. Nor does she have to walk around and smile at everyone. She draws a salary.

"What kind of job do you want to find?" She takes the curriculum vitae form I've just filled out with the help of one of the cheerful volunteers, and starts entering the information. "Have you checked the paper or gone on the Internet to look for a job?" she asks, staring at the screen, as if the computer is the one looking for a job.

"No, I haven't," I say, answering the second question first. "There are too many traps in job adverts on the Internet and in the paper. I thought it would be less trouble to come here."

"You're obviously very careful. But it's up to you to protect yourself. I can't guarantee that any job you hear about here will be trouble-free."

"But aren't you a government agency? If the employers you guys introduce might be scammers, then who can we trust?"

"Scam-prevention is for the police, not the Bureau of Labour Affairs. But we do do preliminary background checks."

"What kind of checks do you do? You get lots of new job adverts every day. How can you tell the legitimate ones from the fake ones?"

The salaried non-volunteer glances over at me bureaucratically. Then she looks back at the monitor.

"You seem more concerned about our jobs in general, and not about your future job."

"I was just curious. I imagined you might have a system or program to batch-process all the complicated job-related information."

"We don't have anything like that."

"But didn't you just say you do background checks?"

"Are you a reporter?"

"No, I'm not. Why do you ask?"

"I thought only reporters would keep asking questions like you are doing."

"And I thought that reporters today don't ask questions any more, that they've lost the ability to doubt." It suddenly occurs to me that if the department Professor Safe founded were still around, it could collaborate with the Department of Journalism on interdepartmental courses. There might be a need for a professional degree programme for reporters, to teach them the importance of comparing and analysing information and the dangers associated with the failure to do so. "Reporters today just know how to copy, paste and send. I think that they should have the ability to judge the quality and truth of the news," I say.

The lady behind counter three gives me a second, defensive, glance.

"Aren't you here to find a job? What's your specialization?"

"Cryptology."

"What-ology?"

"Crypt-ology. I study codes."

"Then can you pick locks?"

"Pick locks?"

"Isn't there like a huge vault in a bank? Don't you have to know complicated codes to be able to open one? I've seen it happen in the movies."

As long as I have a key there is no lock I can't open." I'm sure she doesn't understand the relationship between keys and codes. But I can't help adding: "The lock on a safe or a vault is mechanical, but the codes I study are digital. But it comes to the same thing. The purpose in both cases is security."

"Security…" She nods and types some words into the computer. "So your specialism is related to security. No wonder you're interested in scam rings."

"You could say that my specialism is preventing theft. Is the code on your bank card just your date of birth?"

"How'd you know?"

"I advise you to change it as soon as possible. Or else don't put your bank card and your ID card in the same wallet. If you ever lose your wallet, the thieves will break the code in less than three tries and take out all your money before you have time to notify the bank."

"Sounds pretty scary. But all the money in my bank account was withdrawn by my husband. There's no need for me to change the code." She refuses to accept my simple suggestion and seems unwilling to continue the topic of conversation. "There's a job in a bank that would suit you. But you have to do shift work. Are you interested?"

"How would I know if I haven't done it before?"

"What I mean is that if you want to arrange an interview I can give you an invite card."

"Is my specialism suitable for this job?"

"It's a match. But they have an educational limitation. Maybe you can go and talk it over with them."

"What kind of an educational limitation?"

"They limit you to college education."

"I've got a PhD. That shouldn't be a problem, should it?"

"What they're looking for is someone with college or lower education. But the salary is okay. Do you want to give it a try?"

I take the invite card from counter number three, and look it over as I walk out. It's a piece of white A4 paper with the company's basic information, contact, telephone number, e-mail address. I look at the details for the job vacancy. It really does match my specialism. It says: "Bank Premises Observation, Customer Inquiries Services." As for the position, it says: "Security Guard."

The volunteer lady by the door says to me with the sweetest smile: "Good luck finding a job!"

I walk along the winding alley to my old house, a code violation with a rich, fifty-year history. Wearing a pair of reading glasses, my mother is hunchbacked in front of the computer. She is hunt-and-peck typing phonetic symbols on the keyboard. By her side on the table, there are a number of binders, scrapbooks, official envelopes, and stacks of unbound archival materials.

I do not have to look at the monitor or the documents to know what she's doing. Lately she and a number of the grandmas in the neighbourhood have founded a Community Culture Preservation Association. With the help of scholars, experts, social workers, writers and artists, they have been running around hoping to get people behind them to put pressure on the government. They want to get the abandoned brothel district north of the pailou road rezoned as a cultural park, for which they have even come up with a name. They plan to call it the SEX CULTURE INDUSTRY MEMORIAL PARK. Though this name ended up passing, there was a lot of disagreement during the discussion. One "expert" with a background in economics suggested: SEX INDUSTRY CULTURE MEMORIAL PARK, because sex work was a kind of industry, and every industry had its own culture. His view was derided by other scholars of the "culture creative industries". They saw culture as the be all and end all, the source of everything: without culture there would be no impetus for industry. And that's not all. Some of these scholars wanted to add the term creative before the word industry, because "industry" in itself would objectify sex workers: SEX CULTURE CREATIVE INDUSTRY MEMORIAL PARK. My mother said she and her neighbours couldn't wrap their heads around this chicken-

or-egg kind of issue. They just insisted on keeping the word memorial in the name.

"You've come alone? What about Ling-ling?"

"Amanda took her to an afternoon tea with her friend."

"Why didn't you go?"

"It's a woman's group. I'm not invited."

"There's fruit in the refrigerator. Help yourself." Just like the lady behind counter number three at the employment services place, she's unwilling to tear her eyes away from the screen. Her fingers have not stopped typing information about the history of the community character by character into the computer since I got home.

It's hard to imagine how my mother's attitude towards the neighbourhood could have changed so completely. For as long as I can remember, my mother whined about the neighbourhood, declaring her desire to move the hell away, every chance she got. She hated the lawless, haphazard sprawl of the slum. She hated her neighbours, passers-by, and the women who lived down Carnation Lane. The smell, the humidity and the temperature – nothing could please her. When the sun was out she thought the house was hot and stuffy; when it rained she thought the sound of the rain pattering against the ironskin roof was too loud. Even a breeze down the alley on a cloudy day made her frown. While my father drank and shelled peanuts and I practised calligraphy on the blank part of a poster, she would yell: "What a stink! Can you believe the lack of basic hygiene? If you're not going to wash, can you at least shut your windows? Quit trying to poison your neighbours!"

I don't bother with the fruit, just look for the remote control, and sit down on the sofa. The TV is playing a retrospective on the 9/11 incident. I watch the passenger plane hurtle towards the World Trade Center, lowering the volume so I won't disturb my mother. The volume meter slides from loud to soft to mute. The process only takes a few seconds, but it reminds me of my mother. After spending nearly half a lifetime moaning and groaning about how awful the place was, she finally fell silent, and hadn't mentioned moving away since. These past few years, she's changed a lot, much to my surprise. After I was discharged from the army, she started going to the park to take part in morning exercise, aerobics at first, then Chi Kung. Once Amanda and I got married and moved in to a new apartment tower on the other side of the river, she started going to the local community college to take courses in computers, flower arrangement and photography. After Ling-ling was born, she got involved in community cultural preservation work. She wasn't so moody any more, and stopped sulking about the wretchedness of the surroundings. I guess the change in my mother's attitude towards moving was gradual, like when you press the volume button on the remote control.

Not that this association can explain her change of heart. It's like the television and the remote control: before her invisible volume button was pressed to lower the volume, the power had to get turned on by some invisible hand. I wonder what happened to turn her on, changing how she saw the old neighbourhood?

"You don't have to turn the volume off, you won't bother me. Did you hear me say there's fruit in the refrigerator? Please help yourself."

I opened the refrigerator and took out a plate of fruit neatly arranged in two rows on a crystal dish.

"You're home alone. Why prepare an elaborate dish of fruit and put it in the refrigerator?"

"My friends from the Association often come to visit me. I have to have something ready to serve them."

"You're giving me fruit you prepared for your guests. Does that make me a guest?"

"Don't be silly."

I fork a piece of fruit into my mouth. The almost frozen flesh is almost brittle, not crunchy and soft like an apple or watery sweet like a pear. I suddenly remember the day at Professor Safe's house. I remember my adviser's amnesia. I remember his wife handing him wedges of fruit.

"What kind of fruit is this?"

"It's a peach."

"Are they stone pit peaches?"

"Peaches from Stonepit? You think I'd feed you a ceramic peach? These are ordinary peaches I bought at the market."

21

The Triangle in the Sky

Mrs Chiang bewailed Ilya's disobedience to everyone she met. "Ilya is only in sixth grade and has already entered his rebellious phase."

What had happened? Me and Brand weren't too sure. One day Ilya just refused to practise piano or go to cram school. When his mother started yelling at him, he jumped up and yelled back at her, and then ran out, slamming the door behind him. Dusk came and went, and Ilya had not come home; he missed dinner too. The hours passed, dampening the flame of Mrs Chiang's anger. At eleven o'clock, Mrs Chiang surrendered. She went berserk, searching everywhere for sign of Ilya. She came to my house and knocked on the door. I had not seen Ilya during the day, let alone in the evening. I'd never hung out with him in the evening. Mrs Chiang didn't seem to believe me: she opened her bloodshot eyes wide and kept looking in. She yelled "Ilya" at the ceiling, and wouldn't leave until my grandmother came down, stony-faced.

Then she went and knocked on Brand's door, scaring his father half to death. Brand said that there'd been fewer visitors to the house, but more strangers lingering under the lampposts outside for hours at a time. The illegal addition on the roof was now stacked with posters and fliers and banners that the adults had cut out of white fabric. They attached the big ones to bamboo poles or cut holes in them to make them into vests, and turned the small ones into headbands or armbands. Then they painted slogans on them. When Mrs Chiang came knocking on the roll-up iron door in the middle of the night like a madwoman, Brand's father blanched. He had the back window open, ready to make his escape, and would have jumped out had he not heard Mrs Chiang yelling "Ilya" outside.

"Why was your father so freaked out?" I asked.

"He's afraid the police will come to arrest him."

"But he's not done anything wrong. Why would the police want to arrest him?"

Brand raised an eyebrow at me, narrowed an eye, and said: "Haven't you heard? My father's a revolutionary. Everyone knows that when Founding Father Sun Yat-sen was making revolution in the 1900s, he would escape out the back every time he heard a knock on the door in the middle of the night."

Thank God Brand's father hadn't jumped out the back window to make an escape, because if he had, the person caught would have been Ilya, not him. I thought Ilya was more of a revolutionary than Brand's father. He hid the whole night in our secret base, stargazing in the tree fort all night long. Ilya said that when night had just fallen, he saw the Summer Triangle, a right-angled triangle of three very bright stars: the Weaving Maid in the north, the Cowherd in the south, and the fourth star in the Heavenly Bridge across the Silver River, which the Weaving Maid and the Cowherd, China's star-crossed lovers, are only able to cross on the seventh day of the seventh month of the lunar calendar to reunite once a year. The whole night, he kept watching the triangle tracking through the sky, until it was about to touch the hills in the east.

Brand and I prostrated ourselves at his feet, totally in awe. It wasn't because of his knowledge of astronomy. (Though his mother made him practise most of the time there didn't seem to be anything Ilya didn't know.) We were in awe of the fact that he could describe running away from home in such a matter of fact way, as if it were as natural as taking out the rubbish. Brand had the guts to cut up his father's drum set, and I had the balls to cross the border into the forbidden zone, but neither of us would have dared spend the night outside. It was also so out of character. It seemed like the sort of thing me or Brand might do, not something a role model like Ilya would do. And we'd never expected that our improvised tree fort, if you can even call it that, would ever serve as a place to crash.

Ilya appeared in the tree fort more often and for longer each time. Mrs Chiang went out asking after him so much that everyone in the neighbourhood except for that alcoholic lying on the ground with a bottle in his arm crying for his mama knew that Ilya had changed. It wasn't just that he had refused to walk down the road his mother had paved for him in gold, but that he had learned to be lippy and disobedient.

I never asked Ilya why he suddenly started to disobey his mother, but I guessed maybe it was on account of the piano competition. It must have been an important competition, because it was held in the fanciest concert hall in the city. Me and Brand went to hear him play. It wasn't Mrs Chiang who invited us, but Ilya who told us the time and place and arranged to meet us and let us in. That was the first time in our lives we had been to such a high-class place as a concert hall. We were shocked even before we went in the door, which was three times wider than the roll-up door at Brand's place, made all of glass and even opened on its own. Then we went inside. The ceiling felt as high as the sky, and there was so much space that you could have moved in Brand's entire townhouse with the addition on top without making the place feel the least bit crowded.

Me and Brand stood there in the lobby, jaws slack, watching a group of kids about the same age as us but wearing tails or long white tulle dresses as they scampered around on a plush carpet. By comparison me and Brand were like two little beggars that had stolen into the palace, uninvited guests at an imperial banquet. Fortunately, Mrs Chiang did not see us. It was only because she was talking so animatedly with the mothers of the other little princes and princesses that Ilya'd had the opportunity to steal out, let us in, take us up to the second floor, and sit us in the last row of the balcony in the auditorium.

We sat in the dark, empty balcony, waiting. The chairs were soft and fluffy and bouncy. Me and Brand gripped the armrests and bounced up and down. It was fun, but we only bounced a few times for fear that the creaking of the chairs would break the silence of the room. Ilya said this was a big competition, but only in the first few rows could we see any people, probably the little princes and princesses and their parents. Since the auditorium was mostly empty, the staff had left all the lights off except for a spotlight on a black grand piano on the stage and a little table lamp on the wooden table in front of the first row of the audience. I guessed the backlit silhouettes seated away from us at that table were the judges. When those little princes and princesses had entered the dark auditorium they had become suddenly serious. Just now in the lobby they had looked about the same age as me and Brand, but now they were sitting quietly with their parents in the first few rows behind the judges. I don't know if the lights were too dim, or the kids weren't smiling enough, but I felt that they had suddenly aged, become much more mature. They sat in those plush chairs, but did not bounce up and down to test the cushions like me and Brand. Instead, they sat primly like the adults, eyes fixed on the stage, watching the contestant.

I was amazed these princes and princesses dared to walk all alone onto a big, empty stage, stand in the centre and bow, sit at that grand piano, wipe the keyboard with a handkerchief, and then, with a vigorous nod, cause a beautiful music to flow out from their fingers. None of them needed to look at the music, which I found even more incredible, because the keys all looked the same. Somehow they could tell the keys apart and remember what key to play with what finger at what time, without making a mistake. It wasn't just their hands. Their feet were busy too. Brand whispered that they looked like adults driving a car, sometimes putting the pedal to the metal, sometimes slamming on the brakes, sometimes changing gears. Of course, I knew that the pedals on a piano are not like the accelerator, brake and clutch pedals in a car, but every one of those kids could make his or her fingers race up and down the keyboard, swerving back and forth like it was a Formula One for fingers. I soon discovered the reason why they played so quickly: each performer's time was limited. When the allotted time was up, a bell would sound and the little prince or princess who had been playing well until then would immediately stand up, take a bow and hurry off the stage.

Ilya I guess was the eighth or ninth to go on stage and participate in the Formula One finger race. He was clad head to toe in the formal tails a magician wears, so that Brand and me did not immediately recognize him. But when he started to play we knew it was him, making magic without a magician's hat, transforming his fingers into that frightened spider or that high-stepping egret that stepped out an elegant music. I don't know what piece he played. The only pieces of music I recognized were the themes for cartoons or folk songs played on the radio. I was not much interested in music you couldn't sing. I just knew that the reason why Ilya could play such fluent and beautiful melodies was because me and Brand had helped him build the tree fort so he could spend six hours a day practising. Ilya was really playing wonderfully; he went quicker and quicker, so that even a music idiot like me knew that he was creating tension, preparing for the climax. Just then came the explosive sound of the bell. Ilya cut off instantly; the music vanished, and the spider and the egret disappeared without a trace. I sat speechless and wide-eyed on that overstuffed sprung chair, as if a balloon had been blown up halfway and suddenly pricked. Ilya, like the previous contestants, got up, took a bow, and walked off, without the slightest parting sorrow. Me and Brand looked at each other, incredulous. He had practised so long for a measly three minutes on stage. It just wasn't fair. The judges should have let him finish the piece. It would not have taken up very much of their time.

Ilya did not place in that competition, but the judges gave him very high marks. He got practically the same mark as the girl who got third prize, 86. But Ilya only got 86.2, while that girl got 86.9. Mrs Chiang showed displeasure for several days. Every chance she got she paraded Ilya in front of the neighbours and berated him for being second last. It was incredible. There were a dozen kids in the same category as Ilya, and they all got practically the same mark, 86. The placing was decided by the decimal place. Which is to say, that although the auditorium was so huge, the race of fingers had taken place in a very narrow range.

From then on, Ilya seemed to feel that it didn't really matter if he practised piano or went to cram school. Sure, he spent more time in the tree fort, but we knew he spent most of his time north of the pailou road in the fire access behind that inn. He seemed very fond of that orangutan, me and Brand both felt. Of course, everyone liked the orangutan, but Ilya liked it in his own special way. Everyone enjoyed watching the orangutan perform, so much so that the open space by the gateway had been the most popular spot in the nightmarket ever since the man in the beret had set up there. Brand said that long before the performance began folks moved out benches and stools to get a seat in the first row. People who arrived late were blocked by the wall of people in the audience, and couldn't see even standing on tiptoe. The only way they could watch was to climb up on the base, wrap their arms around the arch and lean back, like a clutch of koalas watching an orangutan perform.

Ilya never appeared in the crowd. Brand told me that all the kids in the area had gone to see the orangutan perform except for me and Ilya. Brand knew I didn't dare ask to go out after nine o'clock to see them hawk the cures because I was afraid my mother would find out I'd been to the forbidden zone and ground me. But Brand could not understand Ilya's absence.

"Maybe Mrs Chiang is pushing him even harder?" I suggested. "Maybe the more rebellious he gets, the more pressure his mother puts on him."

"He had the guts to spend the night outside. How difficult should it be for him to come out in the evening to watch the orangutan perform?"

"Maybe he doesn't want to watch the performance. What tricks can it do?"

"It can clap, smoke, count and ride a bicycle. It can also lie on the ground and play dead. It won't get up no matter how you call, like it's really dead."

"You'd never expect it would be such a good performer just by looking at it. Hard to believe Dodo Pops would be such an effective teaching aid."

"My father said the man in the beret takes a carrot-and-stick approach. With Dodo Pops and a club, he said, you could get an elephant to dance."

Though Ilya had no interest in the orangutan's performance he would go every day to the lane behind the inn where the performance troupe was staying to see the orangutan. Me and Brand just couldn't figure it out. Brand told me he went with Ilya a few times, but soon quit because Ilya would stay there an hour or two, or longer if the man in the beret didn't appear with his bucket of water and suitcase. I couldn't understand how Ilya managed to go there every day. And how could he stand to stay there so long? The fire access was a filthy mess, and that orangutan reeked. And to get there you had to venture north of the pailou road, through the maze of smoky, stinky lanes under the coloured canvas awnings. Ilya was not interested in the nightly performance, nor did he go to the alleyway behind the inn to watch the man in the beret train the animal. Brand said that every time Ilya arrived it was the same as the first time. He would talk to it, hold its hand, and brush the fur on its back and neck. He would try to ease the tightness of the iron chain around its neck. He would climb up on top of the iron cage and sit shoulder to shoulder with the orangutan, like he thought he was an orangutan too.

"The only explanation is that Ilya has fallen in love with that orangutan," Brand said.

"It's possible, because that orangutan is a girl," I said.

"What difference does it make? Even if it were a boy, Ilya could fall in love with it."

"Of course it's possible, though it'd be a bit weird."

"Isn't falling in love with a girl orangutan weird enough?"

"You're right. It seems just as weird," I said. "There must be something wrong with Ilya."

"You can say that again. He's sick," Brand said.

22

The Year We Were Twenty-five

I walk into an alley and see, over someone's wide-open door, a big plastic rain awning, under which clouds of smoke are pouring out of a knee-high censer. Two women are standing there, one holding a black garment over the open flame with a bamboo pole.

Knowing what they are doing, I look down, and am about to hurry past when a little girl makes it there a step ahead of me. Riding a kick scooter, she appears out of nowhere and clacks to a stop by the censer.

"What's that?"

"It's Grandma's shawl."

"Why are you burning it?"

"This way Grandma will have something to wrap around her shoulders when she feels cold."

"What?"

I stop to take a look at the girl, who is no more than four, a couple of years older than Ling-ling. I see her blink and fall silent. I know that she is mystified by the answer the lady, her mother or a close relative, just gave.

I walk out of the lane and think of Ilya thirteen years ago.

Why that point in time? I blink, just as mystified as the little girl in the alley.

Ilya eleven years ago has not left a trace of memory in my mind. After leaving the country he never called or wrote. I didn't know where he was living, what kind of city he'd packed off his mother to. I did not know what language he had learned to speak or what cuisine he was eating. I did not know if he was having a torrid love affair with some beautiful foreign girl. Thirteen years ago, no, not just thirteen years ago, but for a period of six years, Ilya for me pretty much ceased to exist.

So why did I think of that particular point in time?

The next thing that occurs to me is crossword puzzles.

When you are trying to break a code for which you don't have the key, the best thing to do is try local inference. That means trying to decode part of the text, like trying to solve a word in a crossword puzzle, which will make it easier to solve a neighbouring word. Of course, breaking any code also requires observation, association, interpretation, and, no getting around it, a flash of inspiration.

After listening to the conversation between the little girl and her mother, I thought of Ilya thirteen years ago in the moment I walked out of the alley. My intuition tells me that the association is just a hint in a crossword puzzle, and that I still have a big grid of intersecting white lines to fill in by local inference.

Thirteen years ago Ilya was twenty-five. That year, he left Belgium for France, moving from a room with a view of a canal to a room with a view of an old cathedral. Not that I knew this at the time. If Brand had not told me he ran into Ilya just after the latter had relocated to Paris, I might really have forgotten we had a childhood friend living in a faraway land. I wouldn't have known how life was treating him.

Brand met Ilya in Paris thirteen years ago. That year he, too, was twenty-five. He had delayed graduation a year, spent two years in the army and become the first of us to join the workforce. He went to work at a big media production company, where he became Little B or Little Lin, a gopher everyone would boss around. His luck was pretty good, because after less than half a year on the job, he got the chance to go help a producer out on some movie star's on-location shoot in Paris. Brand said that they were shooting on the pavement outside the Luxembourg Gardens. Walking along the forbidding fence, each tall black metal post topped with a golden spearhead, Ilya caught sight of Brand. He joined a crowd of onlookers and watched the shoot for quite a while. He waited until Brand wasn't getting yelled at to go do something before calling out his full name. Brand Lin! Brand wondered if he'd misheard. For months the only names he'd been called were "little this" or "little that" or even "kid" or "you". To suddenly hear his name, in Paris, a place where he didn't know anyone, was surreal. They exchanged a few words. Brand said he was only allowed to stay in Paris for three days, unlike the other crew members, who could stay for two days of sightseeing after the shoot. Ilya said he'd just moved to Paris and was still getting used to it: new surroundings, new school, new teacher. Fortunately, Mrs Chiang adapted more quickly than he. That was all they had time to say. Brand was called to do something, and Ilya, carrying a backpack full of sheet music, crossed the street to a nearby metro station. Neither could fathom why they should chance to meet outside the Luxembourg Gardens, when one had just moved to Paris to study music, while the other was only there to help out for a few days on a film. Just like the little girl in the lane who could not figure out why her mother was burning her grandmother's shawl.

It was hard for her to understand the logic of what her mother said. If you burn a shawl, the shawl is gone, but her mother had said that this way Grandma would have her shawl to wear. Initially that little girl must have thought Mama was fooling her, or trying to amuse her with a contradiction. When she said "What?" there was a conspicuous rise in tone, and she sounded a bit displeased. Maybe she still does not understand what death is. Maybe she thinks Grandma is just sleeping, or has gone out for a few days. But if so why would the adults take the opportunity to burn Grandma's shawl? Maybe she already knows what death means, has cried with her relatives, and is still mourning, but is unable to understand the seeming emotional reversal her mother has undergone. How can they joke around with me at a time like this?

I know she has no idea what her mother's pronouncement means, that the customs of death are still beyond her. To such a young child, invisibility is inexistence. Small children don't know that things that they cannot see might exist somewhere else. Of course, that isn't just a problem for children. Even adults might forget something exists, if they haven't seen it for long enough. Or someone.

And thirteen years ago, I had forgotten about Ilya's existence.

That year, I, too, was twenty-five years old. There weren't any canals or old churches in the world I was living in, just a railway that had been rerouted underground, a pair of roads along the river that had risen into elevated highways, and a skyscraper, still under construction, that would briefly be the tallest in the world. Fresh from a Master's programme, I was summoned to the south to guard a stretch of beach

I had never been to before in my life. That year mobile phones went viral, quickly obliterating another kind of communicable disease we all called a BB call, a pager. That year Ilya's old house was once again filled with music, but now it wasn't classical music played on a grand piano, but popular and folk songs performed by a pair of aboriginal brothers with a phenomenal vocal range. That year Internet speed was starting to be measured in megabytes, and computers had begun cutting into the amount of time people spend watching television. That year Brand's father replaced the manual roll-up iron door with an automatic sliding glass door. Now a local politician, he was entertaining even more than he had done back in the day. The big old cypress tea table had been moved out, and never again would people come to the house to drink tea on the first floor. That was the last year of the twentieth century. And the countdown to the fin-de-siècle exacerbated fear and decadence. Worried about the Millennium bug, some people were getting ready to renounce any human transport system. Others were selling off their possessions and buying plane tickets to some mysterious destination where they would greet the aliens.

So for a time I forgot Ilya. I almost forgot him forever. If Brand had not told me Ilya was in France, and if Ilya had not upon his return to Taiwan gone to the nightmarket, and stood on the stairs to the MRT just as I was walking by, my memory of Ilya might have stopped thirteen years ago. I might have always assumed he had stayed in Belgium.

We might never have got in touch with each other again, out of forgetfulness, laziness or awkwardness. Our friendship might have ended the year we graduated from university. I might not have heard about Ilya after he came back to Taiwan, noticed the posters in the windows of the record stores, or become a regular reader of the music page in the paper. I wouldn't have met his ex-wife, the nurse who encouraged me to get a regular colonoscopy. Ilya would not have met my wife Amanda, and she would not have gone out of her way to make friends with him. He would not have known about my father's death or Ling-ling's birth. He would not have found that although my old house had not been torn down, I had already moved across the river to live on the twenty-third floor of a residential tower, closer to the sky than the earth. He would not have found out about my PhD, which only led to a year of employment as an assistant professor. But he would never know that my colleagues now were maids, mainland Chinese spouses and seniors in the play area in the park.

I'm not a child any more, so I know about invisible things. I know that people I can't see might be perfectly fine, happily existing somewhere else. If my memory of Ilya had really stopped thirteen years ago I might never have found out about his decision to tie a rope into the shape of a minim, put it around his neck, and take his leave of planet earth. To me, his death would never have happened. He would have remained alive forever, to appear every time my memory summoned him.

23

A Wry Along the River

I help Ling-ling on with the helmet, hold her close, and put her in the child seat.

She's so excited. I haven't helped her put the seatbelt on yet, and she's already in a rush to start riding. "Wry! Wry! Wry!" she says. She seems to think that by calling out this verb, even though her pronunciation is none too correct, the bicycle will start riding itself.

A simple plan for a sunny day. Since Amanda feels I shouldn't take Ling-ling to the park so much, and wants me to keep my eyes on her at all times, and since I don't want to sit on a concrete bench roasted by the sun perusing a Costco catalogue, I'll take Ling-ling for a ride along the river, let her get some fresh air.

It's all thanks to the bicycle plague these past two years. It seems that practically every stretch of riverside has its own bicycle path. The riverside park below my house certainly does, but it existed in its own inconspicuous way, winding among acacia groves and grassy meadows, before the bicycle plague began. I only recently noticed it. Our apartment is right by the riverside, but I had never gone through the levee. Looking down at the river from the twenty-third floor was nice, but close range contact was something else. Somehow I never thought to go there before.

It's because of bicycle fever that I noticed this bike path. They widened it to encourage cycling. They came and cut down the lush acacias and dug up the grass dotted year round with wildflowers. Then they paved it over, widened the bike path from two lanes to six. Maybe afraid a plane would mistake this straight strip for a runway, they painted a few stylized white bicycles on the pathway, a pair of circles hanging off a triangle. And every hundred metres, in the centre of the path, they've marked the distance for the cyclists without cyclometers. Worried they still weren't doing enough to promote the sport, they even wrote "Keep Going!", "You're Almost There!" or "Don't Give Up!" As if without such notices people would decide to go back mid-journey, which would mean that they had upgraded the path to the luxury model in vain. The upgrade also meant that I didn't have to walk to the riverside to see it. I could see it from my twenty-third-floor apartment; I could have seen it from a cockpit at ten thousand feet.

But my plan today is not to take that bicycle path. I'll take Ling-ling across the bridge. The bicycle path along the other shore is also visible from the twenty-third floor, but not so showy. It doesn't look like a runway in the desert.

"Where we goin'? Where we goin'?" says Ling-ling, sitting in the "front seat". She tries to look back, but she's strapped in by the seatbelt. Unable to turn around, she starts to twist and squirm.

"Ling-ling, sit still!"

"Where we goin'? Where we goin'? Daddy, where we goin'?"

"We're going for a ride."

"Where we goin' for a wry?"

"Oh, just to look around."

"Where we goin' look round?"

"Let's go see Grandma, okay?"

"Where's Grandma?"

Ling-ling keeps on asking earnest questions and I keep on giving her flippant replies, in an endless loop like the pedals on the bicycle, until we ride onto the bridge and the speed on the downward slope finally shuts her up. "Daddy, lookut me! Wee!" she says, as if the bridge is like a slide in the playground. She slides gurgling off the bridge as I ride her into the playground of my youth.

The bridge was only finished a few years ago, like the MRT station in the nightmarket. There's no place for it on the map of my childhood memory. If you can believe the election brochures, the new bridge was Brand's father's achievement. Elected city councillor, he tore down the Japanese-style house with the mango tree in the garden, along with a few old semi-detached buildings, in order to put up a multi-storey car park. Elected congressman in the central government, he widened the two-lane road that ran past his house into the six-lane motorway that runs straight to the river and feeds the bridge that has made him a legend. Brand's father started out by managing a variety show troupe, but as a politician was a lot more interested in securing funding for infrastructure than in cultural activities, even ones with entertainment value. My mother told me that nobody would dare to call him Variety Lin any more. Everyone calls him Congressman Lin. And Congressman Lin is opposed to their community culture preservation work. He doesn't think that a SEX CULTURE INDUSTRY PARK or SEX INDUSTRY CULTURE CREATIVE PARK will bring the community prosperity. To create the "maximum economic benefit", he advocates tearing down the whole slum and re-zoning it as a mixed commercial-residential area.

I don't plan on taking Ling-ling to see her grandma. I want to ride, and there's no way we can squeeze three people on the bicycle. And I guess my mother is probably busy. She said the cultural preservation organization is under intense pressure, that they're facing a moment of do or die. She even used a few trendy terms from the newspaper. "They want to suppress our cultural agency and historical subjectivity! They say all of us cultural preservation workers are street walkers or working girls. For crying out loud! Look at us, old enough to be their grandmothers. What kind of money are we going to make on the street?"

Ma kept on mentioning "they". Is this the same "they" that widened the bicycle path, I wonder? But I have no time to contemplate it further, because now I, too, am under intense pressure. The new bridge is underused, tempting everyone who drives across to speed up. And the roadwork on the six-lane road stripped away the red brick pavement, paved it over, painted a double line along the edge to indicate that it was a slow lane. (Parked bumper to bumper, it's now an extremely slow lane.) I keep pedalling the only place I can, down the centre of the double lane. I'm between a rock and a hard place. If I ride too close to the slow lane, we might crash into some reckless driver's abruptly opened door. And if I ride too far out, we might get sucked into the traffic that is flying off the bridge, a sacrifice to science, a pointless demonstration of Bernoulli's principle.

Cars honk, as if to tell me I am going too slow. Several times I hear the honk only when the vehicle has gone shooting past. Of course, I know I'm going too slow, unlike these drivers who don't get the Doppler effect. Another thing they probably don't get is that I'm not competing in the Tour de France. I'm riding a six-speed family bike, for Christ's sake.

I get honked at a few times, but I don't feel any need to apologize. It strikes me that this is the first time I've ridden Ling-ling around my childhood stomping ground, and the speed seems right. I very seldom take Ling-ling back to my old house to see her grandma. And when I do, we always go in the car. I drop Amanda and Ling-ling off at the entrance to the alley, and drive to the car park Congressman Lin built. Amanda complains that as soon as she arrives, my mother starts nitpicking, pointing out things Amanda is doing wrong. Ling-ling's not eating enough, she's not wearing enough. What are you feeding her? Don't you know it might rain? My mother's overall point is that she is the child-rearing expert. "Why doesn't she say these things to my face?" I asked. "How should I know? She's your mother," Amanda replied.

Just like I don't know why Amanda's pharmacist father mentioned that the house was his purchase to me and not to her. I've never mentioned it to Amanda. I decided to keep it a secret, but secrets can't bear solitude, and this one is always trying to steal out. It's a low burrowing drone that only I can hear.

But right now I don't mind. Although I'm under enormous pressure, riding between a rock and a hard place, I get to take my daughter on a leisurely spin around the old neighbourhood. I have a weird sense of excitement so great that it drowns out everything else.

"Ling-ling, look! This is where I played when I was a boy."

"Where?"

"On the street."

"Where on the street?"

"Right there." I lift my hand from the handlebar and point up ahead.

"Where right there?" Ling-ling looks where I'm pointing.

I discover that I am pointing at a sign that says: "Seaside Clinic –

Cure Crabs and the Clam."

It would be very difficult to explain to Ling-ling what my childhood playground was like. We grew up on streets packed with adult means of production and transportation. We would crouch by the entrance of a repair shop and watch the mechanics fix the motorcycles, and, if they didn't fix us for getting in the way, we could usually manage to nick a couple of screw nuts or empty oil cans. We would borrow several stools from the squid stew seller to use as obstacles, line them up under the arcade and snake around them on our skateboards. We would collect used drink boxes, blow them up with air, put them out in the street when there weren't any cars coming, and then stand under the arcade, cover our ears and wait for that deafening pop. I don't know how to explain all this to Ling-ling, why I would play in an area that did not have slides or swings or seesaws, at a time when there were no foreign maids or immigrant wives.

Leaving my concrete playground behind, I ride through the watergate and onto the bicycle lane by the river. Ling-ling is now fascinated with my legs. She's hanging her head looking at my legs pumping the pedals up and down. She leans down and reaches out with her little hands.

"Ling-ling, sit straight."

"Sit straight where?"

"Sit straight in your seat."

"Where in my seat?"

It's not a holiday today, so except for a couple of packs of stray dogs on the grass there isn't a single soul in the vastness of the riverside park. I ride Ling-ling along the path past deserted basketball courts, roller rinks, softball pitches and docks. They've covered almost every sizable clearing outside the levee in leisure facilities. They've also reinforced the riverbank. All along the river is a concrete stairway like the bleachers in a stadium. I guess there are two possible reasons for the stairs. First, to seat an audience for a performance on a floating stage. Second, to make it more convenient for people to drown themselves. That inconspicuous bicycle path that I'd seen from the other side of the river runs between the stairway and the recreational infrastructure that extends up the manicured shore as far as the eye can see. There are no irritating signs here saying "Keep Going!" or "You're Almost

There!" But now every so often there is a metal sign by the side of the path reminding you that the place you're in is called Close to the Water Park.

I pedal along the bike path less than three metres from the water. The water is brackish, the smell sickening. I'm surprised, because when I was young the odour and appearance of the river were totally different. It's not the river I remember. I remember the stones on the riverbank used to look clean, white or grey, not black like an ink stone. At the time the river had a smell, but it was the smell of shrimp, a faint fishy odour, not like an open sewer. And there weren't any recreational facilities, just a lot of weedy wetlands or fishponds. It would have been hard to explain the absurdity of the change to Ling-ling. When I was young the river water was still clear, but nobody encouraged us to go to the riverside to play. Now that I'm all grown up they've put metal signs by the river encouraging everyone to get close to the water, but now the water is really unapproachable.

Ling-ling hasn't noticed any of this. She's still leaning over in her chair, but now her hand is dangling by her leg. She has gone to sleep.

I leave the bike path and come to a stop in a little grove. My plan was simple, but things have not gone according to plan. I didn't plan on Ling-ling going to sleep; getting her to take her afternoon nap is always such an ordeal. I find a bench, and sit down, with Ling-ling resting her forehead between my shoulder and my neck. What a pity! Usually during the day after Ling-ling starts napping, I have one or two hours of free time to watch the news on television or check a few websites. My gaze can leave Ling-ling for a while, long enough to relax and rest. But now I'm stuck holding her, sitting on a long cement bench in the park with nothing to distract me from the malodorous river, not even a colourful Costco catalogue.

Perhaps because of a lack of wind or because the river water is too thick for ripples, the surface is still as a mirror, a mirror in which a row of towers on the other side is reflected. Our twenty-third-floor flat, which Amanda's father paid for in cash, has also appeared in the mirror, along with the balcony on which I always feel a bit uneasy. It's so close, only a few metres away from the shore. What a strange feeling. This is the first time I haven't had to look up to see the place I live in.

I reformulate my plan: I'll just sit here holding Ling-ling, appreciating the view.

Except that my second simple plan is disturbed by someone moving outside the grove.

It's an older woman. I don't have to look closely at her clothing or her hairstyle to know that she is elderly, because a young woman wouldn't go for a walk by a deserted riverbank. She probably climbed down the levee, because I didn't see her on the way. She's carrying a plastic bag. It doesn't look heavy, but she walks a bit hunched over, like there are two people sitting on her shoulders. She walks slowly by the grove, crosses the bike path, and descends the stairway to the river. She walks slowly but not at all hesitantly, making a beeline for the water and looking neither left nor right. When she gets there she kneels down on the stairs, as if someone had painted THE END on the ground. She takes several bundles out of the bag, arranges them on the ground, and gets out a lighter. Sitting some way back from the river, I can't actually see what she is holding. I can only guess from her hand motions that it's a cheap plastic lighter she's using to light not a cigarette but a few incense sticks she brought in the plastic bag, and that she's having trouble. It would be easier to light a cigarette, because with the cigarette between your lips you'd have a hand free to nurse the flame. You can't do that with a stick of incense. She tries to light the sticks several times without success. Just now the river was completely still, but now the wind has picked up, filling the plastic bag at her feet and sending it up in the air like a helium balloon. She doesn't notice the plastic bag has fled, just stoops around the flame. A typical older lady might have had a chance to light it, using her ample body to block the wind, but this woman is way too thin, so thin it's a wonder she doesn't get blown away like that plastic bag.

She finally succeeds in lighting the incense. She stands up, holds the stick towards the stinky river, and starts talking really loudly, like she's wearing earphones. The more she says the more worked up she becomes. Suddenly she kneels down and kowtows towards the black surface of the water several times. If she hit her head any harder she would break the skin of her brow. But this isn't the problem that the cement ground causes her: after kowtowing, she walks a few steps along the concrete stair, unable to find a place to stick the lit incense. She soon gives up looking, takes a wad of spirit money, stands it on end, and sticks the incense in. Then she takes another wad of spirit money and releases the string. The spirit money is so much easier to light than the stick of incense. It catches fire on the first try, creating a new problem: how to keep the burning bills obediently in front of her, how to stop them from taking flight. One by one, the bills escape her grasp, tumbling sideways along the stair. She chases them a few times, stomps out a few, and picks up several that have already gone out. This is no place to burn spirit money. The woman is stubborn, but it's her own temper that flares first, not the spirit money. I see her stomping on a bill of spirit money long after it's gone out. I suddenly feel very sorry, as if it's my fault that she cannot conduct the ritual. A breeze blows through the grove; I hear the rustling of the leaves. But the black river water remains unrippled, the reflection of my apartment just as sharp. After the woman finally raises a bonfire of spirit money, she curls up on the concrete stair and faces away from the wind, as if to enclose the fire with her flesh. I can't figure out how she avoids the flame, but I already know why she is burning spirit money here at the riverside. I want to go home, but for now I can't get up. It's not because Ling-ling is still sleeping, but because I'm afraid that if I got up she would see me. Actually, I knew who she was the moment she walked by the grove. I know her: she's Mrs Chiang, Ilya's mother. She knows me, too, and even though I know she would mistake me for Brand Lin again, I desperately don't want to be seen.

$$24$$

The Light in Ilya's Eyes

"Harriet's sick," Ilya said.

Me and Brand looked at each other.

Brand kept nailing his board, and I kept applying my paint. Neither of us replied.

The first month of the summer holidays had already passed. We had thrown up the tree fort in the mango tree. We had lived through two typhoons. And like the old roofs of the code violations, our tree fort had miraculously survived the ravages of wind and rain. Not even a single board fell off. We could have left it as it was, but then Ilya had the idea for us to make a sliding door out of a few boards to fill the hole at the base of the rotten wooden gate. Best paint it the same shade of red as the gate, so nobody would notice there was a way in. We didn't want to attract attention to our secret base.

Ever since Ilya overnighted in the tree fort, he'd cared even more about it than me and Brand. When we built it, he didn't help at all, but now he was actively helping, measuring the size of the gap with a ruler and drawing a blueprint for the sliding door. And he kept on pushing Brand to steal a tin of red paint from the rooftop of his house. Although me and Brand were not opposed to a sliding door, we just thought it was unnecessary. This was an abandoned Japanese house that our neighbours said was haunted. I bet we were the only kids in the neighbourhood who would dare to come close. Even if someone had the guts to climb over the wall and up to our tree fort, our secret treasure trove was unlikely to be discovered. The humid woodpile was alive. If he didn't lift the right board on the first try, he'd get freaked out by the creepy crawlies—the centipedes, termites, stag beetles and longhorns—that called the humid spaces home.

"Harriet's sick," Ilya repeated.

"Who's Harriet?"

"The orangutan. I gave her another name."

"Does it have a cold?" Brand asked. "Or an upset stomach? It looked pretty healthy to me last night."

"Did you go see the show again last night?" I said jealously. "How long are they staying for?"

"Probably just one more week. I overheard my father advising the orangutan keeper to leave a few days early and go find somewhere else to perform."

"Why? Isn't business pretty good around here?"

"My dad said it would be better to make an early exit, cause otherwise there might be some trouble."

"What's that supposed to mean?"

"It means that something big might go down in a couple of days. That's all I can say," Brand said mysteriously.

"You guys aren't listening to me!" Ilya shouted.

After yelling at us, Ilya fell silent. He just kept sitting there at the entrance to the treasure trove, his head hung low, staring at the orange plastic bin with all the treasures inside, not lifting his head to look at me and Brand. Ilya had this ability to control his emotions. One moment he'd be flailing his hands in the air, the next he'd fall silent and freeze, like when we used to play the "one-two-three, I'm a TREE" game.

I was no stranger to Ilya's silences. He seemed to be waiting for something. I remember that time when we heard him play the piano at his place. After he had turned his hands by magic into a spider and an egret on the black and white keys, he fell silent and hung his head, waiting. I knew he was waiting for something, just not what. Mrs Chiang wasn't here to rinse the rice and the greens, and there was nobody to ding the bell if he didn't finish in time. There was just the breeze, the swaying branches, and the faint rustling of the leaves. Brand held his hammer, I my paintbrush, while Ilya sat empty-handed. The three of us just sat there, silent. The smell of wood had appeared in the air, making me a bit dizzy.

"Everyone gets sick sometimes," Brand said.

"And it's an orangutan. Usually when animals get sick they get better on their own," I said.

It was like we'd agreed to read lines in a play, and now it was Ilya's turn. "Harriet's really sick, and she won't get better on her own," he said urgently. Not content with just one line, he continued: "She's not healthy, not at all. Haven't you noticed? You guys think that an orangutan likes to perform tricks in front of an audience? You're wrong. She's oppressed, forced to perform. It's unnatural. An orangutan belongs in the jungle. Nobody should be able to chain Harriet up or put her in a cage." Ilya was getting more and more worked up, and now his whole face was red. "She's dying! I can tell: she's not happy. She's really sick. Haven't you seen her expression? Orangutans can't say what they think, but their eyes can talk. You know what her eyes are saying? 'I don't want to stay here any more. I don't want to practise bowing or riding a stupid bicycle. Do you think that practising the same trick over and over again is fun? If you guys think it's so interesting, why don't you chain yourselves to a cage and see what it's like?'" Ilya said a whole bunch of things. I had never heard him talk so quickly before, and by the end I couldn't keep up with what he was saying. I was just dumbfounded by the speed at which the words were coming out. I recalled the kids in the Formula One race for fingers. Their fingers were pretty fast, but Ilya's tongue that afternoon might have left them in the dust.

Brand listened carefully until Ilya had finished his impromptu harangue. When he had said what he had to say, the faint creaking of the tree fort reappeared, and the air again was filled with the smell of soft, wet wood. Then Brand spoke.

"You're saying that the orangutan should not be chained to a cage?"

Ilya nodded.

"You're saying that the orangutan was arrested illegally and is being detained without due process, deprived of its fundamental freedoms under the tyranny of the man in the beret?"

"Ah…" Ilya was dumbfounded. "I don't think I mentioned the man in the beret."

"Same difference. The man in the beret's keeping the orangutan, and the orangutan is being persecuted. That's not fair, right?"

"Exactly, it's not fair at all," Ilya said, fists clenched.

"So what you're trying to say is that the orangutan should decide its own fate? That nobody should try to act on its behalf?"

"Probably." Ilya thought it over. "That's basically what I meant."

"Well, great!" Brand yelled, scaring me and Ilya.

"What's great about it?" I asked.

"Shhhh!" Brand stood up and looked around. "The walls have ears. We better go up to the tree fort to hold a secret meeting."

There were no obvious walls where we were sitting on the woodpile. But Brand was so serious that me and Ilya followed him up to the tree fort, no questions asked. The three of us sat cross-legged on the narrow platform. Strictly speaking, I could only sit with my left leg up, letting my right leg hang out, because Brand took up half the space in the fort. But because I was sitting on the edge of the platform, I had the best view: I saw the river on the other side of the levee flowing in several streams around the sandbars. I saw something gleaming in the sunlight in the reeds on a sandbar. I had no idea what it was; from that far away, I couldn't make it out. The tide was probably ebbing, or just coming in, though I didn't know how to tell the difference. Outside the levee was another world, a taboo realm that the adult prohibition had rendered unfamiliar. I knew that one day that prohibition would vanish. Maybe our parents would announce the ban had been lifted, or maybe we would go and challenge it the way Brand had sneaked up to the rooftop addition or I had crossed the pailou road. I never expected that that day would come so soon.

"We're going to go and rescue that orangutan!" Brand declared.

He spoke very quietly, probably just a little bit louder than the rustling of the wind through the leaves, at a volume we could never have heard down below, because the further you get from windblown leaves the louder they sound. I did not know why this should be so, or why the suggestion should have come out of Brand's mouth. It would have made more sense for Ilya to make it, and for me and Brand to gasp in surprise in response, not Ilya. There were too many things I couldn't figure out. Everything was messed up.

"Did you just say we're going to rescue the orangutan?!" Ilya cried.

"Isn't that what you want to do?" Brand asked, smiling. "Keep it down. Do you want the whole nightmarket to hear?"

"Yeah… no. But I was thinking…"

"You said that an orangutan shouldn't be locked to an iron cage with an iron chain. That it shouldn't be forced to perform tricks. If you really feel that way, we should think of some way to get it out of there, restore its freedom, and make sure it is never ruled over by a human being again."

"Stop talking crazy," I said, interrupting Brand. "Is it so easy to set an orangutan free? If we get caught, we'll get in big trouble."

"Don't you worry about getting caught." Brand raised his eyebrows and narrowed an eye, looking at me. "Our Founding Father Sun Yat-sen's revolution would never have succeeded if all he thought about was failure."

"But didn't you say the Founding Father used to escape out the back door every time there was a knock in the middle of the night, just like your dad?"

"What are you talking about? We don't have a back door. My dad, he just opened the back window."

"So you're saying your dad is braver than our Founding Father?" I said.

"Yeah," Ilya suddenly said, nodding. "We're going to go and rescue that orangutan."

Me and Brand both stared at Ilya. He'd said the same thing as Brand, but even quieter, so quiet that he didn't seem to use his lips and teeth and tongue to make the sound. It was as if he'd drilled a portal to the lowest stratum of his heart, so that the words could spring out unobstructed. Just then, and I'll never forget it, I saw Ilya's eyes flash, like he had borne witness, like he had really seen something. In the instant of that flash, it seemed like the whole world had shrunk, shrunk so small that nothing was left but the light in Ilya's eyes. The flash was so intense, so brilliant, so piercing it held me enthralled. I dare say that something was blazing hot in Ilya's heart, something like resolution and vision and passion and hope, maybe all mixed together in the throbbing chambers of his soul. Whatever it was, it had set off a light-emitting, heat-releasing, self-sustaining chain reaction. The light and heat had gushed out of his eyes and were showering the surroundings with a stream so bright and hot it seemed capable of melting any substance on earth. On the other hand, maybe the flare in his eyes was just reflected sunlight, just like whatever I had seen gleaming in the reeds on the sandbar. In any case, no matter what the cause, I had never seen Ilya's eyes so bright before, not when he proposed that we build the tree fort, not when he climbed up to the lookout on the highest branch.

"We're going to go and rescue that orangutan," Ilya repeated.

"You said it," Brand said. He patted Ilya's shoulders, gratified and satisfied. "Let's go and save the orangutan and bring it here to live in the tree fort. If the man in the beret comes looking, we can hide it in the treasure trove. And when the man in the beret is gone, the orangutan will belong to us."

"No, the orangutan won't belong to anyone," Ilya said. "The rainforest is where she belongs. She should never appear in a place like this."

"Then what do you think we should do?" Brand asked.

"We should take her somewhere where she does not have to practise all day long, a place where an orangutan would feel at home."

"There is no rainforest here," I pointed out.

"I know," Ilya said. "So the best we can do is take her to the zoo."

Me and Brand glanced at each other. This time, without a hammer or a brush in our hands, we could not pretend to be too busy working to hear what Ilya had said. Sure, I'd been to the zoo before, but only that one time five or six years before when me and Ma and Pa had puttered north on the scooter. I'd given up waiting for my father to lay off the bottle. But even if he had thought to take me to the zoo again, Ma would never have agreed, because now I was more than a hundred and fifty centimetres tall. If the police saw the three of us riding a scooter, they would stop us and write a ticket. Another reason was that the zoo had moved. Not long ago, the zoo to the north had closed, and all the animals were taken out. One night, the elephants, giraffes, zebras, apes, lions, tigers and countless other animals were loaded onto jeeps, vans, container trucks, flatbed trucks and other means of transport. They lined up into a long, mobile menagerie and drove along the deserted streets of the sleeping city, sweeping scraps of paper, fallen leaves and plastic bags into their wake as they headed towards the new zoo, which had just been completed upriver, in the south. In a single night, the amazing world in the north of the city—a world of popcorn, coloured balloons, animal masks and happy childhoods – was left in ruins. None of us knew exactly where the new zoo had been built. I had never been, and neither had Brand or Ilya. Someone said they were waiting until the animals had completely adjusted to the new environment before opening. I had adjusted to not having a zoo to visit a long time before.

"Do you know where the zoo is?" I asked Brand.

"I don't know. Do you?" Brand asked me.

"I don't know either," I said.

Ilya suddenly stood up, almost hitting his head on the lean-to roof of the tree fort. He climbed out of the fort and up the trunk, as agile as a monkey, all the way up to sit astride the highest branch. I would never have dared to climb so high, and Brand was afraid that his girth would snap the tree branches higher up. That perch belonged to Ilya alone. That was his lookout, the place where he saw his future.

"I know where the zoo is," Ilya said.

This time he did not snap off a little twig to use as a conductor's baton. He just extended a hand and pointed in the direction of the river. I turned my head and Brand turned his head and, together, we looked where he was pointing. All we saw was that Ilya's gaze had passed over the levee, the sandbars and the sand dredgers and flown upstream on the sunlight to the place from where the river water flowed.

25

The Night the World Changed

The world started to change the day Ilya said he had decided to go to Europe to study music.

Was that fourteen or fifteen years ago? With the inexorable march of time, it's getting a bit tricky to count the years. With close-fist counting, I have to start opening fingers on my left hand to count past ten.

That year we were about twenty-two. It was supposed to be the year we graduated from college and went into the army, but none of us started mandatory military service that year. Brand chose to delay graduation, and I chose to continue at college, while Ilya, who was exempt from military service, chose to go abroad for further studies. Our world changed due to too many choices.

The change was just a feeling. There had been no obvious objective change in our world. The nightmarket was the same old nightmarket. The railway was the same old railway. The river was the same old river. And the infamous area to the north of the pailou road was still Carnation Lane, the local red light district. The guava girls still sat outside the door day after day rinsing and de-stemming the fruit, still called one-two-THREE as they pushed the fully loaded cart up the rise and across the train tracks. My father was still drinking every day, which didn't matter because he wasn't getting up on stage to give stump speeches like Brand's father or collapsing in the alleyway and crying out for his mama like the father of the guava girls. (If he had, nobody would have taken any notice, because my grandmother had already passed away.) My mother was still going on and on about how she wanted to move away, without doing anything about it. But I was different. Having found a shared rental off campus as soon as I started college, I no longer had to take the spot opposite my father at the dinner table or listen to my mother complain.

Ilya told me he was going abroad under the first street light of the alleyway at the end of which I was renting a room.

The university he studied at was even further away from the nightmarket than mine, but he had not moved out. He still lived with his mother in that shack with a grand piano that cost more than a car, but often came over to chat. I moved a few times, and he was always the first to visit, as if he was more concerned about me than my own mother, and he would get to know my roommates even sooner than I did. I think Ilya had got into the habit of visiting me, which is probably why he showed up every Friday night with beer and takeaway after I got married to Amanda. But though unlike me he seemed in his element on the twenty-third floor, he never stayed the night in our flat, or in any of the rooms I rented in college. No matter how late he stayed, no matter how tired he was, he would always fly off home like a dove. I don't recall that Ilya ever spent the night anywhere else either. Except of course for the summer after sixth grade.

I stood with Ilya under the street lamp, waiting for this rich guy to dump furniture at the mouth of the alley. We had already carried a sofa set back to my place, an unfurnished apartment with three bedrooms, a dining room and a living room that five people were renting. It was completely unfurnished. When we came back from a midnight snack, we saw three fairly new-looking sofas under the street lamp. Dumped beside a pile of rubbish, they were obviously unwanted. Obviously the perfect addition to the living room of a student apartment.

It took me three trips with Ilya to move the sofas. When we were getting ready to move the last sofa, an old fellow who had been standing off to one side staring at us walked over. He said if we needed more furniture, we could come back in a little while, because he still had things to throw away. As promised, there was another set of furniture when we came back: a four-shelf bookcase and a round glass top coffee table. Suddenly there were so many nice things to collect. Too many. Suspicious, I asked the old fellow if he was really just throwing everything away. "Yup," he replied. "Take whatever you can move." He stood under the street light and wiped the sweat from his brow with the corner of his shirt.

"The furniture looks great. There's nothing wrong with it. Why don't you want it?" I asked.

"Of course I want to keep it, but my immigration papers have already been processed. I'm going to Canada and can't take it with me."

"What about after you come back from Canada? Why are you in such a hurry to throw everything away?" I asked.

"I have to hurry; every day counts. If I take my time it might be too late," the old man said.

"What do you mean, too late?" I asked.

"This time the communists just shot their missiles into the Taiwan Strait. Next time they might fall on the Presidential Palace. Hehehe. You guys wait here. I've still got a lot of things to throw away," the old man said.

The old man went upstairs. He lived at the entrance to the alley, in a newish seven-storey building with a lift. It was a short walk, but a world away from the shabby, two-decade-old place at the end of the alley that I was renting. My apartment was quiet and close to the university, but the old man's flat combined the convenience of a major street and the tranquillity of an alley.

"What do you think?" Ilya asked.

"It's great. We've got free furniture to collect," I said.

"I mean about emigration. That old man has decided to leave Taiwan at this of all times. What's your opinion?"

"What opinion would I have? He must be loaded, insecure and chicken-shit."

"And you just claimed you didn't have an opinion. In a single sentence you made three judgements about him."

Under the dim street lamp, Ilya's face looked even thinner, and he was underweight to begin with. He was so thin he'd met the standard for draft exemption. I knew he had an opinion, but I didn't, not really. A lot of things happened that year. Taiwan held its first direct presidential election. In response, the People's Republic of China fired missiles into the ocean northeast of the port of Keelung. Foreign residents were evacuated. America deployed two battle carrier groups from the Seventh Fleet to the Taiwan Strait. The stock market crashed. And I didn't have any particular opinion about any of the above. I was an apolitical intellectual who had just got into a Master's programme in mathematics. All I was concerned about was which professor could direct my thesis, whether I could get a high-paid and undemanding part-time job and how to find a girlfriend. These concerns kept me more than busy. I didn't know how I could have opinions about anything else.

"I'm going abroad too," said Ilya.

"Oh? You're going to emigrate somewhere?"

"No, I'm going abroad to study music. My mother has found me a famous piano teacher in Belgium who is willing to direct my studies."

"Why haven't you said anything before?"

"Aren't I telling you now?"

"When are you going?"

"Next month. What's your opinion about that?"

"I think it's great. What opinion would I have?" I repeated.

Now I remember I felt uncomfortable when Ilya said he was going abroad. Of course, I knew that Ilya would put on his magician's tails someday, stand on a splendid stage, and receive a standing ovation from a packed house. He would turn his hands into a spider and an egret to win fame, fortune, women and power. That day had not come, just like the girlfriend I had not yet met. But I believed it would come, just like I believed that I wouldn't be a bachelor my whole life. I just didn't think it would come so soon. We had been waiting so complacently that when Ilya said he was going abroad to study I felt uneasy. This feeling of unease diluted the sense of joy I had just felt upon finding the sofa set. I thought my discomfort was due to jealousy. Fifteen years later, I feel even more strongly than I did then that I had good reason to be jealous. I was not jealous of Ilya, but of his ability to go abroad. All my college classmates had gone abroad. They had got on the plane, flown east across the Pacific, and landed at Princeton, Harvard or MIT, and were studying with famous professors. A few years later they would fly west across America to land in Silicon Valley or the Houston Space Sciences Center or over the Pacific again to land at Academia Sinica, the National Center for High-Performance Computing, or the elite R&D departments of big tech companies. And me? I was going to stay in Taiwan and go to grad school. I only ever crossed a river, and that was to go from one city to another in the greater Taipei area. I taught a few classes of Life Cryptology. And now I've come back home to call foreign maids, immigrant wives and retirees colleagues.

Indeed, in the context of my current plight, I had good reason to be jealous of Ilya's opportunity, but this wasn't actually the reason why I felt uneasy at the time. It's just like the episode in front of the altar when I was three: the harder I think, the more details I recall. Now I can picture Ilya's face when he told me he was going abroad. With moths and termites swirling around and colliding with the street light, his face seemed to exist in some sort of dreamland, as if he wasn't standing with me in the maw of the alley. When he told me of his decision to go abroad, there was no light in his eyes. Of course, this is a result of comparison. Professor Safe always emphasized the importance of the comparison and assessment of information. Most people are like a broken net: they let information, whether useful or useless, flow out of the holes in the mesh of the net. Luckily, I've been able to fish some memories out of the flow. It's taken me this long, but better late than never. That there was no light in Ilya's eyes was relative. If you had ever seen his eyes that day in the tree fort, so bright that they promised to burn the whole world and everything in it to a crisp, so bright that all that survived in them was resolution and vision and passion and hope, then you would know why, that evening under the lamp, Ilya's eyes seemed so dull. It wasn't just that they lacked brightness. They practically looked like a pair of black holes.

I remember Ilya by the rubbish pile at the entrance to the alley asking my opinion about the idea of his going abroad. Now I know that it was his eyes that made me uncomfortable. I find it difficult to accept, but now I know.

"Not having an opinion is a kind of opinion, and usually shows even more contempt. And often not having an opinion about something indicates contempt," Ilya said. "Do you agree that I lack confidence?"

"I didn't say that."

"I thought you would say that if you have enough faith in the future, it doesn't matter where you go."

"Going abroad is something your mother arranged for you. If anyone lacks faith in the future, maybe it's your mother."

"It's the other way around. She has complete confidence in me."

"That's great. Problem solved."

"When I said she has complete confidence, I meant about the future me. As for the present me, she doesn't think I'm good enough. And that's why she has arranged for me to go abroad."

"Sounds like you don't much like this arrangement."

"I don't like it or dislike it. In any case I'm going to accept."

"For your mother?"

"No, I'm doing it for…" Ilya paused, then said: "I am doing it for…"

It sounded like Ilya had said "Dad". But he was speaking too quietly, so I wasn't sure whether I'd heard right. I didn't have time to ask him to repeat himself, because just then the old man reappeared. This time he didn't move anything out with him, just waved at us empty-handed. "Hey, you two, come here," he said in a friendly voice. "I've got a lot of things I'm just going to throw out that you might want. You want to come up and have a look? You can take whatever you like."

The world must have become a little bit different after Ilya told me he was going to Europe to study music and we visited the old man's mansion. I had not recovered from the surprise that Ilya's declaration had given me when I was sucked into another surprise. First, the lift. Of course, I knew a luxury building like that would have one, but somehow stepping in I felt honoured. I had never had a friend who lived in a building with a lift. The apartment I had rented at the end of the alley was on the fifth floor, and you had to walk up with the power of your own two legs, step by step. And I didn't think there was anything wrong with that. But this old man lived on the third floor, and he didn't have to lift his legs to go up a single step. He just had to lift a finger to press a button and the lift would whisk him up to the entrance to his home.

"Come on in," the old man said as he opened the door. "Please keep your shoes on."

Ilya and I walked into the old man's home on a marble floor. Actually, I felt a bit like taking off my shoes, to see how cool it would be to walk barefoot over the marble, smooth as a mirror. The old man, maybe because he was moving, exempted me from my right to a first time experience. But there were other surprises waiting for us in that apartment. We followed the old man down the hallway, and the two of us turned our heads at the same time to look at each other. The living room was spacious, more spacious than the average apartment should have been. I guessed the owner must have knocked down a couple of walls at least to enjoy such a spacious room. Half of the room was empty, probably because of the sofas we had just moved out. The other half was occupied by a grand piano. It was white, a little bit like butter or pearl, with a gold vine and leaf pattern. And on the walls were quite a few hanging scrolls of calligraphy, an eight steeds painting, and two big Western oil paintings in thick bronze frames. I was unable to judge the Western art, but the eight steeds painting was so vulgar I couldn't get up any interest in the calligraphy. But the white piano was irresistible. The strange thing was that Ilya only glanced at the piano before checking out the hanging scrolls on the walls.

"Hey, hey, you two." The old man guffawed. "Those paintings are worth a fortune, don't even think about it. I've already asked a collector friend of mine to come for them. The piano is the same. It's made by a famous company, and you couldn't lift it if you tried. I have some other things for you to look at."

"The piano at my place is much more expensive," Ilya whispered.

"The calligraphy hanging on my walls at home is a lot more refined," I whispered back.

The old man showed us around his home. The other rooms were pretty ordinary. There were two bedrooms, a kitchen and a dining room. Every room seemed to be lacking something, and what furniture remained seemed out of place. We couldn't cook in the place I was renting, so we had no use for cooking utensils. I did need a wardrobe, but not the one nailed to the wall of this guy's master bedroom. Moving it wasn't an option. Same went for the bookshelf. The old man was talking continuously, telling us to take whatever we wanted and "be my guest". Even without the stuff he'd thrown out, there were still quite a number of things in the apartment. Unfortunately, Ilya and I couldn't find anything useful, and in the end, all we took was the washing machine on the balcony.

"That's all? What about all the other things?" The old man seemed a bit disappointed.

"This is loads." I thanked him, and couldn't help reiterating: "All of the things here in your home are still new. Isn't it a bit strange for you to up and throw them all away?"

"Can't help it, I'm selling the place. The real estate agent said that it'd be easier to get rid of it if it were empty."

"Then why didn't the agent come help move himself? What terrible service!"

"He's too busy. These days he's got people beating down his door begging him to help them sell their houses." The old man walked us to the door, and held it so we could carry the washing machine out. "You two seem like honest young men. Do you to want to buy an apartment? Ten million. If you can come up with ten million New Taiwan Dollars, I'll give it to you. You want to think it over?" the old man asked. He did not look like he was joking.

If I had had ten million at the time…no no, I would not have needed ten million. Probably three million for a down payment would have been enough for me to afford this high-class residence, a prime piece of real estate. And now, fifteen years later, I would be laughing; its value would have quintupled. Now I know that I had stumbled upon the property market at its lowest point, perhaps on its lowest evening. The world had changed: it changed the moment me and Ilya walked without a second thought through the old man's door.

We should have given it serious thought. Maybe at the time if we had made one more or one fewer decision, it would've had a butterfly effect, and our troubles over the past decade and a half would have never been. Maybe I wouldn't be sitting here thinking, what if? Of course, I'm not talking about that luxury apartment.

Ilya's situation was different from mine. Delaying my military service by going to graduate school was my own decision. The decision for him to go abroad to study music had been made on his behalf by his mother. For Ilya, that was a road of no return, a road that couldn't be torn up as easily as the shack he used to live in, leaving nothing behind. But now I can't help thinking that if our conversation had gone some other way that night fifteen years ago, that year when there were too many choices to make, Ilya's life might have turned out different. He'd finished his Bachelor's degree. If he had had a premonition then that one day he would come to fear music, then that's when he should have decided to make a change. If he had chosen a different road, then he probably would not have tied a rope in the shape of a minim, put it around his neck, and left the world behind fifteen years later. Maybe he would have had an ordinary life, and nobody would have known who he was. His face would never have appeared on television or on telephone poles. He would have appeared in the MRT, not in a poster but in person, just like hundreds of thousands of other ordinary people. He would've carried a briefcase or a laptop and squeezed aboard the MRT day after day, finding happiness in the mundane. He would have turned out a bit like my dad: always sitting in the audience, never on stage; and the mourners who would have attended his funeral many, many years later wouldn't have filled three rows.

But so what?

What would have been wrong with that?

26

How to Create Suspense

I seldom recall that secret meeting we held in the tree fort, because that was just the time and place we made the decision, not when and where the most important things happened. Then again, I almost never reminisce about the event itself. I sometimes even feel like forgetting it, to free up space in my memory for the details, whether imagined or real, of my first memory. But now I know that when Ilya spoke, the whole thing had been decided.

Ilya said: "We're going upriver. All we've got to do is follow along the riverbank."

When I say that the whole thing had been decided, I don't just mean the event itself. What I mean is that although we'd decided to do something, that something also decided us: me, Ilya, Brand and that orangutan. Brand said everyone should decide his own fate, that you can't let other people make your choices or live your life for you. But once we'd set things in motion, we were like bowling pins watching that event come hurtling towards us like a bowling ball, a ball that would decide which way we'd fall, and the different directions we would go in life.

Ilya's plan was simple. He said that the zoo was upriver, to the north. We just had to unchain the orangutan, get it out of Carnation Lane, through the watergate, and then we could follow along the river. That was it; he did not go into detail. I was speechless. Obviously it wasn't going to be as easy as Ilya implied. The orangutan's chain was thicker than my finger; even if we could find a pair of bolt cutters, we wouldn't be strong enough to cut it. Not to mention the combination lock. What was more, the orangutan was chained up in a savage neighbourhood of coloured canvas awnings, red lights burning in the doorways, and smoky mists out of a tropical rainforest. Three boys would stand out to begin with, and if you added an orangutan, the difficulty of escape would be greater than the difficulty of making revolution for our Founding Father. Finally, the challenge of going through the watergate to the riverside. We had been forbidden since we were children to cross the levee. Of course, very few children could resist the allure of the river, and most of us had sneaked outside the levee to play a couple of times. But I was certain that Ilya had never been, and knew it would be difficult for him, even though I was all of twelve. That river had taken away his father. His father's motorcycle had been found upriver, and his body in a mangrove swamp near the rivermouth, covered in freshwater crabs and bluebottle flies. I don't know where Ilya had found the courage to go now.

No matter what, there were only three weeks left of the summer holidays. And the man in the beret was leaving in seven days. We didn't have much time. We had to take action right away. Brand divided the three of us into two groups. He told me and Ilya to go deep into enemy territory, north of the pailou road, to observe the orangutan in its incarceration. Our job was to figure out how to release the chains and the lock, and to plan an effective escape route. And as for the weaponry and equipment we would need to rescue the hostage, and the transport and supplies we would need for the escape, those were Brand's areas of exclusive responsibility.

Brand was so excited. I knew he wanted to do something taboo, something that would be a lot of fun to do. Ilya's state of mind was very different. He had resolved to do it, and didn't treat it as a game. As soon as Brand had finished announcing the allocation of duties, Ilya dragged me across the pailou road with no concern for niceties like the fact that to me the place was still a no-go zone.

Ilya had been telling the truth. That orangutan really seemed to be sick. Last time we'd appeared in the entrance to the fire access, the orangutan was on the alert: it had climbed up on the cage and glared at us, baring its teeth. This time it just kept lying on the top of the cage, its two hands resting on a belly so distended it looked like a humungous sky lantern swelling up inside it, ready to burst. Even so, I still didn't dare to get too close to the cage. And the duties that Brand had assigned gave me a good excuse. I told Ilya: "You go check the orangutan, I'll figure out the shortest route to the watergate."

Actually, I didn't have to say anything, because Ilya had already flown to the orangutan's side. There he was, talking to it. Brand had not exaggerated. Ilya wasn't just talking to the orangutan, he was doing it in the gentlest tone of voice, patting its head and squeezing its hand, like he was visiting a loved one in intensive care. I heard the clattering of the chain, the orangutan's answer I guessed. But it might also have been Ilya's doing. At any rate, the sound woke me up: until then I'd been sleepwalking through someone else's dream, but now I had woken up and discovered what a complicated and awkward situation I was in. I looked around, and saw that a few of the women standing in the doorways or behind the windows had poked their heads out or leaned their bodies out to look in my direction. I couldn't be sure if they, too, had heard the sound of the chain rattling, but I was certain that they knew there was an orangutan chained up in the fire access: they'd had an orangutan for a neighbour the past few weeks. Maybe they couldn't get away in the evening to go sit in the public square by the gateway and see the orangutan perform smoking, arithmetic and bicycle-riding, but they must have seen the man in the beret clunking the pushcart loaded with a putrid, fly-harassed orangutan past their doorways.

I hadn't forgotten the girl wearing a white nightgown, but, strange to say, I felt a little bit braver now having made several trips down the lane. Even though I was now on my own in the crowded lane, it wasn't like the first time. Now I went and looked where I wanted. I even dared to walk by the doorway where I had seen that girl. I did not know why I wanted to go there again. I was a bit afraid that she would appear and scorch me with the fire in her angry eyes, but I still felt like seeing her again, I guess maybe because of the orangutan. Unlike last time, now I had a legitimate excuse to be walking here: I was there to rescue an orangutan. Based on Brand's division of labour, my job was reconnaissance: I had to scope out the most convenient route of escape. I did not know any way to avoid a trip down Carnation Lane. If possible, I wanted the escape route to go right past her doorway, so that she could see us in action. Maybe then the fire would die down a bit.

Alas, that girl did not appear. Maybe she was inside, or maybe someone had taken her away. In any case I walked up and down the lane several times and did not see her.

I returned to the fire access, a bit disappointed. But Ilya seemed even more depressed than me. He was squatting by the cage, his face buried in his arms, his arms resting on his knees. The orangutan on the other hand looked much better: it was sitting on the wooden plank on top of the cage, baring two rows of big yellow teeth.

"What's wrong?" I asked, patting Ilya's shoulder.

"He's gone too far." Ilya lifted his head and looked at me with a face full of hurt. "I never noticed. I was just too unobservant."

"How have they gone too far?" I asked.

Ilya stood up, holding the chain in front of the orangutan's chest. He reached over, pushed its head to one side, and parted the red fur of its neck.

"Look, the chain loop around her neck is welded to the chain that ties her to the cage!" Ilya said.

I followed the chain attached to the cage up to the orangutan's neck, around which I saw another chain of the same thickness: the loop. But I didn't see a lock connecting the two; they had been welded together. Ilya showed me the weld. I couldn't imagine how they had managed to do it.

"I don't understand. Why wouldn't they use a regular collar?" I asked.

"They're probably afraid she would be able to release it herself."

"Now nobody could release it, not the orangutan, not even the man in the beret. The orangutan must have to wear the chain during the show."

"She'll have to wear this chain for the rest of her life," Ilya said. "I thought that by undoing the collar around her neck, we could set her free. I underestimated how hard it's going to be."

"Then we have no other choice but to take the chain with us upriver. They can find a way to free it when we get to the zoo."

"I wish it were so simple." Ilya was on the verge of despair. "There's no way we can cut the chain. And we don't know the combination to the lock."

I walked with Ilya back to the secret base, not talking the whole way. My reconnaissance had yielded disheartening results. There was no shortcut between the fire access and the riverside. No matter what, we would have to take Carnation Lane, transport the hostage under the gazes of all the women in the open doorways. And Ilya had discovered that there was no way to release the chain around the orangutan's neck. It could not be cut, and only the man in the beret knew the combination to the lock that attached the chain to the cage. He would never tell us.

I climbed up into the tree fort, but did not see Brand. Ilya followed me up, but only to the platform, not to his lookout on the highest branch. He buried his face in his arms, assuming the same posture as by the orangutan's cage just now. The discovery that the orangutan would have to spend the rest of its life with a chain around its neck seemed to have hit Ilya hard. He hung his head, and didn't say a thing, just like the day his mother invited us over to hear him practise: it was Ilya's familiar posture of silent waiting.

I have to say that Ilya's posture of symbolic emasculation was very effective. Every time he assumed it, he got an immediate response out of me and Brand. This time was no exception. Maybe it was fate, but when I looked at Ilya sitting all curled up like that, there suddenly flashed into my mind a way of opening the lock. I don't know where the idea came from. I had never read about it in a storybook, a children's encyclopaedia or in a textbook at school. I just thought of it. If this was what artists refer to as inspiration, then the intensity of this particular flash of inspiration could feed an army of artists.

"We can open the lock just as long as we know the combination, right?"

Ilya didn't reply.

"And only the man in the beret knows the combination?"

Ilya nodded, but still did not say anything.

I started to talk to myself. "If it were an ordinary key lock, we could find some way of stealing the key. But it's a combination lock, and the combination is in the head of the man in the beret. There is no way to steal it."

Ilya glanced at me listlessly.

"I've got a way to get the man in the beret to tell us the combination,"

I said.

I guess from the expression on my face I looked pretty proud of myself. I'd never been so proud before, not even when my grandmother had bragged about my achievements to the neighbours. I talked a few rounds of nonsense to create suspense, but I was actually dying for Ilya to ask me: "What way?" At that, I would announce the great idea with which luck had blessed me. Alas, creativity is cruel. Young as I was, I would now witness how intense creative competition is. I hadn't had the chance to communicate the crystallization of my creativity when I felt the tree fort shake and saw Brand's bulky body down below.

"I've got a way to take the orangutan to the zoo. I guarantee nobody will discover us!" Brand yelled, climbing nimbly up.

"What way?" Ilya finally said. But he was asking about Brand's way, not my way.

"I found a couple of pairs of wheels. We've got lots of wood here. We live right next to a nightmarket. And I just happen to have several tins of white paint on my roof," Brand announced in a loud voice, completely forgetting his warning about the walls having ears.

"Then what?" Ilya couldn't wait to know the answer.

"Then… We just happen to have here a master of calligraphy," Brand said proudly with a mysterious smile on his face.

I have to give him credit: Brand really knew how to create suspense.

27

In the Communicating Tubes

Professor Safe has gone missing!

His wife calls at seven o'clock in the morning. Amanda and Ling-ling turn over, but don't wake up. I get up to answer the phone. When I come back, Ling-ling has taken my place in bed, her legs wrapped around Amanda's waist. I open the wardrobe and put on a pair of trousers and a shirt.

"Was that your mother? Who would call at such an hour?" Amanda reaches down to feel how absorbent the new nappies are. "Why'd you get dressed? Where are you going?"

"That was my professor's wife. She says Professor Safe has gone missing. I am going to help look for him."

"What time is it? It's so early. Who goes out so early in the morning? And how do you know where your professor went? Shouldn't you call the police?"

"Ling-ling will wake up soon. Mix a bottle of milk for her, 250 millilitres. Remember to put the powder in first to avoid clumps," I say.

Actually, I want to say: When somebody goes missing who cares what time they call? Or: Look at my execution. I head out the door as soon as she calls. But I know I can't say such things. It'd be like attacking her, and would only prove how petty I am. It might also break the peace; Amanda and I have not had a fight in quite a while. We seem to have a tacit understanding not to fight in front of Ling-ling. Instead, we change the topic, cut it short, or simply refuse to reply to the other person's possible provocation.

When I drive out of the underground garage, it's not yet eight in the morning, a rare experience for me in the past two years. Too bad it's a holiday: the streets are empty. There are no middle school students hurrying to school to remind me of my life two years ago, when I would drive the car over the river to another city to teach basic mathematical logic in Cryptology in Daily Life. I should have admitted defeat and let the course be called Life Cryptology. Because there's more to life than logic. Sometimes there's something else, something inexplicable, some hard problems that resist all resolution. For instance, I don't know where my inspiration came from that day in the tree fort. It seemed like an adult me had taken a time machine back in time, put on a cloak of invisibility, slipped into the tree fort, and whispered in my childhood ear a way to break the code.

My idea was pretty complicated. First, we would have to prepare a small lock and put it on the chain when the man in the beret wasn't there. Then we would hide, and wait. And when the time was right, the man with the beret would discover under the combination lock another, smaller lock connecting chain to cage. He would be in a rush because it was almost show time. He would hopefully go find a locksmith or a tool to cut the lock, and would almost certainly forget to put the combination lock back on. While he was away we could note the combination on the lock.

I would discover the principle behind my idea many years later after I entered the Department of Comparative Informatics to start my studies in cryptology. I learned from Professor Safe that I'd used the principle of asymmetrical encryption: the man in the beret was Alice and we were Bob. And the code that would unlock the orangutan was the message that Bob hoped to receive from Alice. The little lock we put on was the "open key", and the key in my pocket the "secret key". If all went according to plan, the man in the beret would discover the lock we had put on only after unlocking the combination lock, and would be so upset he would forget to relock. It was like using the open key to encrypt information. When the time came, we just had to use the key in our pockets, open the little lock, and separate the chain from the cage. Then we could just lead the orangutan away.

I drive along thinking about cryptology just as I would have two years before. As if I would be in class explaining it to students in a short while. Professor Safe's wife said her husband had disappeared at first light. His stainless steel water bottle with peeling paint, his pipe with the plastic straw for a mouthpiece and his flannel suit were gone along with him. "That old fool. I'm almost positive he's gone back to the university to teach. Help me find him and bring him back," his wife implored.

I am about to drive into campus when I get stopped by the guard.

"Hello, sir, what's your business today?"

I've forgotten I don't have a parking pass any more, and don't know how to answer his question. "I've got an enquiry to make," I say.

"It's a holiday today. All the departments are closed." The guard eyes the baby seat, and looks at me suspiciously.

"I know. I used to teach here. Actually, I'm here for someone."

"No matter who you are, you have to get a pass to drive in. First half-hour is free, then forty dollars for each additional hour," the guard says.

I exchange my driver's licence for a temporary parking pass and a time card to put on the dashboard. I feel the novelty of my guest status. For almost seven years, I would drive right in as a graduate student or a faculty member, and sometimes the guard wouldn't even bother to look up. I had such a close relationship with the campus, and now I an an outsider who has to pay forty dollars every hour. It's a strange feeling, like finding myself on the wrong side of a forcefully drawn line. It doesn't seem right somehow. But for now I can't put my finger on what the problem is.

I'm sure the problem isn't the money, especially since I won't have to pay anything: I see Professor Safe in the Communicating Tubes, our nickname for the maze of flower tunnels in front of the School of Management, a few hundred metres down the tree-lined boulevard. I see him from far off, partly because there's nobody on campus, partly because he's easy to identify. With that dark blue flannel suit and that shock of grey hair, he stands out among the yellows, reds and greens of the garden. I could stop right by the Communicating Tubes, ask him to get in, and drive back to the entrance in just a few minutes, well before half an hour is up. But instead, I drive by, turn around the traffic circle and park under a shady tree. I don't want to get out yet, I just want to satisfy my curiosity: I want to know what he's doing sitting there on his own. I see him holding the vacuum flask in his hand, but not the pipe; I guess it must be at the ready in his jacket pocket, as good as ever. Professor Safe is sitting alone on the bench, the only soul in the Communicating Tubes. But his mouth is busy. I see him gazing ahead, his free hand gesticulating to emphasize some point he is making. The scene is, of course, a bit out of the ordinary. Luckily, there's no one in the flower maze but him, or they'd give him a wide berth, an old man talking to himself. His wife should fit him out with earphones so people would assume he was talking to someone on his phone.

I sit behind the steering wheel, and watch him through the windshield sitting on the bench in the flower garden. Watching my adviser talking to himself in the flower garden should be a novel experience, but it feels a bit familiar. As I try to savour the moment, an image glimpsed through another sheet of glass surfaces in my memory. It was at the box office for the cinema where my father worked during the day. I've forgotten the name of the cinema, or maybe I never thought to remember it. I just remember the glass walls of the box office were black, painted with the names and times of the movies in red lettering, and ringed on all four sides all year round by small, tabloid-size posters, all pictures of girls adopting various awkward poses in their underwear. My father sat behind the black glass as if framed by the posters, but since the glass was opaque nobody knew he was there. Maybe that was one of the reasons why he was willing to do that job. I had gone to the cinema several times, but had stood far away, hidden behind a telephone pole or a betel nut stand, trying to peek through the semi-circular ticket window at the base of the glass. I don't know if every child is curious about his father's occupation, but I wanted to know how my father was occupying his time.

I finally get out of the car, cross the road and walk into the Communicating Tubes. Professor Safe must have caught sight of me, because he's stopped talking to himself. He's looking over and smiling, just the way he used to stop and wait for me to sit down when I came in late for class. I know it's because the campus is deserted that he's noticed me. But I can't help wondering whether he knew I'd come when I drove by or when I was peering at him through the windshield of my car. Which in turn makes me suspect that my father saw me when I thought I was hiding behind a telephone pole or a betel nut stand.

"Did my wife send you?" Professor Safe gets the first word in.

"Yes." I nod. "She discovered you were gone first thing in the morning, and guessed you would come to school."

"Look at me: I'm old now, and easily befuddled." Professor Safe laughs awkwardly. "I only realized it's a holiday when I got here."

"You're not old. I used to misremember class time too."

"I'm old enough! I've applied twice to delay retirement. I think maybe next term I might have to offer fewer classes, be less active. I have to hand the baton over to you young people."

Professor Safe's condition seems to be deteriorating. Last time at least he remembered that he had retired and that the new chair was his former student; now these memories seem to have been erased. He points at the empty seat beside him, indicating that I should take a seat. It probably rained last night: I see a few leaves stuck to the wet bench and matrices of water pearls. I hesitate a few seconds, wondering whether I should wipe the bench with a handkerchief, but out of respect for Professor Safe, I just sit down, shattering the pearls into countless water molecules that saturate the denim of the seat of my jeans, conveying a jolt of damp cold.

"Tell me what courses you're offering this term."

Looking in his eyes, I find his expression familiar but farcical. It's familiar because he always used to ask colleagues what they were working on, students what their thesis topics were, and he wasn't just starting a conversation: he was truly curious. "Information is being transmitted all around us all the time," Professor Safe used to tell us. "There's no way to stop it or refuse it, but you can direct it. You've got the right to be selective!" The absurd part is that I feel the flow of Professor Safe's memory has carried me into a time tunnel. Two people who no longer have anything to do with the university are sitting on a campus bench in the early morning on a holiday talking about the classes they are going to offer. I suddenly recall something I remembered in the car while driving in.

"The course I'm offering is called Life Cryptology," I say.

"Oh?" Professor Safe's eyes light up. "It sounds very interesting. Can you let me have a look at the syllabus?"

"There's no syllabus. In fact, I don't even know how to write the syllabus."

"Is it so difficult to prepare? I can help you with it," he says. "What's the main emphasis in the course: life or cryptology?"

One question from my Professor Safe and I am already flummoxed. I am just trying to go with the flow of his memory and poke fun at my pedagogical failure. But the seriousness of his response inspires seriousness in me. "I want to take cryptology as a methodology for the study of life. I don't know if it is feasible."

"Well, you'll have to formulate a definition of life." Professor Safe looks at me. "If you don't explain it, people might think you're researching genetic inheritance. Last time I checked, that was not your specialization."

"Yeah, that's the problem. I don't know how to define life. I've never thought about it before."

That's a lie too. In fact, I have wanted more than anything to know the meaning of life, starting from the sixth grade, after the curtain fell on the orangutan incident. The first time was temporary, like a hive outbreak in childhood. The second time was in high school. That time was much more intense. I know everyone in high school is confused or doubtful about the meaning of life due to hormones. But that wasn't it. It was precipitated by my grandmother's death. She had gone out to sweep the alley, and there I was watching television in the family room, resenting her for talking in such a loud voice with the neighbour. Later the voice stopped, and I looked over and saw my grandmother standing in the doorway, one foot inside the doorway, the other out. She was looking at me, a lost expression on her face. Then, and I've never told my mother or father or anyone about this before, she curled the corners of her mouth in a kindly smile. Right before she collapsed, fell over along with the broom in her hand. Her body must have fallen silently, because all I heard was the clatter of the handle on the ground. Then I heard my mother's scream. Of course, part of what I heard might have been my own yell.

"As I see it, life is the sum of daily life. And our daily lives are full of information," Professor Safe says. "You can't refuse it. If one day you do try to shut it out, then you will have refused to live. And then you'll be as good as dead."

"You mean that human beings live for the sake of various kinds of information? That people are just receivers?"

"Life isn't so simple. Reception is the most basic function. But then you must create information and transmit it. The value of your life lies in how far the information you transmit travels, and how long its influence lasts."

"What if I don't want to send any information to anyone? Would my life then be meaningless?"

"That's impossible, child," says Professor Safe. He wants to give me a smile, but the corners of his mouth just tremble, unable to curl up into an arc. "It's not whether you want to or not. As long as you live, you are sending out information to the people around you. As for whether they want to receive the information, or how they want to receive it, that's up to them to decide."

"It sounds like people's lives are just like the sun," I say. "The sun keeps emitting light and heat, and will do so until the day it dies."

"Well put, Daniel. Everyone is a little sun," Professor Safe says. "Right, how old is your baby now?"

I know our conversation can't continue. For one thing, I'm afraid his wife will worry if we stay out too long. For another, the mechanism in his mind for sending and receiving information is showing signs of entering an infinite loop like a needle on a scratched record. Not just him: my own train of thought has been derailed; no longer "readable", it's deteriorated into meaningless, randomly scrambling code. In my mind flash several faces. My grandmother, my father, and probably my best friend in the world, Ilya. They have all left the earth, while here I am thinking about how they looked when they were alive. Which is strange, because I didn't have to think about them before they died. I could treat them as if they did not exist. Now they are all dead, but I think about them often, for no particular reason. They take up a lot of my time, more than they did when they were alive. There's got to be something wrong here.

We get up from the bench, and follow the path out of the Communicating Tubes to where I parked the car. The pathway has been constructed out of stones that fail to communicate, so it's a bit hard to walk down. "Do you think people who have died can continue to send information to people who are alive?" I say, supporting Professor Safe's left arm, afraid he might trip, shocked to feel how frail, almost insubstantial he is, as if a mere shove would send him sailing through the air. It feels strange to help an old man along like this; I've never done it before. My father died just after turning sixty, not yet old enough to need anyone's support. If my father had lived long enough to need me to support him, would he have got so frail? "If I receive," I continue. "I'm saying if, mind you. If I receive some information, and it has to do with people who have died, how do I know it's not a message they sent me when they were still alive, a message that has been delayed and which I've only now received? Or can someone continue to send me messages from beyond the grave? Are those messages part of life? Should I include them in my research on life cryptology?"

"Your topic is too broad," Professor Safe sighed. "You have to try narrowing it down somehow."

28
Lil' G

I remember this girl.

My memory keeps on running backwards to arrive at my college years.

The girl was Brand's college classmate. I remember she was taller than Brand, with a round, smiling face. She was the kind of girl that's gets on well with guys, the kind of girl that makes other girls green-eyed.

It was only because I was reminiscing about Ilya at the time that the girl's image emerged. I haven't seen her in eighteen years. In fact, our paths only converged on a regular basis in the spring term of our second year. We might not recognize each other as "one time friends" now if we ran into each other on the street. But I still remember she was called Lil' G.

That was what everyone called her. I don't know what G stood for, which shows how close we were. I never even called her Lil' G like Brand and the gang. There were actually only two guys in the "gang", two of Brand's classmates. I vaguely remember what they looked like, but after eighteen years, I have completely forgotten what they were called, even though at the time I called them by their nicknames, just like Brand.

Maybe I can give them names, Woody and Rocky, because one was a man of the pen, the other of the sword.

Like Ilya, Brand was still living at home, but unlike Ilya he never came to hang out at my place. To Brand, my rented flat was too small. If he wanted somewhere to hang out with a bunch of people, the best place was in the music studio on the third floor of his house. At the time Brand's father had already disbanded the troupe and gone on to more important things, so that the studio had become Brand's exclusive preserve. Though there were fewer instruments than there used to be, it was still soundproofed. So even if you held an all-night party in there, you would not have to worry about the walls having ears.

Just like when I was young, I often went to Brand's house, but I wouldn't just waltz on in like I used to. First I would ring the doorbell, if I went there uninvited. But mostly Brand would invite me, and of course Ilya was included. Rocky and Woody often came too. In fact, pretty much every time I went up there, I saw the two of them lounging on the couch, one with a beer in hand, the other with a cigarette hanging from his lips. Just one look would tell you that these guys were Brand's college pals, and that they were just as bohemian as Brand. They had director, producer or screenwriter—artist of one kind of another— written all over their faces, and had to adopt an artist's justified disdain for everything. Lil' G often came over too. In her presence, Rocky and Woody behaved very differently. They still smoked and drank, but wouldn't toss their beer cans and cigarette butts out the window. Instead they'd ash the cigarettes in the ashtray and put the beer cans in the rubbish bin.

Woody and Rocky both liked her, especially Woody. He had her in his bones. But Lil' G? Blame Brand for always wanting to blend different circles of friends. She didn't like any of the boys in her class. She only had eyes for Ilya, who went to a different college.

College, especially the first two years, was the time when Ilya seemed least like himself in his whole life. Or was that the time when his mother was the least like herself? Ilya still lived at home, but clearly had a lot more freedom than before. He didn't have to spend the whole day practising piano, and could go out whenever and with whomever he pleased. We could barely sense his mother's existence. At the time Ilya was pretty cheerful and talkative, no matter whether he was talking with close friends or acquaintances. He could click with somebody in no time, with a constant stream of jokes from his mouth like he'd been accumulating them in his belly for twenty years and couldn't wait to share.

We could never figure out whether Lil' G liked Ilya for his sense of humour or his musical talent. The latter seemed unlikely, as he'd never shown off his ability to turn his fingers into animals on the keyboard in front of Brand's college classmates. Falling for him on account of his sense of humour was a bit risky, because Ilya had never been a funny guy, and might not keep it up. Every time I saw Ilya bending over backwards to liven up the atmosphere and get Lil' G to laugh, I couldn't help a flash of clownish sorrow; I felt sorry for him.

Brand came right out and asked: "Do you like Lil' G too?"

"What?" Woody and Rocky swooshed off the couch. Wearing only a tank top, Rocky came over and put me in a headlock. "You like her, too, don't you? You little pipsqueak! You also want to steal Woody's woman away from him!"

"I wouldn't dare," I said, begging for mercy. Even though I knew he was only joking, my nose was only a few centimetres away from his sweaty armpit. Surrender was my only option.

Rocky released me, returned to the couch and resumed his sprawl, while Woody glanced at me sadly and resentfully. Today was an important day, but Ilya and Lil' G had not arrived yet. Woody must have been wondering where the two of them had got to.

Brand and his classmates had a group term assignment to shoot a twelve-minute short. Brand and the others were so excited, because even though they were only in their second year, they felt like they'd been waiting for this day for years. The four of them, Brand, Woody, Rocky and Lil' G, had formed a clique in their very first term, so they had a leg up on their classmates. Unlike their classmates, who would have to form groups and get used to working with each other, they got right to work on pre-production. They spent quite a bit of time on the script. When I went with Ilya to see Brand, I would see the four of them, heads together under the lamp discussing it. Brand wanted it to be a work of social realism, hoping to use the peculiar neighbourhood in which we lived as a set, to shoot a film about a dissolute college student who saves a child prostitute from the clutches of the mafia. Woody and Rocky seconded his artistic vision. But though they agreed that shooting in the doorways of the moll parlours would be totally cool, there was no consensus about the personality of the male protagonist. Rocky said that the point of the film was combat, so the main character should be tall and strong and powerful. But Woody said that the main character wasn't Superman, no matter how strong he was, and could hardly defeat all of the bouncers in the brothel. The main character should have the bookish mien of a student who defeats the enemy by brains not brawn. But Lil' G was opposed to Brand's great idea. She said they'd never get a good mark with such a clichéd plot. And seeing as how we were just college students, it would be too dangerous for us to shoot a movie in a place like this. Brand said: "Look, we've got a difference of opinion about the characters. Everyone wants to play the male protagonist, nobody the prostitute. Am I right?" He pointed at me and Ilya, who had just come up to the third floor, and said: "Problem solved: our actors are here. Leave the script to me."

Eighteen years later, my memory stubbornly insists on replaying the events of that important day, on which our maiden film was given its debut screening in the soundproofed room the variety troupe used to practise in on the third floor of Brand's house. It was a red carpet affair, just without the red carpet.

Brand had prepared the screen and the projector. The movie was on a tape they'd used a Betacam to shoot, edit and copy. They'd spent a week in the editing room at college, during which time Lil' G went home to the countryside to visit her family. After term ended, she had stayed in the dorm an extra week to shoot the film. After Brand had declared "That's a wrap!" Rocky put his palm on his chest and said: "Don't worry about the post-production, we'll take care of it. You just go on home to see your family, Lil' G."

The time we'd agreed to meet for the premiere had come and gone, and neither Lil' G nor Ilya had shown up. I was shocked by how calm Brand and the others seemed. In the few days of the shoot, Lil' G was always the first to arrive. Brand had made some changes to the script, eliminating the child prostitute, turning the main character into an innocent college student corrupted by his friends. He gets addicted to drugs, gets in too deep. Brand explained that it was a guy flick about male friendships, and that he planned to use reverse narration to keep the protagonist on the run with a few early flashbacks to get all the plot elements to hang together. I couldn't understand the film terminology they were using, like "non-diegetic music", "second person follow" or "montage". Brand and Woody had cooped themselves up for a few days to draw the "storyboard", basically a thick stack of shots, which they handed to Lil' G on the first day of the shoot. Her status had been demoted, from the heroine to set manager. I felt the injustice of it on her behalf. Set manager sounded like flower vase, nice to look at but it didn't really need to be there. Her job was running around doing odd jobs, getting us lunchboxes and so forth. But Brand said in all seriousness that the success of their experimental film was in Lil' G's hands. Lil' G nodded vigorously, while Woody and Rocky smiled derisively. Quite a few times when Lil' G clapped the clapperboard, Rocky the cameraman would be shooting a close-up of her face. "What the fuck are you doing?" Brand would shout.

Woody and Rocky weren't smiling now. They spoke even less than normal, I guess because Ilya and Lil' G were late. Rocky swallowed the last sip of beer and crushed the can with one hand, got up and did a jump shot. Clunk! The can followed a parabolic curve, landing right in the rubbish bin three metres away.

"Good shot," Woody said. "If you had shot that well in the Basketball Cup we would have won the championships."

Rocky ignored him. He turned and asked Brand: "You think we should tell her?"

"Naw. Telling her wouldn't change anything."

"And it's not just Lil' G's fault," Woody said.

I didn't know what they wanted to tell her. I guessed it had to do with Ilya, but couldn't think of anything to do with Ilya that they would want to tell her about but that I wouldn't know. I didn't bother asking; I was used to it. On set, they'd spent most of the time huddled together discussing the next shot, on which everyone had uncompromising views. Unable to participate in their discussions, I could only watch with Ilya from the side of the road and wait for them to order me around.

Finally, there was a clatter of steps on the stairs. I knew it was Lil' G. She was always bouncing around like a rabbit. Ilya walked more lightly, like a cat. Unexpectedly, the first to appear was Ilya, but Lil' G followed close behind. Her face was bright red, as if from the summer heat.

"Nice you could join us! Where'd you go for your date?" Brand asked.

"What date? We just happened to run into each other downstairs," said Ilya, looking relaxed. Lil' G said nothing and offered no explanation or apology. She headed for the couch. Woody got up immediately to yield the seat he'd been sitting in for almost an hour, but Lil' G didn't appreciate his gallantry. She pulled over a folding chair and sat down behind the couch, and Ilya gracefully took the seat on the couch that had been vacated for Lil' G.

And so our very first movie started playing. There was no curtain to part, we just turned off the lights. Brand pressed a button on the remote. First came the countdown, then, with background music, the first shot, of a typical city street. It lasted for about ten seconds, but halfway through something flew out of the distance until it occupied half the screen. That thing was the title of the movie, in Chinglish: *A Busy Thing in the Afternoon.*

I burst out laughing. It was the street in front of Brand's house, with the hardware store, the fried rice noodles and squid stew stand, and the boss lady of the ladies' fashion boutique staring straight into the camera, hands on her hips. It was comical for my neighbourhood to appear in the first scene in a film with a proper name. But Brand had not shot a comedy, and had not joked around much during the shoot. I could see how serious they looked, and how cold the atmosphere was in the room, like they were keeping a vigil. Except, that is, for the grin on Ilya's face. This was normal. After all, the film was Brand's business. Whether they passed or failed had nothing to do with Ilya, and even less with me: I wasn't the star, Ilya was. I forget how they decided to get Ilya to play the leading role, the weak-willed innocent corrupted by his friends into a hopeless drug addict. If you were casting someone weak-willed, I might be the better choice, because I'd always taken a back seat to Brand and Ilya. I might go along with them and yell "hit 'em" or "kill 'em", but I never came up with any of the ideas that got us into trouble. If you wanted someone depressive, Ilya seemed to fit the bill, but as I said he'd changed in college, just like the familiar street in front of Brand's house changed in the film. Once he got to play the role of the college student, he became comical, a regular sunny boy.

I saw a sunny boy feigning depression on screen. I knew the plot, and was expecting a face full of dread and despair, but Ilya was really a terrible actor, however good a pianist he was. He looked more like he had a headache and needed a Tylenol. A head shot zoomed into a close-up of his eyes, and then the running shots of the reverse narration began. That's when I heard Lil' G gasp, very softly, so softly that only I could hear over the undulating drone of the videotape machine and the noise of the film.

"I never imagined a film we cut with such primitive equipment would look so good on screen," Lil' G said.

"It's all in the post-production. We didn't spend seven days in the editing room for nothing," Woody said.

"It's like a girl's make-up," said Ilya. "No matter how ugly she is, post-production can turn her into a fairy."

Lil' G had made herself up, faintly. I wasn't sure where she'd added the highlights. I'd seen her without make-up and thought she was just as good-looking. Me and Brand both thought she'd only started after she developed a crush on Ilya. We'd all got on famously since first year, but she'd only begun using make-up half a year before. A girl's heart was harder to crack than the most secure code to begin with, but why had she suddenly gone and fallen in love with a member of the opposite sex she'd been hanging out with for a year? It would have been easier to understand a sudden change of personality if she'd fallen in love at first sight. She had totally changed, but only a year after meeting Ilya. In addition to the make-up, the way she walked and talked had changed, even the way she looked drinking water through a straw. She had turned herself into a completely different person hoping that someone who already knew her as a friend would like her in a different way. This was really strange.

I wanted to refute Ilya's comment, and not just because of Lil' G's make-up. I felt the same as her: I thought it was a well-made experimental short, amazingly so. At least, it seemed like a movie. I didn't have a big part to play; it was five minutes before I even appeared on screen. Which was no matter. I wasn't the main character, but at least I was a character. In that I'd done one better than my father, who had never appeared in anything in his life. Not to say I knew anything about acting. Those three days we were shooting the movie, I didn't know what I was doing. Brand said there was no need for us to memorize our lines, because there weren't many lines in the script, and mostly it was things like "Fuck!", "Screw you!" or "Stay, if you dare." Brand didn't shoot in order. He jumped around a lot, and each shot was so short it felt like they were trying to save film. We went to shoot in the maze of lanes off Carnation Lane north of the pailou road. When Brand called "Camera!" Lil' G clicked the clapperboard and bounded out of frame like a bunny, and I waited for him to holler "Action!" Then I ran out of a lane, turned a corner, ran past the camera and turned another corner. Then Brand yelled "Cut!" Of course, I wasn't the only person running. Sometimes Ilya would run, and sometimes Rocky and Woody together, sometimes I would run after Ilya. I remember it took us two whole days to shoot the chase scenes. Then came the final showdown, the climactic conflict. I had to overturn a table; Rocky duked it out with Ilya. Brand's shot list had divided the scene into fragments, and I'd never read the complete script, so I didn't know why I was doing what I was doing.

But in the end it came together. Rocky, Woody and I managed to play gangland hoodlums, Ilya an innocent college student. His flight in the film showed how badly he wanted to distance himself from temptation or escape from reality. There was one small problem. Ilya had fled, just like Brand had told him to do, but regardless of whether he was running away on his own or whether he was being chased by the hoodlums, he never looked back. Maybe this wasn't a major flaw, but obviously Brand had never considered the issue. If Ilya wasn't looking back, how was he supposed to know who was pursuing him, or even that there was someone pursuing him? It was a bit like him and Lil' G: Lil' G was sitting right behind him, the back of a chair away, while Ilya just kept staring at the screen. Did he know Lil' G was pursuing him? Maybe it would be too much to say Lil' G was "pursuing" Ilya. Lil' G wasn't pursuing him, but on set she'd been practically stuck to him the whole time. You didn't have to focus a camera on them. It was obvious to anyone with eyes.

But not even Ilya could fail to notice the discrepancy of what happened next, a magic realist effect in a supposedly socialist realist film. In one shot, Ilya, fleeing a crowd of hoodlums, had nothing on his face, but in the next shot, in which he rounded a bend, he was suddenly wearing black-framed glasses.

"Oh no!" said Lil' G. This time everyone heard her.

The surrealist effects didn't end there. In another chase shot, Rocky was five steps ahead of Woody, and in the next shot, Woody was out in front, and Rocky was behind me. Then there was a scene of drug dealing in front of the bus stop. While Ilya was hesitantly getting the money out of the wallet, he was shouldering a satchel, but after a shot of Rocky's nasty leer, his satchel had disappeared. Blooper after blooper. A chair that had been knocked over righted itself; an empty beer glass self-refilled. Like magic.

Woody said: "This is the only way we could cut it."

I heard Ilya laugh awkwardly, but he didn't have anything to feel awkward about. This had nothing to do with him. Set management was Lil' G's job; she was the continuity girl: she was supposed to note all the details in each shot so that the shots would go together.

Rocky said: "Actually, it's not that bad. Maybe the teacher won't even notice."

Brand hadn't said anything. He was just pressing his lips together. You couldn't tell if he was angry or resisting the urge to laugh.

The film reached the final showdown, ingeniously designed by Brand. Ilya was surrounded by Rocky, Woody and me. We were thrashing him. He collapsed, and then struggled to crawl back to his feet. Then Brand cut to a breathtaking shot. Whenever I think of the film, that particular shot is the first thing that comes to mind. For other details of the shoot, and the way it turned out on screen, I might have to think a bit. This shot is completely different: it's like a picture that never fades. In retrospect it completely dominates the other shots. I've always felt this shot was meaningful in some primordial sense, that it was like a master key, a key that would crack all the codes we had yet to confront in life, like the solution to all our problems. After Ilya died I finally realized it wasn't a sign of things to come, just a kind of premonition. I found it breathtaking at the time, but its significance went right over my head. It's so blatantly obvious in retrospect that it could not have been lost on Brand's film teacher.

In one shot, Ilya was lying on the ground with a bloody nose, his white undershirt all muddy. But in the next shot, he was standing up, the blood was gone, and instead of just an undershirt he was wearing a short-sleeved shirt on top. He looked as fresh as an elementary school student on the first day of class.

Lil' G started crying.

"Don't cry. Nobody's blaming you," said Woody.

"Yeah, the teacher might not fail us for it," said Rocky.

Lil' G cried even louder. She grabbed her backpack and fled without watching the end of the film, crying all the way down the stairs.

Rocky and Woody stared at one another. Then they glanced at Ilya, as if they didn't know who should run after her. Ilya maintained perfect composure, sitting on the couch with a smile on his face, as if none of this had anything to do with him. About ten seconds later, Brand finally threw down the remote control and went out to catch Lil' G.

That was the last I ever saw of her. Several years later, Brand told me she'd married some bigshot tycoon from Hong Kong after graduation, and had never gone to see a movie since.

29

Temple Protest

"Something's going down at the temple. The place is crawling with cops!"

Brand burst into the tree fort, yelling excitedly.

At the time, me and Ilya were putting the finishing touches to Brand's idea for a surefire way to avoid discovery. We had spent several days using the four castors that Brand had brought and wood from the bottomless woodpile to build a pushcart with a pair of handles. Brand had also brought a big tin of white paint and a small tin of red paint. Ilya painted the whole cart white, and I used the big brush that I had won in the Counterespionage Calligraphy Competition to paint "SUGARCANE JUICE" in red on both sides. Brand nailed a pair of hinges on one of the top edges, and a pair of knobs on the other side, as if we could open the cover and get out the sugarcane we had stored inside. But actually the only door was at the back, beneath the handles. The door was just big enough for the orangutan to crawl in. In announcing his idea, Brand hadn't forgotten to add that the most common kind of vehicle in the neighbourhood was the pushcart, and that a pushcart was the only way to spirit away an orangutan in broad daylight. I had to admire Brand's ingenious idea, which was both simple and practical. A sugarcane juice pushcart was a big wooden crate with wheels, easy to make, but impossible to see into. But Ilya couldn't put his heart to rest. He said that a sugarcane juice cart without a juice press wouldn't fool anyone, that we should nail on a sheet of metal and mount a steel box with a pair of openings like on a real sugarcane juice cart.

But we had run out of time to find or make a complicated prop like that. Me and Ilya covered the cart with a tarp, and hid it in a dead-end alley. Then we ran for the temple with Brand. But we didn't get much further south than the gateway on the south side of the pailou road before we had to slow down. To a standstill. Amazingly, the streets were packed at a time when they were usually deserted, well before the sun had crawled up to its highest position overhead. We were used to crowds at night. For it to be crowded in the morning, well, we had never seen that before.

We pressed our way through the crowd, wanting to see what was going on at the temple. Brand was right: the temple was surrounded by cops. I thought at first they were soldiers, because there were so many of them, but then I noticed they weren't dressed like soldiers; they were all wearing the exact same khaki uniform and white helmet. I never knew there were so many policemen in the whole city. They had lined up into a human wall, not letting people in the nightmarket street get too close to the temple. Like everyone else, we were stuck outside the human wall, dozens of metres away from the temple gate. We couldn't see a thing. The wall, the trees and the roofs nearby were all covered in people. There was no place we could climb up to see what was going on.

But Brand didn't give up. Head down, he led me and Ilya through the crowd trying to find a gap in the human wall to squeeze through. I didn't feel like going any further. I was scared with all the cops there, and the human wall seemed airtight. It was suffocating. The only direction we could move was sideways, which we did until we reached the place where the human wall met the corner of the outer temple wall. There the human wall wasn't so thick. Brand dragged me and Ilya through a gap between two cops.

"Where do you think you're going?" one of the cops said as he spread his arms to stop us from passing, like the mother hen in the game "eagle hunts the chicks".

"We want to go home," Brand said, looking up at the officer, not even blinking.

"What are they up to?" A police officer who was not wearing a white helmet walked over and asked what was going on.

"They say they want to go home."

"Yeah, we want to go home. We live inside."

"Inside the temple?"

"No, across the street. We're neighbours." Brand spoke on behalf of me and Ilya.

"Let 'em in," the plainclothes police officer said. Then he turned his head and said in a nasty tone: "Hurry home! And when you get home, don't come out again, understand?"

We went through the wall and saw there were actually two human walls, extending from the two corners of the fence around the temple to the other side of the nightmarket street, blocking off the stretch of street in front of the temple. It was far less crowded in that stretch, but there were still quite a number of people walking here and there. They were letting people out, but except for us were not letting anyone in. Cordoned off, the street was empty of cars. We'd never seen it this way before. Usually we would walk down the nightmarket street a few times a day, but this was the first time we had been able to walk down the car lanes and pretend that we were cars. Maybe that was the reason why the people inside the walls didn't want to leave: once they left they would not be able to enter again.

The temple gate was shut; around the gate was another, arced, wall of policemen. At first I thought they were there to prevent anyone from going in, just like the human wall we had just squeezed through. But I soon discovered that it was just the opposite. They had lined up outside the iron gate to prevent the people inside the temple from getting out. Yes, there were people inside: we could see them through the gaps in the throng of cops and the bars of the metal gate. The people were sitting on the ground in the temple courtyard, wearing white vests and holding green banners with white characters. A few of those characters were pretty well written, as nice as the character a calligraphy teacher would do, but some were just all right, neat being the nicest thing you could say about them. Oh yeah, the banners said: "Lift Martial Law!"

"I never thought he'd go through with it!" Brand slapped me on the shoulder.

"Who?" I said, in pain.

"My dad."

"You saw your dad? Where is he?" Ilya asked.

"I haven't seen him yet, but I can see all the things they were storing in my house," Brand said proudly, pointing at the protest signs people were holding. He'd told us about all the things the adults had made in the addition. Now me and Ilya believed him.

We kept looking, trying to see if Brand's father was there. In the courtyard was quite a crowd, of which the people sitting in white vests were in a minority, with a dozen people standing for every person who was sitting. Occasionally they clapped and shouted their agreement or broke into cheers. At first I wondered what they were shouting for, but then I noticed a man with a loudhailer standing on the cement stair that led down from the temple censer giving a speech to the people in the yard. They must be shouting whenever they heard something great in the speech. I could not clearly hear what the fellow on the podium was saying, because with all the people yelling it was just too loud. Not to mention that the police had loudhailers too. But instead of political speeches they were using them to blast patriotic songs.

"Hey, look over there," Ilya said. He motioned for us to look towards the fountain to one side of the courtyard.

"I don't see Brand's father," I said.

"It's not Brand's father! Look! At the man in the hat."

"It's the man in the beret!" I called. "What's he doing here?"

"He must've arrived early, before they blockaded the street and the temple gate," Brand said. "It's a wonder he's still here, after my dad told him he'd better leave early. And here he shows up at the temple."

"If the man in the beret is here, your dad must be here somewhere too," Ilya said.

Brand nodded, with a proud look in his eyes. It looked very much to me like the police were blocking the gate, trapping the protestors inside. I thought they might soon flood in and start grabbing people and taking them away, but Brand wasn't the least bit worried about his dad. He was still beaming proudly, like he'd got an award. I didn't know what he was thinking. We weren't trapped inside the temple, but each end of the street in front of the temple was blocked off by a human wall. We had broken into the inner cordon, a zone neither people nor vehicles could enter. I'd never been surrounded by police before, but I certainly knew what it was like to be trapped. It was just like when I was three years old kneeling in front of the altar. At the time I had been holding a crumpled hundred dollar bill. Now there was nothing in my hand, but I was just as scared.

"If your dad is inside, he won't be able to escape," I said.

"Why would he want to escape? He hasn't done anything wrong."

"Didn't you say he was a revolutionary? Didn't our Founding Father Sun Yat-sen, the greatest revolutionary of them all, flee out the back door when a knock came in the middle of the night?"

"Nonsense!" Brand was angry. "Yes, my dad is a revolutionary; but he would never flee."

As he spoke, the people in the temple courtyard who had been sitting on the ground all stood up. The tension immediately escalated, as the people inside moved towards the gate and the police outside the iron gate blew whistles. The people inside pressed against the temple gate. One of them grabbed its iron bars and started shaking it, eliciting another burst of even more shrill whistling. And the loudhailer that had initially appeared in front of the censer, well, it was now just inside the temple gate. Someone was standing there with it slung over his shoulder. He pointed it at the solid wall of cops and shouting slogans: "Lift Martial Law!" the loudhailer blasted, and the people in the street outside the temple burst into cheers. "Martial Law is Military Rule!" the loudhailer roared, and the people outside cheered even louder. "Open the gate and let us out!" the loudhailer bellowed deafeningly. "Open the gate! Let them come right on out!" the people outside the temple shouted at a frightening volume right in my ear.

We were standing with the people outside the temple and shouting along with everyone else. It seems strange to say, but I wasn't scared any more, and even felt safe. The crowd was cheering, and we were cheering too. It was a lot of fun.

"Open the gate!" the people inside chanted.

"Open the gate!" chanted the people outside.

"Open the gate! Open the gate!" we called. We felt delirious, wondering what was going to happen next. The people inside made as if to rush out, even though they were deadlocked across the gate with the police. They might push the gate open, or simply climb over. They could do it for sure, I guessed, and a conflict might erupt at any time. The standoff couldn't last forever; a spectacular drama was sure to unfold.

But right then, Brand grabbed my arm and told me and Ilya it was time to go.

"Let's get the hell out of here. Now!" he said, clutching my arm.

"What's the hurry?" I said, shaking his hand off. "We just got here. Why should we leave just on your say so?"

"Yeah, and remember how much trouble we had to go through to get in," Ilya said.

"This is our only chance to leave," Brand said.

"What do you mean our only chance? The people inside are getting ready to charge out. Don't you want to see what's going to happen next?" I asked.

"Yeah, they seem ready to make a move. Shouldn't we wait and see?" Ilya asked.

There was another uproar from the direction of the temple gate. Someone really had climbed onto the gate, and was straddling it three or four metres in the air. There was fierce applause from the people standing around us, who were yelling at the top of their lungs. The police at the temple gate didn't do anything right away, as if they didn't know whether to pull the guy down or push him back over.

"No mistake. They've made their move," Brand said. He took a look at the temple gate, and started telling me and Ilya something. Two more people had climbed onto the gate, eliciting an even larger wave of cheering that drowned out Brand's voice.

"What'd you say? I can't hear you!"

"I said it's now or never! We've got to make our MOVE!" Brand shouted. This time me and Ilya heard. The people standing beside us heard as well. Quite a few heads turned in surprise to look at Brand. Someone even gave him a spontaneous round of applause.

30

Operation Orangutan Rescue

I thought we'd made our move after the secret meeting in the tree fort a few days before. But now I knew that was just preparation to take action. Preparing to take action and actually taking action are two different things. It was only when we lifted the tarp on the fake sugarcane juice cart and pushed it north of the pailou road that Operation Orangutan Rescue really began.

We had to do quite a number of things before taking action. Nailing and painting the pushcart alone took a lot of effort. It was actually very difficult to construct a stable crate with just nails and wood. We had to add a few two-by-fours for added support. Of course, two-by-fours were not hard to come by: there were many woodworking shops in the area, where we could go and "borrow" what we needed. The difficult part was Ilya's requirements for construction quality. He insisted we shave off every splinter and hammer nails in at an angle, to prevent anything from scraping or pricking the orangutan's skin or paws. We also spent some time scoping out the advance and retreat routes for the rescue mission and figuring out the combination. That was Ilya's job. He went with my idea: he waited until the man in the beret was gone and added another, smaller lock. Unfortunately, the man in the beret did not react as expected. He saw our lock immediately, but did not go and look for a locksmith. He just fished out a paper clip, unfolded it and bent it a few times, picked the lock that Ilya had put on, and tossed it aside. He didn't even yell or swear, as if he'd seen this kind of thing before, many times. Then he started dialling the numbers of the combination one by one. Ilya was really depressed, assuming that our idea, including my flash of brilliance, had failed. But fate works in mysterious ways. You could say Ilya's luck was good that day, and the man's luck was not, because when he was on the last number a bucket of water, whether it was dishwater or something else, came sloshing down, exploded right by his backside and got his trousers all soaking wet. He looked up and swore, then hurried back to the inn to change his trousers, while Ilya looked on from his hiding place. The lock wasn't open, but Ilya had seen everything, and knew the man had already dialled the first three numbers of the combination. He went right up and tried the numbers on the fourth wheel one by one, until it opened with a click on the fifth try.

Finally, we were pushing the cart towards Carnation Lane. Ilya was wearing a backpack containing the things he'd put in the treasure trove. Brand had an old bookbag he'd run home to get while me and Ilya were getting the tarpaulin off the cart. I hadn't brought anything because I hadn't had time to go home. Brand said that's the way it is when you really take action. Even if you are completely prepared, something needs to happen to set the plan in motion, something like the fuse on a bomb. It's like when you're all warmed up but you don't dare go in the water yet, until somebody gives you a push and down you go. I asked him who had pushed the people at the temple into the water. Brand said he did not know for sure, just that his father was always saying: "Intolerable!" and "Outrageous!" Brand's father must have been holding it in a long time before someone pushed him in.

Brand was right. It was now or never, do or die. We pushed the cart along the pailou road. The road was usually mostly deserted by day, with only a few stores open for business, but today the shops here were all shuttered, while the nightmarket street up ahead was crammed with nervous cops in white helmets and fractious onlookers outside the cordon. The incident at the temple drew almost everyone in the neighbourhood, and the rest had probably locked themselves behind iron doors, not daring to come out. We passed the pailou gateway and turned into the danger zone, not having seen more than a couple of people along the way. I was worried we'd stand out, a trio of elementary schoolboys clattering a creaky four-wheel pushcart along the nightmarket street in the morning. Brand must not have considered the problem. But it was too late to worry about it now, because Operation Orangutan Rescue had already been launched:

there was no turning back. That's the difference between preparing to take action and actually making your move.

Luckily, the incident at the temple had had a big enough impact, and there was nobody to notice us along the way. We almost took a wrong turn, because there was no smoke from the sausage stand, no glow of red light from the parlours, and no human walls of women with gaudy make-up on either side of a squirming mass of men. Carnation Lane was deserted. It was as if someone had taken a broom, swept everything into a dustpan, and disposed of it. We turned a few corners and it was the same: there was nobody there. Once a savage rainforest, Carnation Lane had become a lonely ruin. How quiet was it? So quiet that we could hear the loudhailer and the police whistles all the way from the temple.

The operation proceeded smoothly, too smoothly almost, so smoothly that I forgot we were going to rescue an orangutan and not to pick up someone's younger brother or sister at kindergarten. We reached the fire access behind the inn without incident, and Brand stayed at the entrance to keep a lookout while me and Ilya did a U-turn and pulled the cart slowly in. Too excited to wait for me to open the door to the cart, Ilya had already rushed over to undo the combination lock. There he stood, holding the end of the chain, trying to get the orangutan to come down.

"Harriet, it's time to go," Ilya said.

But the orangutan sat on top of the cage, not moving an inch.

"What's up? Come on!" Ilya walked up and patted the orangutan on the head.

When announcing the plan, Brand had said that as long as we could construct the sugarcane juice cart and push it to the cage, the orangutan would get in, just like that. That's not what happened. The orangutan allowed Ilya to pet it, but kept its eyes on the pushcart parked in front of the cage. I don't know if it felt curious or afraid.

"Come down, Harriet," said Ilya, tugging on the chain.

The orangutan would not come down. It just pursed its lips and shook its head, its lower lip like a rubber pouch that could enclose everything below its nose, from upper lip to nose. With its comical expression and the wrinkles on its face, it looked like a little shrivelled-up old man who had lost all his teeth.

But Ilya didn't think it was funny. "What's wrong with you?" he asked.

"What's wrong with it?" asked Brand, who'd run out of patience waiting for us at the mouth of the lane.

"It doesn't seem to want to leave its cage," I said.

"No, it's not that Harriet's unwilling to leave her cage. I guess she doesn't like the cart we made," said Ilya.

"Why not? There's nothing wrong with the pushcart," Brand said.

"Maybe because there's still a paint smell? Or because we didn't install a window?"

"Have you ever seen a pushcart with a window? And if there was a window, wouldn't it be like announcing to the whole world that we've got an orangutan inside?" Brand was a bit pissed off. "You guys hurry up and load it in. I'll be at the entrance to the fire access to watch for the man in the beret or anyone else."

"No need. Why don't we all pull it onto the cart together? That'd be quicker," I said.

"I don't think that's a very good idea. How would you feel if someone put a chain around your neck and dragged you into a cart?" asked Ilya.

"I agree. We can't just pull it," said Brand. "You two pull the chain, and I'll push it from behind."

"The chain is around her neck. If you pull too hard you'll hurt her," said Ilya.

"If it's in pain, it'll come down. Do you want it to be free or not? Freedom is worth any amount of suffering," said Brand.

Ilya didn't say anything. And that's what we did. To be honest, I admired Brand's bravery. I might not have dared lay my hands on the orangutan's apparently sticky clumps of fur. To say nothing of the danger: if we angered the orangutan, it could use its long, thick arms to knock out all Brand's teeth without taking a single step.

I stood behind Ilya, pulling the chain. Brand was pushing the ape from behind. "Down! Down! We've got to be able to get you DOWN," Brand shouted. But the ape wouldn't budge, like someone had glued it there with superglue. "Pull harder, you two!" Brand said. I don't know if Ilya was trying his hardest, but I dare say I was pulling for all I was worth. The orangutan screamed a few times, gripped the taut chain in its hairy hands and started pulling back. Me and Ilya staggered back a few steps, almost falling. Note to self: don't challenge an orangutan to a tug of war.

"Stop pulling. Look at what her feet are doing," said Ilya.

The orangutan's feet were like two big hands clutching the iron bars of the cage. "No wonder we can't move it," said Brand. He reached towards the orangutan's right foot, hoping to pry open its toes, but each of those toes was like a vice-grip: there was no releasing it.

"What do we do now?" I asked. "Have we got it all wrong? Maybe it doesn't want to leave."

"Impossible," Ilya said. "Harriet wants to go with us. She just doesn't dare to get in the pushcart."

"Are you saying that there is something wrong with the pushcart?" Brand asked. He raised an eyebrow and looked askance at Ilya, squinting one eye. I don't remember Brand ever looking at Ilya like that before. It was a surprise, because I thought Brand reserved this particular expression for me.

Alas, Ilya did not see Brand's expression. He threw down the chain and stood in front of the cage, gazing at the orangutan. "Don't be afraid, Harriet. We've come to take you away from here, far away. You won't be chained to a cage any more. You won't be forced to practise tricks over and over again. You don't like performing in the nightmarket, do you? Come with us and you'll never have to do another show or take another bow. We will take you to a place where you don't have to practise or perform. We can't take you home. Your home is in the rainforest, but we don't have a boat or plane to get you off Taiwan and take you back to Borneo. But we can take you to a place that you will probably like. You might meet some of your friends there, folks who won't tie you up or chain you or make you go up on stage. People will come to watch you, but you don't have to worry about them. You won't have to please them. You can pretend they don't exist. So come on, let's go. Believe me, you'll be a lot freer there than you are here."

As Ilya was saying all these things to the orangutan, me and Brand were standing dumbfounded to one side. We didn't say anything to interrupt him. That orangutan obviously did not understand what we were doing, and Ilya's explanation did not enlighten it. Of course, it didn't understand human language. But Ilya gazed into its eyes and said all these things so sincerely that I thought it still might crawl down from the cage and squeeze into the getaway cart we had made for it. But it did not. During Ilya's persuasion, it kept blinking, lifting its lips and flaring its nostrils. Then it stuck out its tongue to lick the back of its hand. Finally it just looked down and started scratching, hunting for fleas in the fur on its tummy and legs. Ilya finished his appeal, but the orangutan's toes were still clutching the bars of the cage. It gave no sign of relaxing its grip.

"It's no use!" Brand said. He opened his canvas bookbag and got out a banana. "Luckily, I anticipated this might happen."

He handed the banana to Ilya, and Ilya held it in front of the orangutan. The ape reached for the fruit immediately, almost got its hands on it. "No, Harriet," Ilya said. He retreated two steps, held the banana close to the ground and wagged it back and forth to tempt the ape. "Come down here. Got a tasty treat for you. Hungry?" The orangutan hesitated, stood up a bit unwillingly, turned and climbed down from the cage. "Success!" I said. But when the orangutan's right foot touched the concrete ground it immediately recoiled like it had got a shock. It squealed and leaped back up onto the cage with a terrible clatter.

"What's wrong?" I asked.

"You scared her when you said success," Brand said.

"No way, it performs in the square every night. It wouldn't get scared so easily," I said. "Maybe it's because Ilya didn't peel the banana."

"Have you ever seen an ape that needed its bananas peeled? You've seen the man in the beret feeding it bananas, peels and all," Brand said. However apes eat bananas, I saw that Ilya had already started peeling the banana. It reeked like hell in the fire access, but I could still smell the banana. If I could smell it, the orangutan must be able to smell it too. But it did not seem to be tempted. Rather, it turned away from Ilya, lowered its head and went on scratching fleas. "Hello! You stupid ape. For Christ's sake!" Brand said.

"Orangutans aren't stupid, not at all. They are about as intelligent as a five-year-old child." Ilya gave up trying to tempt the orangutan, and just put the banana in front of it. It took it and put small pieces in its mouth one at a time, as if it took everything for granted.

"Turns out it eats pretty civilized, not like last time when the man with the beret was feeding it," I said, feeling a bit hungry myself. Seeing the orangutan savour the fragrant banana bite by bite, I half-hoped it would think to share. "Monkeys do love their bananas. And I almost thought it liked scratching fleas more than eating bananas."

"Orangutans are not the same as monkeys," Ilya said. "Harriet is an orangutan, not a monkey."

"Right, but just like a monkey, its favourite food is banana. Right?" I didn't want to get into an argument with Ilya, so I turned to Brand and asked: "Do you have any more tricks up your sleeve?"

"Nope. We have to think of a way to get it into the cart, and quick," Brand said.

"Banana might not be an orangutan's favourite food. Contrary to popular belief," Ilya insisted. "Actually, they like to eat everything. They're omnivores, just like us. They especially like anything sweet or soft. It doesn't have to be banana."

"Ice cream is the sweetest and softest food of all," I said to Brand. "You have any ice cream in your bookbag? If you don't, can you go get some real quick?"

"Are you kidding? Where am I supposed to get some ice cream now?" Brand asked.

"I meant fruit," Ilya said. "Orangutans like to eat natural things. Harriet would prefer honey to ice cream."

This was too much. Ilya said I couldn't tell a monkey and an orangutan apart while he obviously couldn't tell an orangutan from a bear: he'd got their favourite foods mixed up. I wanted to tell Ilya how wrong he was, when the orangutan proved both of us wrong. Just like last time, someone threw something down into the fire access from above. This time it was a cigarette. It floated down, and fell at Brand's foot. I should say that it was half a cigarette. Some litter bug had lit it, taken a few puffs but was too busy to finish it and just tossed it out the window without crushing it out. The lit butt hit the ground and sparked but did not go out. The orangutan acted immediately. It ignored the last bit of banana, came down off the cage so quickly it was like it had grown wings, landed surefootedly on the concrete ground in front of the cigarette, and reached out to pick it up. It had all happened too fast. It wasn't just that me and Ilya were too slow to react, but that we didn't even know what was happening. The only thing more surprising than the ape's descent was how fast Brand moved to pre-empt it. He leaped upon the cigarette at the same time as the ape jumped off the cage, getting there one step ahead. Blocking the ape's hand with his fat body, he bent down and swiped it up.

"Aha! Is this what you want?" Brand lifted the butt high in the air. He retreated two steps and the orangutan immediately came forward.

"Right, last time the man with the beret gave it a cigarette after it finished the bananas," I said to Ilya. "Look at it. Obviously an orangutan's favourite food is tobacco, not fruit or honey."

"Give me the cigarette," Ilya said.

Brand extended the butt of the cigarette to Ilya, and the orangutan followed it with its eyes. Ilya took the butt, held it up between his thumb, index finger and middle finger, giving the orangutan no opportunity to steal it. Brand and Ilya had exchanged the cigarette in a very comical manner. If they had been wearing sports uniforms, and the cigarette were a lot bigger, it would have looked like Brand had passed him the Olympic torch. And Ilya really did seem like an athlete receiving the sacred fire. As soon as he got the cigarette, he started to run, which caused the orangutan to give pursuit. Ilya was running backwards, and the cigarette butt, which had started out high in the air, got lower and lower. Before I could figure out what Ilya was trying to do, he'd retreated to the getaway cart and tossed the butt inside. Almost at the same time, the orangutan threw itself into the pushcart, dragging its chain behind. Ilya immediately slammed the door shut.

We stood there by the iron cage, dumbfounded. We couldn't believe our eyes.

"What are you two doing standing there like gaping idiots? Let's get the hell out of here!"

"But… you've locked a smoking ape inside. Won't it choke to death on the fumes?" I asked.

"You got a better idea?" Ilya asked. "Let's hurry up and push her through the watergate. We can let her out when we get to the riverside."

What Ilya said made sense. It wouldn't take long to get to the watergate from the inn, and I had the escape route all figured out. We just needed to exit the fire access, traverse Carnation Lane, and turn right onto the pailou road. It was only another fifty metres or so down the road to the watergate. The hardest part would be the narrow, winding stretch of Carnation Lane. We'd originally worried the cart might bump into any number of cranky men in the lane, but today it didn't look like that would be a problem because the protest at the temple had drawn such a crowd, and because the human walls of police had scared all the girls in the doorways away. We pushed the cart out of the fire access, and what with an ape for cargo it had become very heavy. Luckily, the three of us were able to handle it. The only problem turned out to be that smoke kept rising through the cracks between the boards.

"What'll we do?" I asked. "I've never seen a smoking sugarcane juice cart before."

"It's been smoking that cigarette for quite a long time, hasn't it? I hope it hasn't set its fur on fire," Brand said.

"Don't worry, Harriet's not that dumb. Don't forget, she has the IQ of a five-year-old," Ilya said.

"Would a five-year-old child smoke?" I asked.

"A five-year-old child wouldn't smoke, nor should an orangutan," said Ilya, a bit displeased. "We have to keep quiet. Don't mention the orangutan again, or people along the way will overhear."

"There isn't even anyone here," I said, immediately regretting it. We were just a few steps away from the nightmarket street when we heard a voice from behind: "Hey you! Wait a sec." It was a stranger's voice. "Don't worry about him. We've got to get out of here," whispered Ilya. We pushed for all we were worth, but the sound of the footsteps got closer and closer, until right at the entrance to the lane a couple of men stopped our pushcart in its tracks.

"Hey! Didn't you hear us calling you to stop?" one of the men said. He thumped the cart with his hand.

I stood there, holding the handles. I didn't dare make a move, but my legs trembled disobediently.

"Why the hell did you keep walking when we told you to stop?" the other man said. Wearing a white muscle shirt, he had tattoos all over his chest as well as sleeve tattoos on his upper arms: the "hem" was pretty neat, like he was wearing a shirt with tattoos for sleeves. At first glance I assumed that he was wearing a green V-neck short-sleeved undershirt under a white vest.

"We… we really didn't hear," Brand said.

"My ass! Who's your daddy, you little shit? I almost yelled myself hoarse. How could you not have heard?" the man who had thumped the cart said.

"My daddy died long ago," Ilya said under his breath. Fortunately, he spoke so quietly the two men did not hear him. I broke out in a cold sweat on Ilya's behalf, but the strange thing was that my legs stopped shaking as soon as Ilya spoke.

"Quit blabbing with them," said the guy with the tattoos. He walked beside the cart and stopped in front of the lettering: "SUGARCANE JUICE". "Open the cover, kid. Make it quick!" he said to Brand.

"Do… do what?" Brand said.

"Do your old lady. Do what?" Mr Hands-of-Lead said. "Yo' daddy's real parched. Hurry up and pour us each a cup of sugarcane juice. Help us slake our thirst."

I looked at Brand nervously, and discovered he was looking back at me imploringly. Help! his eyes said.

"You got wax in your ears again? Do you want us to do it?" the man with the tattoos said, reaching an arm with a tiger head tattoo towards one of the false knobs that Ilya had installed on the top of the pushcart. In that instant, I wanted to drop the cart, yell and take off, but I didn't because Brand didn't move a muscle, and Ilya stood there like nothing was the matter. I just couldn't get up the courage. The man's hand got closer and closer to the knob, and would realize it was fake the moment he touched it. And that's when the trouble we were in would really begin. I closed my eyes, not daring to imagine what might happen next.

"Wait a second," I heard Ilya say.

I opened my eyes and saw the tattooed guy's hand stop in mid-air.

"Won't do you any good to open the cover, cause we sold all the sugarcane."

"Bullshit! You sold all your sugarcane so early in the morning?" the man with the tattoo said, slightly retracting his hand.

"We were just as surprised as you are. It was all the people at the temple. We stopped by there earlier this morning, and a thirsty crowd surrounded us and sold us out in no time," Ilya said, staring right into the guy's eyes, bravely meeting his nasty gaze. The man didn't say anything, just sized Ilya up. It was the other guy, the one who had pounded the cart, who spoke first. "Fuck! We come here to cool off with a hot little piece of ass, but with all the pigs around none of the cathouses are open. We want a cool glass of sugarcane juice and it turns out they just sold out. It's just not our lucky day!"

"Forget it. Let's go see if there's anywhere else we can go to lay low," the tattooed man said.

Seeing those two mean dudes turning back into the lane, I breathed a sigh of relief. I didn't expect that Ilya would have other talents besides conjuring up animals with his fingers on the keyboard, that he could keep his cool and avert a crisis in just a few sentences. I wanted to praise him aloud, but his eyes told me we should get the hell out of there. Unfortunately, we didn't have the chance, because the two guys turned around again.

"Not so fast!" Mr Tattoos said suspiciously. "What've you got there inside the cart?"

"What?"

"Just now when I was going to open the cover, why were you so anxious?"

"Was I?"

"You're carrying something else in the cart, aren't you?"

I felt the air freeze. The lead-fisted one joined his tattooed friend, with one on either side of Ilya.

"Exactly," said Ilya. "It's not sugarcane we're carrying."

"Then what is it?"

Ilya looked at the man with the tattoos and hesitated a few seconds. "There's an orangutan in the cart. About twenty-five kilos. Probably about the same height as me and my friends here." Then, slowly: "You guys want to open the cover to see?"

"Whoa! This kid has fried his brains," said the guy with the fists of lead. "I never heard of an orangutan in a sugarcane juice cart."

The guy with the tattoos didn't say anything, just stared suspiciously at Ilya. The two of them looked at each other for the longest time, when finally the tattooed guy spoke.

"You're shitting me. You think I'm that easy to fool?" he spat.

"I'm serious. Believe it or not."

"Scram!" the tattooed guy said. "Or we'll dismantle your cart. Believe it or not."

This time we didn't wait for him to turn round and head back into Carnation Lane. We hightailed it out of the danger zone, turning onto the pailou road, heading for the watergate.

31

A Sea of Tranquillity

I open the lens case, take out the new video camera, and raise it to eye level. Ling-ling appears on the 7.5 centimetre LCD screen. She is sitting in the family room fitting together a toddler's jigsaw puzzle on the mat. She looks up at me, then looks down and takes the puzzle apart piece by piece.

"Ling-ling, what are you playing with?" I ask.

She doesn't take any notice of me, just keeps playing: she slams it down on the cardboard box, ejecting the puzzle pieces.

"Ling-ling, what are you doing? Tell the camera."

"I..." she says, thinking hard, trying to fit together a complete sentence. "I pouring it out for Daddy."

"Very good," I say. Obviously she's just playing with a jigsaw puzzle, but she makes it sound like she's helping me.

Ling-ling is two years and two months old. I've filmed her before, but only with a consumer digital camera, the kind without HD video. When we played the videos on the computer screen, they just weren't nice to look at. Ling-ling would look distorted, fuzzy, or even washed out. I had been hoping to buy the newest model for ages, but could hardly propose a big purchase if Amanda did not suggest it herself. She's always been rather obtuse when it comes to new technology. If not for an afternoon tea with her posh friend Monica, she might never have noticed the leaps and bounds modern video technology has been making. Monica showed her how good a toddler can look with the latest technology. "Why don't we buy an HD video camera?" Amanda said. "Our Ling-ling is much prettier than Monica's brat. Filming her with that old digital camera of yours doesn't do her justice."

The time on the display keeps increasing, but I don't know what to ask. I feel like a reporter who's just gone on the beat; I am holding a camera, interviewing a difficult subject.

"Ling-ling, what are you holding in your hands?"

"Jigsaw."

"What's it a jigsaw of?"

"Aeroplane."

"Would you dare take a trip in an aeroplane?"

"No!"

"Why not?"

"Aeroplane… scary," she says, patting her chest.

"Why would you be scared?"

"Cause it might fall down."

"It might fall down? How do you know?"

"A plane can't fly too high, cause it might fall down," says Ling-ling, putting down the jigsaw. "Mummy said I can't climb too high, cause I might fall down."

Beginning several months ago, I've noticed rapid development in Ling-ling's linguistic and logical abilities. Before two years of age, she could only babble and gesture and use onomatopoeia. But now she can use a limited vocabulary to express herself and carry on a conversation, sometimes quite coherently. Sometimes what she says is quite logical. It's just that she still can't pronounce the words precisely: "awopwane", not "aeroplane". Sometimes the sounds she makes leave you scratching your head. For instance she wants to say "juice", but the sound that comes out of her mouth is "choose". Or she wants to say "through" and the sound that comes out is "true". I imagine that in her mind, Ling-ling knows exactly how to say these words, but can't yet use her larynx, tongue and lips to produce the sounds properly. Along the way errors creep in that she cannot control or does not notice. For this reason, Ling-ling might think she has pronounced the word right, but when confused expressions appear on our faces and stay there even when she repeats the word, she gets really frustrated. She might even get angry and stomp her feet, assuming we are misunderstanding on purpose to try to tease her.

"Daddy, could a bee shop me?" On the screen, Ling-ling is holding a jigsaw puzzle of a bee.

"Shop you?" I was flabbergasted. "What do you mean?"

Ling-ling was also taken aback. "I mean shop me," she explained.

"Are you asking whether a bee might sting you? Don't worry, a bee won't sting you unless you get too close and bother it."

"No, I mean would a bee shop me?!"

"Daddy doesn't understand what you're saying. Can you try saying it a bit clearer?"

I see on the screen that Ling-ling has already furrowed her brow. But she has not given up on communicating with me. She points at the puzzle and says: "A bee's tail is so shop. It might shop me."

Finally understanding, I laugh out loud, causing the screen to shake. "Ling-ling, sharp is an adjective, not a verb. You can say something's sharp, but not that something might sharp you. You should ask: 'Would a bee sting me?'"

"Woulda bee ding me?" Ling-ling says, looking at the screen like she's pondering what I just said.

"Would a bee ssssting me?" I correct her.

"Daddy, you ever been ding by a bee?"

"It's not ding, it's sting. Actually, it's stung. No, I've never been stung by a bee."

"Dung."

"Stung."

"Dung."

I give up. The camera keeps on recording, but Ling-ling and I fall silent. Thank God Amanda is at work, or she would insist on a tug of war between sting and stung and maybe even sharp, until Ling-ling got angry or Amanda lost her temper. I am in no hurry to teach Ling-ling too much, and am even worried she might be learning too quickly. I am afraid she'll grow up too fast, figure out too many things all of a sudden, and lose the adorable silliness typical of children of her age. But Amanda doesn't see things the same way, and has recently had a fight with Ling-ling about this very issue, two days ago. Amanda was holding an ice cream cone and an ice cream sandwich, one in each hand. She asked Ling-ling: "Which one would you like?" "I wan bof," Ling-ling said. Amanda immediately corrected her. "You have to say 'I would like' not 'I want.'" "Ling-ling means she wants both of them."

Amanda rolled her eyes at me and kept talking to our daughter: "Mummy knows you would like both, but you can only have one. Come tell Mummy which one you would like, this one or that." Ling-ling said, "I wan bof." Amanda tried to teach her a few more times, but Ling-ling refused to abandon her dedication to bof, and soon the cone and the bar melted into two puddles of milky cream in the controversy of this, that and both.

I slide the zoom lever, focusing in on Ling-ling's hands. Her hands, which on the day of the ice cream incident mopped both tears and sniffle from her face onto the shoulder of my shirt, are now fitting the pieces of the jigsaw puzzle one by one into the cardboard base. I keep zooming closer and closer, and Ling-ling's hands get bigger and bigger. That is one of the powerful features of this new camera: 30x smooth optical zoom with shake reduction can turn Ling-ling's hands into the only focus from the other side of the room. Of course, for me to focus in on her hands, she needs to cooperate. Unfortunately, children at this age find it really hard to sit still and let adults shoot photographs or extreme close-ups. It's almost impossible. I very quickly give up trying to get a close-up of both hands. I catch her right hand holding a piece of the puzzle, then her left hand unoccupied by her leg. I slide the zoom lever again and focus quickly in on her left hand. Monica is right about the features of these new HD cameras: Ling-ling's small, plump hand soon fills the screen. Rosy red, smooth and super-soft. I see a chiaroscuro effect in her backlit hand: the bright part is her translucent fingers, slightly curled, the fine lines on her knuckles only adding to the apparent pliancy of her skin; while the dark part is the back of her stationary hand, where the shadow gets deeper and deeper until it merges with the mat she's sitting on, flowing into a sea of tranquillity. Light and dark meet at the base of her fingers in several tiny reddish-orange bands, like wisps of cloud at dawn.

Then Ling-ling's left hand moves, escaping the confines of the screen. That makes it very hard for me to get her hand back in the shot without zooming out. I shoot a close-up of my own hand. This is not a smart move, because the hand that appears on the screen isn't so nice to look at. The veins are like contorted roots, the knuckles in extreme relief, with bushy hair between the joints; and the skin is dry, lustreless, and covered in a grid of wrinkles like cracked soil. This silly hand has held thirty-eight years of things. I had not noticed how old, rough and yellowish it has become. Shocked, I allow my own hand to wander, yielding the frame to Ling-ling's face. At some point she's stopped putting the jigsaw puzzle together and is looking towards the camera with evident displeasure.

"Daddy, don't take a picture of me. I said, don't take a picture," Ling-ling says.

"I am not taking a picture of you."

"Then what are you doing?"

"I'm filming."

"Then don't fiiilming," she says, extending the vowel.

"All right all right, I won't fiiiiilming." I use the vowel-lengthening trick to distract her so I can keep recording the precious moment, the moment before Ling-ling throws a temper tantrum. Ling-ling dodges left and right and suddenly spies the lens cap I have put on the tea table. "Time to put the cap on," she mumbles. She walks to the tea table, picks up the cap, turns and walks towards the camera.

"Wait," I say.

Ling-ling lifts the black cap, which is nearly the same size as her palm, high in the air and asks: "Whose is this?"

"Whose is that? Mine."

"Where's it go?" she asks, furrowing her brow.

"It goes on the lens."

"Where—is—the—lens?" Ling-ling says in a fierce staccato.

"The lens is… wait!" I have no time to reply. As Ling-ling reaches the lens cap towards me, a round black object gets bigger and bigger, until it fills the screen. Click! The screen goes black.

32

Up the River

It's just like when I recollect the time when I was three years old, kneeling in front of the altar: the more I think about the incident, the more details, both true and imagined, come to my mind. I have to admit that for over two decades, I have seldom thought about Operation Orangutan Rescue. If not for Ilya's funeral, when I saw Brand again and got the chance to sit in his massive blue beetle, his super alloy mobile suit of a convertible, I might have forgotten it completely.

With one memory fragment flying fortuitously after another, I've started filling in the blanks with details, mostly invented. Although they wear the masks of truth, I know they're made up, for who can produce a watertight, all-inclusive account of what happened over twenty-five years ago? After all, the human brain isn't a video camera, and even if many memories are stored as images in the mind, they're out of focus freeze-frames, like sepia-coloured photographs fringed with shadow. If you want to edit them into a cartoon or a motion picture, you have got to use your imagination. I don't know any other way.

The part of the operation, which I only started remembering years after the fact, that I replay in my imagination most often isn't a scene of danger or conflict, or any other funny, frightening or ridiculous interlude, but what happened when we first pushed the orangutan through the watergate and reached the riverside. I even adopt the perspective of the orangutan, imagining how it might have experienced the operation. It gets locked inside a pushcart that smells faintly of paint just for a lousy cigarette. What happened? It gets jostled— forward, back, left, right—every time the pushcart speeds up, slows down or turns a corner. Ouch! Then the pushcart stops and someone starts thumping on the lid. Hey! And then it hears the shouts and cheers of a few little boys and sees the door slowly open. Where am I? It sees the boy that has for the past couple of weeks come every day to visit it, talk to it, hold its hand, pet the fur on its neck and back or even crawl up on top of the cage with it to sit shoulder to shoulder and offer gentle words of encouragement. It gets up the courage to support itself with its long arms, tuck its legs and swing towards the entrance of the cart. At that moment, it sees outside a sky as blue as the sea and clouds as fluffy as candy floss. It discovers soft green turf underfoot, and up ahead an endless wall of grass and shrubbery that was taller than a man and as dense as a rainforest. It must have been thrilled. For the past month it had been spending its days locked up in a dark fire access, and its nights performing in the nightmarket. God knows how long it's been since it's seen this kind of a scene. Had it been taller, or if there were a big tree for it to climb up, it would have seen over the wall to a river that glittered like a yellow brick road. It would have looked upstream, sensing that it just had to follow the shore to reach a place where it could be free and at ease, a place where it would not have to practise or perform.

But that's the Hollywood version. Which is contradicted by the still-like impressions that are seared in my memory, the few true details which need no embellishment. What actually happened after we passed through the watergate and reached the riverbank was anti-climactic. The orangutan didn't move at all when we excitedly opened the door of the pushcart, just cowered in a corner. It had no intention of leaving the pushcart. I'll just skip the methods we used to try to get the orangutan out of the cart, because it was a difficult process, about as difficult as trying to get it into the cart in the first place. The only difference was that me and Brand gave up in the end, and decided to let it stay in the cart.

"Unless another cigarette falls down from the sky," Brand said, looking up, "we'll just have to keep pushing it upstream in the cart."

Although I wanted to see how excited the orangutan would be when it finally obtained its freedom, it was fine with me to let it stay in the cart. At least that way nobody would see it. By the river it was mostly grass and mud, but there was also a concrete path about the width of two cars along the levee. The path was flatter and straighter than the lane and the road we had pushed the cart down to get here, and we didn't see any people or vehicles. We started pushing the sugarcane cart upstream along the concrete path. At first, we pushed it very quickly, practically trotting the entire way, because we were afraid that some villain like the guy with the tattoos or his friend might be chasing us. We ran for at least an hour, around several bends and under several bridges. I don't know if we were just lucky, whether the riverside was usually deserted during the day, or whether everyone had run to the temple that day. For whatever reason, there wasn't anybody there. Before we passed under the fourth bridge, we'd only seen one scooter, and the rider didn't even so much as glance at us, just whooshed past.

We stopped to rest under the fourth bridge. The orangutan still would not come out. It seemed to have decided to live in the pushcart. Ilya worried that the orangutan would get "cart-sick" with all the jolting and rattling. He also wanted to feed "Harriet". Only then did we discover we had not brought anything to eat or drink.

"I brought bananas, but the orangutan ate them already," Brand said.

"You brought a big bookbag, and you only put a single banana in it?" I asked.

"What about you? You didn't even bring anything!" Brand said.

Ilya said we'd better make an inventory of the things we were carrying. We did what he said. It would have been better not to do an inventory, because as soon as we finished it we felt even more deflated. When all of the things were laid out in front of us, we realized that all we had was: a Boy Scout rope, a little pot, a pair of reading glasses, a watch that did not work, a penknife, and an empty plastic water bottle in the shape of a cartoon character; a handkerchief, a baseball and two ballpoint pens; six ten dollar coins, four five dollar coins and ten one dollar coins; a pair of wooden chopsticks, a flashlight, two batteries and a comb; and finally a backpack and an old canvas bookbag, both flat now that they had been emptied out. I had barely brought anything. Only the handkerchief was mine, and a couple of the ten one dollar coins, though I for one certainly could not see the use of the things that Brand and Ilya had packed in their bags.

"Who says they're useless? Don't we need water?" Brand asked, holding up the water bottle. "Come on. Let's go to the riverside to fill it."

Brand wanted Ilya to stay by the levee under the bridge and guard the pushcart and the orangutan inside. Me and him were in charge of getting water. Brand's arrangement wasn't as simple as everyone going together to drink from the river. But I knew that Brand was doing it for Ilya's benefit. This was the first time that Ilya had ventured through the watergate. We knew he would have to get up the courage to confront the river itself. Even if his mother had not forbidden him from walking through the watergate to the riverside, he could not have wanted to get too close to the river that had taken away his father's life. We let him and the orangutan stay by the levee, assuming he would have an easier time of it there.

Me and Brand walked towards the river with the water bottle. We were already quite a long way. Before that day, we had hardly ever played outside the levee. Now we were in completely unfamiliar territory, in what seemed to be a meander in the river. Along our section of the river, it wasn't far from the levee to the water: we just had to walk across a grassy clearing, through a few thickets of grass, and we would reach the iron railing along the riverbank. But the river here was a lot further away: me and Brand walked towards the river, parting thickets of grass and climbing onto a little mound. What we saw from up there was not the river but a large green pond, in the centre of which straggling tree stumps stood straight out of the water.

"There's water here for the bottle," I said.

"Idiot, you can't drink it. Don't you see? It's stagnant: there's nothing flowing in or out," said Brand.

I walked to the pond and saw shadows darting about in the water. "There are fish. Too bad we didn't bring line and tackle."

"The pond belongs to someone. Of course there's fish in it. But I wouldn't dare fish here."

"How do you know the pond belongs to someone?"

"Can't you see those stumps?" said Brand, pointing at the centre of the pond. "Would your typical pond have stumps at the centre? The master of the pond put them there to tell people it's private property. We've got to get out of here."

I only half-believed him: how could he possibly know? A pond by the riverside must be a natural phenomenon, I thought. How could someone put a few stumps in the water and turn it into private property?

We went on walking towards the river. The next thing we saw was a vegetable garden. Black earth had been hoed into parallel mounds, out of which grew stout stems with large leaves. Brand did not have to tell me that someone had cultivated this vegetable patch. I was going to suggest going around, but Brand said: "Hey, it's a sweet potato field. Cover me: I'm going to get some sweet potatoes to take back and roast."

"What good will it do to dig up sweet potatoes?" I said. This time I was the voice of caution. "We've got an orangutan to take to the zoo. We don't have any time to stop and roast sweet potatoes."

Brand thought I was right, and decided against stealing the sweet potatoes. We kept going towards the river, passed by a couple more fishponds and vegetable patches of odd shapes and sizes, and went through gaps in the dense grass, until finally we got to the swift-flowing river. The river was different this far upstream: it was narrower, and there were no sandbars in the middle. Brand made a discovery of his own. Supporting himself on a couple of rocks, he lowered himself onto the mud at the water's edge. I thought he was going to get some water and come back up. I never expected that he would squat between the rocks for a while before suddenly standing up and yelling: "Hey, there are crabs!"

"Really?" I asked. That was really surprising. I never knew there were crabs living right on our doorstep. "Are they big? Where are they?"

"I saw one burrow into the sand. It was really big."

Brand was standing in the mud by the river, so I took off my shoes and socks and joined him in my bare feet. Brand gestured for me to be quiet, squat by his side and observe a tiny cleft between the two rocks. I waited a moment, patiently, and there in the muddy hole between the rocks I saw a pincer, light yellow with a hint of red, belonging to a crab, followed by four black legs covered with bristles or spines or something. But when a crab eye appeared like a lit match in the gap, it immediately recoiled. It'd probably got freaked out by the excited expressions on the faces of the boys who were squatting on its doorstep. "I've got a way of getting it out of there," Brand said. He went on shore, found a stick and came back. Then he prodded the entrance to the crab's burrow, stuck it in and moved it around, which seemed to piss the crab off, because he felt it open its pincer and grab the stick. Brand slowly pulled out the stick, and incredibly the crab refused to relax its grip. And that's how Brand caught it. Brand reached out and subdued it with his bare hands. "Gotcha!" Brand said, proud of himself. The crab was really quite big, as big as Brand's palm, its pincer as big as his thumb. It was still clutching the stick, unwilling to let go. It was like it was brandishing a sword. I looked around, trying to find something to put it in. But except for rocks and mud and leaves and sticks, there wasn't anything there. In my confusion, I grabbed the water bottle Brand had brought, took off the cup-shaped cap. Without saying anything, Brand crammed the crab into the bottle.

I thought the game was a lot of fun, and started hunting for the next prey. There were really quite a few crabs at the riverside. But if they were too small we were not interested. The only crabs that we paid predatory attention to were even bigger than the one we'd just caught. Me and Brand walked like crabs along the bank, sideways and hunched over. Brand's Stick Trick proved very effective. In no time, or in what felt to us like no time, we'd caught a bunch of crabs. Brand would provoke the creature with his stick and I would grab it. Just as I was happily putting the sixth into the water bottle, I sensed that we were being watched, by two people standing on the riverbank.

I raised my head. And saw that it wasn't two people, but a person and an ape.

Ilya was standing there with his hands on his hips. He was looking down, and the orangutan was too. Seeing me and Brand with our feet and hands covered in mud, he asked: "Weren't you two going to go get us some water?" His voice was cold.

"Hey, how did you get it to come out of the cart?" I asked, but Ilya did not reply. "Look at all the crabs!" Brand said, giggling. He lifted up the bottle to show Ilya, and then handed it to him. But the Crab Trick did not work on Ilya. He took the bottle, took off the cup-cap, and returned it to Brand. He did not so much as glance at the crabs inside, which were stepping on each other trying to climb up the walls and escape. Ilya let the orangutan stay on the bank while he went down to the water and ladled a cup. He drank a few sips, then refilled it and gave it to the orangutan.

I didn't see the chain around the ape's neck, and wondered how Ilya had got it off. I crawled back up onto the bank before I discovered that he hadn't. Ilya had put the rest of the chain in the backpack and got the orangutan to carry the chain on its back. I had to admire his ingenuity. This way the chain was not so conspicuous, and the orangutan was no longer so limited in its movements. It was just that it looked really comical wearing that backpack. Me and Brand could not help laughing aloud, which really pissed Ilya off. He threw Brand's bookbag onto the ground and pulled the orangutan along, which just made me and Brand laugh even louder. This is the first time we had seen the orangutan walk, and from behind. Its movements were extremely slow, and it walked with a stoop, its bum twisting with every step. We could not see the back of its head, just the backpack swinging left and right so violently it looked as if it might fly off sideways at any time. Its legs were shorter than its arms, and it walked at an angle on all fours. When it stepped forward with its right foot it was fine, because its right arm would stay on the outside. But when it stepped forward with its left foot, its left arm would end up between its legs. From behind it looked like it had grown a third leg.

"Hey, weren't we going to transport the orangutan in the cart?" Brand yelled at Ilya. "It'd be so much quicker pushing it along the concrete path."

"You think Harriet wants to ride in the cart?" Ilya said, raising his voice. But he did not look back. "We'd better stay off the main path: Harriet will attract too much attention on the concrete path."

We couldn't think of anything to say. All we could do was follow. Brand collected his bookbag and discovered all the things we had made an inventory of inside. Regretfully, I poured out the crabs in the bottle and watched them scurry in all directions.

Ilya was really angry. He was leading the orangutan further and further upriver, not even checking to see whether me and Brand were following him or not.

33

Through the Precipitousness and Darkness of Time

With me supporting her, Ling-ling stands on a metal stool in front of the ice dessert and fruit juice stand. She chooses four toppings for her grass jelly on shaved ice.

Though Ling-ling has liked grass jelly for quite a while, this is the first time I've taken her to the nightmarket for a treat. She's been eating grass jelly my mother brings back from the market. Amanda actually doesn't like Ling-ling to eat this kind of food, and has on more than one occasion told me she's not worried about hygiene. The issue for her is that grass jelly might darken Ling-ling's skin. I know Amanda wants me to tell Ling-ling's grandmother to stop feeding her traditional treats like grass jelly, but I've always kept quiet, because I'm not going to let unsubstantiated Internet claims like "grass jelly will turn your skin brown" interfere with the conspiratorial rapport that has with great difficulty been established between grandmother and granddaughter.

Amanda does not know I have brought Ling-ling to the nightmarket. Instead of coming to have dinner at my mother's, she's gone to Yoga class. This has been happening a lot lately. Sometimes it's when I say I'm going to my mother's for dinner that Amanda says she's going to Yoga class. Sometimes it's the other way around. We haven't had an argument about it. Not even once. Maybe we both know that if we did fight about it that'd be it for us. Of course, if she finds out I've taken Ling-ling to the nightmarket to have grass jelly she might be a bit unhappy. But she can't blame me, because she only said she didn't want me to take her to the park. She didn't mention the nightmarket. Still less do I plan on telling her what places I'm taking Ling-ling to this evening.

When the boss lady single-hands us a grass jelly ice with the requested toppings, Ling-ling squeals with delight. I imagine her face is glowing with the colours of the ice dessert stand. But I don't turn to look at her, because when the boss lady struggles to lean over far enough to hand Ling-ling the bowl, she gives me quite the view. She's wearing a floral print blouse with a slightly loose collar, which sags open to expose, cupped in a black lace bra, a lovely pair of breasts: taut, full, round and glistening slightly with sweat. I must be staring longer than is polite, and I guess she's caught me scoping her out. She can't very well display anger, though, because it's her own negligence. But otherwise she doesn't react. She doesn't gasp or pull up her collar or cover her breasts with a panicked hand or turn away in embarrassment. She just gives me a glance, not hurrying as she straightens up to return her breasts to the cups, so matter-of-factly it's surprising.

After moving my gaze to the boss lady's face, I quickly look away. It is a face that fails to match that pair of breasts. The skin is loose and freckled. Below the slightly protruding cheekbones are several folds of flesh. Her eyelids droop, and crow's feet sprawl from the corners of her eyes. A very high hairline makes her bare forehead the brightest part of a dull face. She is a fair distance away from youth, but where she crosses the line into middle age is in her eyebrow tattoos, which form perfect, pastel purple arcs above her slightly inset eyes. All of which makes her face look at least ten years older than the apparent age of her breasts.

It's just a weather-beaten face, nothing special. At least half the ladies behind the stands in the nightmarket have a face like this. I guess it's because of her age that the lady would be so unstinting in her display of her youthful breasts; but I'm not looking forward to another moment of negligence on her part.

I look back at Ling-ling. I make sure she can grip the spoon to ladle the grass jelly into her mouth and then look around. This time my gaze falls on another woman inside the ice dessert stand. She is wearing a pink vest, denim shorts and flip-flops. She is facing away from the stand at a sink on the wall, washing and stacking melamine bowls with perfectly curved legs and smooth, slender arms that sway like kelp in the tide. Just based on her rear silhouette, I can tell she is young.

My heart beats faster.

Could she be her?

Now I know why I've brought Ling-ling to this particular ice dessert and fruit juice stand. There used to be just a few such stands in the market; now there are more. Some of them are pretty big establishments, with long lines and flashing neon signs, underneath which you might see a banner saying: "Thanks to Channel X Cuisine Critic for Two Tongues Up". Or: "Cheers to Channel O News for the Nightmarket Maven Interview". And so forth. Some of them went ahead and printed their appreciation on the sign, sometimes in a bigger font than they used for the name of the stand. I've always assumed that no matter how the world changes, the most change-resistant place in the world would be the nightmarket. Seeing all the notices of cuisine show reviews and the pictures of the owners posing with celebrities, I may have to reconsider my nightmarket nostalgia, but at least some things stay the same. This particular ice dessert shop, for instance, has not changed with the times. It still has the same simple sign, the same stainless steel frame and the same scratched-up acrylic glass display for the fruits and the toppings. Even the two motorized ponytail fly swishers are the same as they've always been.

To me, it's the same old ice and juice stand. Although I haven't been in the nightmarket for years, I still remember how it looks, and the taste of the syrup. I remember the positions and orientations of every table. I remember other things too. I don't know how many years have gone by, but I can still remember how she looked, the high school girl who would go to the ice shop every day after school with her canvas satchel slung over her shoulder to help her mother with the tables and bowls.

I turn my head right and gaze at the empty round metal stools in front of the stand. The clamour of the nightmarket seems to recede. As the stand quiets down, someone slowly takes shape on one of the stools. It's Ilya in a high school uniform, sitting where he used to sit when we would visit this particular stand after cram school, basketball practice or music lessons.

By that time we'd already changed the blue shorts every junior high school student wears for the colour-coded trousers of different high schools. It was like we'd walked out of a long dark tunnel to see the world suddenly open up. North of the pailou road was no longer a forbidden zone, and nobody cared any more if we went through the watergate. But even though we could go wherever we liked, we weren't so keen on expanding our territory like when we were kids. We'd just arrange to meet at this stand to eat an ice. Were we in tenth or eleventh grade that year? I can't be too sure. I don't remember whose idea it was to stop here for a treat, or for how long we came here to eat an ice every evening. It's so long ago after all, long enough ago for a bad colour photograph to fade to monochrome, to go completely yellow or brown.

My mood perks up a bit. I look sentimentally upon the mnemonic time traveller, who doesn't even glance at me. Though there is a bowl of ice in front of him he doesn't look down either. He just stares through the acrylic glass at the woman inside the stand, following her movements at the sink left and right like an oscillating pedestal fan.

The woman washing the dishes turns. I guessed right. A young woman. She reaches up to part her fringe, unveiling her eyes, which, crystal bright, like a block of ice on the shaver, glisten with a cold, wet light. It's her, no mistake! Even though she looks more mature, and is apparently now wearing make-up to cover the runes time has written on her face, her eyes are the key to her identity. They're a match for the eyes in my memory. I am sure she is that girl from long ago.

"It's incredible! She hasn't changed a bit," I imagine myself saying to Ilya sitting by my side. But when the young woman turns and comes over, Ilya immediately looks down and pretends to spoon his ice, nervously, like a student cheating on an exam who avoids the proctor's glance.

A slight smile plays at the corners of my mouth. I see Ilya beside me wearing a high school uniform, anxiously delivering melting spoonfuls of red bean and milk ice into his mouth. Their gazes must have met just now. Otherwise Ilya's face would not have gone as red as the beans in his bowl. "You useless git!" Brand would have said, but the round stool by Ilya was empty; Brand's high school hologram has not formed. Which was typical, as I now recall. In grade ten or eleven, Brand's dad was still doing time, paying the price of several years of his life for the sake of his glorious revolution. While his father was away, an aunt was in charge of Brand's life, a silent, determined, unobtrusive woman, a woman who didn't seem to have a shadow. Brand had become reticent and taciturn, too, under her care. Except for school, he spent most of his time at home, like a spider in its web in the corner of the room.

Looking at that empty stool, I don't feel sad. The year my grandmother passed away, Brand's father returned in style, stepping over the earthen pot of flame into his townhouse, king of his castle again. And when he went to college Brand left the social circles of his aunt's or his own devising. He, too, became his old boisterous self, that flexible fatso who liked to hook the elastic band to the ground with a single scissor kick to let everyone line up and jump over. But I'm not exactly overjoyed to see Ilya, who has time travelled from high school to appear beside me in holographic form, wearing an off-white short-sleeved shirt, navy trousers and a grass green canvas satchel. There's a black canvas violin bag at his feet. I'm confused as to why he would appear at the same time as me at our ice dessert stand. Since we started high school, the world had opened up for all of us, but the way it opened up for Ilya was different from the way it opened up for Brand and me. His marks on the high school entrance exam were good enough for him to go to a top school, but he chose second best: a school with an experimental music class. We knew that was his mother's decision. Ilya did not need to explain. The piano and violin music in which his house on the winding alleyway continued to swirl starting at sundown every day was all the explanation we needed.

"Hey! What are you doing here?" I ask Ilya.

Ilya lifts his head out of his shaved ice dessert, looking confused. His face is a surprise. Though he is wearing a high school uniform, he doesn't have the face of a callow youth. He has the same face as that night in the bar, the face that said it was afraid of music. A weary, gloomy face, with smile lines, deep creases extending from the sides of the nose to the corners of the mouth that only an over-ripe middle-aged man would have. "What are you talking about? Didn't you invite me here to eat an ice?" he says.

"Didn't you invite yourself?" I ask, not of Ilya in high school, but of Ilya as a middle-aged man who has appeared wraithlike beside me. But I can no longer tell which one I'm talking to. "Shouldn't you be practising piano or violin? Where'd you find the time to come eat an ice in the nightmarket at this time of day?"

Ilya doesn't reply to my question. He just smiles a silly smile and says: "Do you think she knows that we come to this shop just to see her?"

"Who knows?" I blurt. Then I remember that this isn't the first time Ilya has asked this question. That he asked it many years before on a summery night like this one, on a seat at this very ice dessert stand. How did I reply at the time? I can't remember any more. I just remember the question not the reply. Obviously, at the time I was just as concerned about the question as Ilya. "Who knows?" I repeat, probably the only reply my high school self would have been able to give. Wearing a white shirt and a black skirt, she would help shave ice every night, but neither Ilya nor I ever took any action to break the ice. We never wrote her a card or left a note. We never sent chocolates or flowers. We didn't dare strike up a conversation. Though we'd had more bowls of shaved ice than we cared to count, we'd never said anything to her. The slightly fat woman standing behind the stand scooping toppings onto shaved ice and manning the till must have been her mother. Positioned between us and the girl, she swallowed up every chance we might have had to talk. "I'm not sure if she knew that we were looking at her. But I bet you her mother knew," I tell Ilya sitting beside me. "Now that I've got a daughter of my own, I'm pretty sure she did."

Ilya looks at me in surprise. "You mean she's under her mother's watchful gaze all day long, and has to do everything she's told?"

"I didn't say that. Maybe she was happy to come to the nightmarket to help her mother out. Maybe she didn't want her mother to get too tired."

"So you still don't know if she knows we come here to admire her on the sly."

"Does it matter?" I said. "In retrospect, the point isn't whether she knew we were looking at her. The point is that we remember ourselves coming here to look at her."

"Of course, I know I come here just to look at her. Don't you?"

"I used to think I knew, but now I'm not so sure."

"What are you saying? Don't tell me you don't come here to see that girl," Ilya says, staring straight ahead again. He gazes at the toppings in the stand with a silly grin.

I follow Ilya's gaze. The stand is the same as always. But at some point the young woman washing dishes at the sink has changed out of her pink vest and denim shorts into a high school uniform, a short-sleeved white shirt and a black pleated skirt. No, she isn't the same woman. Better say that the woman in the pink vest and shorts has disappeared, and a warp in space and time has allowed the lithesome girl we worshipped in high school to reappear. What an incredible scene! Ilya is a temporal mismatch, with the exhausted face of a middle-aged man sticking out of the collar of a high school uniform, but the girl is not: when she turns I see the exact same face we never dared to look directly at, a youthful face, clean as a monochrome pencil sketch. It is as if someone has gone back to the past and taken her by the hand and brought her on a journey through the precipitousness and obscurity of time to the sink inside this bright ice and juice stand in the nightmarket.

A familiar feeling arises. It's not the feeling you get from a teen romance anime, with rose petals floating down from a hazy sky. That isn't the kind of scene that you would see in a nightmarket that smells of a medley of fried chicken, oyster omelette and medicinal pork chop soup. It's a familiar feeling of doubt. It's not self-doubt. It's not the feeling of inadequacy anyone might feel in the presence of an apparently perfect partner, doubting one has any quality that might match the other. I used to feel a sense of inadequacy like a faint brooding sorrow that incredibly used to force me into an abyss of depression. But after having experienced inadequacy a number of times, I now know it's a natural reaction, and banal: it's nothing special, nothing worth mentioning. The doubt I feel is about the existence of the girl, her appearance at the ice and juice stand in the nightmarket. I mean, why would she appear in the ice dessert stand in the nightmarket after all these years? I don't mean the girl that someone has taken by the hand and dragged through the precipitousness and darkness of time to appear before my eyes. I don't want to break the spell, because I want to keep indulging in the scene; but I know that she and Ilya are both fantasies. They're both figments of my imagination that at the moment I wouldn't bother doubting. My doubt is of a different kind. It's a doubt I felt the first time me and Ilya ever saw this high school girl in the nightmarket. I doubted that it was even possible for such a clean-looking girl to appear among all the disorder and dirt. How could she have? And even if she could have, why had we, growing up in the nightmarket, never seen her before?

"A nightmarket feeds a whole bunch of people. How in the world could you have seen every single face?" In his high school uniform, Ilya seems to have read my adult mind.

"We never saw her in elementary or junior high school," I remind him. "If she lived in the neighbourhood, she should have gone to the same school as us. But we'd never seen her before."

"You know what they say about the eighteen metamorphoses girls undergo. Perhaps we never noticed her because she was an ugly duckling?"

"Do you think she could have possibly been an ugly duckling?" I ask. Ilya immediately shakes his head, recanting the conjecture he has just made. "Her appearance in a place like this always seemed weird to me," I say.

"Her mother is selling ice in the nightmarket; it's right and proper for her to come and help, nothing weird about it."

"Do you remember the twins who sold guavas in the nightmarket? Strange, they were girls, just like her, but I never felt that there was anything odd about them spending every evening behind their stand."

"Isn't that because you've got used to them sitting on the stools washing guavas every afternoon?"

"It's not about that. And it didn't have anything to do with their frumpy looks, I don't think," I say. "It was a basic sense of 'existence', like a chemical reaction, between personal qualities and environment. No matter how you looked at it, the nightmarket was not a good environment, but some people were a perfect fit. They could completely blend in, and wouldn't stand out in any way, like a sugar cube dissolved in a mud puddle. The twins were like that. My sense of their existence was very strong, as solid as cement. I always thought they would grow old with the nightmarket, that as long as the nightmarket existed they would remain there."

"But I don't see them this evening. Where are they, the guava sisters?" asks Ilya. But he is just asking for the sake of it, obviously not interested in the sisters. "I don't really understand what you're trying to say," he says. "I just have the feeling that the girl helping out behind the ice dessert and fruit juice stand won't be here for long. We never used to see her, which means she might never come again. We've just happened to see her at a time when she just happens to be here. Someday soon she might disappear."

"She gave you a strong sense of 'inexistence'. This I can totally understand. I had the same feeling. I never thought a girl like that belonged in a nightmarket."

"Then where does she belong?"

"A better place than this."

"Any place is better than this, right?"

"But it's not an easy place to leave," I tell Ilya. I am thinking of my mother, who used to always complain about the place and declare she wanted to move away but who now has no desire to leave. "Have you ever wondered whether your sense that the girl didn't belong in the nightmarket had anything to do with the fact that your own sense of inexistence was so strong? That the reason why you always came to this particular shop to eat shaved ice was because of how badly you wanted to leave?"

Ilya turns to look at me, his exhausted, adult face apparently surprised a second time. Until now, his gaze has been following the movements of the high school girl inside the stand. "Yes, I should be going," Ilya says, then falls silent. "It's already past my practice time. I better not go home too late." He stands up, shoulders his grass green canvas satchel, picks up the black canvas violin tote and slings it over the other shoulder. "Didn't you say that the point is that we know why we come here?"

Ilya gets up, gradually grows distant, and finally disappears into the crowd. I should say I see the violin case that covers quite a big part of Ilya's body shrink slowly into the distance. I suddenly feel a warm, thick familiarity, like a stiff gust of summer wind. Of course, the scene I'm seeing is still the one I just imagined, because we always used to leave together after eating an ice; neither of us would leave alone. The gust of familiarity I just mentioned must have blown down Ilya's alley. We would walk back together from the nightmarket and say goodbye under the dim light of that squat little street lamp at the entrance to his alley. Occasionally I would look back and watch him walking down the winding alley, which was really no wider than a fire access. I would wonder why the alley always seemed so long at this particular time of day. We would have said our thing before bidding each other farewell, but today we did not. Ilya just up and left, leaving me with a sense of things left unsaid, of something I need to get off my chest. I want to tell Ilya that when I said I "knew"' why we went to eat ice at that particular shop, I meant to say "remember". The main point is that I still remember how we used to patronize the shaved ice stand to see that girl, and that's enough. I have not forgotten, I still remember. Or I should say that I forgot, but now I remember.

Ling-ling finishes her grass jelly ice and whines that she wants to go to the next stand to play pinball. I take out my wallet, get out a bill for the boss lady, and look towards the back of the stand. The girl in the uniform has at some point returned to her own space and time, and the girl with make-up has taken her place. I guess I shouldn't call her a girl. She's a mature woman now, who has started using artificial chemical means to conceal the runes of time. Even if she's as beautiful as ever, and even if the sense of her "inexistence" in the nightmarket is as strong as ever, she's changed. I can't help thinking that even if she knew Ilya and I used to come to admire her on the sly, she must have forgotten now.

I am pulling Ling-ling's hand away from the stand when I am stopped by a voice calling me from behind.

"Hey, I still haven't given you your change!"

I turn my head; the speaker is the boss lady who just now inadvertently showed me her bosom. She offers me a middle-aged woman's smile.

I walk back, reach out my hand, and let her place six ten dollar coins and one five dollar coin, slowly, coin by coin, in my open palm.

"You haven't been here to eat ice in a long, long time," she says.

"Yeah, it's really been a long time," I say, putting her off, not surprised the boss lady should recognize me, given that Ilya and I came to eat ice here practically every single night for over a year. I've said it before:

anyone who's been a parent is all-knowing when it comes to his or her children.

"I remember you. You used to come with your friend to eat ice. Time sure flies. Back then, we were still in high school. And look how big our kids have got now!"

"You… you…" I see the freckled face in front of me sitting atop a fleshy frame, a fair distance away from youth. I'm so surprised I can hardly speak. "Then… so…" I point at the young woman on the other side of the stand. "Is that your daughter?"

"As if! My daughter just started junior high. That's my little cousin come to help out in the shop."

"You… you two look a lot alike."

"You really think so?" the boss lady says, her eyes blooming. "Everyone says we're the flowers of the nightmarket, that we look so much alike we could be sisters."

"What a lovely pair." I put the coins in my pocket and feel the hand holding the change trembling slightly.

"Come again. Next time bring your friend." The lady waves goodbye.

"I will," I say, leading Ling-ling away. As we walk towards the pinball stand, I don't dare look back even once.

34

Going Against the Flow

Ilya said we just had to keep going upstream, but we walked along the riverside all afternoon without reaching anywhere an orangutan might want to live. The sky went from blue to purple, and the sun kept passing behind layers of clouds in the west, appearing for shorter periods each time. Finally, when we saw it wasn't going to come out any more, we started to get anxious.

"Why haven't we made it to the zoo?" Brand asked.

"How much longer do we have to walk?" I couldn't help adding.

Holding the orangutan's hand, Ilya kept walking, not looking back. We kept grumbling until Ilya finally stopped and said, rather crankily: "If you hadn't spent so much time playing by the water, we'd be there by now."

Ilya was right, but only half right. This was the longest me and Brand had ever spent by the riverside, and the furthest upstream we'd ever gone. Everything was new and therefore noteworthy, no matter how ordinary. Besides catching crabs, Brand discovered a dead dog caught in the rocks by the riverside, and then another. Standing quite far away, we took turns throwing rocks at the dogs, which were caught in cracks at the shore or lying on rocks in the river, not only to see if they were really dead, but also to see who was the sharpest shot, the one who could scare away the most flies. Further upstream, we saw a small wooden ferry carrying a dozen passengers towards the other shore. The punter stood aft, pushing a pole twice as tall as he was. Me and Brand waited quite a while on the dock, to see whether the little ferry boat would bring back another load of passengers. But we didn't wait long enough to see the return ferry, just a man swimming over in his birthday suit. At first we assumed he was in a hurry and couldn't wait for the ferry, but he didn't have a bag. He came on shore, took a piss in a thicket of grass and dived back into the water to swim back. We stopped constantly as we made our way upstream. One time we watched one group of fishermen cut earthworms in half, bait their hooks and cast their lines, and another group ride out in a big aluminium tub buoyed up by an inner tube from a truck tyre to cast their net. We hunted for wild duck eggs in the grass. We even skipped stones: Brand managed to fire off a perfect seven, but I kept falling short. We dawdled, it's true, and sometimes we had so much fun we'd almost forgotten why we were going upstream. But Ilya had overlooked the fact that it was never us who stopped and refused to go any further, it was that orangutan, every time.

"If that ape of yours hadn't stopped to rest every few steps, we wouldn't have run off to play," Brand said.

"Yeah, and if your ape'd stayed put in the pushcart we'd be at the zoo already," I chimed in.

Ilya stopped and said: "Harriet needs her rest. Her feet aren't meant for walking, certainly not long distances." I didn't know if Ilya had stopped because he wanted to rest or whether the orangutan was planning on taking another rest on the ground. "The encyclopaedia said the furthest adult orangutans can walk in a day over flat terrain is three kilometres. Harriet's already made good headway in walking so far. If there were trees at the riverside, we wouldn't be able to keep up with her even if we ran."

Again, Ilya was only half right. There weren't many trees tall enough to swing from on our side of the river, but there was a dense grove of tall trees on the other side. The sun made another brief appearance, stretching shadows over the river, casting shade upon us as we slogged upstream. The shade pressed down upon the orangutan, apparently reminding it of something. It shook off Ilya's hand and turned to face the river, hooting and calling so piercingly and resonantly that me and Brand had to cover our ears.

"What's wrong with it? Will you please tell it to stop hooting? Everyone nearby will hear," I said.

"She's not hooting, she's crying." Ilya tenderly stroked the sparse hair on the orangutan's head. "She's in a bad mood. Let her have a good cry. In any case we've walked far enough, and there's nobody around to hear."

"How can an orangutan be in a bad mood? I think it's just hungry," Brand said, rubbing his round little tummy.

I knew the hungry one was Brand. Which was partly my fault, because I'd told him not to pick yams when he had the chance. Except for water he hadn't had anything to put in his stomach all day. Luckily, the orangutan only hooted a few minutes. We kept walking upstream, not mentioning the distance or food. There wasn't much daylight left. Among us we only had a single watch, which did not work. Nobody wanted to be the first to say: "It's almost dark." We continued along the dirt path between the grass and the water, in single file, with Ilya and the orangutan leading the way, but proceeding at a very slow pace. The speed at which the orangutan twisted its bottom with every step had not changed, but I no longer found it amusing; I just quietly held up the rear. The river got narrower and narrower, the scenery more and more desolate, and I felt more and more anxious. It really was almost dark, and we hadn't seen any sign of the fabled zoo. We might have to sleep outside.

Sleep outside! I shivered. We hadn't considered the possibility while we were planning the operation. It hadn't even occurred to me that we might not go home for dinner. What would happen if I spent the night out without saying anything? How would I be punished? I could already picture it: it would be just like when I was forced to stand in front of the altar in the family room for stealing a bill out of my father's wallet. My father and mother and my long-widowed grandmother would pace around me and tell me off in an amalgam of Mandarin and Taiwanese, and poke my head. My mother might start crying and blame my father for not making enough money to move us away from this awful neighbourhood, where a kid in sixth grade would go bad, not only running away from home but also stealing people's orangutans. What would he do next?

At the thought, I felt even more anxious. Unconsciously, I started walking slower, and even fell a dozen steps behind Ilya and the orangutan. Seeing Ilya plodding doggedly upstream, I couldn't help wondering whether he, too, was worried about the possibility of spending the night outside. No, Ilya had spent the night in the tree fort not long before. He'd slammed the door and run away from home and let his hysterical mother search for him all night long. He'd done it once, and he might do it again. No matter how strict his mother was, no matter how closely she watched him, Ilya might still run away from home a couple of times, until maybe his mother would give up trying to control him. Absolutely. Ilya wouldn't mind spending the night outside, not one bit. What about Brand? He'd never done anything like that. Would he dare to stay out, without letting his father know? I imagined he would. Brand kept saying our operation was revolutionary, that it was the resistance of the oppressed. We were teaching the man in the beret a lesson. Just this morning, surrounded by countless policemen in white helmets on the square in front of the temple, Brand's father had unfurled a banner that said pretty much the same thing. Brand's father wouldn't blame him, would he? His father had no cause to oppress a fellow revolutionary, did he? No matter how much trouble Brand caused, his father should say the same thing as he had after the jazz drum incident in just as tender a voice: "I don't blame you. Now you are free. Go out and play." Brand must not have been too worried about how late it was.

I looked back to see whether Brand really didn't give a damn. But I didn't see Brand, just a winding dirt path pinched between clumps of awn grass and the rocky shoreline. It wasn't just getting dark any more, it was dark. There wasn't anyone on the path, just constellations of kamikaze bugs.

"Brand's gone!" I cried.

Ilya stopped, and he and the orangutan turned back to look together. "What happened? Wasn't he bringing up the rear?"

"I don't know. I wasn't looking back just now, so I didn't see if he was following or not."

"Maybe he found something else to play with, or maybe he stopped to rest. Let's wait for him here," Ilya said, apparently unruffled. He looked around to make sure that there was no one around, sat down on a rotten tree trunk by the side of the path, and wiped the sweat off his brow. The orangutan sat by his side, imitating his movements, raising a hairy hand to its face.

I was still standing there looking around frantically, about as far from calm as it's possible to be. If Brand had found something fun to do, he would have taken me along. And there was no way he would have been too tired to go any further. He had the best endurance of any of us. Especially considering the snail's pace at which Ilya and the orangutan walked. Even my grandmother would have been able to keep up! I bet Brand had gone back the other way. What a coward! He must have been so afraid of getting in trouble that he went home without telling us. Revolution, my arse! He was just like the Founding Father of the Republic of China, Sun Yat-sen, escaping out the back door.

"Sit down and wait, and try and think about something else. A watched pot never boils," Ilya said. He opened the backpack on the orangutan's back, and got out a long, thin, mud-caked yam. He didn't eat it himself, just broke it in two and handed it to the orangutan. That's how I found out that when me and Brand had been watching the fishermen or the ferry, Ilya had been stealing yams for the orangutan to eat. No wonder the orangutan was content to follow Ilya the whole day. No wonder hunger didn't drive it to revolution.

I did not feel hungry at all, maybe because my eyes had already eaten too much of dusk. Having swallowed the sun, the hills were so close to us now, and the levee had shrunk. Further upstream, you couldn't even see a levee. The river was still fairly wide, but there was less water in it, just a couple of rivulets wriggling along in the rocky riverbed. It was quiet all around. There were no cars running or people talking, no bugs buzzing or birds chirping, just a faint hiss of wind and water. We had walked the whole day, left the city behind and crossed into the upper reaches of the river. The strange thing was that the zoo had not yet appeared. The zoo would not be up in the mountains, would it?

"Still looking around? Sit down and rest a bit."

"But it's almost dark," I finally managed to say.

"I know," Ilya said.

"But look, we're almost at the end of the levee. Look how close the mountains are. We must be pretty close to the source of the river. Are we supposed to just keep on walking?"

Ilya did not reply, pretending he had not heard me, I guess. Facing away from the river, he stood up, his gaze passing clear on through me.

"Huh?" Ilya said softly, reaching up to scratch his ear. Sitting on the log, the ape imitated Ilya's gesture, scratching the nape of its neck. "This place seems familiar. I think I've been here before."

"You've been here before? Is it on the way to the zoo?" I asked excitedly. Then I stomped my foot. "No, what am I saying? You've never been to the zoo. You've never even gone through the watergate."

"I've been here before," Ilya said, sounding much more sure of himself. He walked up a little earthen mound by the path and gazed at the levee. Then he turned around and cast his gaze towards the pitted riverbed. "This must be the place. I've been here before. Do you believe me? My mother brought me here when I was very small."

"Impossible. Didn't your mother forbid you from going near the river? How could she bring you up here?"

"I don't really remember. It was so long ago, so long that it seems hazy now, like a dream. But I do have some impressions of this place. Strange, the river was pretty wide that time, and the water was yellow, rushing and rumbling down from the hills. I remember my mother got me to kneel on the levee, and prostrate myself before the river. She was holding a long bamboo pole, with a shirt of my father's attached to the end."

Something came crashing down in my mind, call it understanding. "You… you mean this is where your dad disappeared?"

Ilya nodded. "Must've been. I think his motorcycle was found parked on the levee. But the chemical plant that was dumping toxic effluent into the river is gone. And there aren't any backhoes and trucks stealing sand and gravel any more." He looked around again as if to verify his memory. "I remember some other things. I didn't cry, because I had no idea what had happened. My mother didn't cry either. She just started yelling, cursing my father, calling him an idiot, a moron, stubborn, obstinate."

"Why would your mother curse your father?"

"Probably because he didn't know how to go with the flow. 'What kind of river inspector are you?' she often said. 'If you meet a mountain just go around it like a river. You've spent your whole life watching rivers without learning anything from them.'"

"Your father was a hero. Everyone talks about how great he was. Not like my father. He's never done anything to be proud of in his entire life. All he knows how to do is drink."

"I don't remember him any more, and I don't know what was so great about him," Ilya said, his voice faint. "I don't remember him hugging me or holding my hand. I don't remember him talking to me. I think he must have, but I was too small to remember. I wish he'd died a few years later, so I could remember a little more about him. But… I'd rather have an alcoholic for a father than a hero. That way, we wouldn't be forever missing a family member, and I could see him every day."

Ilya walked back to the orangutan and sat down on a rotten trunk by the path. He looked down, slouched, and fell silent, like he had just finished playing a piece of piano music. He was looking at a blade of grass by his foot or a little stone, falling once again into a state of silent waiting. I was familiar with this posture of his, but it was a bit different today. In the past, Ilya could only sit all alone when he finished performing the spider and egret magic on the keyboard, no matter whether he was at home in the shack with tyres on the roof or in a splendid theatre on a spotlit stage. But now Ilya adopted the same posture with an orangutan sitting beside him. The orangutan reached a long hairy red arm around Ilya's neck and put its hand on his shoulder. Ilya looked over, his eyes moistening up. In the dull light of dusk, I couldn't tell whether he was surprised or grateful. Just then, the backpack the ape was carrying sagged open and the iron chain inside slid out and hung down like a snake. Ilya hurried to collect the chain, winding it around his elbow and putting it back in.

I stood there, watching Ilya and the ape, not knowing what to say to comfort him. It was Ilya who ended up speaking first.

"You go back."

"What?"

"It's almost dark. You've missed dinner, but if you go back now, the worst that would happen is that you'd get yelled at."

"What about you?"

"I'm just going to keep on walking upriver."

"By yourself?"

"No, not by myself."

"But what about Brand? He's gone. Maybe he went home. If I go back, too, won't you be on your own?"

"Don't worry about me. You can go back," Ilya said, smiling. "Harriet's here, and my father will accompany me the rest of the way. I'm not alone."

Ilya did not seem like he was sulking or joking. It was like he was earnestly describing something right in front of us. I looked and saw that his eyes were shining again, just like the last time in the tree fort, with a blinding light. At first, I thought Ilya's eyes were burning with resolution and vision and passion and hope, but then I somehow realized the light in his eyes was mainly a reflection. It wasn't the sun; the sun had gone down. It wasn't a lamp; both sides of the river were dark. There were a few residential lights in the distance downriver, but they were too dim to account for the gleam in Ilya's eyes. All daylight had disappeared, and darkness had risen up from the ground to swallow all shadow, yet Ilya's eyes were shining. He must've seen something bright, a ghostly torch, or a peerless sun hanging in the night sky that only he could see. It must be welcoming him to go further.

The idea that Ilya had seen something, no matter what it was, set something off in my heart. A cascade. A flood of hot blood burst into my brain that left me wide awake. Only now did I realize what we were doing. Although Brand had described it as a revolution in our secret meeting in the tree fort, I had always seen it as an exciting game of exploration. I thought it would be fun to cross the line and take the risk of being caught and made to stand in front of the altar, to help free the orangutan from the man in the beret, who used a stick to enforce his domination. Now I realized that the orangutan wasn't the only one the operation was supposed to save, that this was also an operation to save Brand, who seemed to have headed home. And even myself.

"Go back now while you still can see the way." Holding the orangutan's hand, Ilya started walking upriver with comically slow steps.

I watched their receding figures, momentarily speechless. Just then, another impulse bubbled precariously up: I decided to go with Ilya. Only in that moment did I truly join the revolution. It didn't matter how dark it got, or even if we had to spend the night outside. I had to complete this journey. No matter what the price.

"Wait for me!" I called. I ran a few steps to catch up with them.

"What's wrong?"

"I want to go with you!"

"You don't plan on going back?"

"No, I'm going to stay."

"You should know what you're getting yourself into. Won't you be scared if we have to spend the night outside?"

"I'm not scared."

"Liar."

"Aren't you scared?"

"I'm not scared at all."

"You're the liar."

"No, I'm not."

"All right, I'm scared. You admit that you're scared too."

"I'm not scared."

"You're lying."

"Am not."

35

Pretending to Be a Hero

Me and Ilya had got Brand all wrong.

After resolving to resist to the bitter end, to follow Ilya and the orangutan upriver, come what may, I'd only walked a few steps when I heard the sound of someone thudding down the path behind us. We turned to look and saw he whom we thought had skedaddled home, Brand.

"I knew I could catch you! Good thing you guys walk so slow," Brand said, winded. He walked over holding a big plastic bag. The smell of bread wafted into our nostrils.

Brand hadn't disappeared because he was afraid. He'd spied a red bread truck go by on the levee. It wasn't your regular loaf-shaped vehicle, local parlance for a van. It was a true bread truck loaded with fresh bread, the kind that wends its way through the suburbs and countryside peddling bread. "Fresh BREAD, buy some fresh BREAD, you won't regret it!" When Brand saw the truck, he went chasing after it without a second thought. He'd chased it two kilometres before he finally caught it in a traditional three-wing farmhouse with a courtyard for drying grain. He used all the money we were carrying, about a hundred dollars, to buy two loaves of bread and a bag of assorted buns.

"I never thought a hundred dollars could buy so much bread," said Ilya, wide-eyed.

"As if it could," Brand said proudly. "When the boss saw how hard I'd run to catch up, he was moved by my perseverance and stuffed a few more buns in my bag for free."

We had provisions and a full contingent again. We could regroup and make a fresh start. But before we did, Ilya and Brand had another spat. Brand said the bread was fresh from the oven, and we'd not had anything to eat all day, so we should sit down and fill our bellies. Ilya said it was getting darker and darker and we should walk as far as we could before night's curtain closed. I had a better idea than wasting what little light we had arguing and letting the bread go cold. Better to eat as we walked.

So that's what we did. Our jaws went up and down chewing pineapple peel buns, buns with peanut butter or strawberry jam, while our feet went up and down over hill and dale along the rocks, sinks or mounds of the winding riverside path. Even the orangutan, who'd been clutching Ilya's elbow, let go and learned how to eat a slab of apple bread piece by piece like we were doing. I have to say that it was really an enjoyable way of proceeding, like we were on a class trip. The only shortcoming was that the bread slowed us down even more. By the time we'd finished half a bag of bread and our tummies had stopped moaning in protest, the sky was completely black.

At first I thought that my eyes would get used to the dark as day yielded ground to night, or even that I'd see in the dark like a cat. Now I realized how wrong I'd been. Night and day were completely different propositions, and though they blurred into each other there seemed to be a clear line between them. When I finished the fragrant bread, it was like I'd swallowed the last ray of daylight and stepped over the line between day and night without noticing. Just now I'd clearly been able to make out the path. Now the night was pitch black and I couldn't see a thing.

We stumbled along a short distance, then the troop came to a halt. The orangutan suddenly escaped Ilya's grip and sat down on the ground, unwilling to get up again. No matter how Ilya coaxed it, it wasn't moving its bum one inch.

"What do we do now?" I asked.

"Looks like we find somewhere to spend the night," Ilya said, tousling the orangutan's hair. "Harriet's walked the whole day. She must be too tired to move."

Brand took it upon himself to tell us to wait there and he would go round to see if there was a good place nearby for us to camp. He fished out a flashlight and batteries from the bookbag and illuminated the ground by the river and our three faces staring woodenly at one another. Me and Ilya exclaimed: "We have a flashlight! Why didn't you take it out earlier?" Brand smiled a silly smile and said: "Sorry, I just remembered I had it."

I didn't want to berate Brand, because we'd just blamed him unjustly for going AWOL. And now we had another practical tool besides the water bottle, which was a good thing. Not that the orangutan thought so. The flashlight didn't fire up its determination to keep walking. When Brand turned the flashlight on, it held its hands in front of its eyes, pursed its lips and shook its head, stubbornly refusing the gift of light.

Brand disappeared into a thicket of grass with the flashlight, leaving me and Ilya in the dark, which was even deeper now that our eyes had adjusted to the artificial light. Just now we'd still been able to make our way in the dark, but now not even Ilya dared to make a move. Luckily, Brand came back in no time. He bounded along, like he had discovered the new world. For us, his discovery was just as significant, though we couldn't know that in the inky black of night. Brand excitedly pulled Ilya along, and for some strange reason the orangutan was now willing to follow. With the flashlight leading the way, we went through the thicket, down a slope, and over a few rocks and a short bridge of wooden planks, until we came to an unoccupied building. As Brand put it, it was a place with a roof and a door, a place where we could spend the night.

It was a farmhouse at the edge of a vegetable patch. There was a door, but no windows. "Farmhouse" is probably an overstatement. It was just a crude shack the farmer had thrown up to store tools and fertilizer and to sit out the rain. It was barely taller than we were. But to Brand, there was nothing ramshackle about it. Like he was about to show us around his own place, he opened the crooked wooden door and shone his flashlight in. There wasn't much space inside, barely space for half a ping pong table. In the corner was a waist-high blue plastic barrel with a board for a cover and some kind of liquid inside. On the thin wall of panels nailed to a simple frame was a row of hooks hung with a few towels, a coolie hat, two black sunsleeves, a raincoat and rainboots, a pack of coarse cotton gloves in a plastic bag with red stripes, and a mud-caked rechargeable handheld searchlight. On the dirt floor was a hoe, a pick axe, a rake and a shovel, just lying there in a pile like they'd been tossed in from the doorway. Clearly the master of the mansion had, upon finishing a hard day's work, been so tired he'd had no energy left to tidy his little toolshed.

"Pretty good, huh?" Brand said. He turned the searchlight on, and because the battery seemed pretty full, he turned the flashlight in his hand off. "We just have to move the things on the floor out and there will be enough space for the three of us for sure."

"But there's four of us," Ilya said.

"Four of us?" I asked, the skin of my scalp going numb.

"Me, you, Brand…" Ilya closed his fourth finger and said: "and Harriet."

I let out a sigh of relief. And I thought the ghost of Ilya's father might be joining us for the night. Brand laughed and said: "Okay, four including the orangutan. But four makes things a bit awkward. I don't know whether there is enough space on the floor for four of us."

Brand was worried over nothing, because before we'd finished moving the tools out of the shed, the orangutan climbed up onto the board on the plastic barrel. It buried its face in the crooks of its arms, curled into a ball, and in no time had closed its eyes.

Now that our accommodation was ready, I was delirious. At first it was a revolutionary resolution, a willingness to put it all on the line that decided me against going home for the night. But now I was in the mood for camping. I had never been camping before, and neither had Brand. But Brand claimed to know what counted as true camping: you set up the tent, build a bonfire and sit around the fire, singing and dancing and playing games until you're too tired to stay awake and you retire to the tent. I suggested we make a fire too. Brand and Ilya immediately said no. Ilya pointed out we were on the run, and if we made a fire, or even turned on the flashlight, we'd probably get discovered and caught. Brand's reason was simple: we didn't have matches or a lighter, so unless we could make fire by rubbing sticks or sparking stones like savages, we were out of luck.

To be honest, camping without a fire or any fun activities was actually pretty boring. Although it was dark out, it was too early for bedtime. By the light of the moon that occasionally made it through the cloud cover, me and Brand took a turn around the vegetable patch.

At first we were hoping to find gourds or fruits to steal, but there wasn't anything there. The patch was probably about the size of a basketball court. There were trellises and long, well-hoed mounds, but whatever seeds the farmer had planted had only produced a few shoots. Yup, the field was freshly planted. Then we walked to the riverside. Brand turned on the flashlight and shone it on the tranquil surface of the river, sparkling the dark water with innumerable points of light. I'd never seen the likes of it. Amazed, I knelt down for a closer look and saw little shrimp floating head-up in the water. They were motionless, stiff, yellow-eyed.

Ilya didn't come along, saying he had to stay behind and take care of the orangutan. We ran back to tell him our interesting discovery, and found him sitting by the door, his back against the wall, his arms around his knees. He was looking up at the sky, unmoving, a bit like the hypnotized shrimp. Me and Brand did the same. The stars were out, as was the moon. There were clouds, which we could see, and wind, which we could not. The stars and the moon seemed fixed in place, just sitting there in the night sky, paying no attention to the dark clouds below, which kept on floating quickly by.

"If the night were completely clear, and we watched the stars long enough, we'd be able to see them slowly move," Ilya suddenly said. "Too bad! With the interference of the moonlight and the occasional floating cloud, we can't observe the motion of the constellations."

"The constellations won't move, unlike us; we've really come a long way," Brand said, smugly. "Don't you think we've done something really amazing? We've walked all this way to somewhere so remote with just our legs to carry us."

"How far have we walked in all?" I asked.

"I don't know. At least a hundred kilometres," Brand said.

"Stop bragging. The most an orangutan can walk in a day is three kilometres. How could we have walked a hundred?" Ilya asked.

"Why do you think your friend is snoring so loud in the toolshed?"

"I'd be surprised if we walked more than fifteen kilometres today."

"Let's split the difference and say we walked fifty," Brand said with a wink. "That'll freak them out."

Ilya didn't pay Brand any attention. But as for myself, I couldn't help wondering. "Staying out all night should be enough to freak them out," I said, knowing that by "them"' Brand meant our classmates at school. I meant it differently. I did not know what time it was; it had been dark for quite a while. My family must be eating now, I thought. My mother would have wiped the table with an oily rag and set out the homely dishes she had just prepared, maybe not my favourite dish of fried tomato with egg but certainly a plate of pickles for my dad to go with his rice wine. My dad always drank before dinner, not much though, at most a couple of glasses, and regardless he would just keep on eating and drinking until he had to go out on his scooter to all the inns in the area to get the lists of guests. My grandmother would probably not notice that I hadn't come home for dinner either, because for the longest time she had been preparing her own Buddhist vegetarian meals and taking them at the tea table. The only one who would discover that I wasn't there was my mother. Of course, she would call out as she always did: "Help serve the rice, Danny!" And then, without looking back, she would pass the rice scoop and the empty bowls back before discovering that nobody was behind her to take them. Only then would she realize I had not come home. Would that frighten her? I guessed it would. But I wondered whether before she panicked she would berate my father, blaming my absence on the fact that he didn't make enough to move us somewhere else.

At that I realized that the resolution that had fired my soul a couple of hours before had somehow cooled down with nightfall. There were quite a few sounds out here in the dark. We heard frogs and toads croaking, like someone was shaking an ancient bamboo rattle. We heard insects chirping, too, though Ilya insisted that insects did not chirp, that they produced sound by rubbing their appendages together. And we heard the river water hissing, but it didn't seem right to call it river water. This far upriver, I thought, we should call it creek water. Those sounds entwined and echoed through the night, and not even the occasional plaintive bird cry or gust of wind could drive them away or shut them up. Instead of getting drowned out, they got clearer and clearer. I heard a voice in my mind say: You idiot! Who are you, pretending to be a hero? This revolution of yours is not against the man in the beret, or against your family, or even against yourself. It's against the night, the endless, all-encompassing night! Haven't you heard that people cannot understand what darkness is like when it's light? Your rash decision to spend the night out before sunset was the easy part. Now you'll know the bitter taste of regret!

I wondered whether Ilya and Brand were also hearing voices, but Brand had thought of a way to drown out all the noise, both the sounds that echoed through the night and the voices in our head. He picked up a stone, and threw it into the blackness ahead of him. Initially me and Ilya did not know what he was doing, but the point was immediately obvious. Brand was playing Bomb the Pond. The creek that was gurgling past not far from us was deep enough at certain points to form pools of water that were shallow enough to leave a few rocks on the riverbed exposed. The rocks that Brand sent flying into the night echoed back several different sounds. Sometimes it was the sound of a little rock smashing into a big one. Sometimes the rock fell into the sand or the dirt by the creek, a muffled sound. And sometimes the rock fell into the deeper water at the centre of the pond, the best, most thrilling sound of all. It wasn't your typical splash: there was about a second of silence, a quarter rest according to Ilya, between the initial *ker* and the final *plunk*.

That was the sound we liked the best. And so we took turns trying to see who could throw the most accurately. It was a lot of fun playing Brand's Bomb the Pond game, trying to hit invisible targets in the night. Victory and defeat depended mainly on luck; it was as addictive as gambling. We threw stone after stone, until it felt like our throwing arms were as sore as our legs after a day of walking.

This game made us realize something: that besides firelight, making noise was the best way to drive away fear in the night. So we started talking, talking incessantly, talking about everything, talking randomly. We talked about people we knew and people we did not know. But mainly we talked about people who appeared on television. Especially cartoon characters. We talked about Super Dimension Fortress Macross, Saint Seiya: Knights of the Zodiac, Mobile Suit, He-Man and the Masters of the Universe, and Doraemon. Ilya clearly knew a lot less about cartoons than me and Brand, but you could tell he was interested. He kept on asking questions and discussing our answers. I was careful not to mention my favourite cartoon, the Thunder Cats. Although the story of the Thunder Cats fighting the mutants is fantastic, the planet on which those five cats lived exploded, and they had to leave their home and wander through space. Somehow, it did not seem right to mention that story at a time like this. I thought that Ilya would tell us about his father, memories of good times together, or how his dad had heroically tried to stop the bad guys from destroying the world. After all, we did not know very much about his father. But Ilya didn't even mention his father. Instead he talked about Sherlock Holmes and Arsène Lupin. Which led to another disagreement. Me and Brand thought the French thief turned detective was better than his English counterpart, because he was like a divine dragon whose tail you could not see, always giving the slip to any pursuit. Ilya did not agree. He insisted that Sherlock Holmes was the best detective in the world, and that the story of the French detective was a lie.

This was the most serious disagreement we had had in the course of our expedition. We had a huge fight over it, and wasted a lot of time. We fought until even the wind blew up. We fought until the moon and the stars hid for good behind the clouds. We fought until a drastic drop in temperature gave us all gooseflesh. But everyone held to his own opinion, not giving any ground. Still arguing, we got up, returned to the toolshed, shut the door behind us, and turned on the searchlight that the owner of the vegetable patch had left behind. This was the first time this evening that the three of us had squeezed into the toolshed. No, I should say the four of us. The orangutan was still snoozing on the lid of the plastic barrel. No longer curled up into a ball, it had now relaxed and was lying on its side. One leg was dangling over the edge, but it was sleeping so soundly it didn't notice.

Seeing the orangutan fast asleep, we were in no mood to continue our argument. Avoiding the nails sticking out of the walls, we each claimed a corner of the toolshed and sat down on the floor. We kept on whispering, but in fits and starts, with longer and longer rests between our remarks. For a moment, I could have sworn we were back in the tree fort.

36
Tearing Down the Fort

We stood there watching the day they tore down the tree fort. I remember it was pretty hot that day. We all had crew cuts and scorched scalps in the blistering summer after seventh grade.

They had not made the trip just to tear down our tree fort, but to move all of the lumber in the yard into storage. They were sent by the owner of the building supply store. Judging from the way they were working, the owner must have told them something like: "Restore the yard to the way it was before!" or "Don't leave a single board behind." Otherwise, why would they have bothered to climb the mango tree and tear down all of the boards we had nailed to bough and branch?

Of course, we had made the trip just to see them tear down our tree fort. We didn't know until Brand spotted workers on the woodpile and a truck parked outside. He ran frantically downstairs and over to my home like someone who was witnessing a murder. Out of breath, he said: "Our secret base is about to get obliterated. It'll be gone, there'll be nothing left, and we'll never see it again. Do you understand?"

Recalling the incident now, a quarter of a century later, I can only say that at the time Brand was still a child. He overreacted. Actually, we'd stopped playing in the tree fort long before the workers appeared. Our parents didn't forbid us, and the tree fort was still there, but we lost interest in going to the abandoned yard after the curtain closed on the orangutan incident. We let the lookout shake in the wind and bake in the sun. For about a year, we hadn't mentioned our secret base, nor did we seem to care if our treasure trove in the woodpile was still as damp as it had always been. It was like we'd discovered that the old Japanese-style residence everyone said was haunted really was haunted.

Brand must have looked like he'd seen a ghost the night his father was taken away. Though we hadn't seen him at the temple that day, several days later someone came knocking another time on the roll-up metal door in the middle of the night. This time, Brand's father had no plan to flee. Instead of the window at the back of the house, he just opened the door to Brand's room. He woke Brand up and admonished him grim-faced to stay out of trouble, to take care of himself and the family like a man, stuff like that. Then he went downstairs, rolled up the door, and went with the people waiting outside, not to set foot in his own home for the next five years. They also took away all of the things in the rooftop addition, including the printer, boxes of lead type, stacks of leaflets, rolls of fabric, bunches of bamboo poles, clubs and two gasoline drums full of flammable liquid. Those people kept going up and down, and Brand kept following them up and down the stairs, with tears in his eyes. When they finally left they did not pull down the door. Brand hunkered down under the arcade in front of his house bawling. He kept crying until his aunt got a call and came over to take him back into the house.

I did not see any of these things with my own eyes, nor did Brand ever tell me about them. And though I can relate them to you now, nobody ever told me what actually happened that night. I can't remember how I found out about it. Maybe I heard about it from Brand's father himself many years later giving a speech at some election event. Or maybe I read it in an article in a newspaper or magazine. But it's also possible that all I know about him is based on my imagination. I don't mean I imagined the details of the event out of nothing, but that I used inference, extrapolating from what I did know. After all, Brand's father's door was not the only door they knocked on in the middle of the night back in those days. I am not sure why they had to come at night, but they did, and they kept coming. There were many such incidents. When the same pattern keeps recurring, it isn't hard to fill in the blanks, no matter how many blanks there are.

Of course, I did not know any of these things in the summer after sixth grade. I just knew that Brand's father was gone, and the gang who used to steep tea on the first floor vanished. And that everyone's attitude towards Brand had changed, teachers and classmates, even the neighbours. Some of them pretended to be all concerned about him, and looked upon him with compassion in their eyes. But even more people were now afraid of him. They would pretend to look somewhere else if they caught sight of him approaching, or simply turn and take off.

Of course, I wasn't a phony like that and I never turned my back on my friend. To me, Brand was the same old Brand. I even envied him a little bit, almost wished my father had been taken away too. I couldn't help thinking that if he had, he'd finally have something worth telling people about, and I could go around boasting about it. I was jealous of Brand: his father had been taken away by the authorities, just like our Founding Father Sun Yat-sen. A son could be proud of a father like that, like some award he could go around bragging about for quite a while.

The strange thing was that Brand did not do that. He seemed to have realized that a revolution was not child's play, no matter whether it was his father's revolution or ours. He never mentioned either revolution to anyone. He talked neither about his father nor about how many kilometres we'd walked that day with an orangutan. The uninvited midnight visit his father had been paid made a world of difference to Brand, who had fallen from eternal day into eternal night. Under the care of his aunt, for whom safety was the top priority, Brand seemed to have become much more mature overnight, becoming a bit wary, timid and tentative, though he was still a beardless boy whose voice had yet to break.

Brand was no longer interested in our secret base. Nor was Ilya. Following Operation Orangutan Rescue, I never saw Ilya appear in the tree fort, the nightmarket, or under the arcade on the main street, or in any of the places in the neighbourhood where we used to play. I can't really say Ilya changed, like Brand. Actually, Ilya just went back to normal. The winding alleyway along which karaoke machines and Buddhist chant boxes resounded was once again graced with piano and violin scales, often from dawn till dusk, over and over, incessantly. His mother filled up his time with academic classes and music lessons, as before. And as before, she would stop rinsing rice and greens and wait for him to finish playing, just listening quietly in the next room. Never again did Ilya slam the door, or raise his voice to his mother. Several times I heard Ilya's mother talking to him very loudly inside the house. But I only ever heard her voice. Ilya must have had the voice of a mosquito, so helpless it could not even make it through the screen door. Ilya's transformation, or return to normal, made Mrs Chiang mightily pleased. Her face fairly glowed with an irrepressible smile. Probably having forgotten Ilya's brief rebellious phase, she told everyone she saw that she couldn't figure out why a boy on the cusp of his teenage years showed no sign of disobedience. The only time he wouldn't listen to her was when she told him not to practise so much.

After the incident, Brand skipped puberty and entered an early maturity, while Ilya lingered on the threshold of adolescence. As for me, I was the same as always, confused. Even now I'm unsure what impact the incident had on me if any. To my great surprise, I wasn't made to kneel in front of the altar as punishment. The one kneeling in front of the altar was my grandmother. My mother brought out pork hock misua—vermicelli with pork knuckle—and insisted that I finish them at the table in front of my father, who was shelling his peanuts and drinking his rice wine, and all the while my grandmother knelt there, pressing her hands in prayer, prostrating herself, and chanting Buddhist prayers, over and over again, for over an hour. It was as if the person who'd caused all the trouble was her, an old lady with white hair, and her grandson had nothing to do with it.

I wasn't the only one who was not punished in any way. Brand and Ilya were the same. The adults all knew we had gone north of the pailou road, through the watergate and upriver, but nobody blamed us for breaking the taboos or made any new prohibitions for us, as if they'd reached some kind of understanding. Even our biggest fear, that the formidable man in the beret would come knocking at the door to demand compensation, didn't materialize. Just like Brand's father, he disappeared, only earlier. Later I heard he made a getaway the evening of the temple protest, hours after we had rescued the orangutan. As if he'd done something awful and was afraid people would find out, he didn't take his leave of Brand's father, just took all of his own possessions, and a few of Brand's father's possessions, including the stage light, loudspeaker, a curtain and some props, and made a quiet exit. The only thing he left behind was the cage in which he had kept the orangutan. I heard it sat in the fire access behind the seedy inn for many years until it was finally sold off by a scavenger.

There were a lot of things I couldn't understand that year. If they weren't going to hold us accountable, why bother warning us so sternly never to cross the line? If the man in the beret and the other members of the troupe were just going to abandon the orangutan like that, why bother chaining it up in the first place? That's not all I couldn't understand. The occupation of the temple was a total mystery. Why had the authorities sent over a thousand white-helmeted police officers to surround the temple, not letting the protestors out? Why were they arresting people just for writing their demands on their white banners, bandanas, vests and armbands, especially demands that a few years later, after Martial Law was lifted, they would go on to fulfil?

These things defied understanding. Not that we had that much time to think about them. After the summer holidays, we were all taken to the barber, who fitted the three millimetre head on his electric razor and gave us each an erratic crew cut. We put on new uniforms and shouldered new bookbags and walked a bit further to get to the middle school, across the street from the elementary school. Brand and Ilya were put in a different class from me, so we rarely saw each other during the day. Even though we occasionally met in the hallway, we were never in the mood to stop and chat, as we were worried about getting whacked in the following class for failing to make the grade. Those were dark days for us, so dark that we felt we would never see the light of day again. We all lined up in front of the podium with the same style of crew cut and the same cut of blue shorts to get caned on the rear end. Very soon we gave up all hope of resistance and just learned the various skills that they wanted us to learn.

I assumed we had no other choice but to grow up, so when Brand dropped his pretence of wary, quiet and seasoned maturity and became a kid again, charging in breathless to tell me the tree fort was going to be torn down, the old emotions all came rushing back. His frantic, panicked excitement was infectious. I tossed my English and maths textbooks aside, rushed out the door, and ran through the streets. We did not go straight to the secret base. Instead we ran to Ilya's house. We didn't know if his mother would let him come out, but they were going to tear down the tree fort, and we felt he should know.

His mother was pretty friendly. Although she didn't invite us in, she did turn and yell for her son to come out. It was actually Ilya, sleepy, wooden and listless, who didn't seem too happy to see us. "They're going to tear down the tree fort. Do you want to go and see?" I said softly, conveying the information without any of Brand's agitation, I guess because of Ilya's blank expression, not to mention the fact his mother was standing right there. In my heart, of course, I was yelling: Our secret base is about to get obliterated. It'll be gone, there'll be nothing left, and we'll never see it again. Do you understand?

"What tree fort?" Ilya said. And then, like he was recalling ancient history: "Oh, that tree fort. The one that we built last summer."

"What other tree fort is there?" Brand asked, again raising an eyebrow and narrowing his eyes at Ilya.

"When?"

"Now! The workers must be there already," I said.

"They've started moving the lumber. I heard them say that when they move it all out they'll take down the fort," Brand said.

"Oh…" Ilya thought it over before asking his mother: "Can I go with them to see?"

"What's so interesting about tearing down a… fort?" his mother asked.

"It's not a fort, it's the tree fort we built last summer," I said, gesticulating. "We didn't build a residential tree fort, the kind with windows and walls. That would have been too complicated. Our tree fort is a lookout. It's much simpler, but it had to be built high up."

Mrs Chiang widened her eyes suspiciously, looking at me like I had a screw loose. She turned to Ilya and said: "Is watching whatever it is get torn down more important than your piano practice?"

"It is not."

"So do you think you should waste your time on something unimportant like this?"

"No, I should not." Ilya looked over and said very politely to me and

Brand: "You guys go on ahead without me. I think it would be better if I didn't go and see."

"Wait, did I say you can't go?" Mrs Chiang said. "Your friends have come to see you, why don't you go out with them? Just don't forget to come back and practise."

His mother closed the door, leaving us standing outside and Brand surprised, and I knew I had the same expression without looking in the mirror. But there was no change at all in Ilya's face; he seemed to be in emotional isolation. "Let's go," he said insipidly.

Twenty-five years ago, a year after the orangutan incident, we walked in single file under the low awnings along the winding alley. Me and Brand had rushed over to find Ilya, one flustered, the other frantic, but as soon as Ilya joined us, his emotional isolation composed and even captivated us. That was the last time we ever walked to the tree fort. We walked slowly and silently like we were part of a funeral procession. I remember that Ilya led the way, then me, about five or six steps behind, and finally Brand right behind me. If I had suddenly stopped, I might have got knocked over by Brand's girth. I don't remember if it was Ilya who walked too quickly or if it was me who tried to keep my distance. All I remember is that I fixed my eyes on the erratic crew cut on the back of Ilya's faintly green scalp, wondering what erratic thoughts and emotions were seething beneath the apparently placid surface.

Picturing Ilya walking up ahead all these years later, I feel like he was a lot further than five or six steps. My memory, once blurred and effaced only to re-emerge, is a wide angle lens that makes Ilya seem so far in front he could be a mere black dot on the horizon. I'm pretty sure that at that time, erratic thoughts and emotions were seething in my head. I bet there were, but I have now forgotten them, probably because my thoughts and emotions were like my body at the time, a shapeless blob, not fully formed. All I can do now is speculate, and see if I can recover some of the feelings, or the feeling Ilya at the time gives me now. Ilya seemed foreign and silent, distant and abject, his every movement constricted. The Ilya who had once with grand gestures conducted the river water, the sandbars, the egrets and the sand dredgers with a twig from the mango tree had shrunk into an ascetic wearing shackles that he had slapped on himself. I hate to describe my late friend in such terms. But that's the way I see him now. On the verge of middle age, I've finally realized that at thirteen years old, Ilya was like a planet that had been wrenched from its orbit, and was sailing out of the galaxy to which it belonged. I witnessed his departure without ever thinking to try to pull him back. Not that I think I had the strength to pull him or anything else back, but in retrospect I am ashamed that I never even had the thought of trying to reach out.

The workers were still working on the woodpile when we arrived. They were carting away a large load of lumber, but there was still a lot left, every board wet near the bottom of the pile. This was the first time the boards had seen the sun in over a year. The three of us stood in a line outside the faded red wooden front gate of the Japanese-style residence. At some point the gate had gone completely rotten, and had been replaced with a few boards nailed helter-skelter to seal the property, like the criss-crossed rectangular notices the courts put up on condemned buildings. Now the workers had just torn the boards down, so that we could see everything inside. The first thing I saw was the orange plastic bin in which we had kept our treasures, crushed and tossed on the freshly cleared dirt by the woodpile. Once a rubbish bin masquerading as a treasure trove, it was now a veritable piece of rubbish. The lid was nowhere to be seen.

"Our precious treasure trove is no more," Brand sighed.

"Doesn't matter. There wasn't anything in it," I said. "Didn't you take all your stuff out?"

"I did. Didn't you? Ilya?"

Ilya did not reply. Unlike me and Brand, he was not looking at the broken rubbish bin. He was looking up at the tree fort that was about to be torn down but at the time was still swaying and creaking in the wind, as it does in my memory.

"Get out of the way! Don't stand so close!" said a workman roughly. He carried an armful of lumber over to the truck and hurled it on the back.

We backed up several steps, so far we bumped against the wall opposite the gate. From there we regarded the workers. They were both topless, covered in tattoos that seemed inconspicuous on suntanned skin. I was amazed at how they could just pick up a big bundle of lumber and throw it over their shoulders without worrying about splinter or exposed nails. In no time, they had loaded all the remaining wood onto the truck. Then a worker picked up a claw and started climbing up the mango tree, quickly and nimbly as a monkey.

"They're going to tear down our tree fort," I said, my voice trembling. There was no need for me to say it, of course, because Ilya and Brand could see the workman climbing the tree with their own eyes, and knew as well as I did what he was going to do.

That workman seemed in no hurry to carry out the death sentence. "Hey, it's really comfy up here," he said to his companion down below, who was cleaning up with a broom in one hand and a big black plastic bag in the other. "It's got a great friggin' view and a cool breeze. I'm going to have a snooze." He pretended to lie down, and the workman on the ground picked up a stone and threw it up into the tree. "Great, go ahead. I think you'd better leave the tree house be. When you get sacked and can't afford the rent, you can crash here." The workman up on the tree cursed and pulled down a board from the lean-to roof of the tree fort and lugged it at the guy below, who just laughed, jumped away, and immediately returned the courtesy by chucking a few more stones. As the workmen kidded around and stones and boards flew up and down, our tree fort was broken up and torn apart, until soon there was nothing left.

37
The Deluge

We were woken up by a strange sound.

It must have been building up, but none of us had noticed. We were all so sound asleep that nobody, not me, Brand, Ilya or the orangutan, knew how it had crept up on us. When we finally heard it, it was already right over our heads. At first it was like somebody pouring sand on the roof, and then the sand rolled into rice, peas and pinballs, at which size the grains or balls remained, dancing like crazy on the thin, corrugated plastic roof, rumbling on and on.

"What a racket!" Brand said, covering his ears. "It's like being locked inside one of my dad's drums."

The noise wasn't the problem; rainwater had now begun to leak silently in from all around, from the base of the wall, from between the boards, and from invisible holes in the roof. In no time, the walls were wet and black like cardboard soaked in water. Like little snakes, the rivulets of water slithered to the centre of the toolshed, where they coiled around each other to form a little pond. Ilya went to the door to see whether it was light out yet. Hardly had he opened the wooden door when he was half soaked by the onrush of the pouring rain. He immediately slammed the door, shocked. It wasn't light out yet, but we could not sleep any more. The floor and the walls were all wet, and the roof was leaking. We couldn't find anywhere dry to sit, so we each made do with a little bucket for a stool. The orangutan was a bit better off than us, because it had occupied the largest water bucket by far, the plastic barrel in the corner, and there was no way it was moving. And when the roof started leaking, it beat us to the coolie hat hanging on the wall. It now had a shield against the assault of the water droplets.

"Look how comfy it looks," Brand said. "Holy moly! This hairy fellow actually knows to find something to block the rain, and it improvises quicker than us." He reached out to try to snatch the hat, but the orangutan grabbed the brims and bared its teeth. "Well I never! Not above biting the hand that feeds you, are you? How ungrateful can you get!"

"Orangutans live in the rainforest. It's perfectly natural for them to grab leaves to shelter themselves from the rain," Ilya said.

"How can a creature who lives in a rainforest be afraid of a leaky roof?" I said.

"Leave her alone," Ilya said. "There's a raincoat on the wall. We can take it down and cover all three of our heads with it."

We huddled closer together on our makeshift stools, and spread the raincoat over our heads. A leak from the roof started dripping onto the raincoat.

"Didn't you say you had never gone camping before? This is just like waiting out the rain in a tent," Brand said.

"This is not the kind of camping trip I wanted to go on," I said. "Stop hogging the raincoat! My back and bum are all wet!"

"Just hold on a little while longer. We'll set out at first light. The zoo can't be much further," Ilya said.

"What if the rain hasn't stopped when it gets light?" Brand said.

"We just have to keep going upriver, rain or no rain," Ilya said resolutely.

We acquiesced tacitly to Ilya's decision. Waiting out the night wasn't easy. It must have rained for several hours, during which time all I could do was curl up on my upside-down bucket and hide underneath a third of a raincoat, which only kept my head and the backs of my shoulders dry. As the light from the searchlight got dimmer and dimmer, we listened to the unrelenting rattle of the rain on the roof and in our hearts.

Brand had jinxed us by asking "what if?" The roar of the rain showed no sign of letting up by daybreak, let alone stopping. Ilya didn't have to open the door to know it was dawn. The bright rays streaming in here and there through the gaps between the boards and the holes in the roof told us the time.

First light had come and gone, and there we were sitting on our buckets huddling close together under the raincoat. Everyone was waiting for someone else to say it was time to set out in the pouring rain, but even Ilya seemed to vacillate. He just sat there, showing no signs of getting up. It was the orangutan that forced us out into the rain. After a night sitting on the blue plastic tub, it finally stood up, pursed its lips, looked up at a forty-five degree angle, and opened its mouth, revealing both rows of teeth. It yawned for what must have been at least ten seconds. Then it slowly turned around on the cover of the tub, wiggled its narrow little bum to the edge, and, without further ado, started pissing a solid yellow-green stream. Yelling, we jumped up immediately, but immediately wasn't fast enough, and there wasn't anywhere to dodge: each of us got sprayed with at least a few drops of orangutan piss. Before we had the chance to get really angry with it, something even more disgusting happened. The orangutan reached behind it, lifted its slightly protuberant butthole, and took a somewhat shapeless shit on its own hand. Then it brought the sticky stuff by its mouth and started dipping the index finger of its other hand into the lump and sucking it clean, just like the way you dip fries in ketchup.

"Orangutans eat their own shit for breakfast?!" I felt like I was going to hurl.

"Harriet, what are you doing?" This time Ilya did not seem to think that eating shit was part of an orangutan's natural behavioural repertoire. "Stop it right this instant! Don't you know it's disgusting?" he yelled at the orangutan, so worked up he started stamping his feet. The orangutan assumed he was a threat to the good stuff in its hand. Table manners be damned, it pouted at Ilya, plopped the whole lump of shit into its mouth, and started licking its palm.

"Holy shit!" Brand and me screamed in unison. Now the orangutan's hands and mouth were all covered in shit. The toolshed reeked so bad we all wanted to charge out the door.

"Thank God it's still raining. Now we just have to take you out and wash you off," Ilya said. He took the orangutan by the wrist, and, carefully avoiding the shit on its hand, pulled it down from its perch on the lid of the barrel and dragged it towards the doorway. Me and Brand dodged fearfully to the wall. But the bigger surprise was still to come. The moment Ilya huffily pushed open the wooden door, everyone was stunned: water was all we saw. I'm not talking about the rain that the sky had been pouring desperately down on us all night long. I'm talking about a snarling yellow torrent carrying sand and mud and sticks and twigs, churning past us less than five metres away.

"How could this be!" Ilya stood stupefied in the doorway, forgetting about the shit on the orangutan's hand and face. Oblivious to the slanting rain, me and Brand charged out of the toolshed, wanting to see what had happened. The rain beat down upon our faces so hard that we could barely keep our eyes open, but we were still able to see at first hand the situation we were in. The little bridge that we had walked over the night before was gone: the boards on the rocks of the creek bed had been flushed away by the turbulent current. A few trickles the night before, the creek had swollen up into a raging river at least twenty metres wide just overnight. It would be impossible for us to cross it to return to where we had been the night before. Brand rushed to the rear of the toolshed, probably to see if there was any way out on the other side. I followed him around. But as soon as we turned the first corner I was stupefied. The basketball court of a vegetable patch, which Brand had patrolled with the flashlight the night before, had been half-consumed, by an even wider, even more torrential behemoth, terrible to behold. The river seemed to be smoking, forming a layer of mist so thick it was impossible to see across, let alone contemplate wading across to the other side.

"We're… we're doomed!" Brand said, his face ashen.

"Don't panic. Let's figure out what happened first," Ilya said behind us. He had calmed down pretty quickly. He patted Brand on the shoulder, told him not to worry, and walked towards the edge of the water. But he had not taken more than a couple of steps before he started swaying, unable to keep his footing. The ground started to split across Ilya's path, just behind him. "Watch out!" me and Brand yelled, reaching out to grab Ilya and pull him back. In just a few seconds, the crack in the earth was a chasm. We were appalled to see the hunk of soil on which Ilya almost lost his footing, which was about the size of a Mercedes-Benz, slowly slide and tilt into the river. Then, as loose and floppy as a sponge cake, it sank into the ferocious flood. In a second it had vanished without a trace.

Our legs buckled, and we fell back on our backsides. The situation was crystal clear: we were trapped on a sandbar between two mighty rivers. We had thought we had found a nice place to spend the night, not realizing the farmer had built his toolshed on sand. By the looks of things, this must have been a very young sandbar, and by the looks of the tender shoots in the field, it had been recently cultivated, probably just to see if anything would grow. The master of the patch's pioneering spirit, along with Brand's courageous leadership, had left us stranded on an insecure sandbar, like a lonely island. Of course, you couldn't blame it on Brand. Blame it on the rain that had poured down on the hills to the south all night long, on the mountain streams that had converged into a voracious torrent. When it hit the rise of land on which the farmer had hoed his plot, that torrent had divided into two, turning the rise into a sandbar and planing away at the edges like peeling a sweet potato. And then at the base of the sandbar, the two flows came together into a single watercourse and thundered downstream.

"What do we do now?" I asked. Before me, an ocean vast, as a vast ocean of tears welled up.

"What else is there to do besides call for help?" Brand said.

"Call who for help? There's no public telephone here, and there's nobody on the other side of the river," Ilya said despairingly. "Who would come to the riverside in such a downpour?"

We returned to the entrance of the toolshed, sat side by side in the open doorway the way we'd done the night before. But unlike the night before nobody was in the mood to talk. We were dripping wet, and the leak was getting worse and worse. There was no point staying in the shed any more. But the orangutan, hands still covered in the brown stuff, head in a coolie hat, climbed back on the plastic barrel it had occupied all night long. Blinking, it watched the deluge through the doorway. Blinking, we looked towards the opposite shore, trying to find some sign of human activity through the mist.

"Don't worry, they'll find us. They will find out we didn't go home last night and come looking for us," I said. I wanted to reassure Ilya, Brand, and particularly myself.

"Even if they come to look for us, how will they know that we've come so far upstream?" Ilya asked.

"Yeah, how would they know?" Brand asked.

Comfort palled, making the agony of the following silence even more difficult to bear. Pelted by the rain, we kept blinking at the opposite shore. Everyone pursed his lips, as various sounds poured into our ears: the rain, the wind, the roaring waves, the rattling of rolling rocks in the river, like the crushing of dry bones, and the tearing and plopping we imagined hearing as the river whittled away at the sandbar. There were other sounds as well, provenance unknown. At each unidentifiable noise, our hearts skipped a beat and our eyes found one another before staring all the harder into the hazy air towards the opposite shore. We were desperate to see a rescuer, so rapidly was the sandbar eroding. Behind the shed, the low trellises and long mounds, along with the freshly sprouted crops, had all been carried swiftly downstream. In front, the river was almost at our doorstep; we couldn't just sit there forever. Like ants on a griddle, the three of us stood and paced up and down the shrinking shore of the sandbar. I had never actually seen ants on a griddle, but I had read the idiom a zillion times in textbooks and storybooks and found it apt for the panic we felt. I vow never to use the idiom again, and wish to propose a replacement: "like kids on a sandbar". I have no idea how ants on a griddle feel, but I will never forget what it's like for a kid on a shrinking sandbar before a flood, a kid so panicked he can't even cry.

Later, though, we did cry. When the river water loomed so close to the toolshed that I didn't dare to look behind me, there finally appeared a brightly coloured form on the opposite bank. Someone in a red raincoat was walking through the reeds. Perhaps there was a footpath and the person was just passing by, not there to look for us. Regardless, we had to make our presence felt. We yelled as loud as we could and waved our hands and jumped up and down, and rushed back into the toolshed, grabbed the iron buckets we'd used as stools and clanged them together for all we were worth. We were like a man stranded on a deserted island who sees a tanker cruising by. No, it was worse than that, because at least a deserted island wouldn't sink under the ocean waves. We were more and more like kids in a leaky rubber dinghy in the middle of the sea. We still did not know if the red raincoat had noticed us. It was raining and blowing too hard, and the raincoat was too far away. We yelled like crazy, but crazy wasn't good enough, and the raincoat didn't stop. It kept walking, faster and faster, and soon it disappeared behind an ironskin hut. At that, the little dot of red, the last blip of hope on our radar, disappeared, leaving only light grey, mud brown and dark green behind. That's when we started crying, first Brand, then me, and finally Ilya. We knelt down on the mucky ground, watched the river water's unrelenting advance, and wailed.

We cried and cried, not out of fear of the all-consuming flood or even of death. At the time death had not crossed my mind, and I guess Brand and Ilya were the same. We were crying because hope had appeared for a moment only to be dashed. It's a scary feeling, like when you take an ice cream cone from the vendor only to turn and see the scoop fall to the ground, except a hundred or a thousand times worse. We cried and stopped and cried again. Nobody heard us crying. It was raining so hard that we could not see the tears on each other's faces. But we kept on crying, because crying would make the time pass a little bit faster, and make the anguish of waiting easier to bear. That's the last time I ever saw Ilya and Brand cry. I don't know if they cried after they grew up. Whether they did or not, I never saw them. It's after all a rare event to see a grown man cry. I myself have cried many times. I cried when my grandmother died. I cried when my father died. I cried several times after romantic breakups. But I always kept my tears so carefully hidden that neither Ilya nor Brand ever saw. Maybe that was the last time we ever saw each other weep. We could not foresee it at the time, but maybe we sensed it somehow, knowing we should take advantage of the chance to have a good collective cry.

And if on the opposite shore another colour had not appeared, we might've just kept on crying forever. Other brightly coloured figures appeared, not just red, but all the primary colours. And shafts of light, flashing red and blue in the thicket of trees on the opposite shore. After a while quite a few more people appeared wearing raincoats or holding umbrellas, some just standing there, others rushing around piling stuff on the rocks at the riverside. More and more people gathered on the riverbank, and all of them were looking in the same direction: the dwindling sandbar on which we were standing.

38

Mission Accomplished

I saw it coming," Brand said. "I knew he'd do it, sooner or later."
I remember riding with Brand in the convertible that smelled of the perfume from the hot babe in the skimpy skirt. I did not now ask him how he knew, or when. His tone of voice told me he'd known Ilya would make an early departure, for a long, long time. Maybe when he ran into Ilya in Paris. Maybe as early as the summer he cast Ilya in the movie. Of course, anyone who declares that he knew all along in hindsight is probably bragging or indulging in self-promotion. But I never doubted the truth of Brand's tardy prophecy. Even if Brand had said that he knew as early as the day when the tree fort was torn down, or the morning when the fire brigade crossed the river to save three kids on the sandbar, I probably would have bought it, without a doubt in my mind.

It's just that what Brand knew wasn't exactly what I wanted to hear.

I'm not very good at predictions, before the fact or after the fact. My specialization is decryption: how to recover the original message from a code is the mode of thought to which I am most accustomed. I usually start with the simplest approach. When you're breaking a code, the simplest and ultimately the most fail-safe approach is an exhaustive key search, often termed a brute force attack. It's menial: you just keep on sticking in keys, over and over again until it works. Take the man in the beret's combination lock. There were only four dials; the combination consisted of four digits. That is to say, starting from 0000, 0001, 0002, 0003, checking every possibility in order, we had to guess at most ten thousand times.

In theory, a brute force attack can crack any code. But we didn't have that much time. And any code verification mechanism with any rigour will limit the number of mistakes to prevent people with too much time on their hands from cracking the code by brute force. And an ATM is probably the most rigorous: if you enter the wrong code into an automatic teller machine three times in a row, like my mother did one time by accident, the card will get eaten by the machine, and you'll have to wait until the next day before you can go reclaim it. My mother hasn't used an ATM since.

My specialization is recovery, but I can't recover Ilya's life. The even sadder thing is that I seem to have reached a mental limit on how many times I can try. The last time I saw my dissertation adviser in the Communicating Tubes, he advised me to narrow the scope of my hypothetical class on Life Cryptology, to make it more manageable. I knew what he meant, and that he was right. But I've discovered that, though I came up with it, the topic clearly has its own internal resistance to simplification. If I get the chance, I'd like to consult with Professor Safe again and share my latest discoveries about life cryptology. Except that his wife hasn't called since the morning he went missing. Which implies two possibilities. One possibility is that his condition has improved; he is no longer suffering from the assault of amnesia's steganography, and has been able to reassemble his scattered memory fragments into a coherent whole. The other possibility is that his symptoms have got worse, so bad that he's forgotten the way out of the house, or even the history of his relationship with his stainless steel vacuum flask, with his pipe with the broken mouthpiece, or with his wife. I most sincerely hope it's the former, but I don't dare take the initiative to verify. Amanda says my biggest problem is that I lack execution. I admit it. When it comes to Professor Safe, I definitely lack execution.

Luckily, Amanda hasn't been coming over to my mother's house for dinner much in the past little while, or she would have asked how come I failed to inherit my mother's ability to act. My mother's participation in community culture preservation has been yielding great results. The voices of their supporters have got louder and louder. They have more than ten thousand likes on the Facebook page for the Sex Culture Industry Memorial Park, and more than a thousand signatures on a petition they ask people to sign at stands in the MRT station or the nightmarket. Her work has given public representatives like

Congressman Lin second thoughts about urban renewal. Politicians are now worried that by tearing down all the dilapidated houses in the slum they might be ripping up their own electoral base. My mother and her colleagues even held a time travel event, a bit like itinerant theatre, basically cosplay. They went north of the pailou road into Carnation Lane and restored the dilapidated houses along one stretch of street to the way they looked thirty years ago. Then they found a group of college students who support the sex culture industry or sex industry culture preservation to play the hookers and their tricks in a bustling Carnation Carnival. Participants received a piping hot sausage and a "thin skin" lubricated condom just 0.03 millimetres thick.

I never did find that ON button, so I don't know what it was that caused my mother's life to abruptly change direction. Why is she now so dedicated to preserving a place she had hated her entire life? Maybe she is afraid of amnesia, worried that if society collectively erases the history of the neighbourhood, traces of her own life will be wiped away. I don't know whether my mother's efforts count as a recovery operation in the cryptological sense or a rescue operation in some existential sense, but I've always fantasized about trying to relive certain scenes in my own life. I've longed to be able to get in a time travel machine and go back to locate myself at certain personally important moments, and then hide and watch myself from the sidelines, like a stalker or an invisible man. On condition that I could not be discovered or influence the future course of events, I would closely observe myself experiencing some episode. This fantasy is probably juvenile, but it seems worth considering, especially for a "sceptic", as Professor Safe labelled me. Why is it that the person I want to go back and see in the time travel machine is myself and not someone else? Why do I want to relive experiences I obviously still remember? I guess the most likely reason is compromised mnemonic integrity, the necessary gaps in any memory. Memory is skittish, fragmentary and selective, forever incapable of fulfilling the demands we place upon it. So I need a time travel machine and invisibility cloak to go back and stand behind the protagonist to fill in the gaps. I want to be an onlooker, a bystander, a third party. I certainly do not want to go back in time to play the leading role again. I believe that with a few more years of life experience, I should be better able now to understand some of the subtleties that I could not have noticed or which otherwise escaped me at the time, to perceive the meaning in details of body language and gesture. I do not want to go back to square one and have my life to relive in the first person in the hazy uncertainty of the present. I want instead to attain omniscience of certain important events in the past, to know precisely what impact these events have had on me and thereby to place them definitively in my life.

Thus, although I've reached the recall limit for memories of Ilya, I'm more than happy to try again in another way, like imagining myself, a thirty-eight-year-old man with all the intellectual maturity of my age, boarding a time travel machine, setting the destination, and materializing in a crowd of onlookers on the shore opposite the sandbar on which my twelve-year-old self was standing.

In fact, that's just what I'll do.

I find myself standing in a clearing in a grove of trees, feet sinking into soft, sticky mud, which is criss-crossed with ruts and crowded with vehicles. I see two red medium-duty fire engines, a police car, an ambulance, and some jeeps and sedans. The vehicles are all empty, but the warning lights are flashing, and the beacon on the roof of the police car is casting beams of red and blue all around. The rain penetrates the sparse leaves and falls directly onto the hoods, roofs and boots of the cars, rebounding a myriad plumes of spray, as if the cars are smouldering. I follow the footprints, which are jumbled but clearly all pointing in the same direction, soon realizing that the best way to avoid your feet sinking into the mud every step is to follow in others' footsteps. There are some twenty to thirty people at the riverbank, apparently split into two groups: one close to the water, all men, in bright orange or navy rainsuits, the other standing away from the shore, middle-aged and old-aged men and women in red or yellow raincoats, some holding umbrellas. I make my way towards the second group and stand beside a little old lady in a red raincoat who has both hands free to manipulate a string of Buddhist prayer beads. She is staring straight ahead and chanting: "Amituofo, Amituofo, Amituofo, please save us!" The mouths of the people around her aren't idle either. "Jeez! Whose brats are they?" "They ain't from round here, and I ain't never seen 'em before, eh." "Why'd they come all the way out here when the weatherman said a friggin' typhoon was comin'?" "Beats me. I came patrollin' last night and I didn't see a soul." "How many are there?" "Four!" the lady with the Buddhist beads suddenly turns and says. "I come by here early this morning and I seen four kids leapin' up and down on that there sandbar." The local people don't know who the kids are, but you can hear real anxiety and panic in their voices. By virtue of their superior knowledge of the temper of the river, the locals have despaired of saving those four kids. I look across the river at the sandbar and immediately see how dire the situation is. Swollen into a torrent, the creek is much wider than I remember it being, the sandbar the river water keeps nibbling away at shockingly small. It is hard to imagine that just last night it was dry land, even with the shed erected upon it. With the rain pouring down and wind roiling the endless yellow waves, the shed looks like the smokestack of a sunken ship, a useless augury of irreversible fate. I see three children in front of the shed, soaking wet in shorts and short-sleeved shirts. They are kneeling on the ground side by side, facing the shore on which I am standing. Their mouths keep opening and closing, but their voices are absorbed into the wind, rain and river, making it hard to tell whether they are yelling or wailing. They must be crying, because the hungry water has eaten away almost all of the ground beneath their feet, leaving only a dark brown strip aligned in the direction of the flow. The three kids look like they're standing on the back of a mighty crocodile, which might dive beneath the waves at any moment and snap them to bits if it doesn't drown them first. The rescue team springs into action. They can't afford to wait any longer, and have no reason to. They aren't outfitted with rope guns yet, and the black dinghy four of them schlepped over seems meant to stay on the shore: it looks like it would be carried off or capsized if launched into the water. The helicopter they summoned on the wireless can't take off due to the inclement weather. They've decided to launch a brute force attack on the river, with rope as the means of rescue. Wearing a helmet and a flotation vest to which the rope is attached, the first rescuer wades into the water, but before he can make it five steps from the shore he slips in the seething water and is carried downstream. "Pull him back!" the people on the shore yell. Seven or eight men in rainsuits line up on the shore and begin a tug of war with the river. The rescuer crawls back up on shore about thirty metres downstream looking much the worse for wear. So the second rescuer decides to go into the water about thirty metres upstream. He, too, is pulled into the torrent just a few steps from the shore, but luckily he does not lose his footing. He manages to push, pull, kick and glide in a semblance of the motions of swimming. "Swim at an angle against the current! Now swim with the current! Swim at an aaaaangle!" the people holding the rope on the shore yell as they let out the rope. The man in the water drifts towards the sandbar like a kite riding on the wind. "Amituofo, Amituofo, Amituofo," the old lady chants, faster and faster. This time she is obviously praying for the man in the river, because when he makes it across, lands on the sandbar and waves at his colleagues, she takes a brief rest from chanting, presses her solar plexus, lets out a long sigh, before spitting out the final "Amituofo". He seems to have the dire situation under control. That life-saving rope allows them to get several rescuers carrying pulleys and slings and three flotation vests onto the sandbar. "Take the fat one across the river first!" barks a man on this side of the river, and the personnel on the sandbar immediately grab the fat little kid and put the flotation vest on him like they are tying up a piglet. The lady starts chanting the name of the Buddha Amituofo again, not realizing that the most dangerous moments have already passed. Now that the rescue personnel have converged upon the boys and forced them into flotation vests in preparation for a trip across the river in a sling, only the old lady and the boys themselves are afraid. "Pull! Pull him back!" the people on my side of the river yell. The fat kid basically gets carried over. He is trembling from head to toe, and even when he is safe on solid ground, his legs are so wobbly he cannot stand. The second boy is a bit better off, but he keeps his eyes tightly shut the whole way across, not daring to look the raging river in the eye. The third child, the smallest of the three, gives the rescue personnel the most trouble. He seems unwilling to leave the sandbar. More accurately, he is obviously unwilling to leave the toolshed. The rescue personnel have put a flotation vest on him, but he has hidden in the toolshed and will not come out. Standing at the entrance, the two rescuers are facing away from us, making it impossible for us to see what they're doing. But you can guess that they are trying to persuade the child to come out. "What the hell! Hurry up and bring the last brat back." The crowd of onlookers is again anxious, because the ferocious river has renewed its assault on the sandbar, snapping off the tail of the crocodile and carrying it downstream. So the two rescue personnel launch their own brute force attack, charging into the toolshed, and carrying out the child who does not want to leave, one on each side. They drag him to the water's edge and rope him into the sling. It's like the child mustn't touch water, because as soon as he gets plunged in the river, he goes berserk, writhing and screaming, completely unwilling to proceed. The rescue personnel have to stop. With everyone looking on, they slap the child and box his ears before he quiets down and lets the men on our side of the river pull him to safety. "Mission accomplished! The three kids who were stranded on the sandbar have been saved!" a man wearing a navy blue rainsuit reports into his walkie-talkie to a round of applause. The three children are led to the police car, one trembling head to toe, one with his eyes shut tight, and one mute. The vehicles in the clearing leave new ruts in the mud when they leave. The crowd breaks up, everyone following the footsteps they made on the way over, everyone that is except the little old lady in the red raincoat. Still standing on the bank, she is still there when the floodwaters finally swallow the sandbar. "Strange… what about the other one?" she says, manipulating her prayer beads and muttering to herself: "Amituofo, Amituofo, Amituofo… Amituofo?"

* * *

I did end up going to the zoo after all. The three of us went together: Amanda, Ling-ling and I. We got there a little bit late. When I'd parked the car, held Ling-ling's hand and headed for the ticket booth, it was only an hour and fifteen minutes until closing. I could've got there a little bit earlier, but Ling-ling had fallen asleep in the car and I did not want to wake her, so we took another couple of turns around the block. Otherwise I would not have arrived at such an awkward time. Of course, if we had not crossed to the wrong side of the river, if we had noticed a tributary on the other side, and if we hadn't been totally ignorant of the fact that the zoo had moved to a site upstream along that tributary, who knows? I might have got there a lot earlier. If we had known to take the left bank instead of the right, maybe that evening we wouldn't have had to spend the night outside. We might have presented a stolen gift to the zookeepers, who in gratitude might have honoured us with a tour around the zoo in advance of the grand opening.

But I did end up making it to the zoo, two and a half decades late. It was so late in the afternoon when we arrived that the turnstiles were spitting out waves of visitors, both adults and children, their faces all red after a day of fun under a hot sun. The square outside the entrance was crowded. Obviously many people were loath to leave so soon after having seen the animals. Vendors selling snacks and mementos saw their chance. There were children skipping about wearing animal hats or masks, pandas, rabbits, elephants, monkeys and tigers. There were animals with wheels rolling around on the ground. There were wind-up doves flying low through a cloud of coloured balloons. Half the children were single-mindedly blowing soap bubbles into the wind, while the other half, just as single-mindedly, were trying to burst the bubbles by fair means or foul. Half the adults were chasing their children with cameras, mobile phones or tablet computers, trying to get energetic little animals in focus, while the other half were sitting sedentary on anything that could fit a bum. The gaiety in the square outside the zoo was strangely carnivalesque; I'd never witnessed such a scene outside any other theme park. It seemed like exiting at the main gate and leaving that smelly place behind was something to celebrate.

I held Ling-ling's hand, walking against the flow of people into the zoo. Amanda had fallen a bit behind in her high heels; the people going the other way created a powerful resistance to our forward movement. There was another source of resistance that sought to slow our steps, much smaller, from Ling-ling's little hand. She kept looking all around, and every time she saw a child holding a balloon, eating an ice cream or pushing along a push-along animal that played music or rang bells, she would suddenly squeeze my fingers, alerting me that she wanted what she saw, whatever it was. But she didn't voice her desire, just like her mother. In the old days, before my pharmacist father-in-law had paid cash to buy us that new flat, when Amanda and I would walk hand-in-hand down the street, she would often grip my hand like Ling-ling was doing now. I always knew she had been grabbed by something she'd seen in a display window. She didn't say anything, just like her daughter many years later. But the force of her grip was not faint, like Ling-ling's. She often gripped my hand so hard it hurt.

"We have to get a move on. You'll have to wait until we come out," I told Ling-ling.

"What's the rush?" said Amanda behind me. "The zoo is closing. No matter how quickly you walk there is no way you'll be able to see all the animals."

"It's because the zoo is closing soon that we have to step it up." I looked back to explain things to Amanda, then went back to poring over the map of the zoo trying to figure out exactly where we were. "We come to the zoo once in a blue moon. How can we not try to see as many animals as possible? Hurry up, we don't have much time! But we still have time enough to see the most important animals."

"We can come next time if we can't see them all today. I don't get it. Why do you have to be so greedy? Ling-ling isn't even three. There's no way she'll remember which animals she saw."

Ling-ling would remember, I thought, but I didn't have the time to argue with Amanda. It was just like when I went with my parents on the scooter to the zoo at the age of five or six. First impressions are indelible, especially first and only impressions. I can still clearly remember the elephants I saw that time, and the giraffes, the zebras and the camels. If possible, I wanted Ling-ling to see all of these animals on her first visit to the zoo. And on my second visit to the zoo, I wanted to check my memories of those animals many years later, to see if there was any difference between my memory of the animal and the actual animal.

The zoo was unimaginably big, much bigger than I thought it was going to be. Ling-ling got tired halfway through, and refused to walk any further. So I had to carry her. By the time we got to the elephants, I was covered in sweat.

"Ling-ling, look at the elephants!" I lifted Ling-ling high onto my shoulders.

"Elephants."

"Look how long their trunks are. Do you see?"

"Long trunks."

"Do you see how big their ears are?"

"Big ears."

An elephant lifted its trunk and gave a stentorian cry, at which time loudspeakers hidden in the trees or the false rocks made an announcement: "May I please have your attention please? The zoo will be closing in forty-five minutes. We request that you begin making your way towards the exit. We thank you for your visit today."

"All right. Let's go see the next animal." I let Ling-ling slide down my back and started giving her a piggyback to the next stop.

"That's it? But I haven't really seen what an elephant looks like," Amanda said, out of breath.

"We have to keep going. Didn't you hear the announcement? If you haven't seen enough, you can take a closer look next time. We have to go and see some other animals."

"If you want to go, you take your daughter." Amanda had lost her temper. "I don't want to walk any more. I'm going to stop and rest here."

"Suit yourself."

I trotted with Ling-ling on my back to see the giraffes, the zebras, the camels and the other animals I remembered seeing in the zoo when I was a child. And on the way we saw rhinoceroses, hippos and kangaroos, and other animals I did not remember seeing. When we reached our final destination on the map, there was another announcement: "Your attention please. The zoo is now closed. We request that you make your way to the exit immediately. Please do not linger. I repeat. Make your way to the exit immediately. Do not push or shove. Please assist children or elderly visitors. We thank you for your visit to the zoo today. Come again."

Ling-ling and I went through the turnstile and joined the festive crowd. Ling-ling stood timidly before a toy stand, and I let her pick a little white rabbit hat and helped her put it on. I bought a bubble wand in the shape of a monkey too. She couldn't wait to start blowing bubbles. At first she didn't know the technique. Either she didn't get enough soapy water on the ring or didn't blow hard enough, so the bubbles kept plummeting and bursting on the ground. I was anxious to tell her to blow with the wind and hold the wand away from her mouth to avoid getting soapy water on her lips, but I didn't have time to say so, because Ling-ling had already got the hang of it. Soon she was able to blow at least ten bubbles every time. The setting sun cast golden yellow streams from the hills behind the zoo. Ling-ling's bubbles joined the other children's bubbles, rising slowly in loose formations into the blue. I must have looked a bit spellbound watching her, and would have kept looking quietly on like that, waiting for dusk to descend, but Ling-ling wasn't about to leave me idle. "Daddy, now it's your turn to bwow bubbos," she said and stuck the bubble wand into my hand, wanting me to blow bubbles for her to chase in the breeze. I couldn't understand why such a small child would feel so passionate about bubbles. Every time I took a deep breath and released a big bunch of bubbles towards Ling-ling, she was ecstatic, bursting into giggles. She raised her plump little hands, looked up, and raced around among the coloured bubbles, twirling and jumping. As if I had the magical power to make my daughter happy, just by blowing bubbles. So I blew even more quickly, almost continuously, as if blowing bubbles was the most important thing in life and the only thing I should be doing.

Amanda had at some point walked through the turnstile and found us in the square outside the zoo. She did not interrupt our game, nor did she get out the camera to hunt for shots of Ling-ling. She just stood silently to one side, watching us from a safe distance. When I noticed her, I seemed to see her smile at me. I didn't know what she was thinking. Nothing in the fundamental conditions of our lives had changed. The message she was sending me in that smile was hard to interpret, like a code that was simple but extremely difficult to crack. Of course, maybe her smile was just as innocent as a little girl twirling around in a cloud of bubbles, and I had overinterpreted, unconsciously adding encryption. No matter what, I should have given her a smile in return, but I couldn't because my lips had to stay pursed to keep the stream of bubbles flowing.

We played in the square until dusk fell, until most of the cars in the car park were gone. Amanda got in the passenger seat while I buckled Ling-ling up in the safety seat. Then I squeezed into the driver's seat. It was only when I thunked the door shut that I realized I had forgotten to check whether there were any orangutans in the zoo.

9 780993 215483